Here is a dramatic, hair-raising adventure alive with extraordinary people. As only he can, Michener brings the strange and exotic world of the Middle East to vibrant life in this colorful and suspenseful novel.

About the Author

James A. Michener was born in New York City. Brought up in Bucks County, Pennsylvania, he was graduated from Swarthmore. In 1948, while an editor in a New York publishing house, he won the Pulitzer Prize for his TALES OF THE SOUTH PACIFIC. Today he is internationally known as the author of such world-famous bestsellers as HAWAII, THE SOURCE, and THE DRIFTERS as well as CENTENNIAL and CHESAPEAKE.

Fiction

THE BRIDGES AT TOKO-RI

CARAVANS

CENTENNIAL

CHESAPEAKE

THE COVENANT

THE DRIFTERS

THE FIRES OF SPRING

HAWAII

POLAND

RETURN TO PARADISE

SAYONARA

THE SOURCE

SPACE

TALES OF THE SOUTH PACIFIC

Non-Fiction

THE BRIDGE AT ANDAU

IBERIA

KENT STATE: WHAT HAPPENED AND WHY

RASCALS IN PARADISE

SPORTS IN AMERICA

CARAVANS

A Novel by

James A. Michener

FAWCETT CREST • NEW YORK

To Baldanza

1

On a bleak wintry morning some years ago I was summoned to the office of our naval attaché at the American embassy in Kabul. Captain Verbruggen looked at me with an air of frustration and growled, "Damn it all, Miller, two weeks ago the ambassador ordered you to settle this mess about the saddle shoes. Last night the Afghanistan government made another protest . . . this time official. I want you, by three o'clock this afternoon, to hand me . . ."

I interrupted to report: "Sir, a much more serious matter has come up. Last night a dispatch arrived. I've assembled the data for you."

I shoved before him a leather portfolio jammed with papers. Across the face of the portfolio was stamped the gold inscription, "For the Ambassador," and since our embassy owned only two such folders, what went into them was apt to be important.

"Can't it wait till the ambassador gets back from Hong Kong?" Captain Verbruggen asked hopefully, for even though he was our acting ambassador he preferred to temporize.

I disappointed him. "It's got to be handled now."

"What's it deal with?" he asked, for he was a self-made man who disliked reading.

Carefully folding back the leather cover, I pointed to a cable from Washington. "Senior senator from Pennsylvania. Demands an answer. Immediately."

Verbruggen, a rugged, bald-headed man in his sixties, snapped to attention, as if the senator from Pennsylvania had entered the room. "What's he want?" He still refused to do any unnecessary reading.

"The Jaspar girl," I said.

With a disgusted reflex Verbruggen slammed shut the portfolio. "For seventeen months," he complained, "this embassy has been plagued by the Jaspar girl. I'm here to help a nation climb out of the Dark Ages, and that's the job I'm trying to do. But I'm pestered with saddle shoes and Jaspar idiots. There's nothing more I can think of to do on this case," he concluded firmly, shoving the papers to me.

But I forced the papers back to his side of the desk. "You've got to read the dispatch," I warned.

Gingerly he lifted the leather cover and peeked at the peremptory message from Washington. When he saw that even the Secretary of State had involved himself in the matter, he snapped to attention and pulled the paper before him. Slowly he read aloud:

"It is imperative that I be able to supply the senior senator from Pennsylvania with full details regarding the whereabouts and condition of Ellen Jaspar. All previous reports from your embassy are judged inadequate and unacceptable. If necessary, detail your best men to this problem as it involves many collateral considerations. Am I correct in remembering that Mark Miller speaks the native language? If so, consider assigning him to this project at once and have him report promptly, sparing no effort."

Captain Verbruggen leaned back, blew air from puffed-up cheeks and once again shoved the folder to me. "Looks like it's been taken out of my hands," he said with relief. "Better get to work, son."

I lifted the portfolio from his desk and said, "I have been working, sir. Ever since I arrived."

"In a very desultory way," he suggested pleasantly. My boss could never forgo the obvious, which was why he was stuck off in Afghanistan, one of the most inconspicuous nations on earth. In 1946 it was just emerging from the bronze age, a land incredibly old, incredibly tied to an ancient past. At the embassy we used to say, "Kabul today shows what Palestine was like at the time of Jesus." In many ways, our attaché was an ideal man for Afghanistan, for he too was only just emerging from his own bronze age.

Yet I liked him. He was a rough, wily businessman who had made a minor fortune in the used-car racket, and a place for himself in the Democratic party in Minnesota. Four times he had helped elect Franklin D. Roosevelt, and although I was a strong Republican, I respected Verbruggen's tested loyalty. He had given the Democrats some sixty thousand dollars and they had given him Afghanistan.

He was almost entitled to it. While still a civilian he had made himself into a rough-and-ready yachtsman, for boating was his principal hobby, and when World War II struck, he volunteered to help the navy manage its shore installations. By merit and drive he had risen from lieutenant to navy captain and had made significant contributions to the building of our great bases at Manus and Samar. He was a tough bullet-head and men respected him; he had courage, and I could prove it.

My name is not really Mark Miller. By rights it's Marcus Muehler, but in the 1840's when my ancestors fled Germany they decided with that foresight which distinguishes my family that a Jewish name would not be helpful in America, so they translated *muehler* into its English equivalent, and henceforth we were Millers.

As usual, my family was right. The fact that my name was Miller and my face wholly un-Jewish enabled me to succeed at Groton and Yale, so that when in 1942 the United States navy was looking for a few acceptable Jewish officers to avoid having many unacceptable ones forced upon them, they grabbed me with relief and were happy when most of my shipmates never realized that I was Jewish. In how many ward-rooms was I assured by amateur anthropologists, "I can spot a kike every time."

Captain Verbruggen, under whom I served at Manus, watched me for three weeks, then said, "Miller, you're the kind of kid who ought to be in Intelligence. You've got brains." And he personally fought with the brass on the island until he found me a good berth. In 1945, when our State Department also became eager to pick up a few Jewish career men with table manners, my former boss

(4)

remembered me, and in one exciting week he switched me from lieutenant, junior grade, to State Department officer, very junior grade.

Then came the problem of where State should put me, for the typical embassy doubted that I would fit in. For example, I wouldn't be welcome in Cairo or Baghdad, where the citizens hated Jews, or, as it happened, in Paris, where many of our staff felt the same way. At this point Captain Verbruggen, now serving as naval attaché in Afghanistan, reported that he knew Mark Miller, and that I was a well-behaved Jew who would be a credit to the country. "In fact," he said in a cable that was passed widely throughout the department, "some of my best friends are Jews," and he got me. His courage gained the gratitude of President Truman and a nod from the Secretary of State. To everyone's relief I was working out reasonably well, so that Captain Verbruggen looked on me with a certain pride. I was one of his ideas that hadn't turned sour, which could not be said for all of them.

"I haven't been a ball of fire on the Jaspar girl," I confessed, "but when the cable arrived I got everything together. I've reviewed the files and I think I know what's got to be done next."

"What?"

"At four this afternoon I'm seeing Shah Khan. At his home. He talks better there, and if anyone knows where the Jaspar girl is, he does."

"Will he tell you?" Captain Verbruggen countered suspiciously.

"In Afghanistan I expect no one to tell me anything, and what they do tell me, I distrust."

"You're learning." The captain laughed. He looked at his watch and said, "If you've already studied the file, and if you're going to meet Shah Khan at four . . ."

"I'd better get to work on the saddle shoes," I anticipated.

"You'd better. Those damned mullahs are off again on a big religious kick." I was always surprised at Captain Verbruggen's use of the vernacular. He read widely—magazines, not books—and acquired strange phrases. "The mullahs from the mountain districts stormed into town yesterday," he continued, "and they got wind, somehow, of the saddle shoes and they're demanding that our Marine guards be sent home."

"You aren't going to let a few mad priests dictate our policy, sir?"

"The one thing I refuse to get mixed up in is a bunch of fanatic Muslim priests. You don't know them the way I do. Already they're putting a lot of pressure on the Afghan government. I may have to lose my Marines."

"What am I to do?"

"You speak the language. Go down to the bazaar. See what's actually happening."

"Very good, sir."

"And, Miller, if there's any good reason for getting rid of the Marines, let me know right away. Their time's almost up and it might be a friendly gesture on our part to get them out of here. Placate the mullahs at no real expense to ourselves."

I was equally surprised at the precise vocabulary my boss could use when he wished to. "I don't like the idea of placating a bunch of mullahs," I objected stubbornly.

"You won't be," he replied. "I'll accept responsibility, and we'll all be further ahead if I do."

I nodded deferentially and rose to go, tucking the Jaspar papers under my arm, but at the door I was stopped by a command from the acting ambassador. "Let me know what Shah Khan thinks," he said.

I laughed. "There must be twelve million people in Afghanistan who would like to know what Shah Khan thinks. I'm sure I won't be the one to find out." I left the room, then called back, "But I'll let you know what he doesn't tell me."

In 1946 the American embassy in Afghanistan required no large staff, for in those hesitant days the big lend-lease program that was to mark the future had not yet been visualized. We who did serve in the strange and sometimes forbidding city were forced by circumstance to be a closely knit group, because at that time Kabul provided positively nothing for foreigners: no hotels that we could use, no cinema of any kind, no newspapers, no radio with European programs, no restaurants available to visitors, no theaters, no cafés, no magazines. No public meetings were allowed, nor were we permitted any kind of normal social life with our Afghan hosts, for this was prohibited by the Afghans. We were thus driven in upon ourselves and if we wanted entertainment or social life we had to provide it ourselves, looking principally to the personnel attached to the English, French, Italian, Turkish and American embassies. At the end of a long, confining winter during which the city was snowbound, we searched hungrily for any diversion and were delighted when the people at the English embassy, always the most inventive where living overseas was concerned, came up with the idea of reading plays aloud before informal audiences.

Therefore, when I got back to my office in the two-story white building which served as our embassy, I was not surprised to find our pool secretary, Miss Maxwell of Omaha, typing furiously and somewhat irritated when I asked for the well-thumbed papers on the saddle shoes.

"They're over there," she snapped without looking up.

"Could you get them?" I asked.

"Please, Mr. Miller," she protested. "I'm just finishing the play for tonight."

"I'm sorry," I said, finding the papers for myself.

"The reading's tonight," she explained, "and I'm responsible for all of Act Three. The British girls are doing Act One, which is the longest, and one of the Italian girls is typing Act Two. She's finished. I guess they never do any work at the Italian embassy," she sighed.

"You go ahead," I said consolingly, and I noticed that she had in her machine not only the original copy but seven carbons as well. "See that I get one of the first three," I cautioned. "I can't read those last carbons."

"On my machine they're all right," Miss Maxwell assured me. "It's the Italian typewriters that won't strike off seven copies." I noticed that Miss Maxwell was using a German machine, and it did make seven usable copies.

I took the saddle-shoe papers to my inner office

and started to leaf through them, but the top page arrested me, for it said briefly, "Afghan agents have warned us that if the Marines continue to molest the saddle shoes, there will be a murder in the bazaar." This moved the whole matter up several notches in gravity, so I asked Miss Maxwell to summon my Afghan aide, Nur Muhammad, who came quietly into the room.

He was a good-looking, lithe young man of thirty-two, dressed in a western-style blue suit which fitted badly. He had black hair, dark skin, deep-set eyes, a big Afghan nose and extremely white teeth, which he showed rarely. He was a moody, sensitive person who during the two years he had worked at the American embassy had taught himself to speak English. It was generally known that he was in the employ of the Afghanistan government.

"Sit down, Nur," I said. With grave attention to protocol he sat in the chair I indicated, smoothed his trousers, then folded his hands in his lap.

"Yes, sahib?" he said with a deft combination of willingness to help and studiousness not to appear too eager.

"It's about the saddle shoes," I began, and Nur Muhammad relaxed. "You've heard about the latest intelligence?" I continued.

Nur Muhammad betrayed nothing. He was far too smart to be trapped into admitting that he knew anything. He insisted that I speak first. Then he would react to what I had said. "What intelligence?" he asked blandly.

I opened the manila folder on the case and looked at the ominous report. "Some of your peo-

ple have warned us that if the Marines continue to
. . . Well, they say molest. Nur Muhammad, do
you think our Marines have molested anyone?"

Before Nur could reply my door was opened by
a handsome young American Marine who had won
battle stars on Guadalcanal and Iwo Jima and who
now enjoyed, as his reward, an easy job as one of
our two military guards in the embassy. He
stepped in smartly, handed me some papers,
turned professionally, and disappeared. His uniform, I remember, was immaculate and his shoes
were shined.

When he was gone Nur Muhammad replied cautiously, "I wouldn't say by your standards the
young men have molested. But Ramadan is approaching. The mullahs gain more voice each day.
It is they who believe there has been molestation
and if they believe this, Mr. Miller . . ."

I showed him the report. At the suggestion of
murder he drew in his breath.

"Yes," I said. "Murder." Nur Muhammad carefully replaced the paper, then straightened his
trousers once more.

"I would not ignore the mullahs," Nur Muhammad warned. "You see, as Ramadan approaches
they wish to reinforce their power. To remind us of
that power."

"Suppose these suspicions continued? Suppose
the Marine you just saw did . . . well . . . molest?"
I added quickly, "You understand, I'm not for one
minute granting that any Marine did molest."

"You made your position clear on that point,"
Nur Muhammad agreed effusively.

"But suppose the mullahs thought otherwise? Whom would they murder?"

Without a moment's reflection Nur replied, "The saddle shoes, of course."

"The saddle shoes!" I gasped.

"Of course. I must explain, Miller Sahib. In the past the mullahs loved to murder the ferangi, but whenever they murdered a ferangi it caused much trouble for Afghanistan. So they've had to quit."

I was always bemused by the Afghan word for *foreigner*. When the first Asian students saw this ugly word, with its even uglier connotations, the unaccustomed combination of *g* and *n̄* perplexed them, so they invented an expressive pronunciation which included all the letters, heavily fraught with hatred, envy and contempt. Some pronounced it *ferangi*, with a hard *g*, some *faranji*, others *foreggin*, but it meant the same.

"The mullahs will not murder the ferangi," Nur Muhammad assured me.

"I think we should go down to the bazaar right now," I suggested.

"I do not think I should go, Miller Sahib. My presence would endanger your effectiveness and mine."

"I agree, but I'd like to have you there, if danger should erupt."

"What danger can erupt in a Kabul bazaar?" Nur Muhammad asked deprecatingly.

"We just agreed. Murder."

"But not to a ferangi," Nur assured me, and he declined to join me, returning to his regular duties.

When he had gone I called Security to request that our two Marines be excused from duty, and although I met with loud protest, my threat to involve the acting ambassador turned the trick. From my window I watched the two clean-cut battle heroes hurrying toward the exit gate. I summoned Miss Maxwell and informed her, "I'll be in the bazaar."

"Good," she replied, grabbing her hat. "I'll deliver the copies of the play."

I went to the exit gate and asked the guard to hail me a ghoddy, and in a few minutes a driver pulled up with the world's most uncomfortable taxi: a horse-drawn two-seater in which the driver perched comfortably in front on a hair cushion, while the passengers clung precariously to a sloping wooden seat that faced backward. Thin strips of old automobile tires tacked to wooden wheels enabled the ghoddy to travel over the rough, frozen streets.

I've been told that diplomats and military men remember with nostalgia the first alien lands in which they served, and I suppose this is inevitable; but in my case I look back upon Afghanistan with special affection because it was, in those days, the wildest, weirdest land on earth and to be a young man in Kabul was the essence of adventure. Now, as I jogged along in the ghoddy on an unbelievable mission, I thought again of the violent land and the even more violent contradictions that surrounded me.

The city of Kabul, perched at the intersection of caravan trails that had functioned for more than three thousand years, was hemmed in on the west by the Koh-i-Baba range of mountains, nearly seventeen thousand feet high, and on the north by the even greater Hindu Kush, one of the major mountain massifs of Asia. In the winter these powerful ranges were covered with snow, so that one could never forget that he was caught in a kind of bowl whose rim was composed of ice and granite.

Kabul, pronounced Cobble by all who have been there, Kaboul by those who have not, was shaped like a large capital U lying on its side, with the closed end to the east where the Kabul River flowed down to the Khyber Pass, and the open end to the west facing the Koh-i-Baba. The central part of the U was occupied by a rather large hill, which in my home state of Massachusetts would have been called a mountain. The American embassy and most European quarters lay in the northern leg of the U, which I was now leaving, while the bazaar, the mosques, and the vivid life of the city lay in the southern leg, to which I was heading.

As we made our way toward the center of Kabul I was reminded of the first contradiction that marked Afghanistan. The men I saw on the streets looked much more Jewish than I. They were tall, dark of skin, lithe, with flashing black eyes and prominent Semitic noses. They took great pride in their claim to be descendants of the lost tribes of Israel, who were supposed to have reached these mountain plateaus during the Diaspora. But at the same time the Afghans remembered that the ancient name of their country was Aryana, and in the volatile 1930's they were adopted by Adolf Hitler as the world's first Aryans and his special wards. The proud Afghans were able to accept both accolades without discrimination and consequently boasted that while it was true that they were born of the Jewish tribe, the Ben-i-Israel, once they reached Afghanistan they had ceased being Jews and had founded the Aryan race. It made as much sense as what some of their friends were propounding elsewhere.

The dress of Afghan men was striking. The few educated men and officials dressed like Nur Muhammad: western clothes with fur-collared overcoats and handsome iridescent caps of karakul, shaped either like American Legion overseas caps or like fezzes. Other men wore the national costume: sandals which allowed toes to drag in the snow, baggy white pants of Arab derivation, an enormous white shirt whose tails were worn outside and reached below the knees to flap in the breeze, richly patterned vest, overcoat of some heavy western cloth, and a dirty turban, one of whose ends trailed over the shoulder. If they were tribesmen from the hills, they also carried rifles and sometimes wore bandoleers well studded with cartridges. I doubt if you could have found a national capital anywhere in the world where so many men walked the streets fully armed, for in addition to their rifles most of the tribesmen carried daggers as well. Civilization in Afghanistan, as represented by officials who wore the karakul cap, existed on a very narrow margin of survival.

During my first days in Afghanistan I had noticed that whenever I saw a pair of these fierce tribesmen down from the hills, men who had probably killed in mountain ambush, one of the couple behaved in a very masculine manner while his partner was sure to have feminine traits. He walked in mincing steps, kept a handkerchief in one hand,

and carried a winter flower between his teeth.
Usually the feminine partner wore a little rouge or
eye makeup and always he walked holding the
hand of his more rugged partner.

A further glance at the streets of Kabul explained why this was so. There were no women
visible. I had been in the country more than a hundred days and had yet to see a woman. I had been
entertained in important homes, like that of Shah
Khan, but never had I been allowed to see any of
the women who lived there. It was this phenome-
non that accounted for the curious behavior of the
men: having removed all women from public life,
the Afghans realized that feminine traits were nevertheless desirable and so allocated them to men.
On the frozen streets of Kabul I saw just as many
feminine actions as I would have seen on the bou-
levards of Paris, except that here men performed
them.

Of course, it isn't accurate to say that I saw no
women. Frequently as the ghoddy plugged along I
saw emerging from towering walls, whose gates
were always guarded, vague moving shapes en-
shrouded in cloth from head to toe. They were
women, obliged by Afghan custom never to appear
in public without a chaderi, the Muslim covering
that provides only a tiny rectangle of embroidered
lace through which the wearer can see but cannot
be seen. We were told by educated Afghan men,
most of whom despised the chaderi, that the impo-
sition damaged the health and the eyesight of the
women, but it persisted. At the age of thirteen all
females were driven into this seclusion, from which
they never escaped.

I must admit, however, that these ghostly figures, moving through the city in shrouds that were often beautifully pleated and made of costly fabric, imparted a grave sexuality to life. There was a mysteriousness in meeting them and wondering what kind of human being resided inside the cocoon, and rarely have I been as aware of women, or as fascinated by them, as I was in Afghanistan, where I saw none.

It was midmorning when the ghoddy dropped me at the little fortress-like mosque with two white minarets that stood by the river in the heart of the city, and I noticed at the doorway to the mosque three mullahs—tall, gaunt, unkempt men with flowing beards and fierce eyes—who appeared to be guarding the holy place and condemning me, a non-Muslim, for passing so near. When I looked at them politely, they stared back with undisguised hatred and I thought: These are the men who rule Afghanistan!

At this moment one of them, obviously down from the hills, spied something behind me that alarmed him, and he began screaming imprecations in Pashto. Encouraged by his protests, the other two mullahs started running at me, and I hurriedly ducked aside to let them pass. When they had gone, like scarecrows in their long gowns and flying beards, I looked after them to see what had so agitated them, and I discovered that our typist, Miss Maxwell, had driven to town in the embassy jeep and was now hurrying along the public sidewalk with her eight copies of the play we were to read that night. The country mullah had spotted her, a woman without a chaderi, and felt obliged to assault her for this violation of faith. He and his companions, giving no thought to the fact that Miss Maxwell was ferangi, bore down upon her screaming and cursing.

Before I could protect her, the three tall mullahs, their beards and hooked noses making them caricatures of religious frenzy, had swarmed upon her and were beating her with their fists. What was worse—then and in retrospect—they began spitting at her, and rheum from their lips trickled across her terrified face.

I dashed through the crowd that had gathered and began grabbing the mullahs, shouting in Pashto, "Stop it, you fools! She's ferangi!"

I was saved by the fact that I knew the language; the holy men fell back, startled that I could speak to them in Pashto, whereas had I been a mere ferangi who had struck a priest they might have incited the crowd to kill me. A policeman ambled up, never swiftly for he did not wish to become involved with mullahs, and said quietly, "Look here, men. We're in Kabul, not the mountains. Let the woman alone." And the three fanatic mullahs withdrew to guard once more the mosque at the river's edge.

Miss Maxwell, terrorized by the sudden attack, proved herself a brave girl and refused to cry. I wiped the spit from her face and said, "Forget them. They're madmen. I'll find your driver."

I looked about for the embassy car and discovered the Afghan driver lounging unconcernedly along the river wall, from where he had watched the incident. He was sure that I or somebody would halt the fanatical mullahs and that his charge, Miss Maxwell, wasn't going to get seriously hurt, so he saw no good reason to risk his neck brawling with idiot mullahs.

He now sauntered over. "Must I take Miss Maxwell back to the embassy?" he asked in Pashto.

"The Italian embassy," I explained.

"Be careful," he warned me. "The mullahs are dangerous these days."

Before he drove Miss Maxwell away, I congratulated her upon the self-control she had exhibited. People back home made jokes about the softness of Americans, but they should have seen Miss Maxwell that March day in Kabul.

When she was gone, I wandered over to the bazaar, a nest of narrow streets in the crowded section of the city, where almost everything was for sale, much of it stolen from warehouses in Delhi, Isfahan and Samarkand. I derived perverse pleasure from the assurance that new India, ancient Persia and revolutionary Russia were alike impotent to halt the hereditary thieves of Central Asia. When Darius the Persian marched through Kabul five hundred years before the birth of Christ, this same bazaar was selling practically the same goods stolen from the same ancient cities.

There were, of course, a few modern improvements. Gillette razor blades were in good supply, as were surgical scissors from Göttingen in Germany. One enterprising merchant had penicillin and aspirin, while another had imported from a rifled G.I. warehouse in Bombay cans of Campbell's soup and spark plugs for American cars, of which there were beginning to be a few on the deeply rutted streets of Kabul.

But it was the faces that made me think I was back in the days of Alexander the Great, when Afghanistan, astonishing as it now seemed, was a distant satrapy of Athens, a land of high culture long before England was properly discovered or any of the Americas civilized. In these faces there was a sense of potential fire, of almost maniacal intensity, and wherever I looked there were the mysterious forms of women, shrouded in flimsy robes which hid even their eyes.

I was watching the movement of these alluring figures, wondering as a young man should what form was sequestered beneath the robes, when I became aware—how I cannot even now explain—of two young women who moved with tantalizing grace. How did I know they were young women? I don't know. How did I know they were beautiful, and aching with sexual desire, and gay and lively? I don't know. But I do know that these creatures, whatever their age or appearance, were positively alluring in their mysteriousness.

One was dressed in an expensive, pleated chaderi of fawn-colored silk; the other was in gray. At first I thought they were trying to attract me, so when they passed very close I whispered in Pashto, "You little girls be careful. The mullahs are watching."

They stopped in astonishment, turned to look out of the bazaar toward the three gaunt mullahs, then giggled and hurried on. When I turned to look after them, I saw that they were wearing American-style saddle shoes. These must be the girls who had been reported as meeting our two Marine guards in the bazaar, and from my memory of the dashing manner in which the Marines had left our embassy compound, and from the saucy way in which the girls had moved past me, I suspected that matters of substantial moment were afoot, and that the impending meeting of these young people might lead to tragedy.

I therefore set out to follow the girls, and I cursed Nur Muhammad for not being on hand to help. The girls were not moving fast, and from time to time I was able to catch glimpses of them, two figures shrouded in expensive silk, exquisite in their movements, and wearing saddle shoes. They became the personification of sexual desire—attractive, dangerous, evanescent—as they moved gracefully through the bazaar, looking, hoping.

I followed them into the alleyways where karakul caps were sold, those silvery gray hats that made Afghan men seem so handsome and ferangi so ridiculous. "Sahib, cap! Cap!" the merchants cried, falling back with laughter when I said regretfully in Pashto, "It takes a handsome man to wear karakul."

Now the shrouded girls moved lazily, wasting time in the fruit stalls where precious melons from the south were available, and in the dark stalls where cloth from India was on sale. I do not think they were aware of me, following them at a distance, but the movement of those gay, abandoned saddle shoes fascinated me, and I well understood how our two Marines had fallen under the spell of these lively girls.

For a moment I lost them. I turned into a street where there were shops with metal goods—bronze, tin, stainless steel and silver—but the girls were not there. Fearing something not easily described, I hurried back to the fabric center, and finding no one there I turned toward a little alley which led to what seemed a dead end. On chance, I stepped that way and saw a perplexing, haunting sight.

Against the dead-end wall leaned our two American Marines, in bright uniform. Against them, their backs to me, were pressed the two Afghan girls, their chaderies thrown back, their unseen lips pressed eagerly against those of the Marines. The girl in gray had allowed her dress to be pulled partly away, and in the wintry air I could see her naked shoulders. I have never seen human beings so passionately intertwined, and I became aware of the fact that the girls had begun to loosen the uniforms of the Marines and to adjust to the results.

It was at this moment that I saw, from the corner of my eye, the three gaunt mullahs moving through the bazaar, intent upon finding the girls. It would be some moments before they reached this alley, and they might not see it. On the other hand, they might.

"You fools!" I shouted in Pashto, running down the alley. "This way! At once!"

I tried to grab the two girls, partly, I suppose, in order to see what Afghan women looked like with the chaderi removed, but they eluded me, and when they finally did face me, the shrouds were back in place and the girls were as mysterious, as silent as ever.

"The mullahs?" they asked in real fear.

"Yes! Hurry!"

I started to lead them to what I thought was safety, but the two couples, having surmounted the language barrier, had somehow planned their own escape routes, for in an instant, the girls vanished down a narrow pathway that led away from the approaching mullahs, while the two Marines vaulted the seemingly unscalable wall, and I was left alone in the cul-de-sac. I heard the angry mullahs behind me, whipping up a crowd, and on the spur of the moment I had the presence of mind to start urinating against the wall.

This even the mullahs understood, and I heard them cry in frustration from the other end of the alley, "The evil girls must be here." When I made my way through the crowd, I saw along the farther edge two shrouded figures, one in a fawn-colored chaderi, one in gray, drifting easily away from the bazaar. Their silken shrouds flowed in the wintry wind like the robes of Grecian goddesses, and along the snowy footpaths I watched the saddle shoes depart. I was aching with the mystery of sex, with the terrible allure that such undulating figures could evoke. I wanted to run after the girls and protest madly in Pashto that I needed them, that with the Marines gone I would like to make love with them, even in the hurried corner of a bazaar where men paused to urinate.

For the Marines would have to leave Afghanistan. That was clear. Regretfully I watched the girls disappear, then realized with some shame that I was inwardly pleased that the Marines would be sent home. I dismissed the unworthy thought and looked for a ghoddy. To my surprise one appeared promptly, occupied by Nur Muhammad, who had come down to survey matters from a distance.

"Trouble?" he asked blandly, pointing to the

mullahs, who were haranguing a crowd near the entrance to the bazaar.

"Just escaped," I reported. "A miracle."

I climbed onto the sloping seat of the ghoddy and we drove back toward the embassy. As the horse clip-clopped over the frozen mud that served as a road in Kabul, I noticed once more the little open ditches that lined most streets in the city. In them ran the public drinking water, since underground pipes were unknown in Afghanistan. But in the same ditches the citizens also urinated, pitched dead dogs, brushed teeth and washed all food that would be later eaten by the citizens, including ferangi stationed in the American and European embassies. I shuddered.

Ahead of me a man from the mountains, carbine slung over his back, squatted over the ditch and defecated, while not ten yards away a cook's helper, dressed like Nur Muhammad, unconcernedly washed the meat that would be served that night in the French embassy.

"A thing like that is a national disgrace," Nur said bitterly.

"Does the government know who the girls are? The saddle shoes, I mean?"

"Rumors whisper that one is Shah Khan's granddaughter."

"Does the old man know?" I probed.

"He's the one who protested to the ambassador."

"Is his granddaughter pretty?"

"They say she's a beauty," Nur replied. "I haven't met anyone who's seen her."

"Is it true that Shah Khan has openly stated he's

opposed to the chaderi?" I asked, trying to review our intelligence on the man I was shortly to see.

"Of course. That's why the mullahs tried to murder him last Ramadan."

"I have to be there at four," I repeated. Nur said he'd have the jeep ready, and I hurried to report to Captain Verbruggen. We arranged for the two Marines to be shipped out of the country that afternoon. They would ride an open truck down the long, perilous mountain passes to Peshawar, at the Indian end of the Khyber Pass. And in the years ahead they would relate such memories of Afghanistan as would inspire other young men to serve in distant nations.

2

Kabul was superb at the end of winter, particularly when the late afternoon sun rushed toward some rendezvous in Persia, to the west; for then the normal drabness of the miserable mud homes was masked in snow, and the solitary figures with carbines who moved across the empty fields outside of town bore an epic quality which captivated the eye. No stranger, at such a moment, could forget that he was in Asia.

Shah Khan lived well to the west, in a forbidding fortress hidden behind massive surrounding walls at least fifteen feet high. It must have required the forced labor of hundreds of convicts for many months to build the walls alone, for they enclosed many acres. This redoubtable establishment, complete with turrets and its own minaret, lay in the shadow of the beautiful Koh-i-Baba mountains, which were now snow-covered, reminding the foreigner that during the winter this city was practically inaccessible, unless one wished to risk his life on sloping mountain passes where each year many trucks were lost.

At the fortress gate through which one entered to visit Shah Khan there hung a bell cord, at which Nur Muhammad tugged vigorously, sending an echo through the frosty air. Normally the heavy gate would have been operated by some superannuated warrior who had served the owner in his youth, but when Nur yanked the cord a second time I thought I heard the pounding of horses' hoofs. Then, instead of the miserly half-inch through which the guards customarily peered at intending visitors, the gates were slammed violently open and a handsome man of thirty-six, astride a pawing white horse, greeted us.

"Mark Miller! Enter!" he cried in English. He was Moheb Khan, son of the Shah, educated at Oxford and at the Wharton School of Finance and Commerce. He held a responsible position in the Foreign Office, but on this day was affecting the dress of a prosperous mountain man, for he wore sheepskin trousers, an expensive embroidered vest, a long Russian-style fur coat, and a silver-gray karakul cap. He was clean-shaven, sharp-eyed and urbane, the educated Afghan at his best. I had talked with Moheb Khan several times before and had found him sophisticated in learning, dignified in bearing, and arrogant in judgment. He was tall and slim, with a large head marked by wavy black hair in which he took special pride. I respected him as one of the cleverest men I knew.

Whenever I was with Moheb I appreciated anew the fact that the future history of Afghanistan, if left to Afghans, would be determined by the struggle between the many bearded mullahs from the hills and the few young experts like Moheb, with degrees from Oxford or the Sorbonne or the Massachusetts Institute of Technology. I was not at all sure how the contest would eventuate, but it was clear that not only I but also all the people of all the embassies prayed that Moheb Khan and his young associates might win.

"Where'd you get the horse?" I asked, walking into the great compound, which in the nineteenth century had housed thousands of men during the frequent sieges.

"Look at the brand!" he cried, reaching down to shake my hand. "Pardon the glove," he added, "but I'm afraid to drop the reins."

He pointed to the horse's left flank, where a scrawling W had been burned deep into the hair and skin.

"I don't get it," I said.

"Think, Miller!"

"W," I repeated aloud. "I don't know any ranch with that brand."

"It's sentimental!" Moheb laughed. "Think! Think!"

I could not guess what the cryptic brand was intended to signify, and when Nur Muhammad edged the jeep into the compound, the horse shied and darted off across the snowy plain—it would be ridiculous to call that huge expanse of land a garden—and I could well observe the fine horsemanship that Moheb Khan exhibited.

He brought the dashing animal back to the jeep, to familiarize the horse with the sound of a motor car, then leaped with agility to the ground beside me and cupped his hands near my right knee, all in one marvelously synchronized movement. "You ride," he commanded.

There was something that no stranger ever became accustomed to in Afghanistan: the peremp-

tory command of the educated Afghan. "You ride!"
a friend said, and you got the feeling that if you
didn't leap on the horse immediately one of those
omnipresent carbines was going to go off. So I
threw my right foot into the cupped hands and,
leaping upward to match his strong lift, I was
astride the white horse.

At Groton I had taken horsemanship, and I
could ride passably well, but it quickly became apparent that I was not going to tell this horse what
to do. Yet the semi-wild animal loved the feel of a
man on his back, for he tore across the huge field
in such a way as to blend his movements with
mine. I thought: He wants to frighten me, but he
also wants me on hand so that there'll be someone
to frighten. He did not exactly ignore the reins, nor
did he respond quickly. Like a willful child he
must have thought: If I pay no attention to him,
this rider may forget the whole thing. But when I
quietly insisted that he obey my commands, he accommodated himself to them, tardily and with a
trace of rebellion. He was a superb horse, and I
brought him back to the jeep, where Moheb Khan
stood talking with Nur Muhammad.

When the horse was close to the idling jeep,
Moheb suddenly reached for the accelerator with
his hand, jammed it down so that the engine exploded once or twice, thus sending the horse high
in the air. Fortunately I had not yet dropped the
reins, and I tugged at them fiercely to bring the
frightened beast back under control. I was furious
with Moheb for this reckless act—training his horse
at my peril—and on the spur of the moment I dug
my heels into the flanks of the white beast and we

tore across the open land, turning and twisting and cavorting for some minutes. At the end of our exciting ride I brought the horse back to the jeep and called sternly, "Nur Muhammad, turn off the engine."

But before he could do so, Moheb Khan again jammed the accelerator pedal to the floor. This time I held the horse steady, then threw the reins to Moheb. "He's a good horse," I said.

"You're a good rider, Miller. Better than any American I've seen yet." I laughed and he asked, "You don't fathom the brand?"

"Who can fathom the brain of an Afghan?" I joked.

"Not I," Moheb confessed. "But your failure does surprise me."

"Where'd you get the horse?" I asked again, as we walked toward the main house, an imposing mud-walled castle around which clustered twelve or thirteen smaller buildings.

"Some traders brought him down from the north. Said they got him over the Oxus in Russia. I had a man from the Russian embassy out one afternoon and the horse did seem to recognize Russian commands."

"Splendid beast," I said, "Russian or whatever."

Moheb Khan led me through the rugged door of the main house, whose mud walls were more than thirty inches thick. I said, "They must keep you cool in summer."

Moheb replied, "More important, they withstood British cannon for eleven days." He pointed to spots where there were deep indentations. With an imperial afterthought, he indicated to Nur Muhammad where he should wait, then took me in to see his father.

Shah Khan—his name could be translated as Sir Mister and was hardly a name at all—was a slim patrician who had served as adviser to three successive kings. He was thin and gray, wore a trim mustache, expensive Harris tweeds tailored in London, and a heavy gold watch chain across his vest. Normally he spoke Persian, but in dealing with foreigners, he preferred French, for he had attended the Sorbonne; but he was also competent in English, German and Pashto, the language of the countryside. Like all educated Afghans, Shah Khan looked to France as the source of culture, to Germany as the source of military instruction, to America as the source of canned goods, and to England as the fountainhead of duplicity. Nevertheless, it was with the latter country that Afghanistan had always maintained its closest ties, like a husband who hates his wife yet would be lost if she deserted him.

One of the reasons why Shah Khan had taken a liking to me, and confided in me when he refused to do so with other Americans, was that although I could not speak Persian I did speak French, and he could thus indulge his obsession that diplomacy must be conducted only in that language. Today we would speak French.

The room in which we talked was important in the history of Afghanistan and essential to any understanding of the modern nation. Here had occurred spectacular murders which altered the course of dynasty, protracted sieges, secret councils and, strangest of all, Christian weddings under the sponsorship of Shah Khan. They took place whenever some exile from Europe wished to marry a Christian girl from one of the embassies, for there often were no Christian ministers available in Kabul.

It was a rocky fortress of a room, built by a German architect, furnished by a Danish merchant who sold only the best, and decorated by a Frenchman who spent eleven thousand dollars in shipping charges alone. On one wall there was a Picasso, but nothing the French decorator had devised could alter the Germanic heaviness of the room, and it remained a typical Afghan salon.

On the low table from Copenhagen lay copies of the *London Illustrated News*, the *Manchester Guardian*, *Newsweek*, the *Reader's Digest* and six or seven French magazines. Against one wall stood a huge Gramophone with numerous speakers, for Shah Khan loved music, as did his son, Moheb. Another wall contained the principal British, Italian, French and American encyclopedias, as well as novels in five or six different languages.

Shah Khan, who could be as Afghan as his room, asked bluntly, "What do you wish to discuss?"

I showed him the leather folder and replied, "Our government is demanding that we report where Ellen Jaspar is."

"They've been doing that for the better part of a year," Shah Khan parried. He sat deep in a leather chair which his grandfather had purchased in Berlin. Not even the French decorator had been able to banish it from the room, but he had succeeded in staining the leather an objectionable red.

"But this time, Your Excellency, it isn't merely

the government who demands. It's the senator from Pennsylvania."

"Is that important?" the old Afghan parried.

"Well," I fumbled. "Let's say that in America a senator has the same powers that you have in Kabul. Now suppose you sent the embassy in Paris an inquiry. Wouldn't you expect an answer?"

"I certainly would. Moheb, did you know the senator from Pennsylvania?"

"Which one?" Moheb asked quickly. He rattled off the names of the two senators. "I liked them both."

"Are they significant men?" his father asked.

"Very," Moheb replied. The young man was an unusual Afghan, in that while he was a devout Muslim, he also drank alcohol, and he now poured me a drink of whiskey. His father, a Muslim of the old school, felt obliged to reprove his son because the drinking took place before a Christian. Accordingly he spoke harshly in Pashto, whereupon I replied in the same language, "Let the blame be upon me, Your Excellency." This reminder that I spoke not only French but also the Afghan language softened the old man.

"You feel, Monsieur Miller, that this time something must be done."

"Indeed, or we shall all be reprimanded. Perhaps called home."

"Let us suffer the evils that we know rather than flee to those we know not of," Shah Khan replied, paraphrasing Hamlet in French. "Have you new material about this unfortunate girl?"

I checked with Shah Khan and his alert son the facts that our embassy knew about Ellen Jaspar

and Nazrullah. In the autumn of 1942 the Afghan
government had sent a fine young man from Kabul
to the Wharton School, the business end of the
University of Pennsylvania, in Philadelphia. This
Nazrullah, who was then twenty-four—eight years
younger than Moheb Khan—came from a good
Kabul family, was bright, good-looking and en-
dowed with a very comfortable expense account
which allowed him to buy, from a Philadelphia
used-car dealer, a Cadillac convertible painted red.

The young Afghan cut a swath in Philadelphia
society. He was seen everywhere—Merion, Bryn
Mawr, New Hope. At the same time, the solid engineering degree he had earned in Germany prepared him to work for high marks at the Wharton
School.

Moheb added, "In spite of his enthusiastic social
life, Nazrullah was an honor student. I kept tabs
on him, since I was serving in the embassy in
Washington at the time."

"Didn't Nazrullah's time at the Wharton School
overlap yours?" Shah Khan asked.

"No," Moheb explained. "Don't you remember?
You sent him to Wharton because I'd done fairly
well there."

I pointed excitedly at Moheb and shouted in English. "That's it! The W stands for Wharton!"

"Exactly!" Moheb shouted back, and we raised
our glasses.

"What's this foolishness?" old Shah Khan asked
from the depths of his red leather chair.

"Your son branded his white horse with a W. In
honor of his degree from Wharton," I explained.

"Preposterous," Shah Khan growled, plainly irritated by his son's noisy drinking.

"Nazrullah was offered half a dozen jobs in America," Moheb added, "but he preferred to help us out here at home."

"Where'd he meet the Jaspar girl?" Shah Khan asked, fingering his gold chain.

"Those were the years," Moheb reminded us, "when there weren't too many American men available. Nazrullah . . ."

"What's his last name?" I interrupted.

"Just Nazrullah," Moheb replied. "Like so many Afghans, he has no last name. As to the girl. She was a junior at Bryn Mawr. I think he may have met her while he was playing tennis at Merion. She came from a good family in Dorset, Pennsylvania."

"Where's that?" I asked, finding it strange to be asking an Afghan about American geography.

"Small town in Penns County," Moheb explained. "North of Philadelphia."

"They didn't get married in Dorset," I explained to Shah Khan.

"I should say not!" Moheb agreed vociferously. "Her family raised bloody hell. Bryn Mawr did the same. You know what that girl did? In the middle of the war she went to England, wangled her way to India, and came up the Khyber Pass in a donkey caravan. She was married here in Kabul."

"It was a brilliant wedding," Shah Khan remembered. "Have you a picture of the girl, Monsieur Miller?"

From my files I produced several photographs of Ellen Jaspar. As a sophomore at Bryn Mawr she had played in Shakespeare—Olivia in *Twelfth*

Night—a thin, good-looking blonde and apparently graceful. In her junior year she sang in the chorus that co-operated with Fritz Reiner in doing Beethoven's *Ninth Symphony*, and in her surplice with her blond hair peeking from under her cap she looked angelic. There were pictures of her and Nazrullah, she a lovely white and he a romantic brown. And there was one picture of her when she graduated from high school, wide-eyed and smiling, yet somehow apprehensive. I had known a thousand girls like Ellen Jaspar; they adorned the campuses at Radcliffe, Smith and Holyoke. They all did well in English, poorly in mathematics, indifferently in philosophy. They were the vibrant, exciting girls who would seriously consider, in the middle of their junior year, marrying a young man from Afghanistan or Argentina or Turkestan. Most of them, in their senior year, developed more sense and married young men from Denver or Mobile or Somerville, outside of Boston.

"What made her different?" Shah Khan asked.

"We have the reports. Her father says he begged her not to do this thing, and all she would reply was that she was fed up with Dorset, Pennsylvania, and that she would rather die on the sands of the desert than marry the young man from that town who had been courting her."

"Is Dorset so bad?" the old Afghan asked. "I knew many small towns in France, and they weren't exciting, but they weren't bad, either."

"I used to drive out to Dorset," Moheb Khan replied. "I remember it as a lovely American town. Rather colonial in architecture, I recall."

"But you didn't live there," the old man reflected.

(35)

"As a matter of fact, I did," Moheb corrected. "For three days. Ellen and Nazrullah drove me up one Friday afternoon. He wanted the Jaspars to see that in Afghanistan we had many young men who spoke well. It was an agonizing weekend."

"The Jaspars took the whole thing rather dimly?" I asked.

Moheb was about to reply when I received the distinct sensation that some additional person had entered the room. A presence of some kind seemed to hover near me in the heavy battle-room and I thought I saw old Shah Khan looking over my shoulder and shaking his head. I turned in the direction of whoever it was who might be receiving the message, and there was no one. But I did see something I had not noticed when I first arrived in the room. In the hallway, thrown across a chair as an American child might throw her raincoat, lay a fawn-colored chaderi.

"Dimly?" Moheb was echoing. "The Jaspars looked at Nazrullah and me as if we had leprosy."

"What did Mr. Jaspar work at?" I asked. "Wasn't it insurance?"

"Yes. He had that sweet, affable nature that insurance men around the world acquire," Moheb replied. "I liked him, and his wife was equally pleasant. He was also chairman, I believe, of the local draft board. A position of responsibility."

"Later on," Shah Khan inquired, "didn't you advise the Jaspars against an Afghan marriage?"

"Yes. I met them in Philadelphia, and I brought along our ambassador from Washington, and the four of us . . . Nazrullah and Ellen knew nothing of this meeting and did not attend. We discussed the matter quite frankly."

"You told them the truth?" I asked.

"Completely. As I recall, our ambassador was rather unhappy and thought the explicitness of my explanation unnecessary. Told me later I might have damaged our nation's reputation. I told the Jaspars that if their daughter married Nazrullah, when she reached Kabul her American passport would be taken away and she could never thereafter leave Afghanistan, no matter what the excuse, without her husband's permission. That she was an Afghan then and forever, and that she surrendered all claim to protection from America."—

"You told them that as clearly as you are telling me?" Shah Khan asked.

"Yes."

"What did they say?"

"Mrs. Jaspar began to cry."

"Did you warn them about Afghan salaries and living conditions?" I asked.

"I did. Most explicitly," Moheb assured me. "I said, 'Mr. Jaspar, Ellen mustn't be deceived by the fact that in America Nazrullah drives a Cadillac and I a Mercedes. Our government is very generous to us as long as we're abroad, but when we go home Nazrullah and I will get jobs that pay no more than twenty American dollars a month.'"

"Did they believe you?"

"They saw the cars and were sure I was lying. In Dorset, Pennsylvania, as in Kabul, cupidity is the same. The Jaspars were convinced that Nazrullah was very rich."

"What does he earn now?" I asked.

The Khans conversed in Pashto and agreed that Nazrullah and his American bride had begun with a salary of twenty-one dollars a month and that it had now grown to twenty-seven, more or less.

"And I explained the housing," Moheb continued. "I said that for much of her life Ellen would live in a hovel, surrounded by women who despised her for not wearing the chaderi . . ."

"Is it true, Your Excellency," I asked, "that Afghanistan may soon discard the chaderi?"

The old man leaned back in his red leather chair and replied, "You Americans seem inordinately preoccupied with the chaderi. Look!" and he pointed to the chair in the hall. "My own granddaughter wears the chaderi and her mother graduated from the Sorbonne." I looked again at the fawn-colored shroud.

"Does your granddaughter enjoy doing so?" I asked.

"We do not concern ourselves about that," Shah Khan replied.

"But the Russians do," I responded, touching a sore point with the old man. "They say they will force you to set your women free, as they have done theirs."

I knew instinctively that he wanted to speak further on this point, that he agreed with me and the Russians that the chaderi must go or revolution come, but he stopped the conversation with this observation: "I learned today that the young woman from your embassy, Miss Maxwell, was assaulted by three mullahs from the hills. You rescued her, I believe. Then you know how powerful these fanatics still are. The chaderi will remain."

"I assured the Jaspars," Moheb continued, "that Ellen would not have to wear one, but that Nazrullah's family would hate her if she didn't. I also warned them that if Ellen appeared in public without the chaderi, mullahs' might spit at her." His voice grew harsh as he added, "Miller Sahib, I told the Jaspars of every fact relating to ferangi wives in Afghanistan and later on I told Ellen herself. I was as honest as a man could be. I warned her that if she married Nazrullah she would become a woman without a country, a woman without a judge to protect her, a woman with no human rights at all, an animal . . . an animal." He rose and walked with great agitation up and down the fortress room. "And I remember exactly what I said, Miller, because a year later I had to tell another girl, from Baltimore this time, the same dismal story, and this girl had sense enough not to marry me, but your damned Miss Jaspar went ahead and married Nazrullah, and now senators are trying to find out where she is."

He fell into a chair, poured himself a drink and reflected, "This preposterous Afghan government. It says, 'When young Afghans go abroad they must live like gentlemen.' So the government provides huge expense accounts and we buy Cadillacs. What allowance do you suppose I got when I was at the Wharton School? One thousand dollars every month. No wonder the girls wanted to marry us. But when that same government brought me home, you know the salary I got—twenty-one dollars a month. Right now, Nazrullah heads an irrigation project west of Kandahar and earns twenty-seven dollars a month . . . more or less."

(39)

"Is his wife with him?" I asked bluntly.

"Which wife?" Shah Khan asked.

I was startled. "What do you mean, which wife?"

"Didn't you tell the Jaspars about that?" Shah Khan asked his son.

"There are some things an Afghan doesn't discuss in a foreign country," Moheb replied.

"Was Nazrullah married before he went to America?" I pressed.

"He had a family wife, of course," Shah Khan explained. "But that signifies nothing."

"That's not in the file," I protested.

"Enter it now," the old man said. "Nazrullah was married before he met the American girl. That should put the Jaspars at ease." As soon as he had said this, he apologized. "I'm sorry, Miller Sahib. That was ungenerous. I'm as worried as the Jaspars must be. Where is their daughter? They haven't heard from her, you tell me, in more than thirteen months? What a terrible burden on good parents."

The old man began to cry, and wiped tears from his dark eyes. Afghans, I had learned, were very apt to cry on little notice, but these tears were real.

When he had mastered his weeping he added in a beautiful French whisper, "Our family showed the same prudence as Nazrullah's. Before we allowed Moheb to leave for England we married him to a local girl from a good Muslim family. We reasoned, 'Later on, if he also marries an English girl, no harm will be done. When he works in Kabul he'll have a Muslim family and when he's sent to Europe he'll have an attractive English wife.' I remember discussing the matter with Nazrullah's parents. We promised, 'We won't allow the boys to leave home till they've had one or two Afghan babies.' It worked very well."

"Did you explain that to the Baltimore girl?" I asked Moheb.

"No," he replied honestly, "but I suppose it was what drove me to describe so frankly the other drawbacks of life in Afghanistan."

I put my hands squarely on the leather folder and said, "All right, where can the Jaspar girl be?"

Shah Khan ordered a glass of orangeade, a foul sweet drink which abstemious Afghans took in place of alcohol. It was brought, of course, by a befezzed man, for in a country adhering to the chaderi, men must do much of the work usually done by women.

"I've been pondering this problem," Shah Khan reflected. "It isn't easy to obtain news from a city as far away as Kandahar, but we manage. We find that Nazrullah and his American wife . . . you understand that his Muslim wife stays here in Kabul with the children?"

"More than one child?" I asked.

"Yes, he had one before he went to the Wharton School and one after he got back."

I pondered this, then pointed out, "But he must have been living with the Jaspar girl when he had the second child?"

"Of course. But he also had responsibilities to his Afghan wife. She merited consideration."

"So he gave her another baby?" I asked.

"It's difficult to comprehend our attitude toward women," Shah Khan confessed. "We cherish them. We love them. We protect them. And we dedicate most of our poetry to them. But we don't want them cluttering up our lives."

(41)

"I'd think that two wives would do just that," I demurred.

"My life is one of the most uncluttered I know," Shah Khan assured me quietly, "yet I have four wives."

"Four?" I asked.

Something in the way I looked at the old man amused him, for he said quietly, "You Americans picture a man with four wives as leaping from bed to bed till he drops of exhaustion. It isn't like that . . . not at all. Fact is, in some ways I'm worse off than the average American businessman. He marries young, outgrows his wife and gets rid of her. I can't. When a girl marries me, she leaves her home forever and I can't send her back. I've got to support her in my home the rest of her life, unless I divorce her, which would be a public disgrace. So as the years go by I move these good women, one by one, into back bedrooms. In energy and money the American and the Afghan systems cost about the same."

Moheb interrupted, "The Muslim attitude toward women was a response to historical forces, and the interesting thing is that these same forces are acting now to make America polygamous."

Before I could challenge this surprising theory, Shah Khan observed, "Moheb's right. Islam was born in a period when war and ambuscade killed off our men. Each family had a burdensome surplus of women, and Muhammad, with his superbly practical mind, saw there were only three ways of dealing with the matter. Either you converted the needless women into marketplace whores, or edged them into ritual celibacy, or portioned them out as extra wives. Muhammad, always the most moral of men, shuddered at prostitution and gave the women legal status as wives. He chose the flawless solution."

"How does this apply to America?" I asked.

Shah Khan ignored my question. "So under our system I've had to take care of many women . . . wives, brothers' wives, grandmothers. By the way, Miller Sahib, do you know anything of a Quaker school near Philadelphia called the George School? We're thinking of sending my granddaughter Siddiqa there. The other girls have always gone to Paris."

Cautiously I asked, "How old is Siddiqa?"

"How old is she?" Shah Khan asked.

"Seventeen," Moheb replied. "She prefers things American and we thought . . ."

"It's a good school," I said. "Coeducational. Boys and girls."

"It isn't a convent?" Shah Khan asked with some surprise.

"Oh, no!"

"That takes care of America," Shah Khan growled. "Off she goes to Paris. But what Moheb said earlier is true. The forces that drove Islam to plural marriage will operate throughout the world. In France, for example, I thought their handling of the problem was pathetic . . . mistresses, liaisons, scandal, murder."

"But Moheb referred to America," I pointed out.

The young diplomat sipped his whiskey, then reflected, "Do you know the thing which impressed me most in America? The frightening excess of women over men. In some cities like Washington and New York the situation was scandalous."

"You were there during wartime," I pointed out.

"And peacetime," he reminded me. "You not only have more women than men in the population, but you also have an increasing number of young men who remove themselves from the marriage market. Homosexuality, Oedipus complexes, withdrawal from competition, psychological crippling . . ."

Shah Khan interrupted to observe gently, "The point is, Miller Sahib, that brilliant young men like you come to Afghanistan and say, 'Such a quaint land beset by such quaint problems.' When I go to France or Moheb to America we make exactly the same observation."

"And the most quaint," Moheb laughed, "is the way in which your society pretends to be shocked when some man is caught with two wives, legal or otherwise. What do you expect a girl to do when she realizes there aren't enough husbands to go around? Grab someone else's . . . I would."

Since I had not come to Shah Khan's for a lecture on the shortcomings of my country, I asked abruptly, "Then Ellen Jaspar was last heard of in Kandahar?"

"Not exactly," Shah Khan replied. "We know she was there, because one day some mullahs attacked her on the street. Not wearing the chaderi. She distinguished herself by fighting back, and her husband joined her. Between them they kicked the devil out of the mullahs, and I'm glad they did."

"Must have made her popular in Kandahar," I suggested.

"Didn't matter one way or the other," Shah Khan

laughed. "Most of us in government are bloody well fed up with mullahs, but we don't know what to do about them. At any rate, her outburst didn't harm Nazrullah's chances, for shortly he was promoted to the best engineering job in the country. Set up headquarters in the old fortress at Qala Bist."

The old man's eyes misted over at the mention of this great name in Afghan history and he asked, "Monsieur Miller, have you ever seen Qala Bist?"

I hadn't, but I refrained from comment because I didn't want to get the old patriot off on a tirade about the vanished glories of Afghanistan. My trick didn't work, for he said quietly, "This fantastic arch rising from the desert and reflected in the river. It's as beautiful an arch as there is in the world. I much prefer it to Ctesiphon. No one recalls when it was built, but the building it was attached to must have been immense. There's a fort nearby which surely housed ten thousand men, and an abandoned city of perhaps half a million. Now we don't even remember what the city was named."

"What's he doing at Qala Bist?" I asked, for I had learned at previous meetings that when Shah Khan started talking about the lost glories of Afghanistan, reaching back long before the days of Alexander the Great, there was no stopping him. In fact, I had acquired much of my Afghan history from such reminiscences, for unlike those of other men, the reflections of old Shah Khan were founded in fact. If he said Qala Bist had once been a city of half a million, it had been, and now even the history of the city was lost.

"Nazrullah and his American wife went there for preliminary work on our big irrigation project," Shah Khan explained.

Moheb added, "We know that she reached Qala Bist, for we had letters from them. But that was nine months ago."

"What would your guess be?" I asked.

"Judging from what's happened to other ferangi wives"—both Moheb and his father used the word *ferangi* no matter what language they were speaking—"three things could have taken place. Miss Jaspar could have killed herself in despair, or she could have been locked up by her husband with no possibility of escape, not even to send a letter. Or she could have tried to run away. There's a British railroad station, you know, at Chaman, but we've asked there and she didn't reach Chaman."

"Your guess?" I insisted.

"Putting myself in Nazrullah's place," Moheb ventured, "I would suggest these lines of possibility. Nazrullah was very kind to his American wife and tried to soften all the blows her vanity received. He took her as quickly as possible away from his domineering family, where his women must have made her life unbearable. At Kandahar he reasoned with her and helped her adjust to living on mud floors on twenty-seven dollars a month. She wanted to go back to America, but he refused permission, as was his right, and after a series of dreadful scenes she decided to run away on her own account and perished before she reached the frontier. It's happened before."

"But why hasn't Nazrullah reported these matters?" I asked.

"For two reasons," Moheb Khan replied, bowing to his father's judgment. "First, she is only a woman and nothing to get excited about. When he gets back to Kabul he'll explain everything. Second, because he truly loved Ellen Jaspar and still thinks she may have survived and will come back to him."

We sat silent for some minutes and I noticed that the wintry darkness had enveloped us, stealing down from the Koh-i-Baba on icy blasts of wind that ripped across the plain which lay between the fortress walls. Snow eddied in the darkness like the passage of a white horse, and we were alone in the massive room of a massive fort that had withstood shocks from the Koh-i-Baba and from other quarters.

"Would you object, Khan Sahib, if I went to Kandahar and Qala Bist? Some very important Americans insist upon knowing."

"If I were your age, Miller Sahib," the old man replied, "I should have gone to Kandahar long ere this."

"I have your permission, then?"

"My blessing. In spite of the rude comments of my son, we Afghans do get excited about beautiful women. And if she is a ferangi woman, we respect those ferangi who get excited about her, too."

To my own surprise, I asked abruptly, "Shah Khan, have you a photograph of your granddaughter, Siddiqa? The one who wants to go to School in America?"

"No," the old man replied. "We true Muslims

don't like photography. It seems a violation of our religious principles. An intrusion on the essence of a man."

"And especially a woman?" I laughed.

"Yes, it is quite contrary to the spirit of the chaderi. But I will tell you this, Monsieur Miller, she is an unusually pretty girl, and she is the child whom you caught kissing the soldier in the bazaar this morning."

I was shocked by his knowledge of an event which I supposed that I alone had witnessed. "The Marines are already on their way to Khyber Pass," I mumbled.

"If they had not been expelled," Shah Khan replied evenly, proving that his intelligence service covered Americans as well as Afghans, "I would not now be talking with you. Moheb, get Monsieur Miller's jeep."

When the younger man had left, old Shah Khan rose from his leather chair and walked with me to the door. I looked past him for a moment, staring at the fawn-colored chaderi, and the former sensation of overpowering sexuality repossessed me, and I felt dizzy, as if the shroud were exuding its own perfume.

"These damned girls!" The old man laughed. "They douse their chaderies with cheap French essence. To make the boys notice them more. Smell this!" And he picked up the fawn chaderi and smothered my face with it. The perfume was heavy and clung to my nostrils after he had withdrawn the silk.

The old warrior put his arm about me and said, "Monsieur Miller, concerning the Jaspar girl. We do have one bit of additional information. Perhaps I shouldn't call it information. Nothing but absurd speculation, I suspect. Anyway, it's so bizarre, really, that I won't suffer myself to repeat it. Perhaps it represents what happened, but when you get to Kandahar you'll undoubtedly hear the rumor. So you judge for yourself."

"You won't tell me?" I begged.

"I would abhor having in your file my name even remotely attached to such a rumor. I've my reputation to consider. But you're a younger man. You can risk such embarrassments, and I wish you Godspeed." I was always astonished to rediscover that Muslims shared our God in exactly the form we used Him. There it was, old Shah Khan wishing me Godspeed, and there could be no doubt that he was referring to the One God.

"Papers authorizing your travel to Kandahar and wherever else you may have to go in the area will be at your office in the morning," the old man assured me.

"Thank you, Shah Khan," I replied, and when he opened the door leading to the waiting jeep I saw his son, Moheb Khan, once more upon the white horse, leaping and twisting and roaring off across the snow. As he disappeared in a cloud of flakes I thought: That must be the only horse in the world branded with a W for the Wharton School in Philadelphia.

3

In Afghanistan almost every building bears jagged testimony to some outrage. Some, like the walled fortress now owned by Shah Khan, were built to withstand sieges, and did so many times. Others were the scenes of horrible murder and retaliation. In distant areas, scars still remained of Alexander the Great or Genghis Khan or Tamerlane or Nadir Shah, of Persia. Was there ever a land so overrun by terror and devastation as Afghanistan?

Yet of all the buildings which testified to acts of violence none was more evocative than the group that huddled within the British compound, for here scenes of terrible defeat and massacre had taken place, here loyalties were betrayed, here brave men died with daggers across their throats, and the fact that the British still maintained friendly relations with Afghanistan was tribute to English resilience.

In 1946 the British compound was probably the most civilized center in Afghanistan, a fortress of its own well out into the country, with its private gardens, tennis courts and restaurants. It was here that the European community, in which the Americans were grudgingly included, met on long winter evenings to read plays. Tonight, fresh from the typewriters of the English, Italian and American embassies, in that order, the play was to be *Born Yesterday,* a boisterous comedy which had opened in New York only the month before. Ingrid, a stately Swedish girl, was scheduled to read the part of Billie Dawn. An Englishman who imagined that he could talk like an American gangster was to be Harry Brock, and I was to read the part of the *New Republic* reporter.

Italians, Frenchmen and the Turkish ambassador's wife completed the cast, and looking back upon such readings I am still impressed by the intellectual pleasure we had when the snow was so high in Kabul. We were, in a very real sense, cut off from everything that civilized men and women had come to take for granted: books, magazines, theaters, hotels, music. All we had were our own personalities, with what understandings and memories we had acquired through the years; and it was reassuring to discover what a vivid social life was possible under those circumstances. Never have I known better wit nor more exciting conversation than in the crowded little rooms of Kabul. Never have I known a group of people to be so self-sufficient, so enchanting as human beings. In those years I used to see the same two dozen people night after night, and they were rewarding beyond expectation, partly because any escape from them or their individualities was impossible.

On this night our reading—in which we were peremptorily handed pieces of paper we had not seen before and directed to read specific parts, growing into them as the night progressed—was delayed because Miss Maxwell, from my office, was late in arriving, and since she had typed Act Three and was to read one of the minor parts, we felt the least we could do was to wait for her. However, our host, the British ambassador, found Miss Maxwell's tardiness embarrassing since he was at the moment entertaining Sir Herbert Chinnery, the stiff, mustachioed Inspector Ordinary for Asia, whose duty it was to report on conditions at the British embassy in Afghanistan as he had just done for the embassy in Persia, and it was important that Sir Herbert be pleased.

"Don't worry," Sir Herbert said graciously, putting us all at ease. "I've learned that Americans are rarely punctual."

I replied that I was sure Miss Maxwell must have met with some misfortune—temporary, I hoped—for she had that very morning risen at six in order to type her share of the play and had then, at some risk to herself, insisted upon delivering it to the Italian embassy, to which Signorina Risposi could testify. "As a matter of fact," I concluded, "in performing her duty Miss Maxwell was subjected to harsh treatment at the hands of three mullahs . . ."

"The usual?" Sir Herbert asked.

"Spitting, jostling, curses in Pashto," I explained.

"That's the second time it's happened this week," the ambassador said.

"I've a mind to advise Whitehall," Sir Herbert confided, "that all English girls in Kabul go into chaderi immediately."

"Oh, dear, no!" squealed a peaches-and-cream English girl called Gretchen Askwith. "Oh, Sir Herbert. No, I beg you."

It always seemed to me that the British went a little far in their coyness, but Gretchen Askwith was quite the loveliest of the unmarried white girls in Kabul, and it ill behooved me to think poorly of her, for although there were six or eight eligible young European men among the various embassies, I appeared to be the one most likely to win Gretchen's attention . . . that is, if she didn't discover that I was Jewish, a fact which none of the ferangi embassies yet knew.

There was not good blood between the British and the Americans in Afghanistan. The English tolerated us, and that's about all. Captain Verbruggen was thought to be a great bore and unlettered as well. Our secretaries were too pretty and too highly paid. Our Marines were undisciplined. And men like me were much too brash. In fact, about the only thing American that impressed the British was my ability to speak Pashto, but this was diminished by the fact that three of their chaps did too, including one chinless young man who spoke Russian and Persian as well. Still, we were tolerated because our kitchens served excellent food and our bars were generally open.

"There she is now!" Sir Herbert cried, with that boyish excitement that even the oldest Englishmen often retain, but when the door opened it was not Miss Maxwell but an unexpected guest, Moheb Khan. He was now dressed in a blue Bond Street pin-stripe worsted, with handsome brown leather shoes and a London shirting. He had transformed himself into a most proper diplomat, and in this guise presented himself to the ambassador.

"On three occasions, sir, you've asked me to

these readings. May I choose my own time?"

"My dear fellow, you honor us!"

"I hear the play's very funny. I'd not have known about it except that I stopped by the Italian embassy and was told of its merit by Signorina Risposi." He bowed toward the Italian typist, who was quite plump.

"She told you the truth," Sir Herbert interrupted. "Our man in Washington saw it last month. Laughed so much he airmailed me a script."

There was a moment of emptiness, into which the Swedish girl said loudly, "Couldn't we start? Miss Maxwell doesn't participate until Act Two."

"I think it would be better if we waited," Sir Herbert insisted. "After all, the dear girl did much of the typing, Mr. Miller informs me."

Miss Askwith added, "And after her bout with the mullahs . . ."

"Do you think the mullahs are gaining ground in their battle for control?" Sir Herbert asked Moheb Khan.

"No," the Afghan replied cautiously. "On the other hand, they're not losing ground, either."

"Some time ago there was talk of discarding the chaderi," Sir Herbert suggested, and our discussion proceeded from that point. I had found, even in my short stay, that Afghanistan had two topics of conversation which were positively guaranteed to excite participation: the chaderi and the latest cure for diarrhea, for with the kind of drinking water available in Kabul, this latter scourge was sooner or later bound to infect everyone. Sure enough, not long after the chaderi was disposed of I heard Signorina Risposi advising the group.

"A German doctor has invented something much better than entero-vioform. It's called sulfas, I believe. Developed during the war."

"Does it work?" the Swedish girl was asking.

"My theory," Sir Herbert interrupted, "has always been to fill the lower bowel with some bland bulk producer like one of the new mucils. You'd be surprised how this slows down the bowel action."

"Really?" the Turkish ambassador's wife pursued. "I've relied on entero-vioform, and it seems to concentrate rather effectively on the upper bowel. But when it fails, it fails."

The dialogue now switched to French, for one of the scientists in that country had developed a radically new drug which the French ambassador's wife was explaining, and I thought: This must be the only capital in the world where a sophisticated international audience can discuss with all seriousness the control of the upper and lower bowel. Yet no aspect of Afghan life was more significant than this, for when the virulent Asiatic diarrhea, known locally as the Kabul Trots, struck, it was not like a stomach ache back home. It was a sickness which nauseated, embarrassed, debilitated and outraged the human body. In a land where toilet facilities were not excessive, diarrhea was a scourge, and I was willing to gamble that not a single person in that softly lit room, lined with books, was without his or her secret vial of pills and even more secret roll of personal toilet paper.

"What do you do for the disease?" the French ambassador's wife asked Moheb Khan in French.

"It's very simple," Moheb replied in lilting English. "You Europeans are always shocked at our open water supply into which little boys urinate. Or worse. But what happens? From drinking such water most of our children die, and that's neither a curse nor a blessing. They die and that's that. So the life expectancy in Afghanistan is about twenty-three years. But that figure doesn't mean what it says, not really. For if by chance you are one of the babies who does not die, you are inoculated against positively everything. Look about you. See the large number of our men who live to an extreme old age. With the women, I can assure you, it is the same. If you drink our water till you are seven, nothing can kill you but a bullet." He thumped his chest and laughed.

A rotund English doctor, on temporary duty in Kabul, said quietly, "You know, of course, he's not teasing. Take poliomyelitis, which strikes so many children in an antiseptic country like America . . ."

"Here no child gets polio," Moheb Khan insisted. "But you Europeans who come to us later in life, when you've not had the inoculations our water imparts . . . How many cases have we had of polio among the Europeans?"

"Many, even in my time," the fat doctor concurred.

There was a sound at the door, and in a moment Miss Maxwell appeared, flushed from the deep cold and from some experience which had left her stunned. "It's too much!" she cried in a kind of wild exhilaration.

"What happened?" many voices cried.

"This morning," she said excitedly. "The three mullahs screaming at me."

"We know about that unfortunate affair," Sir Herbert said consolingly.

"I didn't mind it," Miss Maxwell said. "I left Omaha to see Afghanistan, and I love it." Seeing Moheb she ran to him and took his hands. "What do you suppose I just saw? Not two hundred yards from the embassy?"

"More mullahs?" Moheb asked quietly.

"Wolves!" Miss Maxwell reported. "Yes, a huge pack of wolves. They were running across an open field where the snow was thick."

"The storms have driven them down from the mountains," Moheb Khan explained. "At this time of the year . . ."

"Would they attack . . . a man?" someone asked.

"They're ravenously hungry," Moheb replied. "In the morning you may hear . . . Well, they are wolves, down from the Hindu Kush."

The concept of wild wolves, running in a pack through the outskirts of Kabul, running until they found a straggler, either animal or human, cast a spell of terror over the group that had gathered to read a comedy. We felt chilly, and Sir Herbert directed his Afghan houseboy to throw on more logs. We felt very close to each other, and our group became more compact. Miss Maxwell, I am glad to say, did not try to monopolize the center of attention. She simply reported, "They were not at all like the wolves in Walt Disney. They were animals, great shaggy, terrifying animals."

"Did they have long teeth?" Signorina Risposi asked.

"I don't know. At such a moment . . . You know, they dashed right at our car. If I'd been driving I

(57)

don't know what I'd have done. But our boy, Sadruddin, was in charge and he blew the horn sharply. Like one huge animal with many legs they swerved away and disappeared."

"Where?" the Swedish girl asked.

"Toward town," Miss Maxwell said, pointing toward where we all lived.

"It's one reason why we built high walls," Moheb Khan reflected in French.

"This is a land of startling contrasts," the French ambassador agreed.

"Do the wolves surprise you?" Moheb asked the general audience in English. "Before we read the play, tell me. Do the wolves surprise you?"

"No," the French ambassador replied in English. "When we come to Kabul we expect . . . Well, we expect the Hindu Kush."

"But we are never prepared for what we expect," Sir Herbert observed. He, too, was willing to postpone the reading of the play. After all, in winter in Kabul it mattered little when a party broke up . . . ten o'clock, or one, or four. "I remember when I was stationed in India. It was before the war." He didn't say, "They were good days, those," but we knew he intended us to think so. "I was hunting in Kashmir and I announced one day that I was going out with my native bearers to bag me a Kashmiri brown bear.

"A man in the bar at Srinagar, a total stranger, asked, 'Are you quite sure you want to shoot a Kashmiri bear, Sir Herbert?' I replied that I intended doing so, and doubtless my manner implied that I was irritated with his question."

The Afghan servant came in to place upon the

fire a few precious logs, and each of us drew closer
to someone else, for the wind outside was audible.
"The stranger rejected my rebuff and asked again
'Sir Herbert, do you know anything of the Kashmiri bear?' I replied, with some irritation, 'It's a
bear. I've seen it at the zoo in Simla. Roger Whats-
hisname shot one.' The man pressed me, 'But have
you shot one?'

"'No,' I replied, and the man said sternly, 'Then
you have no right to have an opinion upon this
matter. Sir Herbert, you must not shoot this particular bear, really you mustn't.' I thanked him for his
pains and marched out of the bar, but on the way
to the shoot, one of my guides asked me in Kashmiri if I had ever hunted the bears of his country,
and when I said no, he suggested that we go back.
This so whetted my appetite that I spurred the
horses and we came to that part of Kashmir where
the brown bears are to be found.

"We hunted for some time and saw nothing, but
toward dusk we came upon a thicket, and although
I didn't get a clear sight on the beast, I could see it
was a bear, and I let fly. I didn't kill the bear, and
more's the pity, for I had wounded it mortally."

Sir Herbert stopped his narrative, and for a moment I thought he had undertaken in his telling
rather more than he had anticipated. He did not
want to continue, that was obvious, but he took a
gulp of whiskey and said, "I suppose no one in this
room has ever heard a Kashmiri bear. He has a
voice like a human being . . . like a woman in extreme pain. When he is wounded, he beats his way
through the thicket crying like a stricken mother.
You can almost hear the words. He moans and

wails and is obviously about to die of mortal pain. It is . . ." He fumbled for words, extended his right hand and punched the air. "It is . . ."

From a place near the fire Lady Margaret said, "It is shattering to the mind. Sir Herbert wanted to leave the thicket, but the bearers warned him that he must finish off the bear. That was his duty. So he plunged in—the men told me—but the bear had limped off into the deeper woods." Husband and wife fell silent, and we listened to the rising wind, blowing down the last of the winter's blizzards.

"I tracked that sobbing bear for about an hour," Sir Herbert said quietly. "It was easy, because constantly the beast screamed and wept. It was positively uncanny. That bear was not an animal. It was all the grieved things that men shoot, the partridges, the deer, the rabbits. I tell you, that bear spoke to me, crying out in its pain. I finally found it exhausted by a tree. Even as I came upon it, it wept new laments. By God, I tell you that bear . . ."

"Did you shoot him?" the French ambassador asked in French.

"Yes. I don't know how, but I did. Then I rushed back to Srinagar to find the man who had warned me in the bar, but he was gone."

"What is the point of this story, Sir Herbert?" Moheb Khan asked. "Surely if tonight we shoot a wolf it will not behave so."

"The point is, Moheb Khan, that none of us in this room was prepared for what we expected in Afghanistan. You, Miss Maxwell, didn't your government in Washington hand you a neatly typed report on Kabul? Mean temperature. Dress warmly. Expect dysentery."

"Yes," Miss Maxwell laughed.

"And it was all the truth, wasn't it?"

"Yes."

"But did it prepare you for today? Getting up at six to type a play because you wanted to be here with us? Being assaulted by mullahs in the bazaar? Seeing wolves rushing at your car?"

"No," Miss Maxwell said calmly. "The reports in Washington did not prepare me for any of that. I never dreamed that I could find a room anywhere in the world as warm, as human as this one. Almost everyone I care for deeply is right here, tonight. As for the mullahs and the wolves, I wasn't prepared for them, either. Right now I don't believe they happened."

"Exactly what I meant," Sir Herbert said, holding his hands up toward the group. "Reality in no way prepared me for the Kashmiri bears. I'm sure that dreadful incident never happened. But, Miss Maxwell, sometime years from now, those wolves will be as real to you as that stricken bear is to me. And to each of us, years from now, Afghanistan will be real, too."

"You make it sound far too difficult to understand my country," Moheb Khan contradicted. "It's very easy, really. All you have to do is read what Colonel Sir Hungerford Holdich said about us in the Eleventh Edition of the Encyclopaedia Britannica." He pronounced the names with exaggerated precision.

"What are you saying?" the Swedish girl asked in French.

JAMES A. MICHENER

"With your permission," Moheb Khan said, bowing to Sir Herbert and taking down from the library shelf Volume I of the Britannica. Opening it to the article on Afghanistan he read in a sardonic accent:

"The Afghans, inured to bloodshed from childhood, are familiar with death, and audacious in attack, but easily discouraged by failure; excessively turbulent and unsubmissive to law or discipline; apparently frank and affable in manner, especially when they hope to gain some object, but capable of the grossest brutality when that hope ceases. They are unscrupulous in perjury, treacherous, vain and insatiable, passionate in vindictiveness, which they will satisfy at the cost of their own lives and in the most cruel manner. Nowhere is crime committed on such trifling grounds, or with such general impunity, though when it is punished the punishment is atrocious. Among themselves the Afghans are quarrelsome, intriguing and distrustful; estrangements and affrays are of constant occurrence; the traveler conceals and misrepresents the time and direction of his journey. The Afghan is by breed and nature a bird of prey. If from habit and tradition he respects a stranger within his threshold, he yet considers it legitimate to warn a neighbor of the prey that is afoot, or even to overtake and plunder his guest after he has quitted his roof. The repression of crime and the demand of taxation he regards alike as tyranny. The Afghans are eternally boasting of their lineage, their independence and their prowess. They look on the Afghans as the first of nations, and each man looks on himself as the equal of any Afghan.

"Now that's all one paragraph, mind you," Moheb Khan warned us, "and I used to wonder how long it would take me to acquire the attributes I was, as a typical Afghan, supposed to have. Crafty, lying, deceitful I was, but what do you suppose kept me from qualifying? That troublesome bit about the bird of prey. How does one transform himself into a bird of prey? Well, I gave up on that first paragraph, but the next one offered hope. May I continue?"

"Proceed," Sir Herbert said.

Moheb Khan smiled, adjusted the heavy volume and read on:

"They are capable of enduring great privation, and make excellent soldiers under British discipline, though there are but few in the Indian army. Sobriety and hardiness characterize the bulk of the people, though the higher classes are too often stained with deep and degrading debauchery. The first impression made by the Afghan is favorable. The European, especially if he come from India, is charmed by their apparently frank, openhearted, hospitable and manly manners; but the charm is not of long duration, and he finds that the Afghan is as cruel and crafty as he is independent."

With a flourish, Moheb Khan slammed the encyclopedia shut and stared at the readers. "You know, there's a funny thing about this. It was written by an Englishman who was totally perplexed as to how we Afghans had managed to thrash the living daylights out of English armies . . . twice. The man who wrote this must have perched himself on a stool in a little room and thought for some time: What kind of men are these Afghans, that they can defeat our armies? And he composed the description of a man who was as unlike an Englishman as possible, and then he wrote it properly in this big book, which I first read at Oxford. And what was my reaction? At that time? I was proud that a ferangi had seen so deeply into my character and had written with such respect. Today, when I am older, these seem like words of hatred or ignorance. They are not. They are profound words of respect from a scholar who simply had to know how we Afghans generated our capacity to fight. Never forget that marvelous peroration: 'the charm is not of long duration, and he finds that the Afghan is as cruel and crafty as he is independent.'"

"Moheb!" I cried. "You've memorized the passage, haven't you?"

"Only the favorable parts," he laughed.

"You think 'cruel and crafty' one of the good parts?" Miss Askwith inquired.

"When you use those characteristics to defend the end word of the sentence, they're good," Moheb replied. "Always remember the end word, Miss Askwith. Independent." Then he laughed easily and said, "But through trying years you English have come to know me as your trusted friend. Otherwise, how would I dare read such an English passage inside these walls, where twice my cruel and crafty ancestors murdered every Englishman resident in Kabul? In 1841 we did that evil thing, and in 1879 we played an encore, and I think it damned gracious of you even to have me here."

"Don't think we English forget the massacres," Sir Herbert said gravely. "It lends a certain spice to life in Kabul. Within these red and crumbling walls. Sort of like living in Hiroshima when an air-plane flies overhead."

"I think we should get on with the reading," I suggested.

"He's to be the star," a young British officer teased. He was my principal rival for the attentions of Miss Gretchen Askwith.

"As a matter of fact," one of the Frenchmen said in French, "he's supposed to kiss Ingrid."

"I am," I said eagerly, "and I'd appreciate it if we got to that part before morning."

"Wise boy," Ingrid laughed. "In the morning I look dreadful."

It was in this mood that the reading began. During the first act, the voices seemed strange, for the Englishman who was supposed to be Harry Brock remained an Oxford aesthete, and Ingrid could be no more than a Swedish beauty with prominent breasts, while the others remained themselves, including me, who never transmuted myself into anything but an eager young man from the American embassy. But the fire was warm. The audience was attentive. And outside there was the smell of wolves, and no one could forget that he was in Afghanistan in the deep of winter, far, far from what he knew as civilization. I think even Moheb Khan was affected by the experience, for at the end of the first act he asked, "Sir Herbert, have the evenings I missed been as good as this?"

"Since I've been here they have," the English-man replied. "Three weeks ago we read *Murder in the Cathedral.* I was asked to be Thomas à Becket."

"Oh, I should like to have seen that!" Moheb

cried. "American college folk are very fond of T. S. Eliot. They adore him as a fellow citizen who became a poet, and respect him for having had the character to flee America, which they would like to do, but can't."

I'm afraid I had fallen rather deeply into the part I was reading, that of the intellectual reporter from the *New Republic*, and I said, "Like Eliot, you fled America, Moheb, but unlike him you regret it every minute."

"Agreed!" the affable Afghan cried. "If there's one thing I like it's fast cars and a sense of irresponsibility. In America I had both, and every day I work here in Afghanistan I regret their passing." He raised his palms in a gesture of submission, then added, "But at some point in our lives, we must grow up."

"I am sure your country will," I replied evenly. Moheb, rather pleased with his earlier remarks, flushed slightly but nodded pleasantly, for he was not the kind of fighter who refused to accept his adversary's blows; he rather respected the man who could strike back.

"Will anyone have more spiced rum?" the ambassador inquired, and as the servants refilled our drinks, and as the fire grew brighter, we reformed our group and the reading of Act Two commenced. By now we were more accustomed to our roles, and the audience accepted whatever peculiarities we exhibited. If tonight Harry Brock spoke not Brooklynese but an exaggerated Oxford—one as bad as the other, I thought—we were willing to accept this convention, and when Ingrid cried, "Would you do me a favor, Harry? Drop dead?"

she sounded exactly like the dumb blonde of all
countries, of all time. By the end of the act we had
created, there in the old fortress, that ambience
which dramatists seek but which so often eludes
them. Actors and audience were one, moving together and accepting each other as equals. Partly, I
think, it was because each person in that warm,
quiet room knew that if he did not achieve some
kind of satisfaction from our play, there was nothing else in Afghanistan to which he could escape.
Either he attained catharsis now, or he was self-
sentenced to days of non-participation. So each of
us reached out to the other, made overtures that
normally we would not have made, because each
knew that for the forthcoming sixteen or eighteen
months we would find joy with our repetitive
neighbors, or we would find no joy at all. That was
why life in Kabul—sans roads, sans movies, sans
news, sans everything—was so profoundly meaning-
ful. We probed the secrets of a few rather than
glossing over the chance acquaintanceship of many,
and each new thing we discovered about our col-
leagues uncovered new significance. For example, I
had never imagined that glamorous Ingrid owned
such a naughty wit.

The conversation that developed after Act Two
was much different from that which followed Act
One. Somehow, the play had insinuated itself into
our intellect and had taken command. We poor inadequate readers had transcended ourselves, and
the characters we were purporting to create had
actually come to life. Harry Brock and his aspiring
blonde were with us in the stout-walled embassy.

"We could use a few of your type in our country," Moheb Khan said to the Englishman playing the part of the junk dealer, and he meant not the actual Oxford boy but his play part, the junk dealer.

"There's a great deal to be said about good old Harry that isn't said in this play," the Englishman agreed. "Miller, how much of the building of America is to be credited to men like our Harry?"

"A good deal, I should imagine, and I think it's rather clever of you to discover the fact. You've not been in America, have you?"

"No, but reading this part makes one recall how inevitably one thinks of Harry Brock as the archetype American. We excoriate him, just as this play does, but we forget that he is also the life force of the nation, whether any of us likes him or not."

Miss Gretchen Askwith threw palpitations into the hearts of various young men by observing, "Really, Mark, you read your part exceedingly well. Have you studied dramatics?"

"In school I was in *Outward Bound*."

"We intended reading that," Sir Herbert interrupted, "but the younger group thought it terribly dated. Do you agree, Miller?"

"I'm afraid I do, but I also think we should read it. It's fun."

"British, isn't it?" Sir Herbert asked.

I did not respond to Sir Herbert's question, for I was looking at Gretchen, and there in the crowded room I had a distinct premonition that Gretchen and I would be thrown together increasingly in Kabul . . . that it would become automatic for all hostesses to invite "Gretchen and Mark," and that sometime in the next years all would be asked to

Shah Khan's great compound, where a tent would be erected and where Moheb Khan would ride up on his white horse to serve as my best man while the marriage was performed.

It was an inevitable progression, Gretchen Askwith and Mark Miller to the altar in Afghanistan; but as I looked at her and saw her blushing, for she must have been entertaining the same premonition of inevitability, her face was obliterated and I saw only a fawn chaderi, smelling of perfume, and a pair of American saddle shoes, and I heard the name Siddiqa, and I looked at Siddiqa's uncle, Moheb Khan, and I knew that it would never happen that I should marry Gretchen Askwith, no matter how inevitable our courtship. I longed to see the hidden face of Siddiqa Khan. I was mesmerized by the flowing movement of her chaderi, by the exquisite sense of sex this child had somehow managed to evoke.

Sir Herbert repeated his question: "Isn't *Outward Bound* a British play?"

"I don't know," I replied. "I always supposed it was by a sentimental American who wanted to sound British."

"You may be right," Sir Herbert replied with the thin smile that served him as a laugh.

The reading of Act Three recaptured the intensity that we had created in Act Two. The laughter at our jokes was rather more explosive than it should have been, and my courting of Miss Ingrid more emotionally received. A good many people in the room were wondering what was going to happen to Ingrid—the person, not the character—and it gave our play an adventitious prurience to have me, one of the unmarried men, attracted to her, even in make-believe.

As we ended our reading there was genuine applause. Our audience was grateful that for a few hours we had provided them with escape, and when the snowy winds whirling down from the Hindu Kush whistled outside, the gratitude increased. I knew there would arise, as had arisen before, a longing not to shatter the illusion of the night, and that we would sit around for hours and talk, hoping to extend the human warmth we had created.

We were astonished, therefore, when Moheb Khan said rather explosively, "Miss Ingrid, may I drive you home?"

The Swedish girl smiled graciously at the Afghan and replied, "Yes."

Within a moment Moheb had his coat and hers. He summoned his driver from the kitchen quarters where all the Afghan drivers were resting, and from the manner in which Ingrid nestled into her fur coat and then onto the arm of Moheb Khan, we intuitively knew that she had allowed the part she had been playing to influence her normal personality. There could be little doubt that Moheb and Ingrid would be bedded down that night. When the door opened and we caught the snowy blast and saw Ingrid move even closer, that last little doubt was erased.

When the door closed, one of the Frenchmen asked, "But isn't Moheb Khan already married?"

"He has two wives," one of the Englishwomen volunteered.

"Both Afghan?"

"Of course. He wanted to marry an American, but it didn't come off."

No one could have anticipated where this line of conversation might lead, but it was forestalled, and properly so, by Sir Herbert, who said, rather petulantly, I thought, "We really ought to read *Outward Bound*. I'll offer myself as the bartender." There was an immediate flurry of casting and a determination as to which secretaries would type out the required copies of which acts. Miss Maxwell, indestructible American that she was, offered to do the longest and others fell in line.

Then Sir Herbert said, "For the young lovers we'll have Gretchen and Mark." The audience looked at us as if we had been set apart, and my former sensation of the inevitability of love in Afghan surroundings returned. Gretchen smiled, a wonderful British smile with white teeth and flushed cheeks. There was a moment of painful indecision, which I fractured by suggesting, "May I drive you home, Gretchen?"

My question was so parallel to Moheb Khan's, the situation was so transparent, that Gretchen flushed again, then laughed prettily and said, "Sir Herbert, you must keep them from talking about us, too."

Sir Herbert grew red, looked at Lady Margaret, then said, "I think you should know by now that in Kabul any pretty unmarried girl is fair game for all sorts of speculation. Are you riding with Mark?"

"Yes," Gretchen snapped saucily. "Yes, I am. Just the way Ingrid went with Moheb." She did not yet have her coat on, but she grabbed my arm possessively.

Sir Herbert smiled wanly and said, "I dare say Freddy and Karl will be damned unhappy about your decision."

"At the next reading I'll ride home with Freddy and Karl," she laughed, slipping into the coat which an Afghan servant held for her.

Lady Margaret interrupted. "But at the next reading you and Mark are to be lovers."

Gretchen flashed her wittiest smile at her superior's wife. "Lady Margaret, haven't you noticed? At the end of a reading the actress is so irritated with her stage lover that she wishes to have no more to do with him. After all, in our play tonight Ingrid and Mark were lovers. But she made no move to go home with Mark. By the time the next reading's finished, I'll be fed to here with dear Mark." With her hand she made a line across her eyebrows. "Tonight, he is my gallant champion, to keep me from the wolves." To my surprise, she leaned forward and kissed me on the cheek.

"Bravo, Gretchen!" Lady Margaret applauded.

"Looks as if you're losing your secretary to the Yanks," Sir Herbert huffed at the ambassador, as I led Gretchen to the jeep which Nur Muhammad had driven up.

Not all the British hands could find quarters in the embassy grounds, ample though they were, and some lived in Kabul proper, in a spacious walled house west of the public square. It was quite the liveliest spot in town, filled with laughter, ponderous jokes which the British overseas so love, and a fairy-tale kind of make-believe which has enabled them to live in reasonable relaxation in almost any portion of the globe. I was often in this house and I remember it now mostly as a center of things hearty. When I first came to know it and its occupants I wondered how a man ever got an English girl into bed. What did they do with her hockey stick? How did he halt her from making very witty jokes about nothing? Now, as I started to ride homeward with one of the prettiest English girls I had ever met, I was bothered by the same questions.

But as we rode over the winding trail that led from the embassy to Kabul, and as we saw to our left the soaring mountains of the Hindu Kush, outlined in snowy moonlight, the trivial problems of courtship left us, and we were two strangers from alien lands traveling across one of the high plateaus of the world. Gretchen moved closer to me, and we held hands as our jeep approached the first houses of Kabul.

Then we saw lights—actual flaming torches—as men hurried to and fro and a wagon with horses approached. There was a crowd in the road, and Nur Muhammad left the jeep to find out what had happened. In a moment he returned to report without inflection, "The wolves found an old man."

It must have ended quickly. Fifteen to twenty wolves, by local count, had struck the man and torn him to pieces within a few minutes. Now they were raging somewhere to the east and soldiers were out to shoot a few, after which the others would retreat. Nur Muhammad drove the jeep past the scene of mutilation and we reached the English dormitory.

Pretty Gretchen said, "Will you come in?" and I said I would, for I knew that on the morning following a reading no one would get to his office promptly, and in the English house there would be fun and good talk and kissing beneath the stairs. But when I started in, I saw Nur Muhammad sitting in the jeep and I said, "Nur, you can go home. I'll walk across the park." But he said, "You mustn't. They haven't shot the wolves yet." And from the east we heard sounds and could tell that something was rushing down the narrow streets, and I did not want to be in the English house that night.

"I'll take Nur Muhammad home," I apologized. "He's been working since dawn."

Almost as if relieved of a heavy burden Gretchen said, "I do think that's best," and I bounded, with improper haste I reflected later, into the jeep.

"Let's find the wolves," I cried to Nur, and we spurred the jeep east of the American embassy and along one narrow street after another until we were on the edge of town, with soldiers well to the south. They were moving slowly northward, hoping to come upon the animals, and we could see lights moving mysteriously along the edge of the river.

We stayed there in the snowy moonlight for some time alone, on the edge of an ancient city with the Hindu Kush rising to our left and the immensity of Asia all about us: to the east the Khyber Pass, to the north the Oxus River and the plains of Samarkand, to the south the bazaars of Kandahar and the limitless deserts of Baluchistan, and to the west the strange lake that vanishes in air, and the minarets of Shiraz and Isfahan. It was a moment of immensity in which I sensed the hugeness of Central Asia, that semi-world with a chaderi over its face, and just as the chaderi of Siddiqa had contained its own perfume, now the crisp, silent night with the flickering lights along the river possessed its particular power. It was the smell of frozen fields, biting on the nostril, the aroma of the bazaar, great and filthy even in the night, and the clean, sweet smell of pine trees that hid behind garden walls. Those were moments I shall never forget, when the vastness of Asia, whose distant mountain passes had sent us the wolves, was borne in upon me and I wondered how I had been lucky enough to draw an assignment in Kabul, the most remote of capitals.

My reverie was broken by shots to the south; gunflashes could be seen. The soldiers must be near at hand. I remember distinctly that at that moment, when the light of the guns added illumination to the crystal, snowy night, I thought: It was nights like this that the Russian writers spoke of, the white nights of Russia. It was a vagrant thought, shattered by a rush of sound.

Moving up from the river, across fields that were now barren, came the wolves: fifteen, eighteen, they were so close-packed I could not count. They seemed not to be running. They were moving as one giant animal, its heads looking out from side to side and finding no food. It was a terrifying, possessive animal that moved across the snow, a force driven by forces outside itself, an embodiment of Asia and the great mountains.

One of the wolves must have smelled Nur and me, for the pack suddenly veered directly toward us, but when its leaders saw not men but the mechanical jeep, whose headlights now exploded with brilliance, the animals shifted course without visible decision, and the gray pack slipped off into the frozen night.

"Here they are!" Nur Muhammad shouted, and the soldiers rushed up. Some shots were fired and I remember mumbling to myself: "I hope they got away."

The Afghan soldiers came to the jeep and conversed with Nur and me for a few minutes, pleased at meeting a ferangi who could speak Pashto. Their officer arrived later in a staff car and it was agreed to leave two men on watch. "It will soon be spring," the officer said in Pashto, "and we'll have no more wolves. Till next year."

It was now about four in the morning, but there would be no sign of daylight for many hours, and Nur started to drive me home, but I said impulsively, "Let's go to the English house!" and we did and as I had suspected the lights were not yet extinguished, and when I knocked on the door the English girls were not surprised to see me. Some men were there talking about the play and I created a stir when I said, "We've been out chasing the wolves. We saw them on the eastern edge of the city."

"Were they fearful?" Gretchen asked, and she seemed then immensely pretty, and I told her of the wolves and of the soldier who said it would soon be spring, and as I had anticipated earlier there was fine English fun, and good talk, and kissing beneath the stairs.

4

Next morning I was awakened by Nur Muhammad beating on my door and crying, "Miller Sahib! Captain Verbruggen has called a meeting for eleven!"

I rose hastily, doused my eyes in cold water and waited for Nur to push open the door with his pot of boiling water for my shave. My face luxuriated in the soothing water, and as I scraped my beard, I asked, "How much time?"

"It's past ten," he warned, and I looked into the hall to greet him, brown, well shaved, dressed in western clothes and karakul cap, waiting to lead me to our breakfast. This morning he was bursting with a special pride. "I'm also to attend His Excellency's meeting," he confided, and I saw that he had used my shoe box to freshen his shoes as well as mine. Such things he was not required to do. He was my official helper at the embassy, but he was a married man and had asked if he could augment his salary by overseeing the servants at my house. "Otherwise, sahib, they'll steal you blind. They're Afghans, you know."

I lived in one of the new houses on the far side of the public park that dominated the north arm of Kabul: to the west lay the British dormitory, within walking distance, while to the east stood the American embassy, also close at hand. When I had finished shaving I slipped into an Afghan robe and went onto the roof of my house to view once more a scene far more important to me than either the British dormitory or the American embassy. I wished to inspect the mountains and thus remind myself of where I was.

I looked first to the west, where the poetic Koh-i-Baba mountains stood shimmering in the sunlight, so near they could almost be felt, so graceful and varied that they seemed like Gothic sculpture rather than real mountains. To the north stood the great, somber Hindu Kush, heavy and foreboding. They had been named, local legend insisted, The Hindu Killers because of what they had done to the natives of India who tried to cross them seeking the profitable trade of Samarkand. Whenever during my working day I caught a glimpse of the Hindu Kush I felt that I was in direct link with the heartland of Asia.

For to the east these master mountains of Afghanistan joined the Pamirs, the impenetrable, mysterious massif that guarded the meeting place of nations; and these in turn led to the Karakorams, most inaccessible of the Asian mountains, on whose flanks lived the Hunza people, the Gilgits and the Kashmiris. South of the Karakorams came the Himalayas themselves on their eastward sweep down the spine of Asia.

Thus each morning when I greeted the mountains I felt myself in contact not only with Afghanistan but with the entire continent of Asia and with my own past: the wartime flights over the Himalayas into China; the intelligence mission into Gilgit, perched in the clouds; the great sea battles off the eastern flank of Asia; and now my job with the State Department in Kabul. I breathed deeply half a dozen times, imagined the ponderous ballet of the mountains as they swept across Asia, and went down to where Nur Muhammad and the servants had arranged breakfast.

For his eleven-o'clock meeting Captain Verbruggen had collected the four members of our staff best informed on the Ellen Jaspar affair. Richardson of Intelligence was there, a tweedy, pipe-smoking gentleman who affected a British-type mustache and who was favorably known for talking sense, primarily because he refused to give any opinion unless it was fortified by documents. He had reached the State Department via the F.B.I. and was an expert in security and Russian intentions. We supposed that he had been assigned to Afghanistan only briefly in order to study the southern flank of Russia where it impinged on Afghanistan. He felt the case of the Jaspar girl to be an intrusion and frequently said so. But now he sat confidently, his hands folded on his own intelligence file, just waiting for us to ask him questions.

Nexler, the subtle brains of the embassy, was also present, a self-effacing man in his late forties and the only one on our staff who enjoyed secure status in the real hierarchy of State. Unlike the rest of us, he had not come to the department from some other job; he had always been a diplomat and found subtle pleasure in reminding us of the gap that existed between him and us. He was an expert in masking his opinions, but we suspected that he deplored the naval attaché as a political hack, held Richardson in contempt as a kind of F.B.I. precinct cop, and regretted me as an unavoidable error in a department that had been forced to recruit untested men to fill new posts. He suffered Kabul in silence, waiting for the day when he would be transferred to a real embassy, say Buenos Aires or Vienna. London and Paris would come later. In the meantime his strategy in Kabul was to speak as little as possible.

Nur Muhammad and I completed the group, and it was to me that Captain Verbruggen spoke first: "Shah Khan's office delivered the papers, so you're free to head for Kandahar."

"I'll go down tomorrow," I said.

"Good. What do you expect to find?"

"Yesterday Shah Khan suggested three different things that could have happened. First theory. She killed herself."

"Is that likely?" Verbruggen asked.

"It's possible. She must have been shocked by the life she was required to lead in Afghanistan. I know I was shocked yesterday by some of the things Moheb Khan said."

"He's the one in the Foreign Office?" Verbruggen asked.

"Yes. Moheb told me something that isn't in our reports. Nazrullah married an Afghan wife before he left for America and had a baby with her."

"We knew that," Richardson said complacently, tapping the file with his pipe.

I was irritated that he had kept information from me. "Did you also know," I asked, "that after Nazrullah and Ellen Jaspar were married, his Afghan wife lived with them and she had a second baby? This could well have caused Miss Jaspar to kill herself. Remember, three years ago the Allison girl did."

The Americans in the room winced at the memory of that dismal affair, and Richardson asked, "Wouldn't we have heard about a suicide?"

"I asked about the lack of information, and what do you suppose Moheb answered? She was only a woman, and when Nazrullah gets back to Kabul he'll tell us all we need to know."

"What were the other guesses?" Verbruggen asked.

I thought: Look at Nexler wincing. A career diplomat would say, "What are the other hypotheses?" I prefer Verbruggen's way.

"Second theory," I said. "She's been locked up by her husband and we won't see her for some years. Remember that this occurred with that English girl Sanderson and that Dutch girl . . ."

"Vonderdonk," Richardson filled in promptly.

"Do you take such a hypothesis seriously?" Verbruggen asked as Nexler raised his eyebrows.

"I certainly do. It's happened before."

Richardson sucked his pipe, then observed cautiously, "Evidence I've collected supports the belief that Nazrullah loved his American wife, did all he could to make her happy. I find no parallel with the Sanderson and Vonderdonk girls. Their husbands hated them and kept them locked up eight or nine years to prove it. I reject this theory completely."

"We're rejecting nothing," Verbruggen said firmly. "This is Afghanistan and no one of us here can project himself inside the Afghan mind. How do you know what Nazrullah might do?"

Richardson nodded amiably, dragged on his pipe, then asked, "Let's concede that he's keeping her locked up. Where? A city like Kandahar? An outpost like Qala Bist?" We looked at one another.

"Excuse me, sir," Nur Muhammad interrupted. "I've reviewed all recent cases of such personal imprisonment. Without exception the jail turned out to be the home of the husband's mother. If you surround a ferangi wife with half a dozen women in chaderi they not only can keep her hidden, they enjoy doing it."

Captain Verbruggen looked at Nur Muhammad as if to say: Whatever we pay you, son, it's worth it. Aloud he asked, "Have we checked the mother's home?"

"Everything possible," Nur replied. "Not a single clue."

Nexler spoke for the first time. "But didn't your government also check in the Sanderson and Vonderdonk cases?"

"They did," Nur confessed, "and they found nothing. But Nazrullah's family is much more modern than the ones involved in those cases."

"Would you rule out the possibility that she's hidden, right here in Kabul?" Verbruggen pressed.

"No," Nur responded quickly. "After all, it was Your Excellency who reminded us that this is Afghanistan. But I do think it most unlikely." The acting ambassador nodded. American officials were not supposed to be addressed as Your Excellency, and by no stretch of protocol did Captain Verbruggen warrant the honorific, but I noticed that all who were so addressed were pleased with the courtesy and reluctant to admonish.

Nexler asked quietly, "Is there no way to visit the family home and check for ourselves?"

The naval attaché turned sharply to his colleague and snapped, "You overlook three factors. In Afghanistan a home is a fort, and if we try to barge in they'll shoot us. The country has no habeas corpus. And most important, Miss Jaspar is no longer of any legal concern to the American government."

"Perhaps we should tell that to the senator from Pennsylvania," Nexler observed dryly.

"He can bully us about the girl," the acting ambassador complained, "but there's not a damned thing we can do to bully the Afghan government. What's the third guess?"

"Shah Khan advised us to consider an eventuality which has also occurred in the past. Miss Jaspar has run away. Trying to reach the British railway station at Chaman. If so, two things may have happened. She reached Chaman, which we know she didn't do because we've checked. She died in the desert, which is the way the two earlier cases ended."

"I don't have their cases," Richardson protested.

"Before your time," I said, and he retreated behind his pipe.

"That finishes your report?" Verbruggen asked.

"Yes, sir," I replied with a finality I did not feel. There remained the matter of Shah Khan's implausible rumor, which he had refused to share with me, but for the moment I concealed this because I wanted our group to explore logical conjectures before speculating on wild improbabilities.

"I'd like to point out," Verbruggen growled with that down-to-earth realism which characterized him, "that your first alternative contains two alternatives of its own, one of which you overlooked. Miller says Shah Khan suggested Miss Jaspar may have committed suicide. I suggest she may have been murdered . . . by Nazrullah."

Nur Muhammad, whom I expected to rise in defense of his countryman, quickly agreed with the logic of this hypothesis. "Not impossible," he said firmly. Then he added, "But I've studied Nazrullah, and it's unlikely he would murder a ferangi."

The acting ambassador nodded. "From what I know of him, most unlikely. But I raise the possibility."

"Thank you, sir," I replied. "As you know, I've never seen Nazrullah, but from what I've read of him he's not the murdering type."

"We're leaping to some rather broad conclusions," Verbruggen cautioned. "Let's all get back to facts."

Richardson coughed and said, "I have a complete report on the Jaspar girl. Naval Intelligence and F.B.I. helped us out." He opened his file ceremoniously, looked at Nexler, and asked, "May I start reading?" Without waiting for consent he began:

"Ellen Jaspar, born in Dorset, Pennsylvania, 1922. Father's in real estate and insurance. She has one brother, three years younger. He seems normal in every way. Enlisted in the army and did well. Now a sophomore at Penn State. We include a photograph of the Jaspars taken in 1943, the year before our subject met the gentleman from Afghanistan."

Richardson detached the photograph and said, "If you're looking for the All-American family, here it is. Even have a collie and a Buick."

When the photograph reached me I saw a family which could have come from any part of America: mother a bit plump but well dressed; father taller and solid-looking; son ill at ease in pants a little too tight; collie dog well cared for; Buick recently polished; daughter . . .

"She's much prettier than most foreign women who marry Afghans," Nur Muhammad reacted.

To my surprise Richardson laid down his pipe and said, "I'd date that one. She stunning."

I looked again. At twenty, Ellen Jaspar was the typical sophomore at a good girls' college like Bryn Mawr. She was lean, well groomed, an attractive blonde, which must have made her additionally impressive to Nazrullah. No one would mistake her for the brain of the campus; she was too good-looking for that. Nor would anyone pick her as the hottest thing at the Saturday dance; she was too intelligent for that. She was, to use a phrase then coming into use, well-scrubbed, for even in the picture she was conspicuously neat, and one felt that she had not prettied herself up for the photograph.

Captain Verbruggen took charge of the picture and asked, "Is there any possible clue as to why she would marry an Afghan?"

Richardson had seen something in the photograph the rest of us had missed, and he said, "She looks to me like a girl who would often whine, 'Oh, Mother!'" Verbruggen, who had a daughter, chuckled, and Richardson continued, "We all know that girls of twelve are driven to anguish by their parents' inadequacies. Thank God this passes. But this girl looks as if she'd maintained this attitude right into her twenties."

I studied the photograph again, and I must admit that I could hear her crying, "Really, Mother!"

The acting ambassador asked, "Do the reports substantiate this?"

"Yes," Richardson replied. "Ellen Jaspar attended public school in Dorset through her sophomore year, and did well. Then she grew discontented with everything and her parents transferred her to a good private school in Philadelphia, where she also did well."

"All-around girl?" Verbruggen asked, implying that only such girls did well.

"Oh, yes!" Richardson assured him. "Hockey, glee club, tried out for the senior play. Boys took her to dances and in the summer she was counselor at a camp. Well adjusted."

"Any desire to travel?"

"None evident, but she did excel in nature work. Led the camp in this respect."

"College the same?" Verbruggen asked. "Hockey, singing, dramatics?"

"You've hit," Richardson said, as Nexler sat silent, looking straight ahead. "Except that in college her singing became good enough for her to join a semi-professional chorus that sang with the Philadelphia Orchestra."

The acting ambassador leaned back and looked at the roof. "Where does the flaw come in? That she would enter such a marriage?"

"We've gone rather deeply into that," Richardson

replied. "First clue we get is from an interview with one of her high-school steadies. Boy who did well in the navy. He told the investigator:

" 'When Ellen came home from boarding school she was pretty stuck up, not socially I mean, because she always stayed a neat kid and we all liked her, but she said screwy things like, "This town is a real bore," and "Can you imagine living the rest of your life in Dorset and going to the country club every Saturday night? Big deal." She talked this way so much that I stopped dating her.' "

Richardson dropped the paper, smiled reflectively and added, "That's his version. The facts seem to be the other way around. It was Ellen who stopped dating him. At least that's what the others reported."

"Is Dorset so bad?" the acting ambassador probed.

"I asked for a report on that," Richardson replied. "Fine town. Good families, good churches, good schools. It's no Tobacco Road, that's for sure. Pearl Buck lives in the next county and so does Oscar Hammerstein. He's the one who wrote *Oklahoma.* There's a little theater not far away. I'd say Dorset was way above average. But when Ellen reached Bryn Mawr her antagonism increased. One of her roommates . . . And here's a point I'd like to emphasize. Not a single person we interviewed said, 'I knew all along she'd do something screwy.' This fact alone is noteworthy. In every investigation you expect to meet the joker who foresaw everything four years ahead of anybody else. In her case, no. Listen to this:

"Miss Jaspar's first college roommate told us, 'Ellen Jaspar was a dear, sweet kid. She was loyal, responsive, and trustworthy. We had three dandy years together and whatever she's done, she's done with her eyes open. And if you come back and say she's committed murder I'm not going to say, it was in her all along. Nothing but essential goodness was in this girl.'

"Her second roommate gave us a somewhat different version. 'Ellen could grow quite bitter about what she called "the inescapable nothingness" of life in her family. She dreaded going back home to marry or live. I'd been to her home several times and I loved the place. Old town, old houses, real good people with lots to do. I didn't understand her antipathy, but I can assure you it was real. Once she exploded, "In Dorset they don't turn back the clocks. They shoot the man who invented clocks." She told me she was determined never to go back there to live, but I used to ask her, "Don't you think New York and Chicago are just as goopy?" She said, "Maybe so. But there must be some place in the world that's different." I never understood her bitterness.'"

"I'm terrified!" Captain Verbruggen cried. "Sounds just like my daughter." He passed around a picture of an intense, good-looking junior from Sarah Lawrence. "You see any difference?" he joked.

"There was this difference," Richardson replied. "In her sophomore year at Bryn Mawr, Ellen stopped dating. Told her roommate, 'I'm not going to marry some jerk whose big vision of life is selling insurance in Dorset, Pennsylvania.' We also have an instructive report from a boy who went to Haverford. Did very well in the army. He told us:

" 'Ellen Jaspar was a real winner. She had a world of class. I took her to several dances in her freshman year and she was practically what you'd call a clock-stopper. Very popular with the gang. Real human too. It she hadn't turned so difficult in her sophomore year something big could have developed. At least I was willing to make the try. What is was that changed her I'll never know. At first I blamed myself, but later on I ran into a lot of chicks who just couldn't get things straight. But I'll take the blame for the bust-up, because I always felt somebody else might have kept Ellen on the track. But I will admit this. I wasn't the man to do it.' "

"It must have been about then that she met Nazrullah," the acting ambassador observed. "How'd it happen?"

Richardson, who rather enjoyed the limelight, went through involved motions lighting his pipe, then explained, "Her first roommate covers that:

" 'In March, 1944, there was this Saturday dance at the Wharton School and some joker invited four of us to go in to Philly. Well, actually he called me and asked me to bring along three warm bodies. So even though Ellen wasn't dating at the time I said, "Come along. You may meet a glamorous Frenchman." The idea struck her fancy and on the spur of the moment she joined us. We went in by train, and at the station my date met me with a jalopy, but there beside him was this dark-skinned fellow with a red Cadillac convertible and a turban. It was too much. Ellen took one look at him, and that was that. They saw one another a lot, then this other Afghanistan gentleman came up from the embassy in Washington and they all went up to Dorset to meet Ellen's folks. It must have been a real fiasco. She came back swearing that she would rather die on the sands of the desert than marry some Dorset jerk. She left college before exams and that was the last I heard of her, except for one week end that summer. She appeared at my home in Connecticut sort of breathless. Nazrullah had gone back to Afghanistan without her, but she had a passport and a couple of hundred dollars. She needed another twelve hundred dollars. Like a fool I let her have it. I've never heard from her since.' "

"Neither has anybody else," Captain Verbruggen growled. "What did her father say?" Richardson was ready with a summary:

" 'My name is Thomas Shalldean Jaspar. I own an important real estate and insurance business in Dorset, Pennsylvania, where my family has lived for seven generations. My wife is Esther Johnson Jaspar, and her family . . .' "

"We can skip the begats," the acting ambassador snapped, so Richardson casually discarded a page and resumed reading:

" 'My wife and I have tried to remember anything that might explain our daughter's behavior, but we come up with nothing. There is no explanation. She was a good girl, never gave us a bit of trouble till her sophomore year in high school, when she got fed up with everything in Dorset, including her parents.

" 'When she reached Bryn Mawr we breathed a little easier, for she fell in with two of the nicest roommates a girl could have and also met some nice boys at Haverford College. Then everything went sour. Refused to date. Didn't go out much, and was downright hateful when she came home, which wasn't often. Her behavior was ridiculous.'"

Here Richardson stopped, drew on his pipe, and observed, "I'm not going to read all of this, but one thing does strike me every time I review it. Whenever Mr. Jaspar comes up against anything unusual, unknown or unfamiliar he describes it as ridiculous. He and his wife seem to have had a rather rigorous definition of what was not ridiculous, and God help anything that fell outside their pattern."

"Thank you for your profound analysis," Captain Verbruggen said. At a normal embassy such sarcasm from an acting ambassador could blight a career, but in Kabul, an irregular post at best, we worked under an irregular discipline which allowed a rather broad latitude for jokes. Verbruggen's wisecrack was directed at himself as much as at Richardson, who laughed easily.

"Excuse me, sir," I interrupted, "but I think we may have the clue we're looking for in *ridiculous*. Since Mr. Jaspar stigmatized everything out of the ordinary with that word, his daughter was compelled by an urge to outrage the system. What was the most ridiculous thing she could do? Find herself an Afghan with a turban and a red Cadillac convertible."

"My dear Miller," Captain Verbruggen said slowly, "when I observed that Richardson's analysis was profound I meant just that, because frankly, what he pointed out had missed me. Now you have made it completely obvious, and I thank you, too."

Richardson relit his pipe, smiled at me and suggested, "Perhaps we should get back to Mr. Jaspar, who seems to have been a completely dull gentleman. Certainly his report is.

" 'At a well-chaperoned dance held at the Wharton School, a fine institution in Philadelphia, Ellen met a young man from Afghanistan and before we had even heard about him she had fallen in love with him. We put detectives on his trail and found that he had a Cadillac, got good grades in college, and that he had been in Germany during the early days of the war. We reported this to the F.B.I. but they said he was cleared and was not a spy. After his examinations the young man . . .' "

Richardson paused and said, "You'll notice that Mr. Jaspar refuses to use Nazrullah's name. Probably considered it ridiculous."

Nur Muhammad observed, "More likely he was confused because Nazrullah had no last name." Captain Verbruggen looked up in approval and Richardson continued reading from Mr. Jaspar's report:

" 'You know the rest. Week before exams Ellen ran away from college and we don't know where she went. She wasn't with the young man, because the detectives kept track of him until he sailed for Afghanistan. Later she turned up at her roommate's in Connecticut with a little money and a passport. She borrowed twelve hundred dollars, which I later repaid, and then went to England. How she managed this we don't know, because at this time ordinary people couldn't get to England . . . I suppose the world is impressed by ridiculous adventurers, especially if they're pretty girls. We haven't heard a word from her since February, 1945.' "

Richardson shook his head dolefully. "No use reading the rest. Poor fellow never had a clue."

"Any reports from Bryn Mawr?" Captain Verbruggen asked.

"Certainly." Richardson brightened, shuffling a new set of papers into position. "Deans, professors, counselors all report the same: Ellen Jaspar presented no problems." Satisfied with the completeness of his responses, the intelligence officer folded his file and smiled.

During the former F.B.I. man's report I had been impressed by the detached air assumed by Nexler, the State Department career man. Now he coughed modestly, produced from an inside pocket a letter which he unfolded with care, and said, "In this case it isn't quite proper to claim that no one had foresight. I made some inquiries at Harvard University, where a Bryn Mawr professor is spending his sabbatical. A routine check by our people there . . ." He turned condescendingly to Richardson and said in an offhand way, "After the meeting I'll give you the letter. It could prove relevant."

Richardson was justifiably furious that information had been withheld from him, but he masked his anger behind the ritual of lighting his pipe. "I'd like to hear what you've turned up," he said with studied amiability.

"Probably of no consequence," Nexler replied deprecatingly. "Comes from an assistant professor of music your people overlooked at the time. Here's what he says now.

" I'm not surprised at what you tell me about the behavior of Ellen Jaspar, and without wishing to appear omniscient I must say that I foresaw almost everything that you report. In fact, I shared my predictions with her parents, but they paid no attention.

" 'When Ellen first joined our group she struck me as one destined for tragedy, but I was not satisfied then nor am I now that *tragedy* was the word I sought. I saw her as a girl of good intention who was determined to disaffiliate herself from our society, and I wondered if she were strong enough to find something better to rely on.

" 'I met her for the first time during the opening of college in 1941. Without my asking she said, "I want to get as far away from Dorset, Pennsylvania, as I can." She spoke with transparent hatred, which did not disturb me at the time, for I encounter many young people who feel this way during their first year of college. But Ellen plunged into the field of medieval music with such intensity that I knew it was not the music she sought. I took the trouble to check with her other professors, and they found her to be normal and above average in performance. I therefore had to conclude that what I had witnessed was merely some temporary aberration.

" 'But when Ellen returned in her second year with increased bitterness, claiming that the world seemed pointless, as if it were interested only in a perpetual Saturday night dance at some cosmic country club, I began to take her malaise more seriously, and I asked my wife to talk with her. Ellen brought her young Haverford boy to dine with us and we found him charming, but were forced to agree with her that his ambitions were as ordinary as her father's.

" 'My wife and I became so convinced that Ellen would fall into serious trouble that in the spring of 1943 we wrote a letter to her parents. We said—and signed it jointly lest it be thought that I was in some way enamored of the girl, as male professors sometimes are with erratic and attractive girls —that we were convinced Ellen might be in for serious psychological disturbance unless a solid attempt was made to reconcile her to her family and her society as represented by her home town. This brought her parents down upon us in full fury. They pointed out that I was not head of my department, that Ellen was doing well in her real subjects, and that it was ridiculous for an assistant professor of music to presume, etc., etc.

" "This was not the first time I had heard this distinction between real subjects and mine, and I confess that I was always irritated by people who raised the issue. Therefore, when Mr. Jaspar shouted for the third time that my letter was ridiculous I quickly confessed that it probably was and asked him to forget the whole affair, which he did. In fact, that December he sent me a Christmas card, and three months later, in early 1944, his daughter met the boy from Afghanistan.

" 'So far as I know I was the only person with whom Ellen discussed her intention of marrying the young visitor. I took her immediately to talk with my wife, and we in turn called in the young man to interrogate him. He impressed us as one of the finest foreign students we had ever met, and if Ellen has fallen into trouble through her association with him, we cannot say, "We told you so." We must say exactly the opposite. We told Ellen, "He's a fine person, but he will not solve your problem." "What is my problem?" she asked, and I said, "You have the disease that eats at our world. You cannot find peace in old conventions and beliefs, yet you are not sufficiently committed to anything to forge new ones for yourself." She looked at me and said, "You may be right. But wouldn't my going with Nazrullah be a step in the right direction?" I told her it would solve nothing, but on the other hand it would not make things worse. That's the last discussion we had.

" 'When you find Ellen you will find that it is not Nazrullah who has wronged her but she who has wronged Nazrullah.

" 'I'll close this informal report with one observation. Ellen Jaspar is sick with the disease that is beginning to infect our ablest young people. She has disaffiliated herself from the beliefs that gave our society its structure in the past, but she has found no new structure upon which she can rely for that support which every human life requires.' "

Primly Nexler handed the letter to Richardson, who accepted it without comment, but Verbruggen blustered, "I'd have acted precisely as the Jaspars did. If my daughter gets A's and B's in her real subjects and a music professor sends me a letter as garbled as that, I'll be as stupefied as the Jaspars were." Then he stared at me with his big, blunt face and demanded, "Miller, does that letter make any sense to you?"

Having heard what he had just said, I didn't want to insult him, so I equivocated. "It's part of the picture, sir."

"What a hell of an answer!" he exploded. "As a father my reaction was the one I just gave. But as an outsider, trying to get a focus on this thing, the music professor's letter is the only one that makes sense." Nexler smiled with satisfaction.

Abruptly Verbruggen turned to Nur Muhammad and said, "Nur, we brought you here today for a fresh look at an old problem. Considering what you've heard, what do you make of it?"

Nur Muhammad was one of the indefinable Afghans who turned up at all embassies. He learned English—or French or German or Turkish as required—had a fair education, quickly made himself invaluable, and was surely in the pay of the Afghan government, to which he reported secretly. Nur was an agreed-upon convenience, for he told the Afghans what we wanted them to know; and through him the Afghans leaked official secrets to us. He had been invited to this morning's meeting to warn the Afghan government that we expected full cooperation in Kandahar.

Nur, who acted as if he did not know that we suspected him of being a government agent, cleared his throat and said cautiously, "Your Excellency, I cling to these fundamentals. Miss Jaspar is not held prisoner here in Kabul. Nazrullah did not murder her. She may be a prisoner at Qala Bist, but that seems unlikely, because remember what I said. Only women can keep a ferangi wife prisoner. Men cannot. I therefore conclude that she has run away to the British at Chaman and has died in the attempt."

"Why haven't we been informed?" Verbruggen growled.

"Nazrullah hopes that she may still be found alive. And remember one thing, Your Excellency. You're not fighting the Afghan government on this matter. It's not a case of Shah Khan withholding information. He too is perplexed."

"Well," Verbruggen warned, "look after Miller in the south. We haven't time to worry about another missing American."

"He shall be my special charge," Nur Muhammad assured him, and from the manner in which the acting ambassador had spoken Nur realized that it was time for him to depart. Graciously, he withdrew.

As soon as Nur was gone, Verbruggen said to me, "While you're down there, there's another matter I want you to look into. Several of the embassies may go together to hire a doctor. We want a ferangi, of course. We've been advised there's a German practicing in Kandahar. What's his name?"

Richardson consulted a memorandum and replied, "Otto Stiglitz."

The acting ambassador continued, "Seems to be a refugee who fled Nazi Germany. But he might have come here to escape British or Russian courts trying war criminals. Anyway, the Italians recommend him as an excellent doctor and if he is, we might work out something. Check him out. Maybe he'll know something about our girl, too."

I looked about the room to insure that no Afghan personnel had entered unexpectedly, then said, "There's one more matter to discuss, sir. Yesterday as I was leaving, Shah Khan took me aside and whispered that he had recently received a rumor regarding Ellen Jaspar so bizarre that he refused even to discuss it. Didn't want it in our files under his name. At any rate, a rumor has arisen substantial enough to survive a trip from Kandahar to Kabul, but so ridiculous . . ."

"You're using Mr. Jaspar's word," the acting ambassador pointed out. "Shah Khan said bizarre. I suppose they mean the same."

"Anyone care to guess what the rumor might have been?" I asked.

"You've obviously been thinking about it all night," Verbruggen pointed out. "You speak."

"Could Ellen have murdered Nazrullah? And is the Afghan government hushing it up?"

Richardson shook his head. "Shah Khan is the Afghan government."

Verbruggen was not so easily satisfied. "Has any American seen Nazrullah alive?"

"Yes," Richardson replied, consulting his notes. "That irrigation expert from Colorado, Professor Pritchard, reported that on his way to ascertain water flow along the Persian border he had talked with Nazrullah at Qala Bist."

"Would he have known Nazrullah if he saw him?"

"His letter refers to him as a fine young man with a beard who graduated from the Wharton School. Must have been Nazrullah."

"Next guess," the acting ambassador snapped.

"Could she have defected to Russia?" I asked. This was 1946 and most Americans would have viewed my question with amazement, for in the States it was not yet recognized that Russia was our major enemy. In Afghanistan, living next door to Russia as we did, we knew.

"The thought's been going through my head," the acting ambassador replied. The Kabul dispatches of 1946 and 1947, if they are ever published, are going to make our staff look like a group of military geniuses. Partly this was because Richardson, our intelligence man, saw things very clearly; partly because Captain Verbruggen had a feeling for military matters; and partly because all of us on the staff could add two and two.

"We know that the Afghans hate communism," I argued, "especially its attitude on religion, but we also know that secret Russian missions have been operating in this country. Now if an American woman let it be known that she was fed up with America and Afghanistan . . . well, mightn't the Russians approach her?"

Richardson tried to light his pipe and said off-handedly, "You'd probably be on better grounds if you investigated the likelihood that she defected to the Chinese. Don't forget that lands controlled by the Chinese Communists touch Afghanistan on the north."

"I think we're up the wrong tree," Captain Verbruggen said. "If she had gone over to either Russia or China, those governments would use that fact to embarrass us. They haven't done so."

"On the other hand, sir," I argued, "this girl's whole personality, her attitude toward her home . . . Everything indicates the kind of person who might turn traitor."

The acting ambassador refused comment and changed the line of discussion radically. "Any chance she's in Europe? Why couldn't she be toasting her heels in Venice with some Italian grand duke?"

Richardson treated this with contempt. "The chances of an American girl's entering India without being noticed, then sailing from Karachi or Bombay, are just not measurable. Can't be done. You want to call the British embassy to check?"

"I withdraw," Verbruggen surrendered. There was silence, after which he turned to me, saying, "You find out what happened, Miller."

"I'll do my best, sir," I said briskly.

"You'll find out," he growled, "or you'll damned well be back in the navy." The group laughed and Richardson left, followed by Nexler. When we were alone Captain Verbruggen put his arm about me and said, "Miller, it would be a feather in my cap if we could get this Jaspar thing cleared up before the old man gets back from Hong Kong."

"I'll do my damnedest," I promised.

"On the other hand," he cautioned, "don't rush things. This is your first big mission. Ask a lot of questions. Learn the country. Don't be afraid of looking stupid, because one of these days we could be driven into war across this terrain, and you'd be the only American who'd ever seen parts of it. Keep your eyes open."

"I will."

Suddenly he cried, with real emotion, "God, I wish I was going in your place. Good luck, kid."

As I left his office I thought: Nexler's dying to get to Paris and Richardson wants to get back to Washington. But Verbruggen and I love Afghanistan. Who cares about the dysentery and the loneliness? For I knew that Afghanistan was the toughest assignment on record. Here was the post which sooner or later tested a man, and for me the preliminaries were over. I was about to plunge into one of the world's great cauldrons.

5

While it was still dark, Nur Muhammad helped me pack the jeep for the trip to Kandahar. We stowed our extra tins of motor oil, the precautionary spark plugs, the rope, an extra jack, sleeping bags and medical supplies. We had requisitioned from the embassy four cases of army K-rations, two spare tires and some jugs of boiled water for drinking. Seeing us on that wintry morning, you would not have guessed that we were embarking on a routine trip from the capital of a sovereign nation to the secondary metropolis nearby. We looked more like adventurers about to set forth in some dubious caravan, which we were.

Before we left Kabul, where wolves had again made forays down narrow streets, I asked Nur if he would drive me past the home of Nazrullah's family, and he obliged. It lay in the southern arm of the city, on the way to Kandahar, and when we drew up before its tall, fast-bound wooden gate, studded with ancient nails and bolts, I realized that I was once more facing the portal of an Afghan fortress. The surrounding mud walls were many feet high, so that nothing inside was visible. No agency in Afghanistan other than force was entitled to break its way into these confines, in which a woman could be kept hidden indefinitely without the assent of any but her jailers.

While we sat in the car inspecting the silent and forbidding gate, we became aware of someone inside the walls who had been alerted by our presence, and after a while a feeble light, obviously from an open flame, was seen glimmering through the chinks in the weatherbeaten gate. The light stopped moving. Someone on the other side was staring at us through the gate. No one spoke.

After several minutes I whispered to Nur, "You suppose they know who we are?"

"They know," he replied. "The jeep means ferangi."

"Why don't we ask where Ellen is?" I suggested, certain that Nur would dismiss the proposal as fruitless. To my surprise he shrugged his shoulders, decended from the jeep and went dutifully to the gate. Even though the unseen watcher must have followed his approach, nothing happened. Finally Nur surrendered and went through the formality of tugging the bell cord.

Inside the stout wall there was a clangor and the light moved. After the customary interval the small one-person doorway that had been cut into one of the larger gates swung open and a thin man swathed in rags and a dirty turban peered out. While Nur spoke in Pashto he listened impassively, then shook his head no. The little door squeaked shut in the darkness and between the chinks I could see the flickering light disappear.

"They don't know where she is," Nur reported, and in our strong headlights I caught my last glimpse of the mysterious wall.

The road from Kabul south to Kandahar was about three hundred miles long and had been in existence for some three thousand years. Judging from its condition at the end of winter in 1946, the last repairs must have been completed at least eight hundred years ago, for each mile of the road involved a particular adventure.

The potholes were so deep that we could travel at no more than twenty, and wherever water had seeped under the rocks, the entire roadbed vanished and we had to set out across rutted fields until the antique roadway reestablished itself. In the darkness we passed many vehicles disabled, their passengers sleeping unconcernedly until spare parts could be procured from Kabul on foot.

Promptly at six, for we were in the vernal equinox, the sun rose over the eastern hills and illuminated the noble, desolate landscape of central Afghanistan. Far to the west stood the Koh-i-Baba range, white in majesty and completely impenetrable as long as snow preempted the passes. Nearer at hand stood an occasional home, a low, mud-brick affair entirely surrounded by walls along whose tops thorns had been trained to grow and broken bottles implanted. Close to the road stretched shreds of fields which in good years might produce scattered crops; but usually rain stayed in the mountains and the farmer's work proved fruitless.

The dominant aspect of the landscape was its color. Everything not covered with snow was brown: the mountains, the mud walls, the land where nothing grew. The human stragglers on their way to Kabul seemed all a dirty brown. Once their shirts, hanging to their knees, must have been white, but much wear and little laundry had rendered them brown. Even the dogs were brown.

We stopped once to watch a group of men playing with one of these dogs, but the beast knew we were strangers and began snarling, whereupon the men picked up small rocks and with prodigious accuracy threw at the animal until he retreated. "I should think they'd injure the dog," I protested, but Nur pointed out that none of the stones had been thrown with force.

"They love their scrawny dogs," he assured me. "Kill an Afghan's dog and he'll track you through the Hindu Kush."

To travel from Kabul to Kandahar at the time of equinox—we were starting our journey on the twenty-first of March, the last day of winter, the first of spring—was comparable to traveling from the snowbound mountains of New York to the spring-drenched warmth of Virginia, for as we moved south we rushed headlong into the Asian spring, and we traveled from snow to flowers. Before the first morning had passed we were seeing blue flowers beside the road and yellow birds speeding across brown fields. The great bleak plains, so recently under snow, were beginning to look almost alluring.

Our first stopping point was the ancient capital of Afghanistan, the storied city of Ghazni, and I use the word *storied* with care, because when it was announced that I had drawn Afghanistan as my first diplomatic post I studied what I could of local history and no existing city captured my imagination as Ghazni did, for from its many-tow-ered walls there had issued in the year 1000, a convenient date to remember, a barbaric conqueror of unmatched vigor. He was known as Mahmud of Ghazni, and every year for more than a quarter of a century this fearful Afghan had led his armies down through the Khyber Pass and onto the plains of India, where he was not once defeated nor even successfully resisted.

The chroniclers said of him, "Mahmud kept the cities of India tethered in the sun like fat cows, which he came regularly to milk." He murdered thousands, swept up the riches of a continent, and transformed his ugly little Afghan city of Ghazni into one of the contemporary centers of education, wealth and power.

I remember that on the day when I first encountered his name, one of the most lustrous in Asian history—comparable perhaps to Chalemagne in Europe—I interrupted my studies to ask some twenty other graduate students then joining the State Department if they had ever heard of Mahmud of Ghazni, and none knew the name. I think it was then that I realized how completely unknown a land Afghanistan was, and I discovered to my chagrin that even learned people were vaguely of the opinion that Afghanistan was an alternate name for Ethiopia. Many of my friends assumed I had been assigned to Africa.

Well, I learned who Mahmud of Ghazni was, and now with Nur Muhammad's guidance I was approaching his city. What a drab, desolate disappointment it was from a distance, a scrawny collection of mean brown buildings surrounded by an ugly mud wall. From where I first saw Ghazni, it looked like a nondescript collection of cattle barns. There were no trees, no cooling river, no spacious approach. It was to remain my major disillusionment in Afghanistan, this dreary, almost forsaken jumble of mud huts that had once been the capital of much of the world.

But when we reached the wall there were compensations, and I must confess that when I stood before the great south gate I did feel a stirring of imagination and an echo, however remote, of the imperial Mahmud. The gate was huge and excellently built. It was protected by two stout round towers whose battlements were slotted for rifle fire and whose windows were mere slits for the accommodation of guns. To stand outside this gate amid a throng of travelers, seeking admission to the city, imparted a sense of history, and I could believe that it was from the security of these walls that Mahmud had issued on his yearly forays.

And when we had edged our jeep through the gates and into the narrow streets, even the dimmest mind could perceive that we were no longer in Kabul, where the embassies provided a spurious international flavor and where German engineers had at least brought the river under control. In Ghazni there were no German engineers and we were in the most ancient part of Asia.

In the little square in which we finally found ourselves, an earthen, unpaved square bordered by dusty shops and a filthy restaurant, every man we saw was dressed in dirty white trousers, knee-length shirt, western-style vest, shabby overcoat and voluminous turban. All wore open-toed sandals of ragged leather, and there was not a karakul cap to be seen. Nor were there any women, not even in chaderi. Men walked by lugging skins and furs, bladders filled with goats' milk, grapes and melons from the south, bundles of charcoal, and odds and ends of country produce. Compared to the bazaar at Kabul, this was mean indeed, for color was lacking, and movement, and foreign goods; but it was impressive in a timeless way and I was not unhappy when Nur parked the jeep and told me to guard it while he went searching for a place to stay, for the road was so bad that we could not hope to make Kandahar in one day and to stop south of Ghazni was unthinkable.

I had been studying the mean little square for perhaps ten minutes when I found myself surrounded by Afghans in tattered clothes, ordinary men from the city who were interested in the ferangi. They were pleased when I spoke Pashto and were telling me that in the Ghazni area it had been a bad winter with little food when Nur Muhammad returned. As he did so, the crowd mysteriously dispersed, and I supposed that Nur had reprimanded them, but I saw what had scared them off was the approach of two mullahs, tall, bearded men in dark robes and scowls of intense hatred. They marched up to the jeep, which they knew to be alien to their interests, and began berating it, not me.

Their fury abated when I spoke to them in Pashto, explaining that I was their friend. Granted this assurance, they relaxed their animosity and began discussing my trip with me. They proved to be pleasant men, and under Nur's careful persuasion they actually started laughing and the crowd regathered. Nur assured them that the ferangi would not molest the girls of Ghazni nor would he drink alcohol. They bowed as they departed, and Nur whispered, "Mullahs could be handled . . . if we had enough time."

Nur now called a little boy to lead me to the front of the hotel while he drove the jeep to a compound in the back, where it could be locked up and guarded during our stay in Ghazni. The boy, dressed in pitiful rags, shuffled along a narrow alley and brought me finally to my first Afghan hotel, which I approached with real excitement. I will say merely that it had no glass in any window, no lock on any door, no water, no heat, no food, no bed, no bedclothes, and no flooring but earth. It did, however possess one characteristic that made it memorable: on the dirt floor of our room were piled five of the most beautiful Persian rugs I had ever seen. They had been woven in Russia at the ancient city of Samarkand and had been smuggled into Afghanistan by itinerant traders who had hauled them over mountains and across deserts. They were poems in thread, three reddish blue and two in stunning white and gold. They had lain on the hotel floor for many years, where the extreme dryness had kept them from rotting, and they seemed now as colorful as when they left the loom. They made the hotel livable and I was dismayed when Nur Muhammad began unloading every item of our cargo, including the two spare tires, onto them.

"Don't lug that stuff in here!" I protested. "What shall I do with it?" he asked.

"Leave it in the jeep," I said.

"In the jeep?" Nur gasped. "They'd steal everything we own."

"You hired two men with shotguns," I argued.

"They're to see that nobody steals the wheels," Nur explained. "Miller Sahib, if we left these spare tires in the jeep, the guards would sell them in ten minutes."

I was disgusted and said, "I'm hungry. Let's go out and get some food."

"We can't both go," Nur replied.

"Why not? The mullahs know you're here as my friend."

"I mean the room. We can't leave it unguarded. One of us has to stay."

I looked out the back window, a mere slit for rifle fire, and pointed to the two big, bearded guards lolling in the empty jeep. "Let's put one of them in the room."

"Them!" Nur exploded. "They'd steal everything we have and shoot us when we got back."

"Then why are you paying them?" I demanded.

"To keep the wheels on the jeep," Nur repeated.

I couldn't hide my irritation, so Nur took me to the front window, another rifle slot, and showed me the hotel courtyard, where forty or fifty hungry-looking tribesmen had gathered. "Miller Sahib," Nur whispered, "they're just waiting for us to leave this room."

It was decided that I should eat first, and it was about three in the afternoon when I returned to the square seeking a restaurant. I use the word loosely, for all I could find was the filthy corner café I had seen earlier. It contained one rickety table, three chairs and a water bottle whose sides could not be seen for flyspecks. Its aroma, however, was another matter, for I had grown partial to Afghan food and this café had some of the best. The waiter, a man in an unbelievably tattered overcoat and green turban, brought me a chunk of nan, a kind of thick, crunchy tortilla made of coarse, nutritious flour and baked in slabs the size of snowshoes. It was, most of us thought, the best bread we had ever eaten, for it was baked in clay ovens over charcoal and tasted of the fields where the wheat had grown. The waiter also plopped down a large dish of pilau, a steaming mixture of barley, cracked wheat, onions, raisins, pine nuts, orange peel and shreds of roast lamb. On these two dishes, nan and pilau, I would exist during my entire trip, and I would never tire of either.

As I ate, men with whom I had been talking earlier reassembled about me. Two sat on the frail chairs. Others stood behind me, and from time to time I offered them chunks of nan, which they used as scoops to attack the pilau. Perhaps seven or eight men thus dipped their fingers into my meal with me, and we developed that camaraderie which is so marked a feature of Afghan life. As I was paying for my meal and bidding my guests good-by, some men in long coats ran across the square, shouting. I did not understand their words and was about to return to the hotel so that Nur could eat, when the men around me became very excited and tugged at my sleeve. I was to follow them. Together we trailed the first men across the square and out of the gates of the city. I remember thinking that I should return to Nur Muhammad, but some evil genius kept me running and soon I was in the midst of a mob converging on a spot outside the gates where a heavy stake had been driven into the earth.

On the far side of the stake, which rose to a height of seven feet, stood four mullahs, including the two who had accosted me earlier. They were mournful, aloof and terrifying. In their beards and turbans they seemed like patriarchs of old, and I was assailed by the uneasy feeling that I had intruded upon some Biblical scene which should have terminated twenty-five centuries ago. The lean, angry mullahs were from the Old Testament. The string of camels placidly grazing by the crumbling walls were of an ancient time, and the crowd of turbaned men, their faces brown from sun, their beards gray with desert dust, could have been waiting for some religious rite in Nineveh or Babylon.

As I looked hurriedly about I could detect only one note that indicated we were in the twentieth century. Outside the gates of Ghazni, jammed into a crumbling fragment of wall that may once have formed part of a fort guarding the imperial city, stood a telegraph pole which carried three precarious wires from Ghazni to Kabul. What I was about to witness could thus have been telegraphed to the whole world in a matter of minutes, but no one in Ghazni, except perhaps Nur Muhammad, would have considered it worthy of report.

The mullahs were praying, and the declining afternoon sun threw handsome shadows athwart their faces. The prayer stopped. From the nearby gates marched four soldiers bearing carbines and bandoleers, leading between them a hesitant, barefooted figured covered by a coarse white chaderi.

In Kabul I had seen pleated chaderies of exquisite cloth with embroidered peepholes for the eyes, and the savageness of the custom was temporarily overlooked; but in Ghazni this chaderi was a coarse, dirty white shroud and the opening no more than a tiny square of cheap mosquito netting.

I was not told who hid inside the chaderi, but it had to be a woman, for so far as I knew men never wore the shroud. Whoever it was must have seen the looks of bitter hatred that greeted her as she passed.

When the soldiers reached the stake, they inexpertly drove several nails into it and lashed their prisoner's hands to these nails, at the same time securing her ankles to the bottom of the stake. When they stepped back, the dirty white chaderi fell completely over the bare feet and the prisoner was wholly masked. She was still free, however, to look out upon the world of hate-filled faces.

Now the four mullahs prayed, and the crowd responded in a ritual I did not understand; but this was followed by a speech from one of the mullahs who had accosted me in the square, and what he said was in Pashto, and this I understood clearly, though what it signified I was not then competent to guess. He shouted mournfully, "This is the woman taken in adultery! This is the whore of Ghazni! This is the raging insult to all men who revere God!" He ended and I stared at the shrouded figure, trying to anticipate what her punishment was to be. If she heard the charge, she did not tremble.

Another mullah stepped forward and cried, "We have studied the case of this woman taken in adultery and she is guilty. We submit her to the judgment of the men of Ghazni." His companions assented, and the first mullah led the bearded men back through the gates of Ghazni and we saw them no more.

I had turned to watch the mullahs and did not see what happened next, but I heard a thudding sound and a gasp. I looked around quickly in time to see that a rather large stone had apparently struck the woman and had fallen at her feet. The gasp must have come from her.

Now the men at my right, the ones who had eaten with me and brought me to the scene, knelt to find stones, and the smaller rocks they discarded, but soon all were armed, and with the same skill that I had seen directed at the dog, they began throwing at the shrouded figure. From all sides stones whizzed toward the stake, and most struck, and it was obvious that punishment for adultery in Afghanistan was severe.

The woman refused to cry out, but a cheer soon rose from the crowd. One powerful man had found an especially good stone, large and jagged, and he threw this with force, aiming it carefully at her body, and it struck so violently in her abdomen that soon the first blood of the afternoon showed through the chaderi. It was this that brought the cheer, but I remember thinking how indecent it was that a human body which none could see should send its blood through the interstices of a shroud and deposit it in sunlight as testimony of punishment.

Another stone of equal size struck the woman's shoulder. It brought both blood and cheers. I felt sickness in my throat and thought: Who halts the punishment?

Then I almost fainted. A large man with unerring aim pitched a jagged rock of some size and caught the woman in the breast. Blood spurted through the torn chaderi and at last the woman uttered a piercing scream. I wanted to run away, but I was hemmed in by maniacs and I had been warned by many accounts that for a foreigner to make one mistake at such a scene might lead to his being killed. I prayed that the men had had enough, and then I saw why the soldiers had hammered the nails in the stake. They kept the ropes from slipping, and when the prisoner fainted, her bloodstained chaderi going all limp, these nails prevented her from falling to the ground.

Surely, I thought, the soldiers will release her now. But they watched impassively while men from all sides gathered fresh ammunition.

The sagging body was struck eight or nine times in the next fusillade, but mercifully the woman could not have known. Now a burly man shouted that he had found the perfect rock and others must stand clear. The crowd obeyed and watched breathlessly as he took careful aim, whirled his arm, and launched his missile with ugly force. It flashed across the fifteen yards separating the men from their target and sped accurately as intended, striking the unconscious woman in the face. Quick blood marked the spot and the crowd cheered.

The blow was so terrible that it wrenched the prisoner's hands from the nails and allowed her to collapse in a heap about the stake. As she did so the crowd broke loose and rushed to the fallen

(115)

body, smashing it with boulders which no man, however powerful, could have thrown from a distance. Again and again they dropped the huge rocks on the fallen body until they crushed it completely, continuing the wild sport until they had built a small mound of stones over the scene, as a pauper family in the desert might have marked a burial.

In a state of shock I returned through the gates of Ghazni. I passed the restaurant where the fellowship had been so congenial and was greeted by the men who had thrown the largest rocks. They were gathering to discuss the execution and congratulate each other upon expert performances. I got to the hotel to find that Nur Muhammad, realizing I had been sidetracked, had sent a boy for some pilau, which he had eaten with greasy fingers. He was now asleep on the Persian rugs, but when I entered the room he wakened like a prudent guard.

"Why are you so white?" he asked.

"A woman taken in adultery," I mumbled.

"Stones?" he asked.

"Yes."

Nur beat the rugs, then put his hands over his face. "What a terrible disgrace! My poor country!"

"It was horrible," I said weakly. "How can you permit it?"

He sat up, cross-legged on the rug, while I sank down on the spare tires. "Don't you suppose we're ashamed?" he asked. "Moheb Khan . . . the king? If they'd seen this . . ."

"Why don't they stop it?" I demanded angrily.

"If they tried to stop it, Miller Sahib, the men

you watched today and their brothers in the hills would storm Kabul and kill you and me and Moheb Khan and the king, too."

"Impossible!" I cried.

"They've done so in the past," Nur insisted. "In Kabul we have perhaps two thousand educated Afghans who know that things like this must end. In Kandahar maybe five hundred. But in Ghazni none. We're outnumbered twelve million madmen to three thousand . . . perhaps five thousand. I'm not sorry you saw the execution, Miller Sahib. You'll understand my country better."

"Will things go on like this indefinitely?" I asked.

"No," Nur said firmly. "Across the Oxus people just like us used to behave the way you saw today. Public executions supervised by mullahs were common in places like Samarkand. But the Communists from Moscow and Kiev said they had to stop. The chaderi was outlawed. Women were freed. Miller, we have ten years to halt these terrible things. If we don't . . . Russia's going to come down and stop them for us."

"Does the government realize this?"

"Of course. Do you think men like Shah Khan are stupid? The government knows it. But twelve million citizens don't." Nur rose and stamped impatiently about the room, picking his way through our scattered gear. "Don't you understand the problems that face a man like me? Right now in Ghazni, a few hours' journey from Kabul, every man who participated in that stoning fully expects to continue doing so for the rest of his life. If you told them tonight that you were going to halt all this, they would kill you."

I was suddenly assaulted by a terrifying premonition and I leaped off the spare tires to grab Nur by the arm. "Is this what happened to Ellen Jaspar?"

Nur relaxed and started laughing. "No, Miller Sahib. If that had happened we'd have known in Kabul."

I said, "I feel sick. Let's take a walk."

"I can't leave the goods," he protested.

"Call one of the guards," I said sharply. "I've got to get out of this town."

"Go ahead. I'll stay here and guard the things."

"I'm afraid to go alone," I said honestly.

"You're wise," Nur agreed, and against his better judgment he started to summon one of the guards. Then he paused to ask, "You assume responsibility for this?" I said I did.

Nur told the bearded warrior, with gun and bandoleer, "If one thing is missing when we return, you'll be shot. Understand?" The fierce renegade nodded and when we left we heard him piling our goods against the door to keep out would-be intruders.

We walked through the square, where the enthusiastic executioners hailed me again, and down to the gate, where I could see the ominous stake rising from the mound of rocks. Dogs were nosing at the blood.

"How long will the body remain?" I asked.

"They'll take it away tonight," Nur assured me. Then he said fervently, "One thing you must understand, Miller Sahib. Today's execution must have looked like a riot. It wasn't. Mullahs study these cases with care and no decision is reached casually. Strictly speaking, what you saw was a planned, legal act of justice. But a horrifying one."

We turned away from the funeral mound and walked south along an old caravan route until we had lost sight of Ghazni. We must have covered four miles when I saw off to the east an unfamiliar sight: something that looked like a flock of large black birds assembled on an empty plain, and I expected the huge birds to take wing; but as we moved closer I saw that we had come upon a tribe of nomads who move back and forth across Afghanistan with the seasons.

"Povindahs!" Nur exclaimed with marked excitement. Running ahead, he called, "Look at those women!"

From a distance I watched the nomad women, dressed in black with flashing jewelry. They moved with fierce grace—I can call it nothing else—and wore no chaderi. They were free, the wild nomads who traveled the upland plateaus of Asia. The sun was setting now, and its red rays illuminated their dark faces, lending them an animal quality of absorbed preoccupation with the world about them. For more than three thousand years their ancestors had moved back and forth across the boundaries of Asia and no one had found a way to stop them.

In their annual passage across Afghanistan the Povindahs must have looked with disgust at the way the Afghans imprisoned their women, hiding them in sacks and treating them like chattels, while at the same time the Povindah women were free to move about as they wished.

"They're an insult to your whole system," I told Nur.

"You're right," he agreed. "But the price they pay for this freedom ~~is~~ appalling."

"They look fairly happy to me."

"They're completely ostracized. When they move through our country they remain a people apart."

"Then why were you so excited when you spotted them?"

Nur laughed. "Afghan men are lured to these black tents like flies to honey. Many of my friends have tried to spend the night in there." He pointed to the tents where the women moved. "But the Povindah men are watchful to keep us away."

One such nomad rode up to us now, on a brown horse. He was a tall dark-faced man with mustaches and a flowing turban. Across his chest were bandoleers and with one arm he pointed a rifle at us casually and said in Pashto, "Keep away!" Nur spoke with him for a moment and he replied graciously, but at the end he repeated his warning. "Keep away!" Spurring his horse, he rode back to the tents.

"He suspected we were government officials."

"Where do they go from here?" I asked.

"They follow the melting snow."

We started to leave when I saw from the corner of my eye a figure in red dart out from one of the tents and disappear behind another, as a bright-colored bird will flash through trees in spring. I turned to look more carefully and was rewarded when a young girl, dressed all in red and bangles, reappeared chasing a goat, but before I could see her well, she disappeared again and I thought: She reminds me of Siddiqa. Like Shah Khan's granddaughter she seemed a person of unusual grace and sexual suggestion.

Nur Muhammad, who missed little, which was why the Afghan government employed him to be employed by the American government, chuckled and asked, "Fascinating, isn't she?"

"Why does she wear red?"

"Shows she's not married . . ."

"Look!" I cried. From behind the tent nearest us the wayward goat burst free and ran directly at us. Hot after him came the determined girl, and some forty yards from where we stood she tackled the animal, rolling him in the dust. I saw her dark skin, her flashing eyes, and two long pigtails which swung in the sunlight as she wrestled with the goat. I could understand the fascination felt by the Afghan men for such a person, and as we watched she skillfully led the goat back to its tether.

"Makes me feel good to know that such people are also a part of Afghanistan," I observed as we walked away.

"They're not our people," Nur corrected. "In the winter they go to India. In the summer they go north. They use us only as a corridor."

"What country do they belong to?" I asked.

"I never considered the matter," Nur replied. "Legally, I suppose they're Indians."

It was night when we approached the Ghazni gate, on whose ramparts flickering lights moved back and forth. It was a solemn moment, at the end of the day, when the ancient city was settling down for sleep, and we paused to watch the towers etched in the glow from some improvised fire where travelers outside the city were roasting a sheep. In after years, whenever I have thought of an Afghan city it has been Ghazni, looming in the darkness.

When we passed the scene of the execution Nur Muhammad begged, "Don't look again, Miller Sahib. This is our shame." And we returned to the square, where shadowy lights illuminated the corner café. We took our seats at the table and good-natured men elbowed up to us to discuss the day's events; and against my will I found myself entangled with these bewildered, half-savage men who were fighting the contemporary world, yet who were so hungry to know about America. They ate our nan and shared our pilau. They told us of the problems facing Ghazni—the food supply, the taxes and the cost of horses—and at the end of our meal they walked with us to our hotel, where they entered and sat for hours, crosslegged on the Persian rugs, talking . . . talking . . .

6

Shortly after dawn we left Ghazni, passing on the way the scene of execution, from which the stake had been removed, for wood in Afghanistan was precious. The stones, however, were left conveniently scattered in case another culprit should be apprehended.

We had been on the road for less than an hour when I discovered an important fact about Afghanistan which none of my reading had discussed; yet it was so fundamental that if one missed its significance he missed the meaning of this country. I refer to the bridges of Afghanistan.

When we came to the first one I did not appreciate its importance. It was a beautiful bridge, built in the early 1900's, I judged, by some expert engineer. It was well designed, contained good stonework and was ornamented by four crenelated towers. Unfortunately, a recent flood had eaten away the approaches to the bridge, leaving it an isolated structure that now served no useful purpose. To cross the river we had to leave the road, descend by gullies to the river, ford it, and reverse the process until we climbed back onto the road. Obviously, in time of storm traffic on the road would halt, but I remember thinking, while fording the river: That's a handsome bridge ... almost a work of art.

Thirty minutes later we came upon an even more beautiful bridge, with eight towers done in the most sturdy style, a kind of military Gothic common to old French and German towns. It was a splendid structure and I studied it with some care, for which I had ample time since its approaches had also been washed away. We were thus forced once more to ford the river, and I could see the bridge from below.

The stonework was exemplary; the joints were interesting because I could not detect how they were sealed. It looked as if the architect had depended upon the skill of his cutters to give him a joint which held of its own friction and weight. Moreover the structure was well designed, with the eight towers adding a striking note. It was a bridge to admire, and only the advent of some unexpected flood had rendered it useless.

But when we came to the third fine bridge and found its approaches gone too, I grew irritated and asked Nur Muhammad, "Are all the bridges like this?"

"They are," he said sadly.

"Why?"

"We call them 'Bridges Afghan Style.' They can't be used."

"What happened?" I demanded.

"Afghanistan's folly," he said, and it was obvious that he wished to drop the matter.

At the seventh washed-out bridge we had to ford a river much deeper than we had anticipated and got stuck in the middle with our bottoms wet and our engine useless, waiting till a truck came along to haul us out. We had nothing to do but study the bridge overhead, and it was perhaps the loveliest of all: its arch was graceful, its turrets solid, its brickwork neat, and its impression substantial.

"Beautiful bridge," I admitted grudgingly. "Who built it?"

"A German. One of the worst tragedies that ever hit our nation."

It was a pleasure to talk with Nur, for he spoke idiomatic English while I was fairly competent in Pashto; for practice we liked a system whereby I spoke in his language and he replied in mine, but when discussing complex subjects each used his own language. To an outsider our conversation would be confusing, for often we switched languages in midsentence. Now, with my bottom wet and cold, I was angry and spoke in harsh Pashto.

"What happened with these bridges, Nur?"

He replied in careful Pashto. "A disaster. We were taking our first step out of the Dark Ages and the Germans said, 'It's stupid to have your two major cities unconnected by a road.' They arranged a big loan and gave us experts who surveyed the road and showed how it could be built. When the king saw the survey, very neatly drawn with little pictures, he approved and said, 'We're a modern country now. We must have a modern road.' Then he asked who would build the bridges, and the Germans lent us a learned professor-architect who had built many bridges, and the work started."

Nur pointed up at the bridge. "He was a brilliant man who demanded the best. Look at that brickwork. You don't find much of that in Afghanistan. It was his idea to mark each bridge with distinctive turrets and ornamentation, for he told us, 'A bridge is more than a bridge. It's a symbol connecting past and present.' He said that towers and intricate brickwork were part of the Afghan soul. In a famous speech he gave in Kabul he said that he had taken the idea of towers from the family forts that mark Afghanistan."

"I didn't see the relationship," I remarked, but Nur pointed down the river toward a private fort and then I knew what the professor-architect had been after.

"He built some twenty bridges," Nur explained as we sat in the cold river—and I mean in the river, for the jeep kept settling—"and all the time he was working, a handful of Afghans like Shah Khan and my father kept warning him, 'Doctor, that bridge is fine for a well-controlled European river, but has anyone told you about our Afghan rivers in the spring?' He replied angrily that he had built bridges over some of the finest rivers in Europe . . . much greater rivers, he assured us, than these trivial desert streams."

Nur looked sadly at the bridge and said in English, "You understand, of course, that this all happened before I was born." Then he explained in Pashto, "But I remember my father telling us later, 'We went to the government and warned them, "Those German bridges will not stand up against our rivers in the spring."' They were told, 'You think you're smart enough to tell a German how to do his job? A man who has built bridges all over Europe?' My father replied that he had never seen a European river and it looked to him as if the

German had never seen an Afghan river, and there the matter was left."

The jeep settled deeper and Nur said in English, "Shah Khan is a learned man and a brave one. In those days he was without the dignity of his present position, but he refused to drop the matter. He told the Germans"—and here Nūr Muhammad reverted to Pashto—"'These bridges are far more important to us than they are to you. They're our first contact with the western world. If they succeed, we who want to modernize this nation will succeed. If they fail, dreadful consequences may follow. Now please, Professor-Architect, listen when I tell you that sometimes in the spring what you call our trivial desert streams roar out of the mountains two miles wide. They move boulders as big as houses. They destroy everything not perched on a hill. And the next day they're little streams again. Professor, build us big broad bridges and leave off the pretty towers.'

"The German professor was furious that Shah Khan would dare speak to him directly. He insisted that a meeting of government be convened, at which he made an impassioned speech. 'I want to tell you that I have sunk my pillars to bedrock. I have built as no bridges in Afghanistan have ever been built before. When the floods that Shah Khan speaks of meet my bridges not one bridge will fall down.' I must say that Shah Khan was a fighter. He replied, 'Professor-Architect, you're entirely right. The bridges will not fall down. Of that I'm convinced. But the rivers of Afghanistan, like the people of Afghanistan, never attack the enemy head on. Your stout bridges are like the British army. Their soldiers were ten times better than ours . . . better fed . . . better armed. But we didn't march up to the British in double file so they could shoot us down. In a thousand tricky ways we surrounded them. They protested, "This is no decent way to fight," and we destroyed them. Our rivers will destroy your bridges, Professor-Architect, because they're European bridges and they're not prepared to fight Afghan rivers. What we want, Professor-Architect, are tricky Afghan bridges.'

"The German replied, 'A bridge is a bridge,' and Shah Khan shouted, 'Not in Afghanistan.' The quarrel was taken to the king himself, and he ordered Shah Khan to shut up. The German ambassador explained everything by pointing out that Shah Khan had been educated in France and was thus emotionally unstable.

"So the bridges were built, and the next year there were no spring floods. For eighteen months we enjoyed a wonderful road between Kabul and Kandahar, and Afghanistan was spurting to catch up with the world. In that second winter there was a great snowfall in the mountains followed by an unusually warm spring, which sent towering floods down the gullies, moving boulders as big as houses. When these floods struck the bridges, the German was proved right. His stone pillars stood fast, as he had predicted. The bridges were as strong as he said. But they were so narrow in span that our rivers simply went around them. All the approaches were gouged out and the bridges stood isolated."

"Why not rebuild the approaches?" I asked.

"We did," Nur replied. "Another flood took them out. So we rebuilt again. Another flood. My father calculated that to keep the bridges operating would require a hundred thousand men working around the year. So after the third flood the government said, 'Let them go. Who needs bridges?' And the dream road that was to have bound our nation together remained an aching monument to the folly of man."

"What happened to the professor?" I asked.

"After the first flood he traveled from Kabul to Kandahar, refusing to believe what he saw. 'I've built a hundred bridges over some of the greatest rivers in Europe,' he shouted. He stood in the middle of one little stream two feet deep and wailed, 'How could this little puddle wash out a bridge?' He refused, even then, to see the boulders which that little puddle had moved down from the mountain."

"Did he leave the country?"

"No, he went back to Kabul and boasted to everyone who would listen that not a single one of his pillars had been destroyed. He made himself what the English call 'quite a bore.' He insisted upon explaining about the bridges. The German embassy finally called him in, and what they said we never found out, but that night he went to his room and blew his brains out."

Nur shook his head sadly, still waiting for a truck to appear. "You can't imagine the tragedy those bridges became. Whenever the government wanted to do some new thing the mullahs and the mountain chiefs would laugh: 'Remember the German bridges!' You're an American and you may not like Germans since you fought them twice, but in Afghanistan they were wonderful people. Most of what we have that's good came from the Germans, but after the bridges even they were held in suspicion. Their effectiveness was chopped in half. Those damned bridges!"

He shook his head, then asked, "By the way, you're meeting a German doctor in Kandahar, aren't you?"

"How did you know?" I asked.

As soon as I uttered the words I could have kicked myself. Perhaps it was the coldness of the river that had made me thoughtless, but the damage was done. Nur stammered, "Well, I just know."

It was a rule in Afghan-American relations that neither side would embarrass the other regarding spies like Nur Muhammad on their side and Richardson on ours. It's true that Nur had slipped when he let me know that somehow or other he had found out that one of my missions in Kandahar was to inspect Dr. Otto Stiglitz; he should have kept his mouth shut. But once he did betray himself, I should never have challenged him. I had humiliated a good friend and an able spy. I was sorry.

He recovered by saying, "In a few miles . . . if we ever get out of this river . . . you'll see a bridge that my father and Shah Khan built. You'll laugh at it, but it's stood for more than thirty years."

A truck finally arrived and shouting men plunged into the river with ropes, which they attached to our front axle. With relative ease they pulled us free, then refused pay. We offered them cigarettes, which gratified them, and with much laughter they assured us that the rivers to the south would give no trouble. "But in two more weeks. Whooo, whooo! Floods everywhere. Road washed out for six or seven days."

When we resumed our journey Nur Muhammad said, "So if I tell you, Miller Sahib, that we have an Afghan way of doing things, and it works, please don't think I'm being obstinate. It's just possible that it does work."

"On the other hand," I argued, "if your country operates on unique solutions which no outsider can possibly understand, and if you use that as an excuse for doing nothing, then Russia will surely move in and make the changes for you."

"That's the battle we're engaged in, you and I," Nur agreed. "May we complete the job before Russia takes over."

"My government's policy is to help you," I said.

"But do be reasonable on one thing, Miller Sahib. We'll soon be in Kandahar, and you'll be forming opinions about Nazrullah. Let me assure you, he's on our side. He understands these matters better than either of us. Don't antagonize him at the beginning. If we destroy men like him, Afghanistan is lost."

"I don't want to destroy him," I snapped. "I want to find out where his wife is."

"So do I," Nur promised. "But in the Afghan way."

I was about to make an acid reply when Nur stopped our jeep at the bridge his father had built across one of the lesser streams, which the Germans had left for later. It was a silly affair that looked like a roller coaster at a run-down amusement park. It was built of wood and showed no evidence of European beauty, but it looked good for a hundred years. I thought: If a German professor-architect designed a bridge like this they'd hang him from the Brandenburger Tor.

"The secret," Nur pointed out, "is the big dips in the road before you reach the bridge itself. See how they work?"

"Not exactly," I replied.

With his forefinger he drew in the dust on the jeep windshield a profile of the bridge, showing a level road which dipped sharply, rose again to cross the bridge, then dipped on the other side. Nur's diagram looked like a scraggly capital W. "You might call it an Afghan bridge. It says to the river, 'I want to cross you, but I know I mustn't pinch you in. So when you want to run wild, go down the dips in the road and leave me alone. The rest of the year I'll leave you alone.' Silly, but it works."

Hesitantly I asked, "But during the flood you can't use the road?"

"Of course not," Nur agreed. "But if you allow the river its way, it closes the road only once or twice a year. Who needs a road all year? Maybe it's better to give it a rest."

I thought of six good answers to this evasion, but I was constrained from using them by one overriding fact: while crossing rivers which the German had tried to conquer my bottom was wet, but while crossing on the tricky Afghan bridge my bottom was dry, and things had been this way for nearly fifty years. I kept my mouth shut.

We were about to resume our journey when a truck came down the road from Ghazni bearing a

strange group of men who were dressed in vivid
clothes of many colors and who wore their black
hair long in the manner of ancient Greek page
boys: thick bangs in front, elsewhere a shoulder-
length bob. The faces of the men were aquiline
and paler than those of the normal Afghan. All
were handsome but there was one young man not
yet in his twenties, I judged, who was positively
beautiful. At first I wasn't sure he was a man and I
must have pointed toward him as the truck crossed
the bridge, for in Pashto he screamed a very filthy
phrase, which caused his truckmates to cheer his
insolence. In acknowledgment he made a pretty
gesture like a girl, but he was startled when I
shouted back in Pashto a phrase equally obscene.
He laughed with gusto, moving his head so that his
long hair flashed in the sunlight. Then he pointed
at me with a languid, graceful arm and shouted, "I
know what the ferangi wants, but he can't have it."
Once more the men in the truck applauded their
special member, and proceeded on their way to
Kandahar.

"Who were they?" I asked.

"A dancing team," Nur replied. "They tour the
country all year."

"The long hair?"

"Traditional. Judging from their clothes they
must be a pretty good team."

We had completed most of the trip to Kandahar
when we overtook a young man in his early twenties, conspicuous because he wore not only the customary baggy pants and long shirt, but also a tattered overcoat made originally for a woman. It
must have been a beautiful coat, with long flaring

panels and a tight waist, and looked as if it might have come from Paris. Wine-red in color, it still possessed an air of grace.

I asked Nur to stop and we invited the young fellow to join us and his eyes widened with pleasure. He climbed in the back and adjusted his coat carefully over the spare tires on which he had to crouch.

"Ever been in a car before?" I asked in Pashto.

"No. It's exciting."

"Going to Kandahar?"

"Yes. To the spring festival."

"Ever been before?"

"No," he replied with a flashing smile. "But I've heard of Kandahar. Who hasn't?"

"Where do you live?"

"In the hills. Badakshar."

"I don't know it," I said to Nur, who with four or five pinpoint questions developed that it was several hundred miles north.

"Must be a dump," he said in English.

"Good place?" I asked in Pashto.

"Oh, yes!" the young man replied warmly. "Last year we had a good crop. In the autumn I sold a horse to the Povindahs as they went south. So I am coming to Kandahar with some money, I can tell you."

As soon as he said this he realized that his boasting might cost him his life, for he did not know who we were, and travelers were frequently murdered when it was known they had money. No doubt it had sometimes happened near Badakshar, and he looked at us fearfully.

"Shut your mouth, you fool," Nur snapped. "This time you're lucky. We're from the government."

The young man sighed and fell silent, but I asked him, "Where'd you get your coat?"

He was a congenial fellow who enjoyed talk, so he said quickly, "It's been in my family for many years. My father wore it to Kabul once. I haven't been to Kabul, but my brother wore it to Herat, which is a large city, he says."

"Where'd your father get the coat?"

The young man refused to answer and Nur Muhammad asked, "He killed a man for it, didn't he?" The traveler said nothing and Nur continued. "A stranger came through the mountains wearing this coat and your father got hungry for it. So he shot him, eh?"

I turned around to look at the young man, across whose face had come a beatific smile. He said, "You government men know everything, don't you? How to raise sheep. How to pay taxes. What roads to build. But you don't know about this coat, do you?" He chuckled and in sheer pleasure wrapped his arms a little tighter about himself.

"Who killed who?" Nur pressed.

The young man laughed openly and wagged his finger at Nur. "No, no, Mr. Government! That's one thing you're not going to know. And before you ask any more questions stop the car and I'll walk."

"Take it easy," Nur said.

"All right," the young man said gravely. "But forget about the coat."

We rode in silence for some miles, then heard a gasp from the rear of the jeep, for our rider had spotted some of the minarets of Kandahar. "It's the city!" he cried.

At first I saw nothing, but gradually the outlines of Kandahar, much older than Kabul, stood out against the horizon, and as we approached the walls I could not say who was the more excited, the young man with the European coat or the man from the American embassy about to engage in his first diplomatic mission.

We dropped our passenger in the middle of the city, a sprawling, dirty, camel-train metropolis whose mud walls looked as they had in the time of Darius the Persian. Nur found us a place to stay, much better than the hole in Ghazni but without the Persian rugs, and when the jeep was under armed guard I said, "Since you already know I'm here to see Dr. Stiglitz, could you find where he lives?"

"Now?" Nur asked.

"Now," I repeated, and he soon returned to lead me down a mean, narrow street where from one dirty mud wall projected the sign.

DOKTOR
UNIVERSITY OF MUNICH

"Want me to stay with you?" Nur asked.

"No thanks."

"Kandahar is rougher than Kabul," Nur warned.

"I can handle myself," I assured him and entered the doctor's quarters.

The waiting room startled me. It was a small, dirt-floored, misshapen room with one bench and two very old chairs, on which sat men in turbans.

One rose to offer me his seat, but I said in Pashto, "I'll stand," and the bronzed faces stared at me. Finally one asked, "Ferangi?" and I replied "American." The staring continued.

After some minutes the door leading to the doctor's office opened and a turbaned man departed. The next patient in line moved in to see the doctor and he must have said that there was a ferangi outside, for the door quickly burst open and a man of middle years and middle height rushed out, not to see me but to inspect me.

"Who are you?" he demanded in crisp, accented English. I gave my name and he drew back suspiciously. "What do you want?"

I tried to say that I'd wait until he was through, but he interrupted, shouting in Pashto, "These damned Americans come here demanding special privilege. They always do. Well, he must wait in line till all of you are finished . . . all of you."

In Pashto I said, "When you're through, Doctor."

My use of the language did not impress him. He stepped back, eyed me coldly and asked cautiously, "What is it you want?"

"Did you ever treat the American wife of Nazrullah?"

He glared at me, drew a protective shell of some kind about himself, and returned to his office, slamming the crude wooden door. In a flash he was back in the waiting room shouting in Pashto, "He must wait in line like all of you . . . to the very end." Once more he slammed the door.

By the time the last Afghan had seen the doctor, darkness had fallen and I was left alone in the shadowy waiting room. The wooden door creaked open and Dr. Stiglitz said graciously, "Now perhaps we can talk."

He did not invite me to his office but he did leave the door open so that some light from the single unshaded electric bulb entered our room. He was balding, with a blond-gray German crew cut, and he had a pipe. He looked more frightened than bellicose, and his forehead was deeply wrinkled. "Yes, I treated Madame Nazrullah. Not quite a year ago. Sit down." He invited me to take one of the rickety chairs while he sat wearily on the other. "Be careful of the chair," he warned. "In Afghanistan wood is so scarce that any chair is a treasure. You can't imagine the trouble I had finding that door. I shouldn't have slammed it so, but visitors make me nervous." He made a conscious effort to relax and asked with some show of generosity, "Now what do you wish to know?"

Before I could speak, the door to the street opened and a thin Afghan in his fifties entered, followed by a chaderi. The woman stood obediently near the door while the man bowed and pleaded with the doctor. "My wife is ill," the man whispered.

"All right," Stiglitz growled in what I thought was an offensive manner. "She's late, but I'll help her." With no enthusiasm he returned to his office, and I moved my chair aside to let the woman follow, but she was left standing in the outer room and it was the nervous husband who joined the doctor. Stiglitz, seeing my surprise, said, "You'd better come in here. He wouldn't like you alone with his wife, and what happens may interest you."

So the American visitor, the German doctor and

the Afghan husband consulted in the inner room while the sick woman remained standing by the door of the waiting room. "Tell her she can sit down," the doctor began, and the husband went to his wife, who obediently sat on the floor.

While he was gone I had an opportunity to inspect the doctor's office. It was a dirty little mud-floored room with practically no medical equipment and one cupboard containing flyspecked bottles of pills. There was a desk made of packing crates and the swinging, glaring electric light bulb.

The husband returned and Stiglitz asked, "Now what's wrong?"

"Pains in the stomach, Doctor."

"Fever?"

"Yes."

"High?"

"No, medium."

"Does she vomit?"

"No."

"Pregnant?"

"The midwife says no."

"Is her period regular?"

"I don't know."

"Find out," Stiglitz ordered, and the husband dutifully returned to the other room, where he sat on the floor to consult with his veiled wife.

While he was gone I asked, "Don't you examine her?"

"A wife? In chaderi? I'd be shot."

The husband returned and said his wife's periods had been regular, so the examination proceeded. Six times the husband was ordered to ask his wife intimate questions regarding her health and six times he relayed his understanding of her answers to the doctor. Once, when the man was gone, Stiglitz confided, "The real evil of this system comes when the husband thinks his wife's symptoms reflect discredit on him. He suppresses the information. And if the apothecary charges too much for the medicine I prescribe he simply doesn't buy it."

"What happens to the woman?" I asked.

"She dies," he replied without emotion. "That is, she dies a little sooner than otherwise."

The husband now decided that he had told Dr. Stiglitz all that was relevant and he waited for the doctor's decision. "It's an amazing thing," Stiglitz said in English, "but after a while you instinctively know what ails the woman and you probably do her as much good as if you'd taken her pulse and temperature." In Pashto he instructed the husband what medication to buy for his wife and the man laid down a pitiful fee, which the doctor accepted. When the man went to inform his wife he left the door open and I could see him kneel beside her and console and reassure her, with obvious love etched on his face. His wife, who must have been seriously ill under the chaderi, breathed deeply two or three times, then rose and followed her husband out of the office.

"Now about Madame Nazrullah," Dr. Stiglitz began. "Since you're interested in her you must be from the American embassy."

"I am."

"And you've been sent down here to spy on me?"

"No," I lied.

"You're lying. Right this minute you're thinking,

What's a man like Stiglitz doing in a hole like Kandahar? Go ahead and spy on me and I'll spy on you."

Before I could reply, Stiglitz hopped up, ran to the door leading to the street, and barred it. When this was done he sat on one of the chairs, using it in reversed position so that its unsteady back formed a chin rest. "Young man," he said. "Will you please bring me my pipe?" He was tired and he looked it.

I joined him in the waiting room and studied him as he lit his pipe. His hands were nervous, but I remembered that this was the end of a long day. His close-cropped head was a little larger than normal, and his hard blue eyes looked at all things with a blend of cynicism and challenge. He was inclined toward plumpness and was clearly no self-reliant German superman. I was disposed to like his quick honesty and felt intuitively that he ought to move to Kabul, where the various embassies could provide him with patients well able to pay. As he had foreseen, the major question in my mind as I studied him was, "What's a man like this doing in a hole like Kandahar?"

"Nazrullah's wife lived in this region for a little more than a year," he reported grudgingly. "Why are you interested?"

"She's disappeared."

"What?" he asked with real surprise.

"Yes. Her parents haven't heard from her in thirteen months."

He began to laugh, not heartily but in disgust. "You Americans! My parents haven't heard from me in four years but they don't go running to the German embassy."

"With an American woman married to an Afghan the problem is somewhat different," I said sharply.

"Any ferangi who marries an Afghan does so with her eyes alert," Stiglitz replied impatiently. "I treated Madame Nazrullah several times."

"What for?" I asked.

Stiglitz looked at me coldly. "She was a well-adjusted, likable young woman. Quite happy with her husband and he with her. I've grown to respect Nazrullah as one of the finest Afghans. Say, Herr Miller, are you hungry?"

"I am."

"You eat pilau and nan?"

"At every chance."

"Good. I'm starved." Then, for the first time, I saw him hesitate, as if he were unsure of himself. "Herr Miller, may I be very rude?"

"You may."

"I wish that the invitation I just extended could mean what it would in Germany. That I was taking you to dinner. Frankly, Herr Miller . . . You saw the fee they pay here."

"I'm taking you to dinner," I assured him.

"No! My own dinner I can afford. But sometimes you ferangi eat like such pigs . . ."

He summoned a watchman, who appeared from a room in the back carrying a rifle and two daggers. Carefully Stiglitz locked the cupboard with its pitiful supply of drugs, then unbarred the door, which the watchman locked behind us as soon as we had left. Stiglitz led me to the public square, which contained an eating place of better than average appearance.

Cautiously he asked, "Do you like beer?"

"Not particularly."

"Good," he sighed with real relief. "I manage to find a few bottles each month and it makes life bearable. So if you don't mind I'll not offer you one. Why don't you have an orange?"

"I usually drink tea."

"Better for you," he laughed uneasily.

When our meal was served, the waiter produced from some well-protected corner a bottle of lukewarm German beer, which Dr. Stiglitz attended to personally. With meticulous care he pried away the top, quickly pressing his mouth over the foaming bottle to catch each drop that would otherwise have been wasted. Next he took a long, slow, satisfying draught, closed his eyes, and placed the bottle reverently on the table close to his right hand.

"What would you have said," I asked, "if I had liked beer?"

He opened his eyes slowly and winked. "I'd have said, 'How unfortunate. In Kandahar the mullahs allow no alcohol,' and right now we'd both be drinking tea. I won't try to explain, Herr Miller, but this is my only contact with Europe. It's so precious . . ."

"Would you have any guess as to why Nazrullah's wife disappeared?"

"I'm not satisfied she has."

"Any rumors?"

"I give no credence to rumors."

"That means you've heard some."

"Herr Miller, I hadn't even heard she was missing."

"You hadn't?"

"Why should I?" he asked impatiently. "They left here last July to work at Qala Bist. Haven't seen them since."

"Was she all right . . . when you knew her?"

"All right?" he asked angrily, licking his fingers. "Who's all right? Maybe she was planning to murder her husband and have a baby by a camel. Who can you point to in Afghanistan and say, 'That one's all right'? She was healthy, she laughed more than she cried, and she was well groomed."

"How do you know about the crying?"

"I don't. Every time I saw her she was laughing."

It was obvious that he intended the interrogation to end, but I could not resist one final question. "Did you know her by her western name?"

Dr. Stiglitz threw down the piece of nan he had been using as a fork and sputtered, "No more! Eat!" He took a long swig of beer.

This relaxed him and he asked philosophically, "Herr Miller, have you ever speculated as to why it was such a terrible punishment in these lands to cut off the hand of a thief? No? The awful part about it was that they always cut off the right hand. Look around this restaurant and see if that gives you an idea."

There were perhaps fifteen eating areas in the dusty room and at each men were eating pilau, but I didn't see the connection. Stiglitz pointed out, "They're all eating with their right hands. See!" He pointed to a rug on which five bearded Afghans were digging freely from a common bowl, and each used his right hand. The left never appeared in motion.

"I don't understand."

"Only the right hand is allowed in the food bowl," Stiglitz said ponderously, like a German professor, "because when a man goes to the toilet he must always wipe himself with his left hand. In lands where there is little water, this is a prudent rule." He took another drink of beer and reflected, "It was a terrifying punishment, to cut off a man's right hand. Automatically it banished him from the food bowl."

I was about to ask the point of this story when I saw two men rigging a string of lights across one corner of the square. "What goes on over there?" I asked.

"That's for the dance," he explained. "Spring festival brings out the dancing boys, the dirty little monsters."

I described the team I'd seen on the truck and he banged his empty beer bottle. "That's the kind. They're all alike. Filthy animals."

"The ones I saw looked fairly clean," I protested.

"Clean? Yes. Even perfumed. But they're cruel little pederasts . . . sodomites. When they come to town they create a great evil."

"You astonish me," I gulped.

"I shouldn't. If you have a society where women are forbidden, men must volunteer for the female functions."

"I was remarking on that the other day. But not in this context."

"This is the context that counts," Stiglitz snapped. "Our handsome dancing boys are all dirty little whores. How could they otherwise afford the clothes they wear?"

The lights were now in position and a stage was being marked off, about which began to cluster several hundred men in turbans and a few in karakul caps. From an alley which was to serve as dressing room a man in his fifties, whom I recognized from the truck, appeared to make a speech.

"Let's go see the little monsters," Stiglitz proposed, and we walked slowly across the square to join the crowd. We were in time to hear the speaker assure us that he had brought to Kandahar the finest troupe of dancers in Afghanistan, who had just finished a season in Kabul, where they had danced for the king. Five musicians came on stage, older men who played flutes, drums and a bucket-like fiddle containing at least twenty strings. The music had a standard Oriental, wailing quality, but also a fierce rhythm quite alien to countries like China and Japan. This was the throbbing music of the upland plateaus, a modification of Indian, Mongol and Greek strains. As sound it was attractive; as rhythm it was compelling.

"I've grown fond of the music," Stiglitz said, "and these men are good." They played for some minutes and induced in the crowd a subtle change. Men stopped talking. Bodies began swaying, and a sense of excitement became almost tangible. Then, with a shout, two young men in candy-striped costumes leaped out of the alley and began a whirling dance in which their long hair stood out straight from their heads. They were unlike western dancers, more controlled in their torsos, but more abandoned in the way they used their extremities and their heads.

I whispered to Stiglitz, "Do you deny they're artists?"

"It's their other skills I object to," he snapped.

During the first half-hour the star of the troupe did not appear and the interval was filled with flying bodies and wild music. The audience seemed to grow impatient and it was clear they were waiting for the young man who had insulted me on the bridge, and I too was waiting for him. The master of ceremonies knew this and took advantage of our anticipation by sending his musicians among the crowd to collect donations in their karakul fezzes.

"What do I give?" I asked the doctor.

"As little as possible," he growled, and I saw him throw in a few small coins, which caused the musician to sneer at him as a ferangi. I contributed a bill and gained a professional, ingratiating smile.

The musicians reassembled and the master announced that we were now to see what we had been waiting for, the premier dancer of Afghanistan. The long thin drums, with goat leather at either end, began throbbing and flutes scurried up and down the register. The music halted and from the alley appeared, in the slowest of rhythmic steps, the young man who had made such an impression on me that morning.

He was dressed in a tunic cut from some rare purple fabric threaded with gold. His trousers were gray whipcord that flowed about his legs as he danced, and his turban was of pale blue silk, its free end flying out from his left shoulder. At this stage of the dance his extraordinary hair was held in place by the turban, but at his shoulders it was free to twist and move in the flickering lights. He was a young man of extreme physical beauty, and I was repelled by him for the reason that he knew he was beautiful and intended using his beauty to create confusion.

The tempo of the music increased, but now the audience did not move and the solitary dancer began to shift his body and his feet more deftly. I noticed that he kept lagging behind the beat of the music, as if he were too languid to keep up, and this gave his dance a quality of sexual boredom and lethargy.

Then the musicians began to shout and hammer their drums in planned frenzy, giving the impression that the boy was being driven to dance more rapidly, and as he did so the end of his turban pulled loose and was soon expanded into a flash of color and a hypnotic gyration that I had to admit was thrilling. No woman in a steamy hall, loosening her garments one by one, ever generated more excitement than this young man did in twirling away his blue turban until his furious black hair was free to whirl out in great circles parallel to the earth. He now intensified his rhythm until he was beating the earth like a drum, his head twisting in ecstasy.

Dr. Stiglitz, who refused to acknowledge his spell, growled, "Probably his last year."

"He's not twenty!" I protested. "He could dance thirty more years."

"You forget. His job isn't dancing. He's here to attract customers for a troupe of nasty little boys.

When they grow too old to attract these swine," he said, indicating the silent, panting watchers, "they're through, and that sweet little man playing the fiddle finds himself ten more teen-age mountain boys who enjoy sodomy."

I felt a little sick at this scientific appraisal of what I was seeing, but such thoughts were banished when I looked across the stage to see in the front row the young man from Badakshar, who stood mesmerized, swaying back and forth in his tattered European coat. I tried to attract his attention, but he was enchanted and could not take his eyes from the young dancer, who now entered the final portion of his performance.

Elbowing my way through the crowd to speak with the young mountaineer, I incurred bitter remarks from Afghans who were similarly bewitched by the exciting dancer, but I ignored them and came at last to the youth from Badakshar. "He's good, eh?" I asked in Pashto.

He did not hear me. He was not aware that anyone had joined him, for he was captivated by the expert who had now whirled about the stage in wide circles, his hair flashing in the night, his gold and purple costume rippling like crests of sand in a windswept desert.

I poked the young mountaineer, and he blinked his eyes. Finally he was able to focus on me, as if from a distance, and he muttered weakly, "Without wings, he flies." Having uttered this, he returned to his trance and watched as the dancer leaped and gyrated into a furious finale. Now even I had to pay attention, for I did not believe that a human body could move so fast and yet maintain control.

The drums exploded and the flutes ran riot. There was a flash of hair and wild eyes and grinning mouth and golden cloth. The dance ended. At my side the young mountaineer gasped and said, "In Badakshar we saw no dance like that." I wished him good night, but I fear he heard no words.

※

———————

7

When I awakened in the morning I saw Nur Muhammad perched on the spare tires, a mirror propped against a knee, a can of hot water at his side, shaving contentedly, for in the hotel at Kandahar there was no bathroom. After admiring his dexterity for some minutes I said in English, "That dancing boy we met on the bridge put on a terrific performance."

"The one who cursed you?" Nur asked.

"Stiglitz said they were all sodomites."

"They are," Nur said methodically. "But the police watch them."

I pondered my next question for some time, then asked, hesitantly, in Pashto, "Nur, would you tell me what you know about Stiglitz?"

He continued shaving, inspected his chin as if today a good shave were important, then dried his face with ostentatious care. Apparently Nur had anticipated this question before we left Kabul and had consulted with government officials as to how he should answer. Carefully he replied, "We first heard of Otto Stiglitz in February of last year. That's 1945. Without any warning he crossed the border from Persia. Had no valid papers and was arrested in Herat. Never been to Kabul. He did carry with him papers that claimed a doctor's degree in medicine from some German university."

"His sign says Munich."

"I believe it was. When the war ended we directed our ambassador in Paris to investigate the matter and he satisfied himself that Stiglitz was a legitimate doctor. His degree was authentic. As I recall, we received a copy of his university record. It was impressive."

"But it's so difficult to get permission to enter Afghanistan," I pointed out. Since we were speaking in Pashto I automatically used the standard pronunciation, as if the word contained no *gh* sound at all. To us who worked or lived in the country, it was Afanistan. "How could an ordinary man like Stiglitz just walk in?"

"You forget," Nur pointed out. "He wasn't an ordinary man. He was a doctor, and we need doctors. He was also a German, and we've always needed Germans. Forgetting the unhappy experience with the bridges, our nation has been built by Germans. We're sometimes called 'The Germany of Asia,' and we're not going to turn away German refugees now."

"You believe he was a Nazi?"

"Weren't they all . . . legally?" Nur asked quietly, as he began to pack away his shaving gear and offer me the hot water.

"That's all you know?" I pressed.

"Obviously, he came to Kandahar and opened shop as a doctor. Local people advise us he's very good. At any rate, we're glad to have him and I suppose he'll stay here for many years."

"Why do you say that?"

"For most Germans, Afghanistan is the end of their road. From here there are few places they can go."

"Not even back to Germany?"

"There least of all."

"How many German nationals have you in the country?" I asked, with a kind of morbid fascination, for although I was no professional German-hater I did have to acknowledge that had I been a citizen of that country in 1937 I would now be dead. And my relatives and many of my friends would also be dead. And since I'm a man who has always found joy in my association with relatives and friends, the thought of their being mutilated and starved and dead was not only morally repulsive. It scared the very devil out of me. Instinctively I feared Germans and always will.

I don't think this sprang from an unhealthy preoccupation with death. From early childhood I had been prepared by my parents to face the fact that people died, and I knew that one day I would; but Jews have a love of continuity—which accounted in part for the delight I took in the history of Afghanistan—and prior to World War II, whenever I thought of myself as dead, I thought of future Millers continuing. "There'll always be some Miller who has tickets to Symphony Hall," I assured myself, and if I weren't among them my absence would be regrettable but not tragic; but if Millers and Goldbergs and Sharps and Weinsteins were not there—if all were gone—it would be unbearable. Had my family not emigrated from Germany we would now all be dead, and I could not ignore that fact.

These personal reflections kept me from hearing all of Nur's reply, but I did catch the figure of more than six hundred Germans reaching Afghanistan, some with exalted credentials.

"All Nazis?"

"That's a matter of definition. Many were decent men and women who hated Hitler and who had scars on their backs and minds to prove it. I talked about this with Moheb Khan . . ." Again I lost what he was saying, for his phrase "I talked about this with Moheb Khan" didn't jibe with my experience of the two men. Whenever I had been with Moheb in the presence of Nur, the former had treated Nur like a servant. Apparently there was much I didn't comprehend about Afghan espionage and I supposed that some day I would find that Nur was Moheb Khan's younger brother or nephew to the king.

"If Stiglitz is so good, why doesn't he come to Kabul?"

"An understanding we have with all refugees. They've got to settle in different parts of the country. Where they're needed. If he proves himself in Kandahar, he could be invited to Kabul."

"Then he's not free to move around?"

"You aren't free to move around," he pointed out. "You had to get permission from Shah Khan."

"I'm an outsider."

"So's Stiglitz. Until he proves himself."

"Is he doing so?"

"Yes." Obviously, Nur wished to say no more on this subject.

But I asked, "What's the average Afghan pay for a visit to a doctor?"

"Possibly eight cents."

"So the refugees don't get rich?"

"Not in Kandahar." Again he ended the conversation, then added with cool calculation, "But if later on he could move to Kabul, then perhaps he'd be able to serve the diplomatic community. Perhaps even officially. And for that he'd receive good pay."

"Do you suppose Dr. Stiglitz would consider coming to Kabul?"

Nur looked straight at me as he filled my shaving mug with hot water. "I should imagine that he dreams of nothing else."

"Could you give me an opinion as to how long his apprenticeship in Kandahar will be?"

"That will be decided by our government . . . and yours, if you should be thinking of employing Stiglitz as embassy doctor." I made no comment.

I was amused when Stiglitz and Nur met at lunch that day. The German was much more careful with Nur than he had been with me, for he quickly guessed that Nur might be an official with some power in Kabul. "It's a pleasure to meet Your Excellency," Stiglitz said ingratiatingly.

"I'm not an excellency, sad to confess," Nur parried. "I'm Miller Sahib's driver."

Stiglitz looked carefully at Nur's western shoes, western suit and expensive karakul cap and decided not to fall into that trap. "I must congratulate Herr Miller on having one of the finest drivers in Afghanistan. I wish I spoke English as well as you, Nur Sahib."

"I wish I were a doctor with a fine degree from

Munich," Nur replied, and the pudgy German radiated gratification.

In succeeding days I saw a good deal of Stiglitz, and the more I saw the more assured I became that the embassies would be getting a good doctor if they got him, and I decided to help engineer his promotion to Kabul. We often ate together, he jealously guarding his bottle of beer, I asking questions by the score, and he was willing to permit this because I paid for the meals.

My questioning assured me of one thing: Stiglitz was no Nazi. He had a humanitarian attitude toward medicine and an understanding of what it could do to alleviate mental as well as physical suffering. He was hungry for philosophical discussion and each night dined with me on nan and pilau, then accompanied me to see the dances, after which we talked till midnight as he smoked his pipe.

One memory of Stiglitz persists when I recall those exciting days in Kandahar: his outspoken disgust over the dancing troupe and the lead dancer in particular. "They're a blot on Afghanistan," he railed, pronouncing the name of his new land like a native. "They represent a deep malaise. By God, they ought to get the women out of chaderi and put this country on a normal psychological basis."

One day at lunch we were discussing this with Nur and he laughed tolerantly. "Every ferangi who comes here has some one thing that ought to be done right away. Dr. Stiglitz says, 'Get the women out of chaderi.' The French ambassador says, 'Educate two thousand more medical men.' The American ambassador tells us, 'Pipe water into the city from the hills.' And the Russians say, 'Pave your streets.' Do you know really what we must do first?"

"What?" Stiglitz asked eagerly. This was the kind of conversation he liked.

"All of them," Nur replied. "Yes! Laugh! But we've got to move the entire nation ahead on all possible fronts. And that requires more brains and more courage than we have available. Pray for us when you go to sleep."

"I've been praying that you'd take me to the house where Nazrullah lives when he's in Kandahar," I said.

"I completed arrangements yesterday." Nur bowed. "Will you join us, Doctor?"

"I would be honored," he said formally. He was about to dig into his pocket for some change when a pleasant thought struck him. "Is the ferangi paying for this lunch?"

"I am," I said. No refugees worried so constantly about money as the Germans. He sighed with relief when I produced the money, and I noticed that just before the bill was totaled he grabbed an extra piece of nan, which he munched as we hiked through the streets.

Nur led us to the typical walled house, where the inevitable gate watcher inspected us grudgingly, then allowed us to pass. The establishment contained no unusual feature: it had a garden, some fruit trees, mud walls, some Persian rugs, and a male servant. There was a big colored photograph of the king and on the table three very old copies of *Time*. The furniture was upholstered in a bilious pink mohair.

Then something quite different happened. From one of the doors appeared an apparently young woman in a pale blue silk chaderi. Dr. Stiglitz showed amazement when he saw the shroud worn indoors, as did Nur Muhammad, who introduced me as the gentleman from the American embassy. In Pashto the shrouded figure said, "I am proud to welcome you to Nazrullah's house." Then she whispered to Nur, who nodded assent, and she called for a male servant, who appeared with two children, a girl four years old and a boy only a few months old.

"Nazrullah's children," Nur said approvingly. "The oldest is the age of my youngest."

"How many children have you?" I asked Nur.

"Three," he replied.

"Is your wife Afghan?"

"It's none of your business," Dr. Stiglitz snapped.

"She's from the north," Nur said obligingly.

It was obvious that we were speaking among ourselves because the presence of the woman in chaderi embarrassed us. Normally any Afghan man advanced enough to bring a ferangi into his home for presentation to his wife would tell her, "You can remove the chaderi, dear." And Mrs. Nazrullah must have wanted to do so. But she was restrained by the fact that Nur Muhammad was an official of the government and might be a man committed to retaining the chaderi. To protect her husband, she had to remain covered.

Nur, on the other hand, was known to me positively as an enlightened Afghan who wanted to see the chaderi go, and he was certainly inclined personally to say to Mrs. Nazrullah, "With us you can drop the chaderi," but he was afraid that someone might report his action to Kabul, and he was not sufficiently well placed in government to establish his own rules.

So two people who knew the chaderi was doomed were thus locked into positions where pragmatically they defended it. I broke the impasse by asking, in English, for I had no idea how a man addressed a woman whom he couldn't see, "Why didn't Mrs. Nazrullah accompany her husband to Qala Bist?"

"Ask her," Nur said, so I restated my question in Pashto.

"There were no quarters for us," she replied softly. It was a curious sensation, hearing words issuing from a shroud.

"I understand," I said, but at the same time I remarked to myself: Ellen Jaspar found quarters.

"Do be seated, gentlemen," she said as the servant appeared with four glasses of orange drink. I wondered: How's she going to drink with a chaderi on?

"We'll be seeing your husband soon," I said. "Can we take him anything?"

"You're very thoughtful," she replied in what I detected as embarrassment. Then she laughed charmingly, and I saw by the wall a box of things already waiting for us to take to Qala Bist.

"Nur's been here before me," I said with what gallantry I could command.

"Yes," she said easily. "He arranged it yesterday, but I'm pleased you have the same idea. I wouldn't want Nur to exceed his prerogatives." Her use of words was so precise that I had to readjust my concept of the Nazrullah triangle. His Afghan wife was no barefoot desert girl hurriedly acquired to have babies which would extend the family line.

"Can you speak other than Pashto?" I inquired.

"French." Then slowly, and with pride, she added, "And a little English."

"Wisely so," Stiglitz grunted. "Some day she'll be an ambassador's wife."

Mrs. Nazrullah didn't hear this and Nur repeated the compliment in Pashto. The veiled figure laughed, then turned to the doctor and asked, "Do you speak French?"

"Yes," Stiglitz replied.

"Do you, Miller Sahib?"

"Yes, madame," I nodded.

"Then why don't we all use that language?" she asked in good French. I looked at Nur, and Madame Nazrullah assured me, "Oh, Nur speaks better French than I."

I must have looked startled, for Nur explained, "Where do you suppose I worked before I worked with you? French embassy." I thought: When the Afghans get hold of a good man they see he gets a practical education.

Dr. Stiglitz remarked, "You come back in three years, Herr Miller. Your man Nur will be speaking Russian."

"Well," Madame Nazrullah said with that hands-folded, businesslike way women can adopt, "I've been told why you're here, Miller Sahib, and I wish I could help you. But I haven't any idea where my husband's other wife has gone."

"Isn't she with him?" I asked.

"I think not," she said.

"And she's not here?"

Madame Nazrullah laughed pleasantly. "No, we haven't had any ferangi wives walled up here in Kandahar for weeks and weeks."

"Forgive me," I said.

"But I suppose if you went back a few years, you might find an example or two. So your suspicions are excusable."

"Thank you."

"I do want to assure you of one thing, and please believe me as a friend who would do neither you nor Ellen harm. She never fought with me. I never humiliated her. During the short time we shared a house in Kabul we behaved like sisters. She used to sing to my daughter."

"Had she been warned—a second wife, I mean?"

"Of course!" the shrouded figure laughed. "On the day we met she kissed me and said, 'You're Karima. Nazrullah told me all about you.'"

"I can't believe it," I said flatly. "No American girl . . ."

Nur interrupted. "Don't speak like that, Miller Sahib. Is what Karima says any more difficult to believe than other things we already know to be true?"

"No. I apologize."

"I know how difficult it must be to understand my country," Madame Nazrulla said softly. "But in your report cling to this fact, Miller Sahib. In Nazrullah's home Ellen was treated with love and respect. She treated us in the same manner."

"Does that include Nazrullah's mother . . . and sisters?"

"For two hours each afternoon Ellen took lessons

in Pashto from Nazrullah's mother. She was an adorable girl and our family loved her . . . all of us." She rose, bowed graciously and started to leave. Her orange drink remained untouched.

"One more question, please," I pleaded. "Have you any guess, no matter how bizarre . . ."

"As to what happened? No. But I will assure you of this. Whatever Ellen did was an act of intelligence. She willed it to occur just as it did occur, for she was in possession of all her faculties and they were extraordinary. She was a brilliant, wonderful person, and if evil has come to her I am bereft, because there is one other thing you must know." She hesitated and I believe she was crying, for she put her right hand to her mouth, or so I judged, for the chaderi masked her motions. "When Nazrullah brought her to Kandahar and left me behind in Kabul, it was Ellen who insisted that I rejoin them. When I arrived she met me and said, 'I was so homesick for the little girl.' Between us, Miller Sahib, there was only love."

She left the room, then reconsidered and said from the door, "Possibly she asked me to come to Kandahar because she knew I could have children and apparently she couldn't. Dr. Stiglitz will confirm that."

The lady in the shroud, whatever her complexion or beauty, bowed and we saw her no more. When she had gone I said, "I expected a barefoot nomad from the Hindu Kush."

"Her sister went to school in Bordeaux," Nur observed.

I turned to Stiglitz and said, "About the matter of having children . . ."

In disgust Stiglitz barked something in German which I did not understand. He turned to leave the house, then snapped in Pashto, "Such matters are no concern of an embassy." Abruptly he left us and stalked off, and I could see that he must have fled Germany for good reason. He was an honest, hard, opinionated man and for him life under the Nazis must have been hell.

Slyly Nur observed, "His way of confirming what Karima said."

"Think so?"

"Include it in your report," Nur advised. "You won't be far wrong."

That evening Nur and I missed Dr. Stiglitz at dinner, but after our nan and pilau we wandered across the square to watch the dancers and I told Nur, "You could take this troupe to New York right now and they'd be a sensation."

"Is that true?" he asked skeptically.

"Of course. That lead dancer could fit into any ensemble I ever saw. Do you realize how good he is?"

"Look!" Nur chuckled during one of the intermissions. "Overcoat Sahib." And there was the young man from Badakshar, still stupefied by the dancer who "without wings, he flies."

My comment about the troupe saddened Nur, in a way I could not have predicted. "In many things we have great talent in Afghanistan. I've heard old men in the hills who could tell long stories better than most of the European novels I read. You say the dancers are good. Do you realize how miserable it is to grow up in a country where there's no outlet for talent?" I felt it best not to comment on this, but Nur asked, "Is it true that in Russia they take dancing teams like this and sometimes give them medals and even send them to Paris?"

"Of course," I replied. "All countries do. In the middle of the war I was in China, where they fought the Japanese all day and went to Chinese opera at night. The Chinese were no better dancers than these men."

"Is that true?" Nur mused. Again, the idea depressed him.

But next morning we received another view of the dancing team, for while I was seated on the spare tires, shaving, I heard my name called in the courtyard. One of the armed guards who had been sleeping in our jeep was announcing that a visitor had come to see me, so I wrapped a towel around my neck and went to the slit window. The visitor was Dr. Stiglitz.

"Let him in!" I called in Pashto.

In a moment the German doctor joined us. "Want to see something unique? Probably nowhere else in the world to see it."

"What's up?"

"Didn't you hear the commotion . . . about four this morning?"

"Yes," Nur replied. "Fighting in the streets. I put it down as a brawl."

"You were half right," Stiglitz said. "It started as a brawl."

"What about?" Nur asked.

"The usual. Men got to fighting over the dancing boys. Particularly the one Herr Miller admired."

"The one I said could succeed in New York," I reminded Nur.

"He succeeded last night," Stiglitz said wryly. "Two men were fighting over him. It ended in murder."

Nur Muhammad swore in Pashto. "Another of those?"

"Yes," Stiglitz replied in Pashto. "I warned our American friend that this boy was evil . . . evil. You never understood, did you, Herr Miller?"

"I didn't anticipate murder," I admitted in Pashto, and for the remainder of the terrifying incident in which we were to participate we continued to speak that language.

Nur Muhammad must have guessed what we were about to witness, but I didn't, for nothing in my reading about Afghanistan, nor even the grisly events in Ghazni, had prepared me for the public square in Kandahar that lovely spring morning. Dr. Stiglitz, having witnessed such an event in Herat, knew what was afoot, and on our short walk to the square asked us to stop by his office, where the armed guard admitted us to a doubly locked trunk from which Stiglitz produced a Leica camera. Testing it by snapping Nur and me in his consulting room, he slung the camera over his shoulder and put on a karakul cap. Then he led us to the square.

Where the dancers had performed the night before, a large group of men had gathered, but now the string of lights was gone and the bare earth glistened rock-like in the sun. To one side stood an elderly man, the focus of all attention. He seemed not to be a distinguished citizen, for his sandals and shirt were tattered and his vest was nearly in shreds, but he commanded attention if only because of the noble manner in which he bore himself. He was surrounded by the mob, yet not a part of it, and all who came close to him offered deference, which he accepted as hereditary right. He was obviously one of the causes why the mob had gathered.

When the sun was well up, there was a beating of drums, not intended as the passionate accompaniment to dancing, for they were somber and of a different timbre, intended to announce the arrival of eight uniformed policemen, grim and forbidding in appearance. In pairs they marched to compass points previously marked by piles of pebbles, and then I saw that each pair had a mallet and a short stake, which was driven into the ground, leaving about eight inches showing.

The drums throbbed again, and from the alley that had been used as a dressing room appeared two mullahs, small, roundish men with clean-shaved faces, quite unlike the gaunt beak-nosed mullahs of the hills. They signaled the drums to cease, whereupon they prayed, first one, then the other. I did not catch all their words, but they seemed to be cleansing the minds of those who were about to participate in a time-honored rite. They also prayed that each of us, seeing this thing, would henceforth respect the commands of God and the precepts of His chosen Prophet. When their prayers ended, the drums beat again and a shackled man, obviously a prisoner, was led forth.

"It's the young man with the coat!" I cried.

Nur said, "From Badakshar!" Then he cautioned me to remain silent, while Dr. Stiglitz busied himself taking photographs of the procession.

The young man from the hills was in a daze. I doubt that he understood what was happening or had happened. He had come to Kandahar with a year's savings and had been engulfed in a whirlpool beyond his comprehension. The guards moved him about as if he were merely an animal.

"Is he the murderer?" I whispered to Nur.

A man to the left explained, "Last night, when the dancing ended, the prisoner tried to buy the dancing boy. But a policeman had already spoken for him. The mountain boy refused to understand that the dancer could not be his. In a blind fury he killed the policeman. Everyone saw him do it. There's no question of guilt. Only of punishment."

"What's the punishment to be?" I asked.

"I wish you weren't going to see it," Nur replied.

"Are you staying?"

"What happens . . . I must report," he said with resignation.

The two mullahs went to the bedazed mountain man and said, "You have committed murder." The prisoner was unable to acknowledge the charge. I didn't know what to expect next.

The mullahs moved to a man whom I had not seen before, a fat fellow with a karakul cap, and asked, "Does the government wish to assume control of this case?"

The fat official replied, "This is a crime of passion. The government is not concerned in any way with this case." He nodded to the mullahs and departed.

Next the mullahs moved to the elderly man in the badly torn vest and announced, "Gul Majid, this prisoner has murdered your son. By the law of the Prophet, he is handed to you for punishment. Do you, Gul Majid, accept this responsibility?"

The old man stepped forward with great dignity, raised his eyes so that they stared directly at the young man, and announced in a clear voice, "I accept the prisoner."

The mullahs said a final prayer, beseeching justice and mercy, and we saw them no more.

The men who had been guarding the prisoner shoved him forward until he was almost touching the old man, and it was now a matter solely between the young murderer and the elderly father of the murdered man, a morality play conceived by desert people thousands of years ago and honored by them through countless generations. State and church alike had withdrawn. It was the guilty and the bereaved, standing face to face, and the crowd, which formed a significant part in this reenactment of the passion play, remained tense and silent until the old man cried in a loud voice, "Let the prisoner be tied!"

At this the crowd broke into a shout of wild approval, and I heard Nur whispering in Pashto, "I wish to God that just once there could be mercy." On this day there was to be vengeance, not mercy.

The young murderer was whisked to the stakes, stretched upon the ground face-up and lashed by ankles and wrists until he was spread-eagled in the manner of St. Andrew at his crucifixion. No further attempt was made to keep this a religious ceremony; we were about to participate in retribution, sure and implacable.

When the young man was securely tied, the guards who had done the job stepped away, to be replaced by a cordon of police, brother officers to the murdered man. They stood at intervals about the prisoner, close enough together to prevent a riot but far enough apart to provide everyone with a clear view. The crowd grew silent and men elbowed their way forward to find good spots from which to view the spectacle.

The father of the dead policeman now stepped forward and stood at the feet of the staked-out prisoner. He mumbled a short prayer, then shouted boldly, "Give me the scimitar." I'm not sure you would translate his word as *scimitar*, but at least it wasn't the word for *sword*, and from his band of associates a man stepped forward with a rusty old nineteenth-century bayonet. In a clear voice the old man shouted, "My grandfather captured this from the British at the siege of Kandahar." The crowd cheered.

I looked down at the young man, who appeared not to comprehend what was happening, for his eyes were glassy and remained in the trance that he had entered at the time of the murder, when he was battling for the favors of the dancing boy. But when the old man's address to the public ended and he knelt beside the young man's head, the prisoner at last saw the rusty bayonet and began to scream.

It was a horrifying, animal scream that came from far back in the history of human development. It was, I thought, exactly the right kind of scream for such a scene, for it put us all solidly in the animal category. "No! No!" screamed the staked-out young man, but we had passed the time for words.

The old man steadied himself, twisted his left hand in the victim's hair, and pulled his neck taut. With the rusty bayonet in his right hand he began sawing at his prisoner's throat, and with each awful passage of the bayonet, the boy's head twisted back and forth, while terrible screams emanated from the throat which had not yet been severed. I thought I would vomit.

Then, by the grace of God, a figure hurried out from the crowd and intervened with the old man. The insanity stopped. I breathed again.

The intruder was Dr. Stiglitz, and he argued with the old man in Pashto, but the impassioned executioner failed to comprehend and looked at the German in bewilderment. Then I saw Stiglitz point to the camera and say in a clear voice which I and the others could hear, "If you work from the other side, the light will be better."

The old man shrugged his shoulders and Stiglitz asked harshly, "You want your picture taken, don't you?" At last the executioner understood, and I watched aghast as he switched his position and started cutting from the other side. The sun was unobstructed.

With four powerful drags of the bayonet the old man slashed the victim's throat and silenced the horrible cries. Then he continued bearing down until the cartilage and bone were severed, whereupon with some awkwardness and fatigue from his exertion he rose, keeping his left hand twisted in the victim's hair, and marched triumphantly about the circle, showing each of us the death's head.

When the old man came to me, I had to look away and found myself looking directly at the sodomite dancer whose alluring performance had launched the tragedy. His face was enraptured as he followed the passage of the severed head. His clothes were as neat as ever and he smelled of perfume. When he caught me staring at him with loathing he flashed his most ingratiating smile and whispered in Pashto, "It was horrible, wasn't it?"

"Herr Miller!" I heard a voice calling. Dr. Stiglitz had seen the sybaritic dancer standing beside me and had come for a picture of us. He worked on the focus for a moment, while the dancer, accustomed to having his picture taken, assumed a dramatic pose and I looked astounded in my karakul cap. I still have the picture, and it serves to remind me that what I have described did happen.

Nur and I walked silently across the square to the restaurant, but I was too shocked to want food. Before long the doctor joined us and said, as if nothing had happened, "I'll have a bottle of beer. Nur can't join me because he's Muslim and you don't like beer." When another of the precious bottles was produced, Stiglitz observed, "I'll have two good reasons to get to Kabul eventually. You don't have these public executions up there, but you do have German beer."

"If the execution appalled you," I asked weakly, "why did you photograph it so carefully?"

"I believe we should have a record," he replied. "All historical processes should be recorded. In a few years what you saw today will vanish. Nur Muhammad will see to that."

"But when you stopped the old man . . . Surely, you could have prevailed upon him."

"Me?" Stiglitz cried. "They'd have killed me."

"They would have," Nur agreed.

"But to ask him to switch sides. God, it's ghoulish."

"I altered nothing," he replied, carefully prying the cap off his bottle of beer.

I was choked with moral rage, and then I began laughing. Deep, gusty, cackling laughter overtook me, and although both Nur and Stiglitz tried to stop me, they couldn't, for I was pointing across the restaurant to the public square, where the old man who had conducted the execution was marching home. In his right hand he held the historic bayonet which had avenged family dishonor, while in his left he held the hand of the sodomite dancer, who walked along bowing to the approval of the crowd. It was not this incongruous mating which had caused me to burst into uncontrolled laughter. At the scene of the execution the old man had discarded his sorely tattered vest and he was now wearing the dead man's overcoat, that beautiful, torn and ravaged but still serviceable woman's coat from Paris. It fitted his spare body well, and he actually looked dapper in his new garment.

"Wait!" I called as he passed, and the old man stopped. "Doctor!" I shouted. "Get a picture of this, too," and I struck a pose between the unlikely pair.

When I rejoined my table Nur Muhammad was so angry that he cast aside his role of polite government aide. "Why did you do that?" he demanded bitterly.

"It was so goddamned ridiculous," I said, suddenly ashamed of myself.

"You're using Mr. Jaspar's word," Nur said acidly.

"What's that? Who?" Stiglitz asked, carefully putting away his camera.

"A friend of Miller Sahib's. Every time he confronts something he doesn't understand he calls it ridiculous."

"I'm sorry," I said.

"Some years ago a Frenchman took a series of excellent photographs . . . in Alabama . . . of a lynching. Was that ridiculous?"

"I was laughing because my nerves were shot," I explained lamely.

"Good. I think that now you may be ready to discuss your problem seriously."

"What do you mean by that?" I asked angrily.

"You've seen the terror of my nation. Now let's talk about Ellen Jaspar."

"I'm willing," I said in some bewilderment.

"Let's have no more diversions. No more amusing yourself with old men in public."

"I apologized," I snapped.

"Good," Nur said grudgingly. "When you ridiculed the old fool and the evil young man I thought . . ."

"I think it was the coat . . . It rounded out the story."

"I've forgotten the incident," Nur said. "Don't you remember it as the way we live in Afghanistan."

"We can talk frankly, then?" I asked.

"You always could, with me," Nur replied.

"The other day when I spoke with Shah Khan he

confided that he had heard rumors that something extremely bizarre had happened to Ellen Jaspar . . . so bizarre, in fact, that he wouldn't even repeat the rumor."

"What rumor?" Dr. Stiglitz interrupted.

"The one I asked you about the first night."

"I told you. I have no speculation," he growled, returning to his beer.

"Have you?" I asked Nur.

"As I told you before, she's run away and perished."

"You're honestly convinced that she didn't die at the hands of fanatical mullahs?"

Nur was plainly irritated. "Miller Sahib," he protested, "you asked me that last week in Ghazni, and I swore it could not have happened. Don't you take my word for anything?"

"What we just saw," I said quietly, pointing toward the headless corpse which would lie on the ground till sundown, "permits a man to check answers, doesn't it?"

"Not when the answers have already been verified," Nur replied.

"But the mullahs?" I repeated.

Nur laughed pleasantly. "Those two mullahs happen to be among the finest men in our priesthood. They were acting in strict accordance with Afghan custom, but they know public executions like this can't continue indefinitely. And when it comes time for men like you and me to end them, they'll be on our side."

"They will?" I asked incredulously.

"Of course. I've a brother who's a mullah and a lot better citizen than I am."

"I'd like to meet him," I said brusquely.

"When we get back to Kabul, you will. Miller, you miss the secret of Afghanistan if you think that Islam is a religion which condones what you've just seen."

"It's a damned fine religion," Dr. Stiglitz interrupted in Pashto, where the oath was more colorful. "Matter of fact, I became a Muslim last year."

"You did?" I asked in undisguised surprise.

"Why not? This is my home from now on. It's an exciting country with a profound religion."

"You've surrendered Christianity?" I asked with an abhorrence which I didn't try to mask.

"I repeat," he began in Pashto. Then for some inexplicable reason he started speaking French. "I repeat," he said in French, "why not? A religion is not something eternal. It's got to function in a given time in a given place. If it doesn't function, it's no good and you'd better get another. Have you ever considered how your Christianity functioned in Germany? The total perversion of society it permitted? The mass executions? The horrible betrayal of humanity? I swore when I reached Herat, 'If Christianity can't do any better than it did in Munich, I'll take whatever religion they use here. It can't be worse.' Actually, it works out rather well."

Nur added something that astounded me. "I suppose you know that Ellen Jaspar also became a Muslim?"

Before I could speak, Dr. Stiglitz said, "Sensible girl. We talked about it the last time I saw her. She said she found great solace in her new faith. Called it 'a desert faith.' When I asked

(175)

her what she meant by that, she said that Christianity had become a convenient ritual for those who overeat on Saturday, commit adultery on Saturday night, and play golf on Sunday." Ellen's description, when delivered in French, sounded witty, ugly and profound. "She said she needed a religion much closer to original sources. One thing she said impressed me. She pointed out that Islam, Christianity and Judaism all started in the desert, where God seems closer, and life and death are more mysterious. She said that we are all essentially desert animals and that life is meant to be harsh. When we live in an oasis like Philadelphia or Munich we become degenerate and lose touch with our origins."

"Would you return to Munich . . . if you were free to do so?" I asked.

Dr. Stiglitz looked at me with contempt. Nothing he had so far said implied that he was barred from returning to Germany, but his self-committal to a new world permitted only one conclusion, and I had publicly stated it. He was angry with me for having done so and replied in German, "No, I would never return to Germany." Then he translated into Pashto.

At this point the pilau was served, a rich, steaming dish with extra pine nuts and raisins, and although immediately after the beheading I had been repelled by the thought of food, with the passage of time I had grown hungry, and we three dug into it with our fingers, achieving a kind of hard brotherhood as we did. Dr. Stiglitz was then forty, Nur Muhammad was thirty-two and I twenty-six, but because each of us had a certain integrity which he was willing to protect, we were growing to respect one another, and I was happy to be with them. Indeed, I was proud to be with them, eating in communion after a ritual execution.

"You must not think of Islam as a religion of the desert," Nur warned. "It has much vitality and the world has not yet heard the last of it."

I was driven to ask an impertinent question. "If a new state of Israel is fashioned out of the desert, will you Muslims be able to accept it?"

"You can trust the Jews to look after themselves," Stiglitz said bluntly, and the brotherhood that had been burgeoning collapsed. I was shocked that a German refugee would make such a statement publicly, but what followed shocked me even more: "And if they should need help, men like you and me would help them. They deserve a country of their own." He returned to his beer.

"The Muslims won't like it," Nur reflected, "particularly the Arabs. I won't like it. I don't want Jews taking part of my homeland. But the alternatives I like even less. We Muslims will give the Jews a little . . . not much, but a little."

After a while I remarked, "We have no proof at the embassy that Ellen Jaspar became a Muslim."

"Many ferangi wives do," Nur replied. "We see no reason for official comment one way or the other."

"They do?" I asked.

"Of course. You Christians always think that conversion goes one way. Right here you see proof to the contrary. Dr. Stiglitz from Germany and Ellen Jaspar from Philadelphia."

I began to laugh again, this time nonhysterically.

"What about that beer?" I asked, pointing at the half-empty bottle.

"A German can be many things," Stiglitz explained robustly. "A Catholic, a Jew, a Lutheran, a Muslim. But always he's a beer drinker. I have a dispensation from the mullah . . . the one you saw today. He's an understanding liberal."

✳

———————

8

Two substantial rivers ran through the part of Afghanistan in which I was traveling, the Helmand, which started in the Koh-i-Baba west of Kabul, and the Arghandab, which flowed down past Kandahar. It was at Qala Bist that they met to combine forces for a dash across the desert, and it was at this confluence, in the most ancient times, that a powerful civilization developed. From the way Shah Khan had described it, I would have wanted to see Qala Bist even had I not known that Nazrullah was working there and that Ellen Jaspar had vanished from that point.

The ruins lay only seventy miles west of Kandahar, but since many of those miles were across open desert, Nur Muhammad had our jeep packed before dawn and we drove out of Kandahar with the first rays of sun. We must have made an impressive one-jeep caravan, for we had now discarded western clothes and were dressed like desert Afghans, except that we kept our karakul caps. I was impressed by the road west, for it led through fruit groves and well-established farms, each protected by high mud walls with box-like structures at the corners.

"What are the boxes for?" I asked.

Nur laughed and said, "Those are melon fields."

"I still don't get the boxes."

"They're for the lookouts," he explained. "Growing melons in Afghanistan is extremely difficult. During the entire month they're ripening the farmer has to station armed men at each field to shoot thieves."

I must have looked as if I thought he was teasing, for he added gravely, "My father raised melons, and at the age of nine I stood night watch with a shotgun. Otherwise every melon would have been stolen."

"Why do you permit such thievery?" I asked.

"We're a brigand society," Nur said. "Our king doesn't rule in Kabul the way your president rules in Washington. In this country we murder kings."

We had now reached the village of Girishk, where we were to leave the pleasant melon patches and turn south across the desert. For me this was a rare moment, for we were about to enter upon the great world-desert that sweeps from Central India across Arabia, through Egypt, over the Sahara and on to Morocco, where it is finally halted by the Atlantic Ocean. I had not previously seen this enormous desert, and now as the early sun showed me the windswept land and the burning rocks I knew I was entering a new world. This was the universe of shifting sand, the mournful camel chewing sideways, the men in dirty white. I remember with great clarity my first impression of this vast desert and my astonishment at its enormous vistas.

The segment which we had struck was in some ways an ideal introduction, for it was both smaller than the better-known deserts of Arabia, Egypt

and Libya—less than two hundred miles on a side
—and more savage. It had no oasis, no vegetation
and no protective rocks. It was a bleak, barren
waste across which the wind howled perpetually,
and to be lost on it meant death, a fact which was
amply proved each year, and it was from this re-
morseless character that the Afghan desert had ob-
tained its lurid name, which I hesitate to repeat,
since it sounds so exhibitionistic: The Dasht-i-
Margo, the Desert of Death.

We had traversed the dangerous wastes for
about two hours when we saw ahead a sight that I
knew was coming but which nevertheless startled
me. Rising from the desert, along the shores of the
Helmand River, stood the arch of Qala Bist, an
enormous clay-brick structure rising high in the air.
A thousand years ago it had formed part of some
Muslim edifice, but even the memory of the
mosque was lost. Yet there the arch stood, so tall it
seemed impossible that a desert people had built
it. It was the more surprising because it was an un-
supported arch, a lofty, soaring flight of brick composed in beautiful proportions, and when we
stopped the car to admire it I told Nur, "You had
some architects in the old days."

"Wait till you see over there," Nur laughed, and
as we approached the suspended arch I began to
see the outline of a great deserted city: walls that
crept up from the river and enclosed enormous
areas, turrets of majestic size, and battlements that
once accommodated thousands of soldiers.

"What is it?" I asked.

"Nobody knows."

"You mean it's just there?"

"It's one of our smaller deserted cities," Nur assured me. Pointing westward across the desert he said, "On the other side, where the Helmand disappears, there's an empty city seventy miles long. No one knows who built it, either, but there it is."

"What do you mean, where the Helmand disappears?"

"This river," he said, indicating the powerful flow at our feet. "Out in the desert it just disappears."

"Into what?" I asked.

"Into air. The Desert of Death is so dry that the river runs into a lake that just dries up." I looked at him suspiciously and realized he was not teasing, so I dropped the matter, but the city before me could not be casually dismissed.

"Who built this?" I probed.

"It's always been here," Nur laughed.

"No name?"

"No. Qala Bist is our modern name for the arch."

"It's a masterpiece. If we had something like this in America, we'd make it a national park."

"You started about a thousand years too late to have something like this," Nur laughed. "We do have some ideas, of course. Possibly it was the winter capital of Mahmud of Ghazni. He was rich enough to have built it. But I agree with the experts who argue that it must have been here for a long time before Mahmud's day."

"And that's all that's known?"

"You see what I see," Nur replied defensively. "There was a great city in the desert, and now even its history is gone."

The idea tantalized me and I was about to say,

I'm going to find out what happened here, when I saw on the ramparts above me a young man in his late twenties, dressed in desert costume and turban. He was waving to us and Nur cried, "It's Nazrullah," and I saw that he wore a mustache and beard. On the city wall he made a fine figure and could have been a young captain of the guard a thousand years ago.

"Eh, Nazrullah!" Nur shouted. "I've brought an American with me . . . from the embassy." This news somewhat deflated the young man on the wall, for he ceased waving; but then his pleasure at seeing visitors overcame any hesitancy, and he scrambled down from the high wall and ran forward to greet us.

"Nur Muhammad!" he cried with real pleasure, and they embraced in a manner that satisfied me that my driver was no ordinary Afghan. Nazrullah then turned to me and said in English, smiling warmly, "You are welcome to my humble abode, such as it is, four hundred rooms."

We laughed and Nur said in Pashto, "This one speaks our language. And he's come to spy you out for the evil fellow you are." It was apparent that Nur desperately wanted us to get along.

Nazrullah extended his hand and said generously, "You're most welcome! Drive this way. We've cut a breach in the wall and you can bring your jeep into the city." And he led us to the opening.

There he climbed in with us, for his camp site was far inside the walls—three-quarters of a mile, I judged—and as we traveled I tried to study both Nazrullah and his extraordinary city. He was an attractive fellow, not so tall as I but more wiry and better coordinated. He had a mercurial brilliance, in both gesture and speech. His hair was rather long, possibly because barbers were rare in Qala Bist, but he was extremely clean, even though he was living under unusual conditions. He seemed a well-organized man and I could understand the high regard in which Moheb Khan, Nur Muhammad and Dr. Stiglitz held him.

The deserted city was equally impressive. Stout walls many feet thick and sometimes twenty feet high swept over rolling ground for some eight or nine miles, enclosing an area which once contained substantial farm lands, water systems and separate villages for menials. The brick city itself was a confusion of palaces, minarets, fortresses and what must have been administrative centers. I can best describe it this way: By the time I had seen one complete set of related buildings I thought: This is the city. But it wasn't, for it was connected by ramparts and forts to a larger segment, and this was repeated six or seven times.

After a considerable drive we reached a large field contained within the walls, and here Nazrullah had pitched his tents, from which he was conducting surveys of the area that was to be irrigated by water taken from the Helmand River. He had at his disposal two jeeps, three engineers and four servants. No women were evident, but one tent, finer than the others, must have been the one in which Ellen Jaspar had lived when she came to Qala Bist nine months ago, and where possibly she still remained. I tried cautiously to study this tent without attacting attention, but I failed, for Nazrullah volunteered, "That's where I live. Let's unload your gear."

"Don't let us inconvenience you," I apologized.

"You're my first guests from Kabul," he replied expansively. "Of course you'll stay with me." He threw back the flaps of his tent and bade us enter. I remember two things: the floor was covered by an expensive Persian rug, and on the desk stood a portrait of Ellen Jaspar dressed in the surplice she wore when singing Beethoven's *Ninth* with the Philadelphia Orchestra. Nazrullah made no comment about the photograph.

He indicated where we were to sleep and sent his servants to fetch our gear, which they unpacked for stowing in cardboard trunks which Nazrullah had acquired in the bazaar, but as they worked I saw in another corner a trunk made of leather, stamped with the initials E.J. It was locked, so I could not tell whether it was empty or full, but it seemed to be waiting for its owner to return.

Nazrullah now took us to a tent some distance from the others, and here, seated on rugs, we had our inevitable lunch of nan and pilau, but this was different, because near the tent the cook was operating an oven that must have been more than a thousand years old, and for the first time I saw how nan was baked. A conical mound of clay, looking exactly like a beehive with the top cut off, rose above a shallow pit in which charcoal was kept burning. The opening of the beehive gave access to the inner sides, which sloped over the coals, and it was against these sloping sides that the raw dough was fixed, though why it did not fall onto the coals I never understood. I asked Nazrullah and he said, "By trial and error the desert people developed this stove three or four thousand years ago. The dough is just sticky enough to cling to the sides and the fire is cool enough not to bake the bread too quickly. It's obviously impossible, but it works." The hot bread was delicious.

After the meal, when our greasy fingers had been washed by servants, we returned to Nazrullah's tent, where he said reflectively, "It's been my salvation, living here on the edge of the desert. After Germany and America, it's reminded me of what Afghanistan is. Do you know what it is?" he asked me directly.

"Until I saw the Desert of Death I thought I knew. A mountainous land marked by inhabitable valleys and plateaus."

"Precisely. That's what I thought it was. But four-fifths of our nation looks like what you see outside these walls. Desert, cut by rivers. And wherever we can lead those rivers onto the desert, we're rewarded a thousandfold. Before you came here, Miller, did you realize that the Afghan is probably the world's best irrigation expert?"

I said I hadn't and he continued, "We waste hardly a drop of water. The skill of our peasants is unbelievable. They take a little stream coming out of the mountains and lead it hundreds of yards to irrigate a field, then take it back to its main bed so that others can borrow it farther down the mountainside. One insignificant stream will be used many times."

"I've never seen that," I replied.

"My job is to do on a grand scale with the Hel-

mand what the farmers do so well with little
streams. We're going to build a gigantic dam up in
the hills and capture all the water you see going to
waste out there."

The concept had inflamed his imagination, and
with boundless vitality he rushed us out of the tent
and over to the city, where we passed through silent streets that must once have been glorious with
ribbons from India and furs from Russia. We
climbed stairs that were almost as good now as
when erected and came to a vast reception hall, its
walls still marked with murals, then entered the
battlements which troops could have used that
night. Nazrullah moved quickly, for he was familiar with the ancient city, but I was tardy because I
wanted to absorb the implied splendor of the
place. It was incredible that men had ruled here
whose dynasties were forgotten, that a city of this
magnitude could have perished without leaving in
the records even the name by which its enemies
described it. As I caught up with Nazrullah on the
battlement I said, "Must give you an eerie feeling,
living in a place like this."

"It does. No matter how indifferent you are to
history, when you live here you speculate."

"Any conclusions?"

"None. I don't have to solve the past." He
pointed down to the river that ran along the foot of
the wall on which we stood. "My job is to get
water out of that river."

"What'll you do with it when you get it?"

He pointed beyond the river to the bleak desert,
where wind was churning up the sand, and I supposed that he was going to say that farther out lay

an arable district. Instead he replied, "What looks like desert down there is potential farmland. Wherever we can lead the water, we can grow crops. When we're through, this land will be as valuable as it was when this city supported perhaps half a million people. They lived by irrigation."

"You think so?"

"Look!" he cried with infectious enthusiasm, and he intended that I look upstream where old embankments proved that the Helmand has once before been tapped for irrigation purposes, but I saw instead a curious procession of tall mounds that led away from our city toward a group of small mountains some twenty miles to the east. The mounds had obviously been made by man, because they appeared at regular quarter-mile intervals, and since each was of considerable size, and there were eighty or more visible, I was looking at a project of magnitude, whatever it was.

"What are you staring at?" Nazrullah asked.

"That chain of mounds," I replied.

Nazrullah thought for a moment, then banged his right fist enthusiastically into his left palm and cried, "Miller, are you game for something exciting?"

"The ambassador told me to look around."

"You'll be the only American who's ever done this." He ran to a point from which he could call to Nur Muhammad: "Nur, you want to go with us through the karez?" He pronounced the strange word in one syllable to rhyme with *breeze*, and it had an instant effect upon Nur.

"Not me! And if Miller Sahib has any sense, he won't go either."

"He's already volunteered," Nazrullah shouted enthusiastically, "and if he goes, you'll be shamed."

"I stand before my ancestors shamed," Nur laughed. "You uphold the honor of Afghanistan. I'm a coward."

We hurried through the deserted city and climbed into one of Nazrullah's jeeps, which he raced expertly through the breached wall and onto the desert. Soon we were pulled up beside one of the mounds, which was built of mud brick rising to a height of fifteen feet or more. A crude ladder led to the top.

When we had climbed it, I saw inside another ladder, much longer than the first, leading down to darkness. Nazrullah dropped a pebble, which splashed in water, far below us, and I realized that we were perched atop a shaft which led to an underground stream.

"Down we go!" Nazrullah cried like a college boy, and I watched his excited face, its beard covered with dust, disappear. I followed, and when I reached bottom found myself standing on a narrow edge of earth bordering a clear stream of water only faintly illuminated by sunlight seeping down the shaft.

"Is each of the mounds like this?" I asked.

"Yep," Nazrullah replied, proud of his American colloquialism. "It's an underground irrigation system bringing water down from the hills. You game to crawl through to the next mound?" He must have seen my apprehension, for he flashed on a light and added, "We've cleaned it out for just such expeditions."

I looked at the low ceiling of the tunnel and discovered that once we left the mound, which permitted us to stand, we would be walking in very stooped positions—duck-walking, we had called it as children—and I wasn't sure my legs would take it. "You won't feel it . . . in a quarter of a mile," Nazrullah assured me.

"Here we go," I cried, more bravely than I felt, and bent over to creep duck-wise into the tunnel.

My back quickly began to ache and, as I feared, my leg muscles became numb, but lithe Nazrullah was pushing ahead with such enthusiasm that I had to follow. At midpoint we could begin to see slight indications of light from the next mound and this encouraged me to bear my pain; it also permitted me to see the construction of the tunnel. Its ceiling was protected in no way and was held in place merely by the cohesion of clay, and whenever I bumped it with my head, bits of earth splashed into the water. I thought: This thing could collapse at any moment, and I began to feel my throat constricting.

Fortunately, we reached the next mound and I was able to stand erect. My feet were soaking wet and my back creaked as I stretched it, but I was too stiff to want to climb the ladder immediately, so we stood in the small shaft of light and breathed the cool air.

"Now you understand why Nur refused the invitation," Nazrullah laughed.

"I'm glad I came. Who invented the idea?"

"Maybe the Persians. More likely the Afghans. It's the best way known to transport water across a desert. If we tried to do it on the surface, the sun would evaporate it all."

"How old is the tunnel?"

"Assuming that it was used by the city, which it probably was, the hole we're standing in could have been dug twelve or thirteen hundred years ago."

"Let's get out of here!" I cried.

"Of course, it's been redug many times. The tunnels do collapse," he said brightly.

"I wondered about that as we were crawling through," I replied.

Nazrullah held the ladder by one hand and said, "The karez system was very costly of human life. Water experts would go to the mountains and dig at likely points . . . sometimes seventy feet down, but because they were experts they usually found water. They would then calculate where that particular level would work itself to the surface, and they would dig these underground tunnels for ten to twenty miles, following the natural line of the water's flow."

"Why didn't the ceilings fall in?" I asked.

"They did, frequently. The one we crawled under could collapse at any moment," he said without emotion. "In desert regions men who worked the karez formed a special caste. They lived under special laws, ate special food, had extra women. Mullahs and police were powerless to molest them, for generally they lived short lives and when they died, usually of suffocation, for they never shored up the ceilings and trusted to luck, their few possessions and their women were passed along to the next karez man."

I was beginning to feel the approach of claustrophobia and started up the ladder, increasing my speed when I saw how fragile the clay bricks were under which we had been standing. When I regained freedom I gasped deeply, then saw Nazrullah smiling, his beard gray with dust. "Lucky I didn't tell you that when we were halfway through," he apologized.

"That tunnel is going to fall on me every time I go to sleep for the next month." I laughed thinly.

"I've thought of that myself," Nazrullah confided. "After a series of collapses they often had to beat the men with whips to drive them back into the karez. At the beginning of the system the kings ordained that any boy born to a karez man had to inherit the job. In some districts they were branded at birth."

"You live in a rugged land," I remarked, shivering in the hot sun.

Nazrullah climbed down the outside ladder and sat with me in the shadow of the mound. "It is a cruel land," he admitted. "The existence of this karez reminds us how cruel. But even today in Afghanistan I could show you things that would shock you."

"I've seen some of them," I assured him.

"What?" he asked suspiciously.

"In Ghazni . . . a woman stoned to death. In Kandahar a young man committed murder over a dancing boy. They cut off his head . . . with a rusty bayonet."

"You've been initiated," Nazrullah said without inflection. He seemed wholly composed, but his inner tension was betrayed by quick gestures and the nervous movement of his beard. "I force myself down to the karez occasionally so that I may remember the heritage of human suffering we're trying to eradicate. If I'd known you'd seen the executions I wouldn't have dragged you into the tunnel, but I find I can't talk with ferangi who haven't had some similar experience."

"I've had three now," I said. "We can talk."

"I think we can," he agreed, "and I'd like to say two things. It will require some words, but like your journey through the karez, it may be worth it.

"I went to Germany at the age of twenty. Before that I'd been educated by private tutors whose main job, it seems to me now, was to impress me with the moral depravity of Afghanistan and the timeless glory of Europe. I knew no better than to accept their indoctrination at face value and reported to Germany fully prepared to exhibit my tutors' prejudices. But when I reached Göttingen I found that the true barbarians were not the primitives who stone women in Ghazni—and we have some real primitives in this country—but the Germans. From 1938 through 1941 I remained as their guest, to witness the dreadful degeneration of a culture which might once have been what my tutors claimed but was now a garish travesty. Believe me, Miller, I learned more in Germany than you'll ever learn in Afghanistan.

"As you know, I went from Germany to Philadelphia, where half the people thought I was a Negro. What I didn't learn in Germany, you taught me. Why do you suppose I wear this beard? Before I grew it I made a six-week experiment. I decided to be a Negro . . . lived in Negro hotels, ate in their restaurants, read their papers and dated Negro girls. It was an ugly, ugly life, being a Negro in your country . . . maybe not so bad as being a Jew in Germany, but a lot worse than being an Afghan in Ghazni. To prove to Philadelphians I wasn't a Negro, I grew this beard and wore a turban, which I had never worn at home.

"My education was worth every penny my government paid for it, because after six years in Göttingen and Philadelphia I positively hungered to get home and go to work. Miller, we can build here just as good a society as the Germans or the Americans have built in their surroundings."

I looked at his surroundings: a bleak desert, a muddy river, blazing empty hills, an abandoned city. Because I had seen Afghanistan, I appreciated the Herculean task he had set himself.

"The second thing I want to say is this," he continued with fervor. "Having made my transition from a boy who wanted to escape Afghanistan to a man who fought to get back, I find daily joy in being here. Imagine, at twenty-eight I can be appointed head of a project that will revolutionize this part of Asia. In Philadelphia a man at a cocktail party offered me the stirring job of helping to sell shoes. 'You're enthusiastic,' the man said. 'Women will go for that beard.' Miller, I'm here in the desert because I want to be here. I want to stir the earth like the karez men stirred theirs . . . fundamentally . . . in the bowels . . . at the bottom of the ladder in a deep hole. And if the ceiling collapses on me, I don't give a damn."

There was another moment of tension, then he laughed and said, "We'd better drive back," but when we tried to enter the jeep, the metal was so hot we could not touch it, for we were really in the desert, and if the ancient karez men had not dug their perilous tunnels, water could never have crossed this land and the city could not have existed.

In the days that followed, Nazrullah talked eagerly about all aspects of life in Afghanistan, but whenever I broached the subject of his wife, he was adept in putting me off. Ellen was not at Qala Bist, however; of that I was satisfied. If Nazrullah did not respond to my overtures on the subject, he did take every opportunity to let me see the kind of man he was, and as I watched him with the engineers and the workers I knew that I was observing a man who had matured far beyond his years.

He had an enviable capacity to elicit from others their best efforts. I understood why the shoe company in Philadelphia had wanted to hire him and why a German engineering firm, looking to the future, had recently written to ask if he would represent them in Asia. He had a quick smile, an infectious wit and a generosity of spirit that was engaging, and I could now understand his effect upon a junior at Bryn Mawr, bored by her native surroundings. It was reasonable that Ellen Jaspar had fallen in love with him, but it was not reasonable that she should now, because of him, be in serious trouble, if indeed she were alive.

In a way, I was sorry that I had interviewed Nazrullah's Afghan wife in Kandahar, for if that silken, shrouded voice had not convinced me that she and Ellen had been friends, it would now be easy to conclude that only the shock of discovering a previous marriage had unnerved Ellen. But if relationships were as placid as reported, and if Nazrullah were as congenial as he seemed, what dark force operating on this trio could have occasioned tragedy?

It was also interesting for me to compare Nazrullah with Nur. The former had been set free psychologically by his travels abroad, while Nur was still uncertain of himself, because of an insular limitation which he was working desperately to correct. Nazrullah utilized a broad, frontal approach to problems and for an Afghan was markedly outspoken, partly because he was honest and partly because he lacked the ability to maneuver, whereas Nur was a master of manipulation. The big difference, however, lay in their concept of what process would lead to their country's salvation. Nur, the traditionalist, whose brother was an enlightened mullah, felt that Afghanistan would be saved through the rededication of the individual and the moral regeneration of Islam. Nazrullah, in our long talks in the tent, argued that what happened to the Muslim religion was no great concern of his. From having studied various religions at first hand, he suspected that any of the three great desert religions, Islam, Christianity or Judaism, was as good as any other but that Islam was rather better fitted for the social structure of Afghanistan. "But what's going to save this nation is the creation of a contemporary world—a new economic system, a real representative form of government, dams, roads, farms . . . the things that we can create."

As he said this he snapped his fingers and cried, "Miller, to show you what I mean, I'm going to take you to the site of the new dam. How soon can you start?"

Nur protested that the location was too far away, but Nazrullah would not listen. "You've got to go there anyway. Saddle up the jeeps!" He dashed about camp and within fifteen minutes had a major expedition assembled. "You're going to see the future of Afghanistan!" he promised.

We roared out of the old walls in a caravan of three jeeps because Nazrullah felt that any penetration of the desert in machines was so inherently perilous that group protection was advisable, but on this day nothing happened. We reached the junction town of Girishk, from which we struck off across forbidding land on a trail that jeeps could barely negotiate. Finally we ground to a halt at a goat trail, where we left the jeeps under guard while we climbed on foot to a high elevation, from which we could see, far below us, the roaring Helmand River as it carried the spring thaw through a narrow cleft in the mountains.

"To build a dam, a great dam such as the American and German experts advise," Nazrullah cried, pointing with a stick, "requires two things, a gorge and a mountain close by. Down there you see the gorge, with steep, solid walls, and over there you see one hell of a mountain."

"What's the relationship?" Nur asked.

"You build a road from the mountain to the gorge. Then you lead that road over a temporary bridge that crosses the gorge, high up in the air. Then you dynamite the mountain rock by rock and haul it in trucks to the bridge, where you drop the rocks into the river. And after you do this day and night for three or four years, you have a dam."

He showed us where the road would be built

and where the bridge would be slung, high above the rapids. "For seven months trucks will dump rocks off that bridge and nothing will happen, because the river will wash our boulders downstream as if they were straw. But one day the rocks will begin to hold, and the river will start to back up— just a little. But on that day we have it strangled. Then we can do with it what we will."

He called for his field glasses, which enabled me to see bench marks already cut into the cliff north of where the dam would be and other marks south, many feet above the present water level. "Any idea what that's to be?" he asked, and when I admitted my ignorance he replied, "That's the tunnel. While we're throwing in the rock, we're also digging that tunnel, and when the river starts to back up, it gradually rises to that level, and runs away through the tunnel. Then we move in hundreds of trucks and throw thousands of tons of rock into the ravine, pack them with earth and after some years concrete the exposed face and find ourselves with a dam."

It was difficult to visualize the completed dam, it was of such magnitude, but Nazrullah had surveyed the ground so often that to him the gigantic structure already existed. Pointing to a mark hundreds of feet above the river he said, "The water will rise to there. We'll collect the floods in the spring, when they aren't needed in the fields, and release them in the summer, when they are. And the beauty of this system is that every pound of water that drops through our tunnel will generate electricity which we'll send over the mountains to Kandahar."

Remembering that primitive city I predicted, "In Kandahar they won't be using much electricity."

"Ah! That's where you're wrong!" Nazrullah cried. "In Germany we made a study of fifteen primitive societies"—I liked his using the word *primitive;* our ambassador had forbidden us to do so, claiming it insulted the Afghans—"and we found that when irrigation dams were built in primitive areas, the financial experts always fought against wasting the money to add generators at the same time. They argued, 'The people are so primitive they'll have no use for electricity.' In every instance, within five years the original output of electricity, which the experts had called wasteful, was being utilized and further capacity was required. If we can get electricity to Kandahar, they'll find ways of using it. Progress creates its own dynamics."

The concept was so new to me that I asked for an illustration of a primitive society where this had happened. "I'll give you a classic," he said instantly. "The Tennessee Valley Authority."

"I'd hardly call Tennessee primitive," I argued with some asperity.

"I would," he replied flatly. "The hill region anyway. I made a study of it, on the spot, and in its way, compared to New York, it's as primitive as Girishk compared to Kabul. And the T.V.A. found it couldn't make electricity fast enough."

I was not satisfied with his description of part of my country as primitive, having always reserved that word for other nations, but I was impressed by his excitement about his job and the poetic insights he brought to it. For example, he stared down at the river which now ran wild through the gorge and said softly, "Isn't it a gripping idea, Miller, that on the day we drop our first load of rock into that turbulent river it'll have no idea of what's happening? Rocks like that have been falling off the cliffs for a million years, and it's washed them aside. But these rocks will be different. They'll be the beginning of something not even that river is strong enough to halt. And we will continue . . ." He hammered the air with his fist, visualizing the enormous aggregation of rock that would ultimately jam that gorge and tame the river.

He turned to Nur and me with dancing eyes. "Each day we must throw similar rocks into the human river of Afghanistan. Here a school, there a road, down in the gorge a dam. So far our human river isn't aware that it's been touched. But we shall never halt until we've modified it completely."

As I looked down at the turbulent Helmand, rushing freely between the cliffs, it seemed to symbolize the wild freedom of Afghanistan, and I said half to myself, "It's rather a pity that such a river must be brought under control."

Nazrullah grabbed me by the arm and whipped me about. "What did you say?" he demanded.

"I said, It's a shame such a river has to be dammed."

"That's incredible," he muttered, not in surprise or anger or any other emotion that I could recognize. "That's really incredible, Miller." He snapped his fingers, tugged at his beard and stared at me as if trying to reassemble fragments. "Those are the exact words Ellen said while standing here." He bit his forefinger, then added with impatience, "You damned Americans are so sentimental. You've organized your own land to the limit, but you criticize others who want to organize theirs."

"I was speaking symbolically," I protested.

"So was Ellen," he snapped. "What you both meant was, The more modern Tennessee becomes, the nicer it would be to keep Afghanistan a primitive place where we could come to observe the peasants. Well, Miller, we're going to change it . . . profoundly."

"I want you to. Perhaps Ellen meant that old-fashioned ways are always better. A lot of Americans believe that nonsense. But I don't."

"What do you believe?"

"That it's always sad to see freedom lost. As for change, that's why we have an American embassy in Kabul. To help you make the changes, yet stay free."

"You'd better help," he warned. "Because if you try to hold us back, Russia will be eager to jump in and help us."

"To what?" I asked, but he had turned away and now stamped angrily down the mountain trail. When he reached the jeeps he jumped into one and roared down the dangerous trail to Girishk, leaving Nur and me to ride with an assistant engineer, who drove us back to Qala Bist. But often as our jeeps passed and repassed on the desert I caught sight of Nazrullah, brooding in silence, the knuckles of his left fist pressed against his bearded chin.

9

Our caravan had barely come in sight of Qala Bist when we spotted a strange jeep speeding at us from the walled city, throwing a cloud of dust across the desert. It was Dr. Stiglitz, driven by an Afghan military officer, coming out to intercept us as quickly as possible.

"Where's Nazrullah?" the German shouted as he drew close.

"He's back there," I cried.

The four jeeps drew together in the desert and Stiglitz said in German, "I bring you bad news."

He and Nazrullah continued talking in German, but I caught the fact that something had happened to the American engineer Pritchard, who had crossed the Desert of Death some months before to measure the spring flow of the Helmand River. I waited impatiently while the two discussed the problem, and finally they took cognizance of me. "Sorry, Herr Miller. My visit really concerns you."

"How?"

"There's an official message for you," Nazrullah replied, and he spoke to the Afghan officer, who handed me a paper containing directions which the

American embassy had phoned down to Kandahar military headquarters that morning. It said:

> Miller. Proceed immediately to The City, thence to Chahar, where Pritchard broke his leg three weeks ago. See if the German Dr. Stiglitz can accompany you at our expense, but travel in at least two jeeps because earlier investigators dispatched by the Afghan government have not been heard from. Obtain fullest local advice before attempting journey.

It was signed by Verbruggen and I could imagine his rough, worried voice on the telephone. I asked Stiglitz, "You know what's in the message?"

"Of course."

"You'll go?"

"I'm here."

"How much?" Before he could reply I led him away from the others, where he stood silent for some moments. I was certain he had guessed why I had called on him in Kandahar and I knew he wanted me to carry back a good report which might enable him to jump from Kandahar to Kabul, so he would be disposed to request a low fee in hopes of winning my favor; on the other hand he was a trained doctor and proud of his German degree, in addition to which the cost of German beer in Kandahar was not trivial, so that he had reasons for asking a substantial fee. It was a delicate problem, and the poor pudgy man was not equal to solving it. I grew ashamed of myself, especially since I was a Jew and he a German.

"I'm sorry, Doctor," I said. "I should've spoken

first. Two hundred dollars plus twenty dollars for each day beyond five that we're out."

Stiglitz breathed deeply, and I judged that my offer was more generous than he had dared to demand. "I accept!" he said, continuing with profuse thanks which became almost embarrassing. "You've no idea, Herr Miller, how those damned Afghans rob me for my beer."

"Agreed." Then I asked the Afghan soldier, "Are you driving us?"

"He is not!" Nazrullah protested. "I am." He drew his staff about him and shot a series of questions: "What's the state of the moon?" "Which of our jeeps is in best condition?" "Miller, will you turn over your K-rations to us?" "Water, crowbars, tow ropes?" When he had satisfactory answers he looked at his watch and said, "We'll leave Qala Bist in forty minutes. We're taking Miller's jeep and mine. Nur Muhammad to drive one. I'll drive the other. Stiglitz and Miller the only passengers. I want everything assembled in front of my tent at once. O.K.?"

He jumped in his jeep and sped for Qala Bist, leading us through the ponderous wall and across the fields to the camp. As he ran for his tent he shouted, "Nur, stay with me," and in the next minutes I watched two Afghan gentlemen assume command of an expedition that could turn out disastrously if anything went wrong. Nur, who understood jeeps, took care of matters in that area, while Nazrullah checked the logistics, then supervised the packing. "Turbans for the ferangi!" Nazrullah shouted, and one of the engineers solved this by lifting two from the heads of the servants. "You'll need it," Nur assured me as I packed mine.

It was still several hours before dark when we approached our loaded jeeps, where Nazrullah consulted for the last time with his staff and with the Afghan officer. Taking a map he drew a tentative line from Qala Bist across the desert to an extended area marked simply The City. There he turned his line south until it reached the remote village of Chahar. "We'll be going this way," he announced in Pashto, "and if anything should happen, I promise I won't be far off this route." He watched while Nur and the officer traced the route on their maps.

"Now," Nazrullah asked sharply, "where do you think the missing men could be?"

He stared at his staff, at Nur, at the officer. The latter spoke: "Ten days ago we sent two men in a jeep . . ."

"One jeep?" Nazrullah asked, tugging his beard.

"Yes."

"Great Jesus Christ!" Nazrullah snapped, uttering an oath quite inappropriate for a Muslim, something he had picked up at the Wharton School. "One jeep?" He stabbed at the map. "Driving across that?"

"Yes," the officer replied, unruffled. "They left Kandahar ten days ago, drove to Girishk, and started across the desert on this course." On Nazrullah's map he drew a firm line which converged on our projected course about halfway across the desert.

Nazrullah reflected and said, "With the lines

running that way we might spot them anywhere during the second half."

I added, "If they're broken down, they'll probably have a flag waving that we can see."

Nazrullah looked at me with compassion, then asked, "Did they know the desert?"

"Yes."

"They the type who follow instructions?"

"Best men we had."

Nazrullah studied the map for some minutes. "I want you to change my route just a little. We'll drop up here and take a look." He drew a jog to the north, almost off the desert, and said, "We'll never be far from this route. Salaam aleikum." With that he spun his wheels in a tight circle and sped for the wall. In a few moments we were entering the desert, headed west for the setting sun, a simple caravan of two jeeps, each marked by high poles from which fluttered large squares of white cloth.

The Afghan Dasht-i-Margo was not a desert in the accustomed sense, for although it did contain vast unbroken stretches of sand, it was also an accumulation of shaly detritus laid down by deteriorating mountains which had eroded through millions of years, so that across the desert we found bands of this shale sometimes half a mile wide along which our jeeps could race at forty miles an hour, while we saw on either side the glorious sweep of traditional dunes that characterize the usual desert.

An additional feature marked this desert: When we were well into its heart we could not see a single thing growing nor any shred of human existence. There were no lichens on the rock, no seedlings in crevices, no shrubs, no birds, no gullies touched with a little water, no lizards, no eagles, no oases of any kind. There were no fence poles nor relics of forgotten homes nor even stones laid in a row. There was only the most blazing, heat-racked emptiness I had ever seen. I remember thinking once, when we were surrounded by dunes: In the polar regions they at least have frozen water and insects. Here there's nothing . . . except heat.

"How hot is it?" I asked Nur.

"Hundred and thirty, but it isn't the thermometer that worries us," he said as he studied the desolate landscape. "It's the wind." He checked some drifting sand and said, "Wind's thirty miles an hour. Later it'll grow to fifty. That's what kills you on the desert."

I now began to appreciate the flags that Nazrullah had provided for our jeeps, for as our caravan moved across the desert we were frequently separated, since neither driver could be sure that what looked like a potential road would turn out to be so; and often it was the driver in second position who found the successful trail, whereas what had looked good to the first man had turned into a wall of impenetrable sand. When this happened, the unsuccessful driver would whirl about, look for his companion's flag, and set off in hot pursuit. Neither waited for the other, but each felt responsible for seeing that the separation did not become too great.

"Is it possible to work your way into a real dead end?" I asked.

"Sure. Probably what happened to the missing men. In this business you need that other flag."

We had been on the road for well over an hour when Nazrullah, whose jeep was now in the lead, stopped abruptly and waited for us to join him. He signaled for silence, then pointed to a small herd of gazelles—not more than fifteen—that had penetrated these dreadful wastes where I had been unable to see a shred of forage but where they were acquainted with hidden areas that no man had yet identified.

At first I didn't understand why the gazelles fascinated me, but I sat spellbound watching the small, delicate animals standing gracefully on the face of the burning desert. What could they be doing? What did they signify? Afghanistan had untold valleys where an animal could find forage. Why were they here? And why was I so moved by seeing them?

One of their lookouts spotted us, and with a disembodied grace the small animals leaped, exploded in the dying sunlight, twisted, turned and fled like wraiths across the desert. I had never before seen such flawless motion, and as they sped away like the sound of retreating music, one female, small and without horns, ran toward us with a breathless poetry, then saw the jeeps and turned in mid-air, throwing her sharp hoofs to one side as she changed direction. As she did this marvelous thing, I was forced to cry out, for I saw that she was colored like the chaderi Moheb Khan's niece had worn, and she was not an animal at all, she was not a gazelle, but the embodiment of the hunger I felt. In this cruel land of recurring ugliness, where only men were seen, the gazelle reminded me of womanliness, of girls at a dance, of the mystery of half the world. I watched her go in matchless grace, darting this way and that until she vanished behind a distant dune, and there were tears in my eyes and I felt I could not tolerate the awful loneliness of the desert. I was lost in Asia. I was forsaken on the high roof of the world and the gazelles had been a sighing, drifting premonition.

Then I heard Nazrullah saying, "They must have come down from the caravanserai," and we took out our maps to discover that we were near the jog that Nazrullah had drawn to the north. "There's a chance the other two might have made for the caravanserai." And we turned north.

The sun was just setting when we reached the top of a dune from which we could look down upon one of the sights that has always inspired the traveler in Asia: a walled caravanserai looming out of the dusk at the end of a long journey. It remains unforgettable: a gaunt, square, mud-walled sanctuary built around a central open space where animals of the caravan were sheltered. One leg of the wall comprised a fort devoid of windows but well supplied in recent centuries with slit holes for rifle fire. Entrance was by a solitary gate, a handsome structure built in fine Arabic proportions. The serai had been erected hundreds of years ago, possibly even in the days of Muhammad, and through the centuries had served continuously, for it stood at the edge of the desert near the end of a little gully in which grass grew and stagnant water accumulated, and to it had come, as we now came, thou-

sands of caravans needing protection for the night.
It was a rule of the desert that whoever succeeded
in entering a serai was safe for the night, no matter
what antagonist he encountered inside, and there
must have been many stirring tales of blood enemies who shared sanctuary here under unexpected
circumstances.

As we approached the gate, Nazrullah halted the
jeeps and he and Nur debarked to study, on hands
and knees, all the surrounding sand, entering the
walls to continue their search. After a while they
reappeared and said, "They didn't get this far."

I hoped that this was a sign that we were to
move on, for whereas I had found the ruins at Qala
Bist so immense as to be commanding, I found this
old deserted caravanserai a place of brooding quiet
that was in a sense terrifying. Possibly I was still
influenced by the gazelles, possibly by the haunting loneliness of a desert twilight, but the idea that
a wayside inn had once flourished here but had
now lost its reason for being was at the moment
too gloomy for my acceptance.

"Are we leaving?" I asked hopefully.

"We'll eat here," Nazrullah replied, and he took
us to the fort, where he and the doctor began laying out blankets on the earthen floor. Nur lit two
Coleman lamps, whose incandescent glow showed
the high roof of the caravanserai to good effect,
and if anything were calculated to make me feel
gloomier than I already did, it was the way the
flickering light threw enormous shadows on the
mud walls. I thought: Genghis Khan could come
through that door, and he'd be right at home.

Two-thirds of the way down the hall, a stout circular column about twelve feet in diameter rose from the floor and continued through the roof. It was built neither of wood nor of mud but of plaster, and our lights played upon its uneven surfaces in exciting patterns. "That's a beautiful column," I remarked. "What's it used for?"

"Famous, too," Nazrullah replied without looking.

"What for?"

"Manner of construction," he replied.

"What's unusual, the plaster?"

"The insides."

Dr. Stiglitz interrupted. "What's inside?" he asked, and years later when I reconstructed that night I became convinced that somehow he knew what the answer was going to be.

"It's not pleasant," Nazrullah cautioned. "Want to hear it before dinner?" When I said yes, he continued, "Some time around 1220, Genghis Khan . . ."

"I just thought of him!" I cried.

"How so?" Nur asked.

"I was looking at those shadows and thought, If Genghis Khan came in now, I wouldn't be surprised."

"He was here," Nazrullah laughed.

"What about the pillar?" Stiglitz asked.

"Genghis Khan destroyed Afghanistan. In one assault on The City he killed nearly a million people. That's not a poetic figure. It's fact. In Kandahar the slaughter was enormous. Some refugees fled to this caravanserai . . . this room. They were sure the Mongols wouldn't find them here, but they did." His voice resumed its flatness.

"And the pillar?" Stiglitz pressed.

"First Genghis erected a pole right through the roof. Then the Mongols took their prisoners and tied their hands. Laid the first batch on the floor over there and lashed their feet to the pole. All around. That's why the pillar is twelve feet across."

"Then what?" Stiglitz asked, perspiration standing on his forehead.

"They just kept on laying the prisoners down, one layer on top of the other until they reached the roof. They didn't kill a single person that day, the Mongols, but they kept soldiers stationed with sticks to push back the tongues when they protruded. And while the pillar of people was still living—those that hadn't been pressed to death—they called in masons to plaster over the whole affair. If you'd scrape away the plaster you'd find skulls. But the government takes a dim view of scraping. It's a kind of national monument. The Caravanserai of the Tongues."

No one spoke. The meal was ready but no one seemed hungry, so finally Nazrullah said, "I tell you these things only to explain the terrible burdens under which Afghanistan has labored. Our major cities have been destroyed so many times. Do you know what I expect . . . seriously? When a thousand men like me have rebuilt Kabul and made it as great as The City once was, either the Russians or the Americans will come with their airplanes and bomb it to rubble."

"Wait a minute!" I protested.

"I'm not speaking against Americans . . . or Russians. You won't destroy us in anger. Genghis Khan wasn't angry at us when he destroyed The City.

Neither was Tamerlane or Nadir Shah or Baber.
And I'm not downcast because we're doomed to be
destroyed again." He shrugged his shoulders. "It's
inevitable. We go on building while we can."

He laughed and inspected the cans that lay
opened on the blankets. "I for one love American
K-rations. But please, gentlemen, you must see to it
that Nur Muhammad and I get ones that contain
no pork."

"Tonight," I said with some embarrassment, "everyone has pork and beans."

"Then Nur and I shall make a great show of
picking out one shred of pork each and placing it
upon your plate . . . thus. 'Please take this pork
from us, Miller Sahib, because we are Muslims.'
But the rest of the pork I shall jolly well keep on
my plate, because I love it." We ate as a family
group, two Muslims, a renegade Christian and a
Jew, and my sense of loneliness was erased, but
when it came time to clean the dishes I noticed
that Dr. Stiglitz, who sat facing the pillar, had
eaten little.

It was after our meal that I learned with pleasure that we would not stay in the serai but were
pushing across the desert in the cooler night air. As
I left the refuge I said, "One nice thing about it.
It's the only building I've seen that I can date. It
was here in 1220."

"Probably been rebuilt since then," Nazrullah
said without further comment.

We went into the night and for the first time in
my life I saw the stars hanging low over the desert,
for the atmosphere above us contained no moisture, no dust, no impediment of any kind. It was

probably the cleanest air man knows and it displayed the stars as no other could. Not even at Qala Bist, which stood by the river, had air been so pure. The stars seemed enormous, but what surprised me most was the fact that they dropped right to the horizon, so that to the east some rose out of dunes while to the west others crept beneath piles of shale.

While I was staring at the unfamiliar stars, Nazrullah borrowed a light and wrote the following note on a scrap of paper in Persian, Pashto and English:

On the evening of April 11, 1946, we stopped here to seek evidence of the missing soldiers but found nothing.

Using a sharp piece of shale, he wedged the message into the door and we started up the gully to the desert.

Then I understood why Nazrullah had halted our caravan at the serai; while we were listening to the explanation of the pillar the burning wind had abated and the moon had brightened and was nearly full. It now stood well above the horizon, a huge center of light which made our trip across the desert possible. It was an unworldly experience, with moonlight reflecting from the dunes as if it were day. I noticed that we now traveled at less than twenty-five miles an hour, and since the path looked just as good as it had in the afternoon when we did over forty, I asked why and Nur explained, "At night we can't spot the gotch."

"The what?" I asked.

"Gotch. A flaky white substance that comes in big patches. I think you call it gypsum."

"That's worth something, gypsum. It occurs in piles?"

"Desert's full of it, always in patches. That's where Genghis Khan got his plaster for the pillar."

"So that's what gypsum's used for," I mused.

"Mixed with water it's useful," Nur cautioned, "but don't hit it when its dry."

At this point we heard a horn blowing insistently, and I looked about for Nazrullah's flag. It was stationary in a valley ahead and he was signaling us not to follow. "He's trapped in gotch," Nur said. "In this light you can't see the stuff."

"Did we pass some this afternoon?"

"Acres of it," Nur assured me. "But then it was no trouble."

We parked our jeep and hiked ahead to where Nazrullah was stuck. "Nothing serious," he said. "The wheels slow down . . . pooosh."

I knelt to feel the gotch and found it a flaky powder, very soft to the fingers and providing no traction for a spinning wheel. "Here's the rope," Nazrullah cried. "Give me a little tug."

We edged our jeep carefully forward, attached the rope, and with no trouble pulled Nazrullah free. When he drew up beside us he warned, "If you hit this stuff at more than twenty-five you may break a nose."

"If we do hit," Nur added, "protect your face. We stop very suddenly."

It was now our turn to lead, and we set forth upon one of the few flawless journeys a man can take: to be moving over the desert at night when the great stars are overhead and a white moon illuminates the ghostly world; to be rising suddenly from a depression and on the crest to see a great sweep of desert appearing like a cross between a blizzard of snow and a garden of white flowers in spring; to watch the rise and fall of dunes as they make their poetic march across the shadowy horizon. Most impressive was the silence, the absolute silence of the desert at night. No insects marred it, no night birds whispered, there was no echo of wind nor sound of distant thunder. If we stopped to reconnoiter, we could hear Nazrullah's jeep chattering unseen behind some hill, and I remember once when we had worked ourselves into a cul-de-sac of sweeping dunes how the sound of our engine echoed from each as we tried to fight our way to passages that did not exist. We were hemmed in by floating sand, but as we studied our position I caught sight of Nazrullah's flag whisking past us on the correct road.

We had proceeded thus some forty miles deeper into the desert when I thought I spied something unusual off to the north. I watched it for some minutes and at first took it to be a pile of shale. Then I drew Nur Muhammad's attention, but he had been concentrating so intently on gotch that at first he saw nothing. Finally his eyes adjusted and when they did so he said, "It's a jeep!" And I saw that he was right.

We then faced the problem of how to flag down Nazrullah, who was well ahead of us. We could drive faster, but that might pitch us into gotch. We could blow our horn, but would they hear? I suggested, "Let me get down and stand here, so that you can find the jeep when you come back."

Nur looked at me in horror. "In the desert?" he asked.

He flashed his headlights, whereupon Nazrullah's jeep promptly turned about, and when he had joined us, he asked, "What's up?"

"Miller found the jeep," Nur replied. Then he added, "He suggested that he get down and wait here till I caught you."

Nazrullah looked at me and groaned. "My God!" Then he looked toward the ghostly jeep and said, "I hate to go up there."

Slowly we drove north and it soon became apparent that we were entering a huge concentration of gotch. Nazrullah called out, "Drive back and plant your flag on the hard surface." We did so and then reassembled our little caravan and moved cautiously forward.

Even from a distance we saw what we had hoped not to see: two men sitting in a jeep. They had bogged down in gotch, had tried to pile stones under the wheels, had probably burned out their clutch.

We hiked across the soft gypsum and reached the uncanny sight: two men fully dressed for desert travel, resting in their jeep, their eyes wide open but completely dried out. They had been dead for eight or nine days, but rarely had the hand of death been placed so gently upon two human beings, for the desiccating wind, blowing constantly through the day with a hundred and twenty or thirty degrees of heat, had completely mummified the bodies.

"We'll leave them here," Nazrullah said finally. "Nothing'll harm them now."

I studied the bodies for clues, but there were none. The jeep contained ample food, some gasoline, but no water. Nazrullah said, "Shift him over, Miller. I'll see if the clutch works." With some apprehension I lifted the driver away from the wheel, while Nazrullah slipped in and started the car. The dead man weighed little. The engine choked, coughed, started. There was no clutch. "Poor bastards," Nazrullah said. "Put him back."

When we were back at our jeeps he said, "They may have lived two days . . . no more. Miller, if you leave a jeep even for twenty yards in this climate, you're dead."

Nur asked in Pashto, "I wonder who blamed the other?"

The idea was so unexpected that we all stared at Nur, but we were also forced to look back at the dead men, and whatever hideous recriminations may have passed between them were now silenced. The younger of the two had been driving.

When we stopped to recover our flag Nazrullah said with real sadness, "Foolish, foolish men, to take one jeep across this desert. Miller, why don't you ride with me on this leg?"

After we had taken the lead I asked, "Did you know them?"

"Fortunately no. I'd hate to think my friends were so idiotic." We drove for some time, then he chuckled. "It's rather fun riding with Stiglitz. He's so German."

"Is it true that he's a Muslim? Or is he just kidding?"

"Why not? He has to live here the rest of his life."

"How do you know that?" I asked.

"The minute he steps across our boundary, the English will arrest him, or the Russians."

"Nazi crimes?"

"Naturally."

"Guilty . . . or just charges?"

"We've seen the legal papers. That is, the government has." He said carefully, "I'd say the charges weren't hypothetical."

I pondered this for some minutes and wondered to myself: If the Afghan government has the dossier, why hasn't it been shared with our ambassador, who's obviously looking Stiglitz over as a possible doctor? I didn't want to ask Nazrullah about this directly, but I did hit upon what I considered a neat alternative: "Surely the British must know about him, if they've threatened to arrest him."

"They do," Nazrullah laughed, for he had guessed the purpose of my question. On his own he added, "As a government, they know his record, and if they could catch him in India, they'd arrest him. But if he gets clearance for Kabul, which I'm sure he will, the embassy people as individuals would consult him medically." Dryly he added, "I'm sure your ambassador would behave the same way—arrest him in New York but use him in Kabul."

"You're probably right," I said noncommittally.

We dropped the matter there, but later Nazrullah observed, "You expressed surprise that Dr. Stiglitz had become a Muslim. Surely, if I'd stayed permanently in Dorset, Pennsylvania, with Ellen's people I'd have become a Presbyterian."

The fact that he had mentioned Ellen of his own volition startled me, but his casual attitude toward abandoning Islam seemed even more striking, for I was then in the days when I believed that Muslims, Christians and Jews were destined not to shift back and forth, so I argued, "Could you really have become a Christian?"

"For six years in Germany and America I was a Christian in everything but formal conversion. Suppose you lived in Afghanistan permanently, wouldn't you pray as a Muslim?"

I thought: Wouldn't he be amused if he knew whom he was asking this question of. That conceit produced my next question: "But if you were to work in Palestine with the British, could you become a Jew?"

"Why not? If the facts were known, probably half our Afghan heritage is Jewish. For hundreds of years we boasted of being one of the Lost Tribes of Israel. Then Hitler decreed us to be Aryans, which gave us certain advantages."

"What's your own opinion?" I asked bluntly.

"I think we're a delightful hodgepodge. Have you heard our marvelous myth? In the valleys west of Kabul we have a concentration of the Hazara people. Know what we believe about them? We claim that every Mongol who ever settled in Afghanistan—and there must have been millions—settled in those particular valleys and never once intermarried with any of us. A thousand years of racial purity. If the truth were known, I'm probably descended from the bastards who plastered up that pillar."

"You mean you could become a Jew?" I repeated seriously.

"I probably am a Jew," he insisted. "And a Mongol, and a Hindu, and a Tajik. But I'm also a hundred percent Aryan, because I have a certificate from Göttingen University to prove it."

We lapsed again into the deep silence of the desert and the faint stirrings of a brotherhood that was developing between us. Then I asked what I know Nazrullah intended me to ask when he suggested that I ride in his jeep: "Where's Ellen?"

"She ran away."

"You know where?"

"Not exactly."

"You think she's alive?"

"I know she is," he said, clenching his hands on the steering wheel. "I'm morally sure she is." From his actions and manner of speech I had to conclude that he was still in love with his wife, hungrily, deeply; yet I found it almost comical that I should worry about a man, no matter how much I respected him, who was worried about his second wife when he had a perfectly good wife waiting for him in Kandahar. It all seemed so Muslim. I was then too young to know at first hand any of those average American men who deeply loved their wives but who could at the same time become agonized if something untoward happened to their mistresses. It was the same problem in two different guises, but at the time I didn't know it.

"She hasn't written to her parents in thirteen months," I said.

With a certain grim humor he asked, "Have you met her parents?"

"No, but I've read their reports."

"Then you know." He smiled as he recalled them, then added, "They're like this, Miller. If they'd seen that pillar at the caravanserai they'd have cried, 'Goodness, something ought to be done about that,' but they'd never have understood if you replied, 'About Genghis Khan you can't do anything.'" He grew painfully intense and said, "There wasn't a thing they could have done about Ellen. They were fated to lose her. I was fated to lose her. And there wasn't a goddamned thing that any of us could have done to prevent it."

I waited till the signs of his bitterness vanished, then asked, "Is she still in Afghanistan?"

I remember distinctly, and at the time I remarked upon it to myself, that before Nazrullah answered he leaned out to look at the stars, both west and east, then said quietly, "I'm sure she is. Yes, she's in Afghanistan."

I wanted to pursue the matter further, but at this moment I saw to the west, where Nazrullah had peered in search of his wife, a star that seemed brighter than the others and pointed it out to my guide. "Good," he said, halting the jeep till the others could overtake us. When they did he pointed to the star and said, "The City."

I looked again at the star and none of us except Nazrullah knew that it was a light and not a star. "It's a light at The City," Nazrullah said. "We'll camp here."

"If it's so close, why don't we finish the drive?"

"It's sixty miles away," Nazrullah replied.

"Impossible," I protested, but Nur supported his friend.

"When you first see something like this, you can't believe it. The light may well be sixty miles away."

"It is," Nazrullah assured us. "Let's get out the sleeping bags."

I looked for low ground that would give me some protection from the wind that was rising, but Nazrullah led us to the highest part of a small hill and when we were prepared for bed he explained, "Tonight we saw two men who died in the desert from sun and heat. For everyone who dies that way, a hundred die from floods."

Stiglitz and I looked at each other in the white moonlight and Nazrullah continued, "Once every three or four years it rains over some part of this desert. In a way you never saw before. Terrible, shattering. A wall of water builds up thirty feet high and destroys everything before it. Moves whole dunes from one place to another, and anything caught in a low spot is crushed."

We looked at the gullies with new respect as he finished, "Probably hasn't been any water down there in five hundred years. But just south of here —due south, as a matter of fact—Alexander the Great was marching his troops home from their conquest of India. They camped in the desert and in four minutes a wall of water swept over them, killing two men in three. This is a tough country, Miller. Don't sleep in gullies."

At dawn we rose and headed west, and when I saw the last sixty miles of terrain I appreciated why Nazrullah had left Qala Bist in a hurry, for we could not have traversed at night what now faced us, and if we had tried to drive through the heart of the desert at midday, the heat would have been unbearable. In these last sixty miles the sand had largely disappeared and we were forced to pick our way through heaps of shale which thundered the day's heat right back at us. The humidity was down to nearly zero and a strong wind dried us out as we moved across the blazing dasht. Nur Muhammad warned me, "Be careful not to bump your nose. The mucus dries up into little needles which puncture the skin. Bad infection." Warily I touched my nose, and he was right. The thirsty air had sucked away all moisture, and my nose was lined with needles.

At one period I thought I would collapse if we didn't stop for a drink, but Nazrullah fell back to warn us, "We've plenty of water and cans of fruit juice, but we're not going to touch it until we're sure we'll reach The City today." He must have seen my disappointment, for he added, "You can discipline yourself, Miller."

So we pressed on, parched with heat. In the States I had never known anything like this, a heat so forceful that it seemed to fight with you for all body moisture. I could feel water evaporating from my skin, and my thoughts constantly returned to the soldiers who had perished in the jeep: This damned wind sucked them dry as they sat there.

Slowly I began to exercise the discipline of which Nazrullah spoke, and I began to find ways to adjust. I wasn't as thirsty as I thought, nor as near dead as I feared. I was on an ugly mission across inhospitable terrain that would kill me if I gave it a chance, but there were many ways to survive, and Nazrullah now taught us one. "We'd better put on the turbans," he suggested, and when we had done so he produced a canister of river water, not for drinking, and from it poured water directly onto the turbans until they were dripping down our necks. We then drove on.

The turban, about eight yards of cloth, held a lot of water and released it slowly, lowering the temperature of our heads as it evaporated. I thought: This is the way to lick the heat. But within twelve minutes the voracious wind had sucked all moisture from the cloth. So we stopped again and sloshed on more river water, and for a while we were cool, but after ten or twelve minutes the turbans were again dry.

At last we reached a narrow pass that dropped down between rocks, and having descended this canyon for about a mile, we reached a low plain and saw ahead of us trees and signs of life and a village, beyond which lay an ancient city and a large body of water. We cheered and blew our horns, for the transit of the desert was completed.

A few Afghans in dirty desert dress straggled out to greet us, but we did not stop. "Tell the sharif we'll be back!" Nazrullah called, and we sped for the lake, where we quickly undressed and lay in the water, so that our bodies could absorb the liquid they had lost.

"Look at him!" Stiglitz said after a while, and I saw Nazrullah far out from shore, where the water came only to his knees. When I caught up with him he said, "You can walk completely across, if you care to."

It was here, in this vast shallow lake, that the

great Helmand River ended, for the desert sun and wind evaporated the water as fast as the mountains near Kabul delivered it. The powerful Helmand simply flowed into the desert and died. I hadn't believed it when Nur told me, but here it was, the death of a river. In late summer even this lake might be gone.

When we dressed, the sharif joined us. His title was pronounced *sha-reef*, with the accent on the second syllable, and he brought us melons and fruit, which in their richness, dripped juice from our chins. He listened impassively as Nazrullah explained the location of the missing jeep, and said that he'd dispatch a scouting party. No one was much perturbed about the deaths; if men crossed the desert often enough, some were bound to die, and many from that area had done so.

Talk then turned to the American engineer Pritchard, and we were all brought into the conversation. The sharif reported that twenty-two days ago the American, who worked at Chahar, seventy miles to the south, had broken his leg while taking water levels. It was originally intended to haul him to this village on a stretcher for a trip across the desert, but the sharif at Chahar had felt that local practitioners could heal the leg, and no stretcher was dispatched. A week ago news came to the village that an infection had set in.

"Did the broken bones puncture the skin?" Dr. Stiglitz asked.

"We were told so," the sharif replied.

"And they tried to treat a case like that?"

"They've been doing it for three thousand years," the sharif grunted. He sent a servant to fetch a man who hobbled in on a leg that had been broken three weeks ago. "We fixed his."

Dr. Stiglitz examined the leg and said in Pashto, "It's as good as I'd have done."

Nazrullah asked, "You'll send a guide with us?"

"Of course," the sharif said, and he ordered servants to refill our water bottles. "But I wouldn't travel in this heat."

"We have to," Nazrullah replied. And we were off.

I have said that when we dropped down off the desert we saw a city by the lake. What we actually saw was one of the marvels of Asia, The City, and we were about to explore a fair portion of its incredible length. For more than seventy miles this nameless metropolis stretched along the lake, the marshes and the river that formed the western boundary between Afghanistan and Persia. At the dawn of history it had been a stupendous settlement. In the age of Alexander it had been one of the world's major concentrations, and he had camped near its bazaars. For a millennium after his departure it flourished to become one of the prime targets of the Mongols, and Genghis Khan had once slaughtered most of the people in the area. Tamerlane . . . all the others had ravaged the treasure, and now it stood in majestic silence, mile after mile after mile.

I thought: We're probably in error, calling this a city. It must have been like Route One between New York and Richmond. At intersections there were towns, and some were sizable, but much of the distance must have been interurban, so that city merged into town and town into rural area, with always the roadway itself hemmed in by buildings of some sort. Here the roadway had been the Helmand River, and now as we traversed it we saw the relics of The City.

At times there would be walls of substantial height running for miles, broken by majestic gates and marked with niches in which, before the Muslims outlawed human statuary, depictions of local heroes had stood. At other times we saw municipal buildings which might have sent emissaries to Jerusalem a thousand years before the time of Herod. And everything we saw was withering in the dry air, an inch or two eroding every hundred years.

There were rugged forts, obviously built by the Muslims: against unorganized shepherds from Persia they must have been impressive; against the skilled troops of Genghis Khan they probably lasted a day or two, at most, after which all the defenders were slaughtered.

We drove along the entire length of The City, and I cannot recall many moments when we were out of sight of really noble monuments. The architecture was solid and secure, wholly fitted to the bleak terrain, and the impression was one of dignity and organization. Qala Bist, at the eastern edge of the Desert of Death, had stunned me with its magnificence. The City, on the western edge, left no such impression. It was so huge, so beyond normal comprehension, and yet so intimate—I felt that men had actually walked these streets and collected taxes in these buildings—that no reaction was required. There it was. Damn it all, there the stupendous thing was, abandoned in the desert the way Route One, two thousand years from now, might reach in shadowy grandeur from what used to be New York to what used to be Richmond.

If the early morning heat on the desert had been oppressive, the heat we experienced at noonday along The City was almost unbearable. Of it I will say only this: Whenever we came upon an irrigation ditch or an arm of the river, we jumped from our jeeps, held our watches and wallets over our heads, and plunged fully dressed into the water, soaking in the moisture through aching pores. We then took with us large cans of dirty water, which we poured over our turbans as we rode, but as before, any relief was temporary, for within a few minutes we were once more completely dry. At least ten times we jumped into the ditches, and if we had not been able to do so, we could not have continued our journey. We would have been forced to seek protection in one of the vast, vacant buildings and wait for nightfall.

After one such dunking Nazrullah again asked me to ride with him, but he would not speak of his marriage. He wished to discuss the old days, when The City flourished. "It probably had trade with areas as far removed as Moscow, Peking, Delhi and Arabia. It was never the superb city that Balkh was, but it must have been impressive. What do you suppose killed it?"

"Genghis Khan," I replied with confidence. "In school I read about him, as a name, but never appreciated what a devastating force he was. He stood before your city and shouted, 'Here I am!' and pretty soon there was no city."

"No," Nazrullah laughed, "you give good old Genghis too much credit. Now Balkh, the best city we ever had . . . He did destroy that. But not this place. Nor Herat. He wiped out the population, but people are easy to replace and Herat still exists. He didn't wipe out The City. Something else did that."

"Plague?" I hazarded, for my mind was not yet geared to Central Asia.

"Three hypotheses are predominant, not mutually exclusive," he said slowly. This was the kind of talk he liked, arguing in Germanic patterns, like most learned Afghans.

I interrupted him, laughing. "It just occurred to me, Nazrullah. I've been with you and Moheb Khan and Nur Muhammad for some time now, and none of you ever says, 'By the beard of the Prophet,' or 'By the blood of the infidel,' or 'Allah shall be revenged.' I don't believe you're real Muslims."

"I have the same complaint against you," he replied seriously. "Not once do you or the ambassador say 'By cracky' or 'Gee whillikens.' We're living in a denatured age."

"Proceed, Son of the Prophet."

"That reminds me of something amusing," he said. "For a while I dated a Penn coed whose sole knowledge of Asia was that fine ballad 'Abdul Abulbul Amir.' Funny thing was, she made about as much sense as any of the others."

"What did wreck The City?"

"First, this used to be the world's foremost example of irrigation. I think Alexander commented on that. You can see relics of the old system everywhere. Over there, for example. Probably a reservoir. But people got lazy. They didn't keep working on it. They felt that what had worked for a hundred years was good enough for the next hundred years. They stopped cleaning the ditches . . . built no new dams. They guessed right. For a hundred years, no trouble. But the death warrant had been signed. Genghis Khan can't be blamed for that. The people had grown fat and lazy.

"Second, and I place much emphasis on this, there was salt. If you irrigate a piece of land long enough, the constant flow of water must deposit salt, so that each year you raise a crop, you deteriorate the land that made the crop possible. Therefore I don't blame the lazy people entirely. Maybe the salt was just too big a problem to handle. In some future century, perhaps, all of Colorado and Utah will be useless because the men of this century were such good farmers. Your salt levels are rising ominously. Behold, Denver, Colorado!" And he pointed to the ruins.

"The third reason is the most tantalizing of all. Goats. Those damned goats are the curse of Asia. God gave us a fertile land, covered with magnificent trees and soil rich enough to feed all men. But the Devil got even by giving us just one thing. Goats. And they took care of the forests. Ate all the young trees. And the rich fields. Ate the cover off and turned them to deserts. Probably the most destructive animal ever created. Much more dangerous than the cobra."

"But how would goats affect The City?" I asked.

"When this was a metropolis," Nazrullah explained, "the hills you see must have been covered with trees. Brisk business in timber and charcoal. Excessive cutting killed some forests, but goats

(231)

took care of the rest. So today in Afghanistan we have almost no forests. Do you suppose we live in mud houses on purpose? They're miserable, but we have no wood. All the time I was in America I wondered, 'What is the goat in America?' I found out. It's the man who destroys your forests." He paused, then observed, "You defeated Germany in this war, but in the future Germany's bound to win. Because Germans plant trees."

I tried to lead the conversation back to Ellen Jaspar but was forestalled when our guide, perched on the spare tires behind my ear, sang out that we were approaching Chahar, where Pritchard lay. We looked for a ditch and plunged in to refresh ourselves, then stood on the bank as the monstrous wind sucked us dry, and when our turbans were no longer wet we replaced them with karakul caps. We straightened our clothes to make ourselves as presentable as possible, and while we were doing this I asked, "Why all the falderal?"

Nazrullah replied, "Down here you impress the sharif, or you get nothing." As we drove into the village he added, "We're so far from Kabul that government doesn't actually exist, except in the person of this brigand who rules as he wishes. Who's going to drive across that desert to correct him?"

It was an attractive village with an oversized caravanserai and cool pomegranate trees whose blossoms sent me an unfamiliar fragrance. The sharif came out to greet us, a huge fellow well over six feet in height, and I thought: How often we choose tall men to govern us.

And this sharif governed, that was obvious. As

absolute monarch of a tiny kingdom, he had his own army, his own judges, his own treasury. Since he lived so close to Persia and so far from Kabul, his little kingdom used mainly Persian coins and Persian stamps. "Dozens of these principalities remain in Afghanistan," Nazrullah explained, and I understood why, in Chahar, the evacuation of an American with a broken leg was impossible. When you got sick here, the local medicine man cured you, or you died.

The sharif led us to a low, stifling hut tucked away in a corner of the caravanserai, and there on a straw mattress laid over a rope bed we found the gaunt, gray-faced American engineer John Pritchard, a wiry man in his late forties. Nazrullah held out his hand and said, "Hello, Professor. The American embassy's sent a man to get you out of here."

"I'm willing to go . . . right now," the sick man replied. The sharif's servants had kept him clean, fed and shaved, but he was in pitiful shape and I sensed at once that he was close to dying, for his left leg, exposed to dry air to speed the healing, had been punctured by two fractures and was now clearly gangrenous. The skin was taut and greenish.

Dr. Stiglitz hurried to the bed and studied the leg for some minutes, smelling his fingers as he did so. He then probed the man's groin and armpits. When he was done he placed his right hand on Pritchard's shoulder and said quietly, "Herr Professor Pritchard, the leg must come off." The engineer groaned and his face went even whiter than it had been.

Stiglitz continued, as if to convince the rest of us, "In my opinion there's no chance on earth to save this leg. I'm positive other doctors would agree. I'm sorry, Herr Professor, but you must know." Pritchard made no further sound; he must have expected such a decision.

Stiglitz added in a dispassionate professional voice, "We face a difficult choice, for which we are all responsible—Pritchard, Nazrullah, Miller. I can take the leg off here, but where would you recuperate? Tell me that. Or I can medicate the leg now, then rush you back to Kandahar, where the operation could be performed much better and where you could recuperate at ease. In that case the question is, Could you stand the trip across the desert?"

Each waited for the other to speak, then Pritchard said firmly, "If I stay here, I will surely die."

Stiglitz asked, "Then you want to go back to Kandahar?"

"Yes! Yes!" Pritchard cired.

"What do you think, Nazrullah Sahib?" Stiglitz continued.

"I'd like to ask one question," Nazrullah countered. "Professor Pritchard, you remember what the desert was like. Do you feel strong enough to cross it now?"

"Yes!" Pritchard repeated. "If I stay here I'll die."

"We'll take you to Kandahar," Nazrullah said firmly, and when the decision was reached he became once more his efficient self. Looking at his watch, he said crisply, "We must get back to The City before darkness. We'll sleep there. Start across the desert at dawn. You fellows up to it?" Nur and Stiglitz said they were. Then he addressed Pritchard directly: "This is the last chance. You're sure you can cross the desert?"

"Right now," the engineer replied.

"We go," Nazrullah announced.

But I was appalled, both at the decision itself and at the hasty manner in which it had been reached. "Wait a minute!" I protested. "Dr. Stiglitz, is Professor Pritchard qualified to make a decision like this?"

"I am," Pritchard interrupted. "I've waited here too damned long. If I stay here, I'm going to die."

"Have you ever crossed the desert?" I asked, betraying my nervousness at intervening in such a matter, for I was the youngest present.

"I'm here, aren't I?" Pritchard asked contemptuously.

"You remember the heat?"

"Look, Miller, I refuse to stay here. Let's get going."

"The heat?" I shouted. "Have you ever crossed in daytime?"

"Yes!" the sick man shouted back. "I can take it."

I appealed to Dr. Stiglitz. "You know very well, Doctor, that intense heat and movement will increase the danger from that leg." The German was silent and I shouted, "Don't you?"

"Yes," Stiglitz grudgingly assented. "And every minute we don't operate increases the risk."

"That's what I thought," I said weakly. I felt as if I were going to burst into tears. Very quietly I said, "We'll operate here—right now."

Stiglitz spoke solemnly: "But the risk to his life is just as great here, Herr Miller."

"For God's sake!" I cried. "Give me an answer, yes or no."

"There is no answer, yes or no," the German replied stubbornly. "There is risk. There is risk here and risk there. I cannot decide." He turned to Pritchard and asked gently, "You know you're in grave danger, don't you Herr Professor?"

"Three days ago I thought I was dead," Pritchard said. "I'm not afraid any longer. In your opinion, Doctor, which way gives me the best mathematical chance?"

"That I cannot answer," Stiglitz insisted. "You and your American adviser must decide."

The sick man looked up at me, and I almost had to turn away, death seemed so close. "Young fellow," he said quietly, "I calculate my own chances as being best if we go to Kandahar."

I was so certain that once we got that leg on the desert it would insure his death, pumping poison constantly throughout his body, that I could not accept either his answer, or Nazrullah's assent, or the doctor's impartiality. I knew we must take the leg off at once. In my anguish I looked at Nazrullah and said, "Could we walk in the garden a moment?"

"You're wasting time," Nazrullah warned me.

"I need your advice," I said.

"You have my advice . . . Kandahar."

"Please," I begged.

Against his will I led him out beneath the pomegranate trees, sweet in the spring, where I had a chance to confront the hard quality of his mind.

"You're the American in charge," he said harshly. "You must decide . . . in fifteen minutes."

"But, Nazrullah, you're a scientist. You know that a leg like that is pumping poison right through that man's blood. He can't possibly get to Kandahar."

"The doctor thinks he can. I think he can. We should leave."

"But if we do decide to operate here, will you arrange things for us?"

"Absolutely, Miller. I'll stay here a month if necessary. You make the decision and I'll abide by it. But make the decision."

"Help me do what's best," I pleaded. "There's a man dying in there."

"I can't do your job for you," he said coldly.

"Could I see the doctor again? For just a minute?"

"Stiglitz? He's incapable of a moral decision. He said clearly: The facts are these. You decide."

"What did he say the facts were?" I asked, sweating nervously. "I want to hear them from him again before we decide."

"No!" Nazrullah cried. "You can't evade your responsibility."

"Please, review with me what he said. I don't have it clear."

"He said," Nazrullah repeated impatiently, "that Pritchard would probably die, whether we amputated his leg here or hauled him across the desert to do it."

"He never said that!" I protested in real confusion.

"He implied it. He believes it. And if that's true,

which I'm sure it is, the problem becomes simple. What's best for your country and mine?"

"That's a hell of a way to talk about a man who may be dying."

"Miller, he is dying. What's best for you and me to do? Speak up or we're leaving."

"Wait a minute. Let me think," I pleaded. "Nazrullah, we know he wants to get out of here. How much weight should I put on that fact?"

"The whole weight, Miller. If he stays here he knows he'll die."

I hesitated, then said firmly, "All right. We take him to Kandahar."

"That's your decision?"

"Yes. Let's get started. Right now."

"Please put it in writing."

"What are you trying to do?" I cried.

"Things like this often end badly," Nazrullah said cautiously. "Americans like to blame Afghans . . . make us look stupid. If a stupid decision is being made, you'll make it, and you'll put it in writing."

"I'm not afraid," I said bravely, feeling much older than twenty-six. "But in that case I've got to talk with Stiglitz and Pritchard."

"You have ten minutes," Nazrullah said. "After that we stay here . . . for many weeks."

We returned to the sick room and I asked Dr. Stiglitz to join me in the garden. He protested but Nazrullah said in German, "Go ahead."

"Your honest judgment, Stiglitz, and you can't evade now. What's best for this man?"

"This is a decision I cannot make," Stiglitz insisted stubbornly.

"That's a hell of a position for a doctor to take."

"It's the only one under the circumstances," he said defensively.

"What are the circumstances?" I shouted, losing control of my patience under the hammering I was undergoing.

"Pritchard is going to die," he replied bluntly.

"I say that if we take the leg off right now he'd have a chance."

"You're right."

"And if you haul him through the desert death is almost inevitable."

"You're right."

"Then for God's sake, let's go in there and operate."

"I warned you, Herr Miller, that this is not a decision I can make. Pritchard is convinced that if he stays here any longer he will die. His spirit is worn out . . . can you understand that at your age? Worn out. It might be wiser for him to risk the journey to Kandahar if it restores his hope."

"Who can decide this?"

"Pritchard."

I returned to the room and told Nazrullah, "I'll write out the order in five minutes."

"You'd better," he said.

I went to the sickbed and before I spoke to Pritchard I looked at the bleak walls of the Caravanserai and smelled the stale, baked air. I would not have wanted to live in that room, even in health. But to have lain in that stifling heat for three weeks while local practitioners ruined my leg, to have watched it swell and grow green,

(239)

would have been intolerable, and now to face the prospect of six more weeks would kill my spirit.

I sat on the bed and told Pritchard, "I guess it's up to you and me. Here or Kandahar?"

"I know I'm in bad shape. But if I stay here . . . what'd you say your name was?"

"Miller. I'm from the embassy." Then I had an idea. "You know, Professor Pritchard, the ambassador himself sent me here. He's deeply worried about you."

"I didn't know anybody gave a damn." He turned his head, unable to control his tears. "Jesus, Miller, this is the end of the world."

"I can see that," I agreed.

"How the hell did I get here?" he mumbled. "Making a water study for a nation that just don't give a damn."

"Don't say that. You wrote to us about Nazrullah. He's a fine engineer."

"The guy with the beard?"

"Trained in Germany," I assured him.

"Some of the best come from Germany," he said in the approving manner of practical men who recognize excellence wherever developed.

"You're determined to make the run to Kandahar?"

"If I stay here I'll die."

"You appreciate the risk?"

His spirit cracked. Rising on one elbow he shouted, "If you're afraid of your lousy job, I'll put it in writing. I want to get the hell out of here."

"I'll do the writing," I said, feeling miserable, for I knew I was condemning him to death. I called

Nur Muhammad to bring my brief case, and on official paper I wrote:

> Chahar, Afghanistan
> April 12, 1946
>
> I have this day ordered the American irrigation engineer John Pritchard to be transported to the hospital in Kandahar, so that medical attention unavailable here may be given his badly infected left leg.
>
> Mark Miller
> United States Embassy
> Kabul, Afghanistan

Feeling sick at what I had done, I handed Nazrullah the directive. He read it twice, showed it to Stiglitz and Nur Muhammad, and folded it carefully. "We'll leave in ten minutes, sleep at the edge of the desert and start our crossing as soon as we can negotiate that bad approach."

He had overlooked one fact. John Pritchard refused to leave his post until his water-level records were collected. "That's why I came here," he said. "If they want to build that dam, they'll need these records." To my surprise, Dr. Stiglitz supported him.

"A scientist should keep records," the German said.

So I was led by a guide to a spot two miles down the Helmand, where John Pritchard had been collecting the data on which Nazrullah would build his dam. More significantly, perhaps, Pritchard's word would form the basis for riparian treaties between Afghanistan and Persia, who had threatened war over the river. We found a small shed, boiling hot, some water gauges, a sheaf of irreplaceable records. The guide warned me in Pashto to watch the steps leading to the shed, for it was here that Pritchard had broken his leg; and as I stood in this lonely shack, this veritable end of the world where the temperature was daily above a hundred and thirty, I thought of all the careless speeches made in Congress about the cookie-pushers of the State Department, those striped-pants boys who haunt afternoon teas, and I wished that some of the arrogant speakers could have seen the work that John Pritchard had accomplished for our nation and for Afghanistan.

"Was Pritchard a good man?" I asked the guide. It was a kind of judgment he had not previously been asked to make, and he was confused. Finally he said brightly, "Yes, he could handle a gun with skill."

I was to ride with Nazrullah in his jeep, while Nur and Stiglitz supervised loading Pritchard in the back of theirs. As they did so the German said heartily, "If I ever saw a man with a good chance to get across the desert, it's this one."

"We'll make it!" the engineer called as we set forth, and it became my duty when we stopped to pour as much water as possible over the stricken man, thus keeping his temperature down, but before we had traveled far he became partially delirious and asked that I ride with him, as he wished to speak of America.

Thus we rode past the brooding, empty buildings of The City, and in the cooler evening his fever abated and we talked. He was from Fort Collins, Colorado, and had spent each autumn hunting in the Rockies. He was, he admitted, a fairly good rifle shot and had bagged elk, bear and mountain goats. He had a low opinion of the latter and felt they did more harm than good. He was optimistic about one thing: said he knew a one-legged man in Loveland who had no trouble hunting.

"I'm the kind of man," he said, "who won't give up till I learn how to walk with a wooden leg." But at the next stop Dr. Stiglitz decided to give Pritchard a knock-out pill, and the engineer fell asleep.

10

As soon as morning light permitted, we negotiated the canyon, and when the sun was well ablaze we were on the desert, stopping frequently to pour water on our turbans. At first I rode with Nur and the sick man, keeping his body under wet compresses, but he grew constantly worse, and at one of the water stops Stiglitz insisted upon changing places with me so that he might supervise the invalid. The more drastic steps he took to keep Pritchard alive worked. At the start of our trip I had given the engineer no chance to live, but apparently I was going to be proved wrong.

I now rode with Nazrullah, and after we had discussed Pritchard's leg, he asked me bluntly, "What else do you need to know about my wife?"

The question startled me, for I had been devising stratagems whereby I could trick him into comment, and for a moment I could not think clearly, so I repeated lamely, "She ran away?"

"Yes. Last September."

"That's eight months ago," I stammered.

"Seems longer," he reflected, rubbing his beard. In his soggy, formless turban he looked quite Asiatic.

"Why did she run away?"

(244)

"You wouldn't understand," he replied with a nervous laugh. He wanted to be helpful, but the facts were so preposterous that he was unable to evaluate them, so he kept silent, reminding me of the worried Afghan husband who had hustled back and forth between his sick wife and Dr. Stiglitz: he would report only what he himself understood.

I appreciated his efforts at good will, for the conditions under which we rode made conversation difficult. The desert was intolerably hot and we were both gasping for air. "This must be hell on Pritchard," he observed.

"It's what I was worried about yesterday," I reminded him.

"We've been through that!" he cautioned. "I have your order, in writing."

"Did you warn Ellen Jaspar that . . ."

"That I was married? Yes."

"The other day in Kandahar I met your wife, your Afghan wife, that is."

"I know. Karima told me about it in her letter."

"How could she send a letter?" I asked, like a movie detective trapping a suspect. "I saw her only a short time before I left."

"The messenger who brought Dr. Stiglitz also brought her letter," he explained, and I had to laugh at my own suspicions.

"I'm sorry," I apologized. "This whole thing seems so shadowy."

"To me it's even more so," he confessed.

"Then what Karima said was true? You did tell Ellen?"

"Whatever Karima says is apt to be true."

"Is she a beautiful girl?" I asked for no obvious reason.

"Very. It was stupid of her to wear the chaderi. I don't require it."

"I suspect she was afraid of Nur Muhammad."

Inappropriately, Nazrullah began to laugh and I must have looked at him with censure, for he said, "I'm sorry, but when you mentioned the chaderi I remembered something which explains Ellen rather better than anything else I could tell you. I sympathize with your suspicions. You're sure that I mistreated her and that my family kept her prisoner and that she's walled up somewhere pining for freedom. Miller, when she arrived in Kabul, all of us . . . everybody . . . tried to make her feel at ease. You know what she did? On the morning after the marriage she came down to breakfast wearing a chaderi."

"What?"

"Yes, at breakfast. A very expensive silk chaderi which she had asked a dressmaker in London to make from a picture in a book. She was going to be more Afghan than the Afghans. My family tried not to laugh, and I had tears in my eyes to think that she was such a good sport. We explained that you don't wear a chaderi at breakfast. But I had one hell of a time keeping her from wearing it on the street."

He laughed in memory of that bizarre event as a father laughs during a business lunch when he recollects his child's mistakes. "You may have heard that one day in Kandahar the mullahs spat at her. When it was all over, she started to cry, not at the mullahs but at me. 'If you'd let me wear the chaderi,' she whimpered, 'this wouldn't have happened.'"

"I don't understand."

"None of you Americans understand what an extraordinary woman Ellen is. Obviously her parents didn't. Nor her professors. Don't call her a girl any more. She is a woman. I doubt that she was ever a girl. She is a rare human being who sees through to the essence of God. I suppose you know that on one of our first dates she told me all about the atomic bomb."

"You met her in 1944," I checked. "At that time there wasn't such a bomb."

"She invented it," he said cryptically.

I looked at him askance and he was about to elaborate when the rear jeep signaled us to stop, and in the moments we waited for them to overtake us he added, "Ellen foresaw that if the nations continued their madness, they would be forced to invent some super-terrible weapon. She even described it rather accurately. 'It's the age of air, so they'll deliver it by air, and it'll wipe out whole cities.' She added that there was no way to prevent it and probably no way to escape. She said, 'I hope I can get to Afghanistan before they destroy us all.' At first I thought she was using us as a refuge . . . because we would be the last place bombed, but that wasn't her idea. She told me, 'There isn't going to be any refuge, and if I'm to die, I want to die in Afghanistan, which is as far away from our pitiful civilization as any place I know. Let's live and die close to primitive things.' I suppose that's what she had in mind when she protested my building the dam."

Dr. Stiglitz walked gloomily to our jeep and said frankly, "He won't make it, Nazrullah. He wants Miller to ride with him."

But I was so close to probing Nazrullah's secret that I protested, selfishly: "I want to talk with Nazrullah . . . just a little longer."

Stiglitz said without expression, "Pritchard wants to talk, too. To an American."

"Forgive me," I said, and when I took my seat, close to the engineer's fevered head, I started applying towels, but he merely gasped and rolled his eyes at me. He was very close to death.

Finally he whispered, "I can't breathe." Nur was weeping.

"I can't breathe either," I assured the dying man. "This heat."

"With you the cause is different," he replied lucidly. "You don't carry a leg that's beating like a drum. I can feel it pumping poison."

I bit my tongue to keep from reminding him that he was repeating my words. I said, "We're better than halfway through the desert."

"I want you to give my wife a message," he said with painful effort. "She lives in Fort Collins. Damned good woman. Tell her . . ." He winced, as an almost visible pain streaked across his face, driving him to incoherency.

I soaked his turban and applied wet rags to his leg. The river water was used up and I proposed to Nur, "We've got to use some of our drinking water." Nur looked at me is dismay, studied the desert ahead, then listened to Pritchard moan. I saw tears start down his cheek and dry to salt in the desperate air.

"If he needs water, give it to him," he said in Pashto.

I poured some of the drinking water over Pritchard's head and he regained consciousness long enough to dictate jumbled phrases to his wife. She was to consult with a Mr. Forgraves in Denver. The kids must graduate from college, both of them. Then, for some reason I didn't understand, he went into a long discourse about a new kind of paint he had seen described in a technical journal. It would cure their cellar problems once and for all. Be worth two hundred dollars but he thought she might get it for less.

"Pritchard," I broke in after the paint monologue, "I think I'd better get Dr. Stiglitz."

"Don't. If I'm gonna die, let me die with my kind, not some goddamned Nazi." He started shivering. Then a dreadful sweat broke out across his face and little rivulets of perspiration accumulated, to be evaporated instantly in the swirling heat.

"I'm burning up!" he shouted. Nur Muhammad, who heard the conversation, began to cry openly and finally stopped the jeep.

"I will not drive a man to meet death," he sobbed as he stood bareheaded in the sun. "If death wants this man, death must come . . . here."

In a kind of frenzy I saw the jeep ahead pulling away, so I blew the horn repeatedly. "Knock off the noise, you kids," Pritchard cried.

Nazrullah caught my signal and whirled about on the blazing dasht. "What the hell's the matter with you?" he stormed at Nur.

"I will not drive a man to meet death," Nur stubbornly repeated. Taking a small rug from his gear, he spread it on the sand and, kneeling westward to Mecca, prayed.

"He looks awful," Nazrullah said and Dr. Stiglitz hurried over to check the delirious engineer.

A strange, desert prayer came to my lips, silently: "Oh, God, spare my countryman." At the mumbling of these words, John Pritchard died.

I looked distractedly at Nazrullah, who shrugged his shoulders and said, "It was a chance. Nobody thought it was a good chance." The callousness of this remark made me want to storm at the incompetents who had permitted this disgraceful suicide, but that obligation was taken from me by Nur Muhammad, who wept, "You're all criminals. Bringing this doomed man onto the desert."

This was too much. I shouted, "If you thought that, why didn't you say so?"

"Nobody asked me," he sobbed, and it occurred to me that if he had once supported my argument, we never would have left Chahar and Pritchard would now be alive. But I knew why he had remained silent: he had been afraid to contradict his social superior, Nazrullah, so now we were on the desert with a dead body to deliver . . . remorselessly assaulted by the noonday heat.

Nur Muhammad was quite incapable of driving, so I took charge of the second jeep, the one with the corpse, and we headed for Kandahar, but when we reached about forty miles an hour on the shale I suddenly saw looming ahead a field of gotch, which I swerved sharply to avoid, recalling the soldiers who were dead for not having done so, and I threw the jeep against a series of jolting rocks which snapped the front axle.

Nur Muhammad went to pieces, berating himself for the fact that he was not at the wheel in this difficult terrain and cursing fate because the corpse had been thrown out of the jeep and now lay in horrible contortion on the dasht. Nazrullah, in contrast, was superb. He quieted Nur, absolved me of blame, and helped Dr. Stiglitz load the corpse into the workable jeep. He then quietly studied his map and informed us, "The Caravanserai of the Tongues must be a little distance to the north. We'll tow the broken jeep there and decide what to do."

But while we were attaching two ropes Dr. Stiglitz said, "Why don't we drive back and take the front axle from the jeep of the two soldiers?"

Nazrullah stopped sharp, dropped the ropes and stood in the blazing sun considering the alternatives the German had suggested. Clutching his beard he mumbled, "Why didn't I think of that? Stupid. Stupid." He walked away from us, positioning his opened hands as if they were two jeeps. For a long time he strode back and forth across the desert, then returned to us.

"For three reasons we must go directly to the caravanserai," he said. "First, I'm not sure we could find the other jeep if we wanted to."

"It's right back there." I pointed.

"It's more than forty miles," he corrected, "and sometimes you can't find things a second time in the desert. Second, we don't have enough water to double back and forth. But most important, suppose the sharif's scouting party has already been there? Suppose we go back and find that the jeep is gone?"

Saying no more, he completed tying the ropes, then hauled us up to the Caravanserai of the Tongues, into which we limped at four that afternoon. His note was still fastened to the door.

We pushed the jeep into one of the honeycomb rooms, then held a council in which Nazrullah explored the alternatives available to us. We decided that two men in the good jeep must try to get back to Qala Bist, taking Pritchard's body along. It was no use risking four lives. The other two men, with what food could be spared, must remain at the caravanserai with the damaged jeep until such time as a rescue party could return. "There's only one question," Nazrullah concluded. "How shall we pair up?"

Learning from the past, I responded quickly: "I'll write an order and accept full responsibility. Stiglitz and Nur will stay here. Nazrullah and I will drive to Qala Bist."

"Reasonable," Stiglitz grunted.

Nur Muhammad, still shaken, wrecked that plan. He sniffed, "It's my duty to stay with Miller Sahib."

"Your duty is discharged," I replied in Pashto.

"No! You are in my care," Nur insisted.

"The whole argument's irrelevant," Nazrullah said. "If anyone must cross the desert it's got to be the Afghans. Miller and Stiglitz, stay here. Nur, jump in the jeep." Nur started to voice some new objection, but Nazrullah shouted a phrase remembered from his American education. "For Christ sake, scram!" When Nur was settled, Nazrullah and I hiked with the water jugs to the stagnant pool that provided a meager supply for the caravanserai. "Can you live on this stuff for three or four days?" he asked.

"You get back here before then," I joked, but I remembered the terror that Nazrullah felt about being on the desert with only one jeep, so I took all the jugs of sweet water and gave them to him. As I did so I said, "Keep this crate away from the gotch."

As he drove off he assured me, "When I come back to get you, Miller, I'll answer all your questions about Ellen. That's a promise." He headed the jeep back toward the desert he dreaded, and I last saw him speeding eastward, his lone flag whipping in the furnace-like air.

At dusk Dr. Stiglitz and I ate a frugal meal and drank a little of the brackish water. We could exist on it, but the prospect was not attractive. We then went out to watch the blazing sun sink behind the dunes and sat together in the refreshing coolness until the great stars appeared, and the white moon. We were about to retire when Stiglitz whispered, "What's that?" And we heard a soft sound, as if a human being were creeping upon us.

We remained very silent, and then saw moving into the moonlight a small group of gazelles, more graceful now, perhaps, than they had been in sunlight. They had been feeding somewhere to the north and were returning to the safety of the desert, where none of their predators could surprise them. They formed such a contrast to the ugly death we had witnessed, that both Stiglitz and I watched them for many minutes. Then, with an unexpected clap of his hands, he startled the little beasts and they leaped and spun in the moonlight, vanishing at last over the dunes.

"Exquisite," Stiglitz whispered, and for the first time I felt some kind of identification with the German. I still wanted to know why he had made the incredible decision of hauling Pritchard onto the desert, and I was about to question him on this when he said, "It's after nine. Let's get ready for bed." We entered the vast caravanserai and lit our Coleman lamp, studiously avoiding the ghostly pillar at the far end of the fort. But it was there.

I said, "You surprised me at Chahar when you refused to make a medical decision . . . when the facts were so clear. Once Pritchard carried that leg into the desert . . . he was doomed. Why didn't you support me?"

"Was he doomed?" Stiglitz asked cautiously.

"Of course he was. Even I saw that." Something in the way I spoke shattered the empathy we had felt while watching the gazelles. Perhaps Stiglitz suspected that when I returned to Kabul I would use Pritchard as an excuse for not recommending him to our ambassador.

A darkness came over his face and he asked contemptuously, "So even you could make that diagnosis, eh? Well, let me tell you, my young friend, I couldn't make it. And I've been a doctor damned near as long as you've been alive. There are many diagnoses you're not qualified to make, Herr Miller."

Without warning he rose and stamped off to the pillar, taking with him our only carving knife, which he scraped vigorously against the plaster, as if driven by some harsh compulsion.

"Nazrullah said it's a national monument," I warned from the opposite end of the room.

"It's a universal monument," he corrected me, "and I'm going to see what's inside." He spoke with determination, then called, "Come here, Miller. It's a human skull."

Against my better judgment I walked slowly down the room, lugging the Coleman lamp, which Dr. Stiglitz grabbed from my hand to hold against the pillar. Behind the inch of plaster I could see a rounded bone. "Is that a skull?" I asked.

"Yes. How many bodies would you estimate are in this pillar?" Before I could answer he did a most ghoulish thing. He planted the lantern in the middle of an open space and said, "This will be the central pole." Then he lay flat on the earth, his toes near the lantern, and commanded me: "Mark where my shoulders come." When the scratches were in the earth, he shifted his body so that I could mark off a new shoulder, and so on around the imaginary pillar.

"Well," he concluded with some satisfaction, "that makes thirty bodies jammed into one layer. Now how many layers?" He stepped back to calculate the number of tiers required to reach the roof. "Perhaps forty-five layers." He paused and a slow look of horror crossed his face. "My God! There's over thirteen hundred people in that pillar."

We sat on the floor, surveying the grisly monument, and I was struck by the grip it had on Stiglitz. Finally I asked, "When Pritchard died, did I see you crossing yourself?"

"Yes."

"You were a Catholic?"

"In Munich, yes."

"Yet you turned apostate?"

"Of course. Since I'm to live here the rest of my life."

"Why?" I asked bluntly.

"Surely you've been told, Herr Miller," he said with contempt. "That's why this pillar fascinates me. Gives me hope."

"What do you mean by that?" I asked.

"It proves what I've always suspected. The things we did in Germany . . . the really dreadful things, are what men have always done." Before I could express my disgust at excusing the civilized man Adolf Hitler by citing the barbarian Genghis Khan, he added, "In each civilization some men run wild. If we're lucky, we control them early. If not . . ." He pointed to the pillar.

We spent the hours before midnight discussing this theory, and he marshaled strong support for his idea that what he had seen in Germany was a recurring sickness which might strike any nation at any time. I argued against this theory of inevitability, but he was adamant in extending it.

"To be specific," he said, "I haven't been to America but I've seen your films and read your books. I'm positive that in your country there would be no difficulty in finding S.S. volunteers for the jobs of collecting Negroes and throwing them into concentration camps."

"Wait a minute!" I cried, condescendingly.

"Herr Miller!" he replied, pulling my face close to his. "Don't you know in your heart that you could do to the Negroes what we did to the Jews?"

I said quietly, "Don't judge us by the fact that we have a few sick people."

"You have an endless supply," he assured me. "We turned ours loose on Jews. Some day you'll turn yours loose on Negroes."

"But never Buchenwald," I resisted.

"In the beginning, never," he agreed. "Your sensibilities would not permit it. Your Bill of Rights . . . But after two or three years of total propaganda . . . the president, churches, newspapers, cinema, labor unions . . . don't you understand that you would find many Americans eager to shoot down Negroes with machine guns?"

"No," I announced confidently.

"Herr Miller, you're an idiot," he stormed. To my surprise he leaped to his feet and rushed to the pillar, which he banged with his fist. "Do you think that Genghis Khan started with this pillar? No. He marched step by step until this pillar was nothing. I could find in any American city you care to mention men who would be glad—joyous, shall we say —to be led step by step until they were building this pillar with living bodies. Do you think we Germans started out one day by building pillars? No, Herr Miller, no! Do you think I started with this?" He beat the pillar until I expected his knuckles to come away bleeding.

Breathing hard, he came and sat beside me. It was now past midnight and we were both worn by the tragic day on the desert, but the pillar kept us awake, and Stiglitz said softly, "Do you really think, Herr Miller, that the reports the Allied governments have on me started with a pillar like that grisly thing? Oh, no! I was a fine, respectable doctor in Munich, married to the daughter of an important businessman . . . a member of the church. My wife and I saw certain promotions available through the Nazi party and we joined. Many prudent men and women did. It was easy at first. The Jews, whom we all despised"—he told me this in a confidential voice, as if I would appreciate why any reasonable man would despise Jews; indeed, as if our hating them together made us brothers—"were merely to be sequestered. That was all, sequestered.

"One day they asked me to check the health of the Jews they rounded up, and I did so, very carefully. Believe me, Herr Miller, if I found a Jew who needed an expensive medicine, I said so, and there are many Jews alive today solely because I prescribed expensive medicine for them." He nodded in confirmation of his own plea, and I judged that he had often conducted this dialogue with himself. There were Jews living today because of what Dr. Stiglitz had done for them, of that I was sure.

"If I were ever brought to trial," he assured me with great confidence, "the health records of the City of Munich would show case after case where I saved the lives of Jews. It's all there . . . in the reports."

He looked at me beseechingly, a tired, pudgy man with turbaned head, wrinkled brow and worried eyes. I thought, perhaps, that he was perspiring, but he was sitting with his back to the lantern, and all I could see was shadow. Persuasively, cautiously, his words resumed: "Unexpectedly other problems arose. A Jew was to be certified mentally deficient so he could be sterilized. The government wanted me to designate a complete stranger as three-quarters Jewish so his property could be confiscated. I'd never seen him before, but he was obviously Jewish . . . you can always tell a Jew. So step by step my soul was corrupted."

He was driven by some deep hatred back to the pillar, which he hammered with his open hands. "Miller," he cried in a hoarse shout, "do you suppose that the man who applied this plaster over living, breathing mouths started with this job? Do you believe that you're immune?"

"To killing Jews, yes!"

"Ah, but the Negro is your Jew. Are you immune there?"

"Of course!" I shouted in disgust.

"Herr Miller, you're a liar! You're a self-deceiving liar!" He beat the pillar again. "This is your pillar, too. This is the pillar of Americans and Englishmen and Germans alike. I couldn't have built this alone, you know."

To my embarrassment his voice began to choke, as if he were going to burst into tears of confession. Then, thank heavens, he gained control of himself and rejoined me on the floor. It was now about two in the morning and in the flickering light of our Coleman lamp I could see his drawn face, weary yet driven to further revelation, and in some strange way he looked as he had that night in the square at Kandahar when he was condemning the dancers. I could hear his voice speaking the words but this time applying them somehow to his own history: *They're cruel little sodomites. When they come to town they create a great evil.* What

ugly passage in his own life among the Nazis did
that repeated phrase illuminate?

Toward four he got to the heart of his chronicle:
"Finally, when we were winning the war on all
fronts—it was 1941—they came to me and said,
'We're looking for a director of research. Military
problems of the gravest significance. Involved is
the final destruction of England.' What could I
say? I was flattered.

"They gave me a fine laboratory in Munich. I
could live at home." He seemed to savor, here in
the Afghan desert, those bright visions of a happy
German home life in Munich. "I could live at
home," he explained persuasively, as if eager to
convince me. "I had to take the job, you can see
that. At first it was routine experiments on
colds . . . very sensible, very productive. I believe
they're selling in America now a cold remedy that
came from my researches. I convinced myself that
I was helping win the war.

"I enjoyed other successes and then one day in
1943 they asked me to explore a purely theoretical
question: How much cold can a human being
tolerate? Now that's a nice question. A very important one, militarily speaking." He paused a long
time to stare at the pillar, then laughed in a high-
pitched giggle. "Without my knowing it, we were
about to conduct pragmatic experiments on the
same subject . . . at Stalingrad." He laughed
openly. Undoubtedly he had used the joke before.

"A fascinating medical question, Herr Miller," he
said reflectively. "How much cold can a human
being tolerate? Yesterday, for example. You were
very hot . . . thought you couldn't take any more.

But Nazrullah said, 'You can discipline yourself,' and the thermometer rose fourteen degrees and you did discipline yourself. How much heat could you have stood? That's a nice question. How much cold . . . I remember the exact phrasing because I wrote it down the day they posed it. You see, Herr Miller, I have a love for keeping records. Yesterday I could sympathize with John Pritchard when he said, 'I must have the records.' Because it is only from careful records that science can . . ." His voice broke and he dropped his head in his hands. His turban fell off and I could see the gray hairs on his stubbly head; I could see his shoulders moving up and down, silently. Finally he put his hand on my knee and said, "The English captured my records. I was meticulous. I was meticulous."

For some minutes we said nothing, then he rose, overcome by a terrible emotion which I did not try to specify, and walked about the pillar several times, his mouth moving as if he were making a speech. The flickering light—the Coleman lamp gives a very white light and throws facial shadows in deep relief—made him look old. Suddenly he leaned against the pillar and issued a flood of words: "In the cage there was this Jew. About fifty years old, a fine human being. His name . . . you can check this in the records . . . was Sem Levin. I had tried all sorts of experiments and had proved what required to be proved, but I had not applied my findings to an average, healthy man like the older soldiers in our army. So I chose Sem Levin. I chose him right from a nondescript group in the cage. I told my aide, 'That's the man! Now we'll see what's what.'"

He hesitated. He could look from the pillar to where I sat and he must have seen the horror and revulsion rising in my face, but he could not silence himself. "Each morning we put Sem Levin completely naked into a room whose temperature could be exactly controlled. We dropped it lower and lower. After eight hours' exposure we discharged him and he returned to the cage filled with nondescript Jews. At first he merely dressed and talked with them. Later, when he joined them blue with cold, two fat middle-aged Jewish women began caring for him. They took his frozen body and held it between them, as if he were a baby. Everyone in the cage who had clothes to spare piled them over the three Jews, the two fat women and shivering Sem Levin.

"I grew to hate this tough little Jew, because each time he entered that room he announced quietly, 'I am still alive.' And when he said this, the Jews cheered, no matter what we had done to them that day. 'I am still alive.' Now it became with them a matter of honor to keep him alive. They saved food for him. Massaged him. Stole medicine for him. And from their resolve he too became determined not to die.

"No man could have withstood what he withstood. He'd come back to the cage with his dirty little penis shriveled up and blue, and he'd say, 'I am still alive.' And the fat women, remembering their husbands dead somewhere in Germany, would take him in their arms.

"It was at this point, when pneumonia was about to begin, that he started greeting me each morning with the same statement. Very polite. 'Good morning, Herr Professor. I am still alive.'"

Stiglitz leaned against the pillar, weak with horror. Then he said in a ghost-like voice well suited to the silent room, "And all the time my filthy wife was going to bed with anyone who had a little authority." He looked at me with the beseeching face a man uses when he is beyond personal salvation and asks help of a priest or a rabbi. In a kind of wail he protested, "But I was honest about the experiment. I could have killed Sem Levin any time I wished, and silenced that speech: 'I am still alive.' No, I held rigorously to the schedule as planned. We lowered the degrees day by day. My records will show that . . . exactly as planned.

"Much later than anyone would have dared predict, this dirty little Jew"—ten minutes ago he had been a *fine human being*—"contracted pneumonia. He should have died. By all human precedent he should have died. But those fat women somehow infused life into him. All that I took away they gave back. On the last three days he could scarcely make his voice heard, but he rasped, 'Good morning, Herr Professor. I am still alive.'

"Finally we broke him. Would you believe it, Miller, he spent three days stark naked in a room two degrees above zero, your system."

Neither of us spoke. Then, in a wild rage, he shouted, "That's why, you stupid American, I could not make the decision yesterday. John Pritchard would have refused to live if we had left him there. If Sem Levin could refuse to die, why couldn't Pritchard refuse to live? Tell me that, Mr. Know-it-all."

"What happened?" I asked in unconcealed horror.

"He died. Two full weeks after we had predicted . . . fourteen days . . . he died. The man in charge was so infuriated with the fat women that he sent the whole cage full of Jews away."

"Away?" I shouted. "Say it. Where?"

"Away," he repeated dully. Then quickly: "I don't know where he sent them. He signed the order . . . the other man."

"Stiglitz," I said quietly, trying to keep control of myself, "you're lying."

"No, no, Herr Miller. It was he who signed the order."

"You're lying," I repeated, not moving.

"No, before God, he signed the order. For Sem Levin I was responsible. That I admit. The records will prove my guilt regarding him. But the others . . ."

"Stiglitz!" I screamed, driven to my feet by an impulse outside me. "I am a Jew!"

He stared at me in awful disbelief, then drew back against the pillar. He tried to laugh, as if I were joking. He moved his mouth to speak but could say nothing, and failing, ran behind the pillar for protection. "Herr Miller . . ." he gasped weakly.

"I'm going to kill you," I threatened, making a lunge at him, but he used the pillar adroitly to protect himself, and I did not touch him.

In the large room there was no furniture, no weapon of any kind except the knife he had used for scraping away the plaster. It had been left lying on the earth near where I stood, but I didn't see it. To my surprise, Stiglitz left the protection of the pillar and made a lunge at me. I felt I could handle him, although he was heavier than I, and I got set to tackle him head on, but my preparation was useless, because he had no interest in me. With a swoop, he fell on the knife and leaped to his feet, jubilant.

"I'm going to kill you," I repeated slowly. "For Sem Levin and the others in the cage." He grinned at me, holding the knife awkwardly with both hands before his chest, and I made a strong feint to the right, then a drive to the left, aiming a kick at his groin. I caught him well and sent him down in a screaming heap, with the useless knife still held before his chest. Had there been a chair in the room, I would have killed him then, beating him to death, but since I had only my hands, I refrained from leaping on him. Instead, I started kicking at him savagely as he lay huddled on the floor. Then, with a second feint at his head, I drove in with a powerful kick at his stomach, straightening him out and sending the knife softly into the dust. I made a football lunge at him and caught his throat in my hands.

I was about to strangle him when the great door of the serai creaked open, admitting daylight and a tall Afghan. With a deep voice he asked in Pashto, "Who would fight in a serai?" I looked up and saw above me a dark-faced man with mustaches and a flowing turban. Across his chest were bandoleers and in his belt a silver-handled dagger.

"Who would fight in a serai?" he repeated.

"There was no reason," I replied in Pashto, scrambling to my feet.

"Good," he cried, and with a deft kick of his booted foot spun our knife against the wall, where it fell quietly to earth. Recovering it, he jammed it into his belt beside his own and said, "The knife I will keep."

As he spoke, other men began filing into the fort and finally a woman, tall and stalwart, with bangles in her nose and no chaderi. Then I recognized who the intruders were: the Povindahs I had seen at Ghazni, and this tall man with the two daggers was the one whom Nur and I had met that day on horseback.

He seemed to recognize me too, for he turned away and strode to the door, where he issued commands which I could not hear. When he returned, additional men appeared bearing bits of wood and utensils, which they carried to the center of the room, where a substantial fire was started.

When it was well ablaze, with smoke drifting out a hole in the ceiling, three Povindah women marched in with that wild, matchless gait I had admired in Ghazni. They were dressed in good gray blouses and black skirts, and since they passed close to me and wore no chaderies, I stared at them and found them handsome . . . not beautiful in any way but handsome.

After they had taken their places about the fire another Povindah entered, and she was not only handsome; she was bewitching, a saucy pigtailed girl of seventeen or eighteen, dressed in red skirt and pink blouse. We looked at each other, and I recognized her as the girl chasing the goat at

Ghazni, and I saw that in her nose she wore no bangles and that her face was extremely clean and sensitive. She kept looking at me as she moved toward the fire and seemed to smile, as if she recognized me, and the grace of her movement reminded me of the gazelles, who could twist and turn at any moment, and so we stared at each other until the man with the bandoleers cried roughly, "Mira!" And the girl went to him for instructions which I did not hear.

She either did not understand what the leader directed or she thought his words unwise, for she stood perplexed, whereupon he gave her a shove and cried, "Mira, do as I say." He propelled her from the serai and I had to assume that he was angry with her for having paraded before me, but I was wrong.

For soon she appeared at the door bringing with her a most beautiful young woman with blond hair, fair complexion and sparkling blue eyes. She was obviously not a Povindah, even though she was dressed as one in black skirt and bracelets. It had to be Ellen Jaspar—tanned from long hours of marching in the sun, slim, vibrant, more challenging even than her photographs.

I can't recall now what I had expected Ellen to look like: vaguely, I had supposed she would be brittle, or obviously neurotic, or reticent with an overt fear of sex, or generally odd-ball like the typical college girl who reacts negatively to the world. She was none of these. Not a single cliché of the sterile revolutionary was visible in this unmarked, wonderful face, and I could hear Richardson of Intelligence saying in the embassy: *I'd date that one. She's stunning.*

Then I understood why her husband, when I had asked him on the desert if she were in Afghanistan, had looked first to the eastern and western stars, judging from them that it was the season when his wife would return to this country with the march of the nomads. Any man who had ever known Ellen Jaspar would keep in his mind a schedule of her movements. It was to this band of Povindahs that she had run away, and I stepped forward to introduce myself and to tell her that I had come to rescue her. But before I could speak, she nodded slightly, as if she already knew who I was, and hurried past me to where Dr. Stiglitz remained in a dazed condition on the ground.

I remember clearly that her lips started to form a word, then stopped. On her second attempt she cried, "Dr. Stiglitz!" He looked up, saw who it was, and more or less collapsed, hiding his face from what he could scarcely believe.

She knelt beside him, took his hands and gently pulled him from the ground. "Are you all right?" she asked.

"Madame Nazrullah, I can't believe . . ."

Having restored him to his feet, she left him abruptly and came to me, her blond hair peeking from beneath an embroidered Asian cap. Standing before me she said graciouly, "I'm Ellen Jaspar, and you must be Mark Miller from the American embassy."

"How did you know?" I asked in some confusion.

"Our people followed you at the execution in Ghazni," she explained.

In some strange way her composure made me feel out of place, and I didn't know what to say. "I'm glad to find you alive," I fumbled.

She suppressed a smile and said, "The savages have treated me rather well." Then she moved to the side of the tall leader and linked her arm with his in one of those automatic gestures which cannot be explained but which betray everything . . . only a woman who is living with a man ever makes that particular movement. Ellen Jaspar had run off with the leader of a nomad caravan, and it must have been this improbable rumor that had reached Shah Khan in Kabul. Little wonder that he had refused to repeat it or have it attributed to him in our embassy records.

"This is Zulfiqar," Ellen announced.

"Is the feud ended?" the big nomad asked Stiglitz and me. When we nodded he cried, "Then let us eat!" And I had my first meal with the nomads.

11

We had not finished breakfast when two Povindah boys with darting eyes and quick gestures—the kind who steal you blind in a bazaar—came yelling that a jeep was hidden in one of the rooms. The Povindahs piled out to see the vehicle and Zulfiqar demanded, "Whose is it?"

"Mine," I said.

"Why is it here?"

I pointed to the broken axle and explained, "I hit rocks on the dasht."

"What were you doing on the dasht?"

The Povindahs gathered round, and since Dr. Stiglitz was still unnerved by the unforeseen consequences of the pillar, I had to explain Pritchard's death in Pashto. Having done so, I began translating into English for Ellen, but she interrupted, in good Pashto, "I learned the language."

When we returned to our breakfast, Zulfiqar surprised me by inquiring bluntly, "Now what do you want to ask us about Ellen?" He pronounced her name gently, in two careful syllables: *El-len.*

I turned to Ellen and asked, "When you first saw me . . . how did you know who I was?"

Zulfiqar replied. "They told us in Ghazni."

"No one in Ghazni knew what I was doing," I protested.

At this Zulfiqar laughed and indicated with his thumb that Ellen was to speak. She brushed back her blond hair and chuckled. "Two minutes after you arrived in Ghazni, Mira saw you in the bazaar."

"There were no women in the bazaar at Ghazni."

"Mira is everywhere."

"Is that true of all Povindahs?"

The indulgent smile on Zulfiqar's face disappeared and he banged his extended fingertips onto the rug from which we were eating. "We're not Povindahs!" he exploded. "That's an ugly name given us by the British. It means that we're permitted"—his voice assumed much scorn—"permitted, if you will, to cross into their lands. We are the Kochis, the Wanderers, and we ask no nation's permission to cross boundaries. It was we who established the boundaries, centuries ago!" He subsided, but warned me quietly, "We are the Kochis."

Ellen resumed: "Mira saw you in the bazaar and sprinted back to camp to warn us that a ferangi was in town. She already knew that you were from the embassy, had a jeep, traveled with an Afghan driver who worked for the government, and that you were headed for Kandahar. Don't ask me how she knew."

I looked at Mira, whose dark eyes were flashing satisfaction. She smiled, but said nothing.

"When you attended the stoning of the woman, three of our men were spying on you. Later they talked with your armed guards. They found you were headed for Qala Bist, and when you hiked out to our camp at the edge of Ghazni, I watched you from the tents."

Zulfiqar smiled again and said, "She wanted to speak then, but I argued, 'No. Don't spoil his fun. He's a young man. Let him go to Qala Bist. Find out for himself. Let him follow us across the desert. He'll talk about it the rest of his life.'"

I was struck by his shrewdness and recalled the things I would have missed: Kandahar, the arch at Qala Bist, The City, and this caravanserai. In some way I must have betrayed my thoughts, for with a twist of his hand he imitated a man fighting with a knife and observed, "A caravanserai at dawn . . . who would steal this from a young man?"

I looked at Zulfiqar with new respect and reminded him, "You offered to answer my questions. Why is Miss Jaspar here?"

With no resentment he explained. "Last September we camped for three days at Qala Bist. On our way to winter quarters at Jhelum. And this American woman came out from the fort to visit with our children . . . with our women. She spoke some Pashto and our people talked. She asked them where we were going, and they said, the Jhelum. She asked by what route, and they told her Spin Baldak, Dera Ismail Khan, Bannu, Nowshera, Rawalpindi. As we were leaving she came to me and said, 'I'd like to travel with your caravan!' I asked her why, and she replied . . ."

"I said," Ellen interrupted in Pashto, "that I would like to march with the free people."

I turned to Ellen and asked in English, "Is he married?"

In Pashto she replied, so that all the nomads

(272)

could hear, "It seems I can love only married men." Then she pointed to one of the handsome older women and said, "That's Racha, Mira's mother." It was thus made obvious to all what my English question had been, and thus I began my acquaintance with Ellen Jaspar in irritation and embarrassment.

The older woman, with a golden bangle in her nose, bowed gracefully, and I felt like a reproved child. I thought: I'm two years older than Ellen Jaspar, but she makes me feel like an infant. I remember that as I finished this thought, I happened to look across the rug and saw that Mira was smiling at my confusion.

When we finished eating, Zulfiqar asked Ellen in Pashto, "Is the fat one a doctor?" Ellen replied that he was, and Zulfiqar said, "Ask him if he'd look at some of our people." Ellen said, "Ask him yourself. He speaks Pashto."

"I'd be happy to help," Stiglitz volunteered, eager to reestablish himself after the fight at the pillar.

Zulfiqar announced, "The doctor will look at your sores," and the Kochis lined up to show him torn fingers, scarred legs and teeth that should have been yanked earlier. As I watched Stiglitz work, I was again impressed by his skill in handling sick people and I was torn between admiring him as a doctor and hating him for what he had once done as a doctor; while on his part he began to revive his hope that in spite of last night I might still recommend his employment by our embassy. Once he looked at me with a half-smile and asked in English, "For a people without doctors, the Kochis are quite healthy, aren't they? They get along very well without doctors."

I felt it unnecessary for me to put him completely at ease, so I ignored the question and had started toward the door when I was met by a travesty of a nomad, one of the funniest-looking men I ever saw. He was about five feet three, scrawny, unshaved, dirty, and clothed in the grimiest rags imaginable. He wore his filthy turban with one end almost to his knees and grinned through broken teeth and a left eye that had a scar dropping three inches from the corner to his jawbone. He shuffled along in sandals that almost fell from his feet and nodded obsequiously to all.

He had been bitten by something, and showed his left arm to Dr. Stiglitz, who asked, "What happened?"

"That damned camel!" the man railed, spitting between his black teeth.

"Looks like you've been chewed," Stiglitz mused, looking at the ugly, extended wound.

"This is Maftoon," Ellen explained. "He tends the camels. What happened, Maftoon?"

"That damned camel!" the little man repeated.

"He has great trouble with the beasts," Ellen laughed. She spoke rapidly with Maftoon and he nodded. "One of the camels gummed his arm," she said.

"Don't you mean bit?" I asked.

"No, I mean gummed. Camels have no upper teeth, you know. At least not in front. When they get mad at you, and Maftoon's are always mad at him, they gum you."

"What are you talking about?" I asked.

"Come along," she volunteered, and she took me out to the camels, where she threw bits of nan at them, so that they opened their mouths wide to catch the food and I could see that she was right. In front the beasts had strong lower teeth but no uppers, only a broad plate of hard gum against which they bit to chew off grass or other fodder. In back, of course, they had grinding teeth.

"I never heard of this," I said, looking for a baby camel that I could inspect more closely.

"Try this one," Ellen suggested, and she called an enormous brute some nine feet tall at the hump, the female with a bad disposition who had attacked Maftoon and sent him to the doctor. "This old devil hates Maftoon but gets along well with me. Hey, hey!" she called, and the huge beast came close, lowered her head, and nuzzled Ellen for a piece of nan. The split upper lip opened and Ellen pressed her thumb against the hard flat gum, then threw a chunk of nan, which the camel caught. "You try it," she said, and I took the nan and got the old camel to open her mouth. The plate against which her lower teeth hit was hard as bone.

"Extraordinary," I said as the big beast ambled away, but as she did so she caught sight of little Maftoon coming from the doctor, and she began to make noises, showing her irritation. I say "make noises" but I'm sure that isn't the right phrase: the camel uttered a sound that was a combination groan, growl, gurgle and grunt. And it was clear that whereas Ellen and I could inspect her teeth, Maftoon had better stand clear.

"Watch!" Ellen whispered, as the little camel

driver took off his turban and threw it on the ground. He took off his long shirt, his tattered pants, his sandals, everything until he stood quite naked. Then he moved back and waited while the embittered camel shuffled up, smelled the clothes and began kicking them violently. She bit them, stamped on them, spit at them and then pushed them about the sand with her head. When she had vented her spleen she stalked majestically away, gurgling and grunting.

When she was gone, Maftoon recovered his clothes, dressed and went in pursuit of the placated camel. When he reached her head he scratched her neck, she gurgled amiably, and the two walked off toward the meager pasture.

"What's it all about?" I asked.

"The old camel drivers believe . . . and it seems to work . . . that a camel bears terrible grudges. Maftoon and the old lady had a fight, and even though she gummed his arm, she'd attack him again and again unless he allowed her to fight his clothes. She's satisfied and tomorrow he'll be able to load her again."

We followed the little man and his camel for some distance, then sat on rocks to watch the animals graze over land where I could see nothing. Ellen said, "I never tire of watching camels. I suppose it goes back to my Sunday school in Dorset, Pennsylvania. At Christmas we traced camels on the wall. Goodness, that seems years ago."

My interrogation of Nazrullah had been so constantly postponed that I was determined to learn as much as possible in my one day with the Kochis, so I launched right in: "Why won't you write to your parents?"

She was expecting some opening attack like this and replied easily, "What could I tell them?" She looked at me pleasantly as the bright sun illuminated her well-scrubbed face. "If they couldn't understand a simple problem like Nazrullah, how could they possibly understand this?" She pointed to Maftoon, the camels and the caravanserai.

"Perhaps I could understand."

"Not likely." She spoke with a contempt which erased the pleasantness I had observed before.

"Nazrullah is still very much in love with you. What happened?"

"He's very kind. He's very tedious," she replied.

I was irritated by her assumed superiority and was about to comment on it when I saw at the caravanserai gate the tall figure of Zulfiqar, spying on us, but after a while I had to conclude that he was not spying, for he seemed neither jealous nor suspicious; he looked as if he were glad that Ellen had found a chance to talk with an American. I thought: Wonder what they talk about when they're alone. Aloud I asked, "Can Zulfiqar read and write?"

"Books, no. Figures . . . better than either of us."

She said this in a bored manner implying that no further comment from me would be welcomed, so I observed, "Nazrullah seemed one of the ablest men in the country."

"He is," she said with equal finality and equal boredom. Then with a show of real warmth she added, "His wife Karima's even better."

"I met her . . . in chaderi."

"Karima! She never wears chaderi if she can help it."

"I had a government official with me."

"That's how it works," she observed, reverting to a monotone. "Karima observes the custom to protect Nazrullah, and he assures the government that he approves in order to protect Karima."

It was a neatly phrased summary, but I remembered what Nazrullah had said on the desert: *On the morning after the marriage Ellen came to breakfast wearing a chaderi.* Probably I should have kept my mouth shut, but she had gone out of her way to irritate and embarrass me, so I remarked, "Nazrullah told me that when you first came to Afghanistan you wore the chaderi."

She blushed angrily, blood coursing across her beautiful face. "Nazrullah talks a lot," she said.

"Karima talked a lot, too," I continued. "She told me that while you were still in America you learned that Nazrullah already had a wife."

She laughed uneasily. "Why are you American men so preoccupied with such trivialities? Of course I knew he was married. This proves, Mr. Miller, why you could never understand my reasons for leaving Dorset, Pennsylvania."

"Any chance of my understanding why you left Nazrullah?"

She looked at me steadily, almost insultingly, with deep blue eyes, then laughed. "No one who works for the American embassy could possibly understand."

That did it. "If you were a man," I said coldly, "I'd bust you in the nose. Why don't you have the decency to tell your parents where you are?"

My bluntness shocked her and she bit her knuckles, then toyed nervously with the embroidery on her blouse. "Your question is a sensible one, Mr. Miller, and it hurts. My parents are good, decent people and I'm sure they mean well. But what can I possibly write to them?" She looked at me with the first compassion I had seen since we started talking, but it quickly faded. "Would you suggest something like this?" she asked brightly, as she began reciting an imaginary letter.

"Dear Mumsy and Dadsy,

I have run away from Mr. Nazrullah because he's one of the most boring men on earth, and I'm sure his other wife thinks so too. He could move right into Dorset without causing a ripple, because he believes like you, Mumsy-wumsy, that God wants men to have big cars, that electricity makes people happy, and that if you sell enough canned goods, tensions will cease. You were deadly afraid of him, Dadsy-wadsy, but you shouldn't have been. He's your twin brother and if you'd recognized a good thing when you saw it, you'd have fought to keep him, not me. Because he could sell insurance ten times better than you ever did.

> Your loving daughter,
> Ellen
> Bryn Mawr 1945, busted out

P.S. I am now living with a man who has no home, no nation and no responsibility except ninety-one camels. His wife made me the most adorable gray blouse you ever saw in your life, and I'm wearing it as I hike over the Lower Himalayas. I'll write to you next from Jhelum when we get there eleven months from now.

> Your Ellie"

She looked at me bitterly and said, "If you think that would put them at ease, send it to them. Frankly, I haven't the guts."

I was disgusted with her. She sounded like a freshman I knew at Mount Holyoke, except for two things: the other girl's father sold stocks and bonds in Omaha, and in her sophomore year she got some sense. This Jaspar girl was irritating, and I said something which must have made me sound foolish: "When the years pass, you'll be old. What will you do in a Kochi caravan then?"

"What will Senator Vandenberg do? He'll be old. And you . . . what's your first name, Miller?"

"Mark. Groton and Yale."

"That's just dandy. If there's anyone I like to meet in the middle of the Afghan desert it's a Yale man. Tell me, do you honestly believe that in my home town of Dorset, Pennsylvania, there's a basic good, while here in Afghanistan there's a basic evil?"

"I believe that anyone does best when he clings to his own nation, his own people . . . and his own religion. I understand you gave yours up."

"Presbyterianism is not difficult to give up," she replied.

"A moment ago I said to myself, She sounds like a Mount Holyoke freshman. I put you about four years too high. You sound like a high-school freshman."

"Damn you!" she snapped. "I'm sitting here among the camels thinking: That poor dear boy, Mark Miller. Groton and Yale. The years will pass and he'll be stuck in some pothole like the embassy in Brussels. And he'll be old. And he'll have missed

(280)

the whole meaning . . . the whole goddamned meaning." She looked at me sadly and said, "You're a young jerk and you're already prematurely middle-aged and I'm terribly sorry for you."

I stared at her. I said nothing for at least four minutes, just stared at her. Finally she shrugged her shoulders and said, "I surrender. Get me some paper. I'll write the letter."

I asked her if she would come inside, but she replied, "I never get enough of this free air," and as I entered the caravanserai to get some paper from my brief case I met Zulfiqar and told him, "She's going to write to her parents," and he replied, "I asked her to, months ago."

I handed her the paper and she sat scrunched up on the rocks, biting my pen. Then, as she started writing freely and easily, I had a second chance to study her. If I hadn't just heard her bitter comments, I would have sworn that she was exactly what I had guessed when I first saw her in the caravanserai: a lovelier, more beautiful, more delightful person than we had seen in the embassy photographs. She simply did not look like a disgruntled post-adolescent. She was a mature, sensible-looking woman with a plenitude of charm, and if I could have erased her recent conversation I could easily have agreed with her enthusiastic roommate, whose report I now recalled so clearly: *Ellen Jaspar was a dear, sweet kid. She was loyal, responsive, and trustworthy.* It sounded like the Girl Scout oath, but now Ellen came to a difficult part of her letter and a scowl crossed her face—a harsh, belligerent scowl—and I could not possibly kid myself into thinking that I was dealing with any Girl Scout.

"Will that do?" she asked, thrusting the finished letter at me. I took it, turned away from the bright sunlight, and read:

Dear Folks,

I'm terribly sorry I haven't written sooner, but some rather dramatic things have been happening and frankly, I found it almost impossible to explain them to you in a letter. Let me say quickly that they leave me happier than I have ever been, in better spirits, secure in all things. I love you very much.

My marriage to Nazrullah didn't work out too well, but it was not because of his unkindness. He was an even better man than I told you, and I am terribly sorry to have hurt him, but there was no escape. I am now with some wonderful people whom you would like, and I'll tell you all about them later.

To show you how crazy this world can be, I am now sitting with a herd of camels on the edge of the desert talking to a perfectly delightful Yale man, Mark Miller, who will send you a fuller letter of his own explaining all that has happened. He will tell you that I am happy, healthy and alive.

Your loving daughter . . .

Thinking of my own close-knit family in Boston, I could have wept at her inability to communicate with her people. I returned the letter and said, "Sign it, and I'll airmail it from Kandahar."

But before writing her signature she let the pen hang idly and mused, "God knows, Miller, I told them the truth. I am happy, healthy and alive. And if I were to grow old as pleasantly as Racha has done, I'd be content."

She signed the letter, addressed the envelope carefully, then bit the pen for some moments. Extending the sealed letter provocatively toward me, she waved it twice, then studiously tore it into minute bits, which she scattered among the camels. "I cannot send such evasions," she said hoarsely.

We stared at each other for some time and I saw in her eyes hatred, bitterness and confusion. But as I continued to look at her, these ugly attributes vanished and I saw merely the appealing gaze of an attractive, perplexed young woman. I said, "I'll write to them."

"Please do," she replied.

I returned to the caravanserai, where I faced one of the more difficult decisions of my misson: on the one hand I was dead tired from the long, tragic day on the desert followed by the sleepless night at the pillar, so that my whole autonomic system demanded that I fall asleep; but on the other I awaited the momentary arrival of a rescue mission led by either Nazrullah or troops from Kandahar, so that before the rescue party took me away I wanted to see as much of Kochi life as possible. I forced myself to stay awake, watching the children and the older women working at their jobs. I thought constantly: I'm probably the only person from the American embassy who ever saw the Kochis close-up. I can sleep tomorrow.

But when I looked at Dr. Stiglitz, spread out on the floor by the pillar, it became impossible to fight sleep any longer. I dropped on the hard-packed earth and almost immediately lost consciousness. My last memory was of Racha throwing a shawl over me.

I awoke in darkness and my first thought was: Good! If the rescue party hasn't made it by now, they won't come till tomorrow. I can stay with the Kochis tonight. The big room was filled with the smell of cooking, for Zulfiqar had ordered a substantial fire, around which many were working. Then I became aware of someone sitting beside me, and it was Mira in her red skirt, and when I stirred she said in Pashto, "Zulfiqar told me to keep the children away." Then in broken English she said, "Ellen tell me English few words." She spoke in a lilting, pleasant voice that sounded as if it belonged to a younger girl, and she had a gamin smile. When I reached out to inspect her attractive pigtails, which no other Kochis wore, she smiled with pride and explained, "Ellen fix my hair American way." She pronounced Ellen's name as her father did, in two gentle syllables.

In Pashto I asked, "Does Ellen work in the camp?"

"All work," she replied in English, followed by Pashto: "Have you come to take Ellen away?"

"I wanted to, but she won't come."

"I am so glad."

"Who told you I was going to take her away?"

"We've always known she would leave some day," Mira replied. "Look how she works."

Ellen, not knowing that I was awake, was busy at the fire, the antagonisms of her letter lost in work. Zulfiqar had killed a sheep in honor of the ferangi and it was roasting, with Ellen in charge to see that it didn't burn. From time to time she stuck a long fork into the flanks and tasted it, smacking her lips as she did so. Children stayed close to the fire, begging her for stray pieces of mutton, as if she were their mother, while against the wall lounged Kochi men, waiting silently for the unscheduled feast. Other women were preparing pilau in stone vessels, while Dr. Stiglitz and Zulfiqar were opening K-rations, whose tops were promptly licked clean by other children. Except for the American cans, it was a scene that dated back to the beginning of man on the plains of Central Asia.

"We eat!" Zulfiqar announced, and it was exciting to watch Ellen, relaxed and motherly, standing by the roasted sheep and passing out portions as if she had done so all her life. From time to time, with greasy hands, she brushed her blond hair back from her moist face, appearing as feminine as any woman I had ever seen, and I recalled her words from the destroyed letter: *I am happy, healthy and alive.* Clearly she was, and when it came time to serve me she smiled as she gave me a chunk of well-browned meat.

"Be sure to try the nan," she advised, as I helped myself to pilau.

Mira led me to a rug where the leaders were sitting, and I found a place across from Dr. Stiglitz, beside whom Ellen would sit. Later, when I tasted the nan Ellen asked, "Delicious, eh?" I replied that it had a nut-like flavor and she explained in English that it had been baked directly over dried camel dung. "Can't you taste it?" she pressed, and I

(285)

could. In Pashto she said, "It is of the earth. It is of our life."

Zulfiqar nodded and said, "The sheep you're eating . . . we raised."

Later I told Zulfiqar, "Ellen wrote the letter to her parents, but tore it up." Ellen added, "Zulfiqar understands. I can't explain Dorset to him, nor him to Dorset."

The big Kochi chieftain said, "You write, Millair."

"I will . . . tomorrow."

My mention of this word evoked a sadness, and at our rug nothing was said; each looked at the other with a sense of strangeness. Mira broke the spell: "What will you tell her parents?"

"What should I tell them?" I asked the group, and to my surprise it was Racha who spoke.

"Tell them," Zulfiqar's wife said, "that now we head for the Oxus and in the winter back to the Jhelum. We live between the rivers."

"But don't call it the Oxus in your letter," Ellen warned. "They'll go crazy looking for it on their maps. Correct name's the Amu Darya . . . about a thousand miles from the Jhelum . . . and we make the round trip each year."

"Two thousand miles?"

"Each year."

"You ride the camels?" I asked.

This occasioned great laughter and Ellen explained, "Only the babies ride camels. The rest of us . . . we walk." She indicated Zulfiqar: "He has a horse, of course, but he must ride back and forth watching the animals."

"Do you mind the walking?" I asked.

Ellen indicated her legs tucked beneath the black skirt. "They get very strong," she assured me.

"How long has your clan been making this trip to the Jhelum?" I asked, and Ellen consulted Zulfiqar.

"There is no memory," he replied.

"Where exactly is the Jhelum?" I asked.

"Far over the border in India," was Zulfiqar's answer, which caused me to burst into laughter.

The big Kochi looked at me quizzically and I explained, "At a meeting in the American embassy we were trying to guess where she might be." I indicated Ellen, who said in English, "I'll bet you were." Quickly she translated the joke into Pashto, and the group laughed.

"And this important officer said"—I imitated Richardson's pipe-puffing, self-assured style—"'The chances of an American girl's entering India without being noticed are just not measurable.'"

Zulfiqar chuckled. "The British! A million of us pass back and forth each year and no one knows where we go or how we feed ourselves."

Ellen added, "We're the wanderers who make fools of petty nations."

"Where are you headed now?" I asked.

"Musa Darul, Daulat Deh . . . in twenty-five days, Kabul. Bamian, Qabir . . ." Then he added a name that excited my imagination, for I had known it from boyhood days: Balkh, in ages past the greatest name in Central Asia.

"Balkh!" I said, and for a moment I daydreamed of how it would be to visit Balkh, but my fantasy was broken by Ellen, whose unpredictable behavior I was about to witness for the first time. Because our argument over the letter had become acrimonious, I expected her to be resentful, but to my surprise, and for reasons I could not decipher, she said quietly, "We go right to Kabul." Zulfiqar nodded, and from something in the way he acted or from some nuance in Ellen's speech, I received the impression that I might be welcomed on the march to Kabul. I leaned forward to broach the matter and Mira did the same, as if she were anticipating hopefully my reaction to one of the most tenuous invitations ever extended.

"You go right to Kabul?" I repeated. No one spoke.

Then Zulfiqar said quietly, "You're young. They'll send soldiers to fetch the broken jeep."

I turned to consult Dr. Stiglitz, whom I had continued to rebuff, and he said in English, hoping to win back my approval, "He's right, Herr Miller. You should see the mountain passes. I'll stay with the jeep."

Ellen contradicted: "You must come too, Doctor. We could use you in the caravan."

Zulfiqar leaned back and surveyed the ceiling, then asked Racha, "Could we use such a doctor at Qabir?" Racha studied the German and nodded, whereupon Zulfiqar warned, "We won't reach Qabir for many weeks. Will you join us?"

Dr. Stiglitz licked his lips and replied weakly, "Yes."

At this, Zulfiqar ended consultation with the women. "You two," he demanded of the ferangi, "how much money can you share with us?" I had two hundred dollars Afghan and Stiglitz much less, but he pointed out, "The Americans owe me money. When you pass Kandahar on the way back this autumn . . ." Zulfiqar reached out and gripped the doctor's hand.

But before the agreement was sealed I felt, for some reason I could not have explained, that it was my duty to warn Stiglitz of the risk he was taking. I led him away from the table and said, "With me it's simple. If Verbruggen gets mad, I'm sent home. I'll gamble, because from something he said I think he'll understand. But with you, Doctor, if you antagonize the Afghan government . . ."

"I'm a sick man, Herr Miller," he said weakly. "You know how sick I am. Unless I can find a rebirth . . ."

"You could be thrown out of the country," I warned. "You know what that would mean."

"Unless I can purify myself . . ."

"You're placing a great burden on the Kochis," I pointed out.

"Zulfiqar knows that," he argued. "He will use me as I will use him."

"I wonder what he meant, Could we use him at Qabir?"

"I don't know," the German replied. "But I must make this trip. It will be my salvation." And we rejoined the others.

As we did so, Mira came to me and said, in the dying light of the fire, "The Kochis would like you to join us, Miller." Then in English she added, "I like it too."

"I'm going to," I said.

We sat as a group by the embers and I repeated the story of the pillar, to which Ellen responded, "That's no surprise. One more outrage in a long series." Zulfiqar inspected the exposed skull and others satisfied themselves that bodies were immured in the pillar, but no one seemed perturbed.

At bedtime I had my first doubts: Suppose Nazrullah arrives with the rescue party? I'd have to go with them. Suppose the ambassador blows his stack when he gets back from Hong Kong? This could finish me with the State Department. Suppose Shah Khan makes an official protest? I'd be packed out like the two Marines. Then I heard Zulfiqar's powerful voice announcing, "We will move forward at four in the morning." Somehow this set my mind at rest. Nazrullah was not going to intercept me, and once I started north with the Kochis, it didn't matter what the ambassador and Shah Khan thought. They couldn't do a damned thing about it till I reached Kabul.

I was awakened by the fearful clatter of Kochis preparing to launch their caravan for another day. Protesting camels were loaded with trade stuffs. Black tents were struck and folded. Animals in the courtyard were herded onto the trail, and children were assigned tasks to which they attended promptly to avoid stout blows from Zulfiqar. If I had ever thought of nomads as lazy, such ideas were dispelled that morning.

As we were about to leave the serai I recalled how careful Nazrullah had been to post messages which would explain to others where he had been and what he had accomplished, and it occurred to me that I ought to extend him the same courtesy, so I scribbled a brief note stating simply that I had found his wife in good health and that I was hiking to Kabul with a caravan of Kochis. Would he advise our ambassador? "That'll give the old man something to chew on when he gets back," I chuckled, but when I told Zulfiqar what I was about to do he went suddenly pale—I mean he turned almost white—and ordered me to stay where I was while he went to consult the leaders. Sometime later he returned, badly shaken, and asked me to redraft the note omitting any reference to Kochis. I did so, and he asked Ellen to read it, but she could scarcely keep from laughing. She said cryptically, "It's accomplished its purpose," but he asked for further minor changes and at last I carried it with a bit of string to the jeep, where I tied it to the steering wheel.

In darkness we started our journey north, an ageless caravan heading across an ageless land. In the lead, with checkered vest and French overcoat, rode Zulfiqar on his brown horse, complete with dagger, German rifle and leather bandoleer. On the camels rode several infants and one sick woman in her late fifties. The rest walked, slowly, comfortably, tending the sheep or keeping the ninety-one camels in line. Donkeys burdened with panniers chugged along, and behind them marched Ellen Jaspar, wearing stout army-type shoes, and Mira, in sandals.

The busiest person in line was jagged-eyed Maftoon, flapping back and forth along his string of camels, checking the ugly beasts to be sure their burdens were riding properly. I was to discover that during each day's hike, some one of the camels was outraged at Maftoon and made his frenzied life miserable: the ugly beast would not rise, would not lie down, would stray from the caravan, would fight and gurgle and protest. It was amusing to watch Maftoon as he tried to keep his camels in line.

At dawn the sun made Ellen's blond hair shine like gold, and she knew she was a beauty among the dark Kochis, for she carried herself with dignity. She had developed a healthy stride and her broad shoulders swung in the morning sunlight; but she was not alone in her beauty, for beside her with matching stride and jet-black hair hiked Mira, daughter of the chief and a notable person in her own right. She sensed instinctively when I watched her, and this pleased her, for occasionally I would catch her whispering to Ellen and pointing at me.

A day's trip was about fourteen miles. Except in the desert, where all travel had to be at night, we walked from pre-dawn till about noon, stopping at predetermined spots to which the Kochis had been returning for years, and this pitching and striking of tents became the dominant beat of the day's rhythm. I volunteered to help with the camels, for the preposterous brown beasts continued to fascinate me, and I often sat for hours watching them chew, with flopping jaws that seemed to lack all terminal attachments.

Once, when I was observing the frowsy old female who had attacked Maftoon, it occurred to me that the forlorn beast with the droopy eyes looked exactly like my Aunt Rebecca in Boston. I could hear her whining as I left for Afghanistan, "Mark, be careful. Find yourself a nice Jewish girl." Like the camel, Aunt Rebecca uncovered an endless supply of things to complain about, her eyes were jaundiced, and she chewed sideways. If she had had a coat of hair, I'm sure it would have been as bedraggled as the camel's. It was uncanny how much alike they were, and I was fond of them both. I started calling the camel "Aunt Becky," and she responded in a way that infuriated Maftoon. She would nip at him, bump him, cry bitterly when he approached her, then turn to me and be as docile as an indulgent old woman. I made her my special charge and often hiked beside her during the long marches.

My legs grew strong. I acquired a good tan and my sleep was unbroken. My appetite was unbelievable and I had never felt better. I thought: No wonder Ellen joined the Kochis.

But any illusions I had about the nomads as noble savages were dispelled on the sixth day, when we reached the outskirts of the little bazaar town of Musa Darul, for as soon as we struck camp six Kochis and four camels, including Aunt Becky, headed for town and in due course returned with an unprecedented supply of melons, meats, shoes and other necessities. That day we had a choice lunch and all would have been well, except that in mid-afternoon Dr. Stiglitz approached me while I was talking with Mira, and pleaded in a begging manner: "I'm hungry for tobacco. This empty pipe drives me crazy. When you mail your report to Kabul, could you get me a little at the bazaar? I have no money." I replied that after my nap I would see what could be done.

I mailed my report to the embassy, then wan-

dered through the bazaar, seeking parcels of tobacco, and an old Afghan said, "I know I had some
right here, but I must have misplaced it," and I
was about to leave empty-handed when I was ov-
ertaken by a thin, ingratiating Afghan who spoke a
little English.

"Sahib, you got car?"

In Pashto I replied that I did not, whereupon the
salesman assured me, "I have a bargain you can't
resist, sahib. You owe it to yourself."

"What is it?"

"Wait till you see," he whispered, taking my arm
and leading me to the stall of an accomplice. There
amid karakul caps and fabrics from India, were
six relatively new automobile tires. "Quite something, eh?" he asked admiringly.

I was startled by the tires. How could they have
reached Musa Dural? Then off to one side I spotted a jeep carburetor, an oil filter, a jack, a complete set of tools and practically everything else
that could be removed from a jeep frame. There
was even a steering wheel, to which was attached
my letter to Nazrullah.

"Where'd you get these?" I asked.

"Just came in this afternoon," he said happily.
"From Russia."

"You've got a bargain here," I assured him, as
I ticked off some twenty separate items which I
knew were going to be charged against my salary
in Kabul. "But you may have to wait some time for
a customer," I warned him.

He laughed and said, "Five weeks, six weeks. If
nobody wants them, we'll ship it all to Kabul." I

winced as I thought of myself wandering through that bazaar, buying back these useful items.

"You send them to Kabul," I said with resignation. "Somebody'll be sure to need them."

I stormed back to camp and the first person I met was Ellen Jaspar. "These damned crooks!" I bellowed. "They invited me on this trip solely to steal my jeep . . . piece by piece."

Ellen tried to control her laughter but couldn't. "What did you think they wanted, your charm?" she chided.

"Did you know what they were up to?" I asked in outrage.

"Didn't you?" she countered. "Remember the panic you caused when you said you were tying the note to the steering wheel? Didn't you see me laughing at Zulfiqar, who tricked you to stay inside? Miller, when you started for the jeep, the steering wheel was already packed . . . on Aunt Becky."

I felt humiliated. "You mean they stole my jeep and hid it on my own camel?"

"Miller, you should have seen those Kochis unpacking the wheels off Aunt Becky and propping them back onto the jeep until you tied the letter to the wheel."

"It's going to cost me a month's salary," I said ruefully.

"That's cheap, for a trip like this. And don't protest to Zulfiqar. Strictly speaking, what he did was a breach of honor and he's ashamed. No man should be robbed in a caravanserai."

I was about to raise hell when Mira came in to

hand me something. It was three packs of smoking tobacco. "I got them at the bazaar . . . for doctor."

I looked at Ellen and asked, "How did she get them at the bazaar? She has no money."

Ellen replied, "Mira is very quick."

12

I was deflated by my discovery that the Kochis had invited me to Kabul merely to steal the wheels off my jeep, but I soon forgot my irritation. For one thing, after Musa Darul the terrain became more interesting, since we were heading up the Helmand valley, which would ultimately deposit us near Kabul, a valley that few foreigners had seen. It lay west of the barren plains of Ghazni and east of the towering Koh-i-Baba mountains. No roads traversed it and for days we saw no villages and often only the barest of trails.

As we hiked, I grew to appreciate Nazrullah's complaint about the goats of Asia, for weeks passed and we saw not a single tree in what seemed otherwise almost virgin territory. Once great forests had covered these hills; there were historical records of that fact; but slowly the goats and the greed of men had denuded even the remote plateaus, leaving only rocky bleakness. I often wondered how our sheep existed as they plodded from one barren pasture to the next, but like the hungry camels, they usually found something.

In our caravan there were about two hundred Kochis, and on the march we were strung out over several miles, with camels and sheep predominant, so it was Zulfiqar's responsibility, as inheritor of this clan, to ride constantly back and forth, supervising our progress. He offered a striking appearance: tall and dark, with heavy mustaches, and a rifle to maintain his authority. On the trail he wore a white turban, but his conspicuous traits were his taciturnity and his smile. He smiled because he knew that keeping his people contented was half the battle; he kept his mouth shut to cultivate the legend that he knew more than his followers.

When the Kochis had served me roast sheep at the caravanserai, I did not appreciate how special the meal was, for the nomads ate poorly. At breakfast we had hot tea and a slab of nan, on which we hiked for twelve or fourteen miles, after which we had a meager helping of pilau lacking meat. In the evening we had curds and a little nan with some shreds of meat, if any was available. We lived close to the poverty level and seemed to thrive on it, but the children were perpetually hungry. I worried about this until Ellen pointed out, "They don't have protruding bellies. They're wonderful specimens," and I had to agree that what little they got nourished them, but I also noticed they were starved for fat and would avidly lick up any scraps, even if they had fallen to the ground.

Three aspects of nomad life distressed me: the Kochis were dirty; they were unkempt; and they made no attempt to develop intellectual interests. The wild free life of the wanderer left much to be desired.

The baggy trousers and flapping white shirts of the Kochi men were rarely clean, while the felt skirts of the women were apt to be streaked with dirt and tangled with briars, which they ignored. They washed infrequently, but I must admit that the extreme dryness of the air prevented offensive odors from accumulating. In my own case, with the humidity at two or three I could wear a shirt for more than a week because nothing could happen to it except a downright accident: there was no soot to soil the cloth and it was anatomically impossible for perspiration to collect. The minute it appeared it evaporated. I suspected that many Kochi garments were worn for months at a time without washing; only thus could they have become as dirty as they did.

The slovenliness of the Kochis was principally shown in the way they managed their hair. Women rarely combed theirs and men wore shoulder-length bobs which flapped with any vigorous movement. Their heads, men's and women's alike, were actually matted and probably worse. I often thought how much fun it would be to run the whole clan through a barber shop some afternoon to see what surprises would turn up.

As for the life of the mind, the speculation about good and evil, the judgment of past and future, there was none. Since they could neither read nor write, and since there was no radio, conversation was limited to the chance events of the caravan: the birth of sheep, the straying of a camel, the long march, outwitting the border guards and who stole what at the last bazaar. Days sped into months and months into years without any extension of the group intellect. It may be that the Kochis were supremely happy in their rough adaptation to nature; I often found them boring, and I had the ungenerous suspicion that Ellen Jaspar found comfort in the caravan partly because against their illiteracy she could stand out as a person with desirable skills. In any event, I noticed how often she came to Stiglitz or me to escape the dullness of the Kochis and to talk philosophically with an educated person.

There were two exceptions to this tradition of dirtiness, slovenliness and apathy: Zulfiqar and his daughter Mira were alert mentally and far above average in cleanliness, largely due to Ellen, who cut Zulfiqar's hair and tended his clothes. As to Mira, she kept herself well groomed partly because Ellen gave her instruction and partly because she mimicked whatever Ellen did in the way of cleanliness or personal adornment.

She owned several changes of costume: red dress, blue dress, gray felt dress; blue, red, white, green blouses; filmy gray, brown and white turbans; and an extra pair of sandals that she wore only when heading for some village bazaar off the caravan trail. Best of all, she had acquired a stout comb with which she managed her black hair and a washrag which she applied to her clear and even skin. Her face was brown and she wore no makeup, but her eyes and brows were so black that in comparison her face looked more creamy white than brown.

On the trail I often walked with Mira, whose job it was to help mind the sheep, which represented a large proportion of the Kochi wealth, and to swing along beside her as she chattered in Pashto or broken English was delightful. I tried repeatedly to fathom her narrow world and soon discovered that she knew nothing of history or other school subjects and had no desire to learn. But she did not share the apathy of the other Kochis, for she knew much about Central Asia and in all matters affecting the Kochis was an expert. Skilled in trading, witty in negotiation, and a master in the care of animals, she confessed a major sorrow: her clan had but one horse, and it was assigned to Zulfiqar.

"A man like you should not walk with the rest of us," she told me. "In your own country you would be a chief." I asked her not to feel sorry for me and reminded her that I did have a jeep, which in some ways was better than a horse. She considered this for a moment, then concluded, "Where we go a horse is better."

"Don't worry. I like to walk."

"A chief ought to have his own horse. Look at my father! Would he be so powerful without a horse?"

But if there were disappointments in nomad life there were also congenial surprises and none was more appealing than Maftoon, the cockeyed cameleer. We had marched five days toward Musa Darul when I happened to see a camel halted for no reason that I could ascertain. I therefore started across the meadowland to retrieve the beast when I saw, crouched down between her hind legs, Maftoon, with turban awry, mouth open, and on his face an expression of almost heavenly bliss. With his right hand on the camel's teat, he was squirting a flow of milk directly from the udder into his mouth, drinking at the rate of about a quart a minute.

"What the hell are you doing, Maftoon?" I shouted.

"Hungry," he said, halting the flow of milk and looking at me with his good eye.

"Get up! That milk's for the babies." He made no effort to leave his lunch, so I added, "And by the way, Maftoon, I've found out why Aunt Becky tries to bite you so much. You abuse her."

The little man stayed crouched between the camel's legs and looked at me with an expression of sorrow and disgust. "I abuse that beast?" he stammered.

"Yes!" I insisted. "I've listened to you the last three mornings. It's a wonder she didn't gum your arm again."

"You listened . . . to what?"

"To Aunt Becky, complaining of the way you overload her, mistreat her. Damn it all, Maftoon, get away from that camel and listen to me."

Reluctantly the little Kochi left his meal, stood up with his turban reaching his knees, and to my surprise laughed at me. "Tomorrow," he said, "you'll load Aunt Becky." With that he left.

Next morning I was routed out of bed by the little cameleer and taken to where his beasts were being loaded. Aunt Becky, one of the largest animals we had, still rested on the thick callus built up on her chest, her pedestal it was called, and she was loath to leave it, but when she saw that I was to load her, and not her enemy Maftoon, she seemed as happy as a mournful, droopy-eyed, coat-shedding camel could; but as soon as I placed the first blanket on her—it must have weighed about three-quarters of a pound—she let out a sob that would have broken the heart of Nero. It was almost human, a wail of protest against the harshness of the world. I slapped her muzzle, and placed on the blanket a few items that she could hardly have felt, and her groans increased to the point of despair. She really sounded like my own Aunt Becky back in Boston, complaining of the Irish politicians, the Italian grocers, the Jewish merchants, and the ingratitude of her family. "How can I possibly bear this awful burden?" Becky the camel sobbed. No matter what I put on her back, the groans increased, and when she was burdened much more lightly than she had been when running over the desert with my jeep, she struggled to her ungainly feet as if this were her last day on earth; for me she would make that extra little effort and then collapse in a heap before my eyes. I gave her a slap and felt more kindly toward Maftoon. At eleven that morning Aunt Becky was striding along the trail with as much joy as a camel ever exhibits and gave me a pleasant nuzzle as I went past.

The next morning Maftoon summoned me again, and this time as soon as I approached Aunt Becky she became apprehensive that I was about to torture her once more, so I placed on her broad, hairy back a handkerchief. It had barely touched her when she began to rage in protest: "Oh, this is more than a poor camel can bear!" she seemed to say. A stranger listening from a distance would have sworn that I was pushing hot swords into her great bulk, and this kept up all during the loading; so on the third morning I said to Maftoon, "Let's see how much this ugly beast can carry." And this day we loaded her down with well over eight hundred pounds. Her protests were exactly the same; her reluctance to rise identical; and her loping, carefree performance on the trail no different from before. In fact, once we got her started, it was hard to stop her. She loved the heft of the burden and again nuzzled me as I went by. After this indoctrination I decided to leave the camels to Maftoon, and it was well that I did, for when it came time to unload Aunt Becky her dim brain remembered that today she had been mistreated, and she started mauling Maftoon. Luckily he escaped, but soon I saw him naked before the camel while she attacked his clothes. When he was dressed he warned me, "Miller Sahib! You better undress!"

I laughed at the suggestion, but as I approached the huge camel she started for me. Maftoon interceded and, since he had made his peace, saved me. Prudently I undressed and stood by while Aunt Becky kicked the very devil out of my clothes. She bit them, spat on them, and even urinated a little. The next morning we were friends again.

Caravan life provided moments of pride and arrogance: as dawn was breaking we would reach some rise in the trail from which we could look down upon a sleeping village, where dogs would spot us and begin to bark. A few men would appear to see what had agitated the dogs and, seeing the Kochis coming to town, would signal their neighbors, whereupon the villagers would rush about in a frenzy, moving indoors anything that might be stolen. Women in their chaderies would dash out to grab their children lest they be kidnaped, and families would remain cautiously by

doorways as women stared through veils waiting
for the approaching nomads. An excited hush
would fall over the village, at whose outskirts the
first Kochi camels were already sniffing.

At such entries Zulfiqar rode at the head of the
column, a handsome figure with his rifle slung inso-
lently across his pommel. He affected not to see the
frightened families and ignored the pestilent dogs.
Behind him came the lumbering camels, with Aunt
Becky thrusting her big, inquisitive face from side
to side, followed by a large group of Kochi men;
then the sheep and most of the women; finally the
donkeys, the children, and the rear guard of armed
men. It was an impressive caravan when seen in
the close confines of a village street, but what outraged the villagers, men and women alike, was the
brazen manner in which our nomad women
marched handsomely forward with no chaderi.

When Zulfiqar's clan moved through a village we
had with us three additional elements for arousing
suspicion and disgust: there was Ellen Jaspar, obviously not a Kochi; there was Dr. Stiglitz, and
what was he doing in such a motley group; and
there was the young American who marched with
the beautiful nomad girl in the red dress.

Several times infuriated mountain mullahs
dashed among us to spit at Ellen as they had done
at Kandahar, but she had since learned to ward
them off indulgently. She understood the moral
and mental pressures these fanatics were experi-
encing in a changing world and she wished to do
nothing that would exasperate them, but if Zulfiqar
saw them coming, he patiently cut them off with
his horse, whereupon the long-robed mullahs

would back against some mud-walled house and curse our passing.

When the villagers tried to abuse Stiglitz or me they got a sharp surprise: we swore at them in Pashto, claimed to be light-skinned Kochis, and warned them to mind their own business. Sometimes they stopped dead and stared at us, whereupon we laughed and they laughed. Braver men among them would run beside us, asking if we were ferangi, and at such times we would confess that we were German and American, and the animosity would vanish. Occasionally some young man in the village who wanted to comprehend his world would march with us for miles, even to our camp, asking a hundred questions. Such men became our friends, and even if I had not mailed my report to Kabul, these inquisitive men would have got the message to our ambassador, by word of mouth from one village to the next until it crossed Afghanistan. It was such a rumor that had reached Shah Khan in Kabul: "Traveling with the Kochis is a blond ferangi."

We had reached the halfway spot on our march to Kabul when we came upon an especially pathetic village, where I had a chance to see for myself the gentler side of Ellen Jaspar's honest concern with human problems. It was not yet dawn as we moved down the main street, glaring back at frightened faces which peered at us through darkness, and Ellen whispered, "It does my heart good to compare these suspicious villagers with our free nomads."

"I agree. I get a positive bang out of marching through a village like this."

"Just think!" she cried with real intellectual excitement. "In a few years Afghanistan will destroy prisons like this"—she indicated the tight-barred houses—"and the country will go back to the ancient freedom of the caravan."

I should have allowed the subject to drop, but I was struck by a fundamental contradiction in her thinking: the idea that freedom could be preserved only by turning back the clock. I could hear her arguing with Nazrullah at the site of the future dam: *It's a shame that the river must lose its freedom,* refusing to realize that only when the river was harnessed and used could Afghanistan know the real freedom of release from poverty. Therefore I said, "I'm afraid you have it backwards, Ellen. Afghanistan will never gain a single freedom by reverting to the caravan. It will save itself by generating true freedom in the villages."

"How?" she asked with some contempt.

"Roads, books, Nazrullah's electricity."

"Oh, Miller!" she cried passionately. "You misunderstand history and the nature of man. We are born free, like the nomads. But step by step we insist upon crawling into little prisons on little streets in mean little villages. We must destroy these prisons and restore the nomad spirit."

"I'm sorry, Ellen. What you want is impossible. What we must do is go into the villages and rebuild them on a basis of freedom. We must go forward. We can't go back."

"But in Pennsylvania, my father is the village. In Afghanistan these surly people are the village. Will books and electricity cure my father . . . or these clods?"

"Only books and electricity can do it."

She stopped in the middle of the road, pressed her right hand to her mouth, and weighed my arguments. Light from one of the houses, reflecting on her bracelets, flashed across her lovely face. "Miller," she whispered generously, "in part you're right, but you forget that men like my father . . ."

I was not allowed to hear her rebuttal, for out of the shadows darted a pretty little girl of nine or ten, less fearful than her elders. Running through the darkness, she caught Ellen's hand and cried in Pashto, "Your bracelets are beautiful." With a gesture of instinctive warmth, Ellen caught the child, swung her in the air, kissed her, and held her in her left arm while she took off one of her bracelets to give the child.

It was a moment I cannot forget. There in an alien street, beset by enmity, Ellen cradled the child in timeless pose: a lovely young mother holding in the darkness a child who intuitively trusted her; and I was forced to recall Karima as she said: *Ellen knew that I could have children and apparently she couldn't. Dr. Stiglitz will confirm that.* I wondered if this were true, and if so, did it account for her essential barrenness of spirit?

My reflections were shattered by the agonizing shriek of the child's mother, who burst upon us screaming, "The Kochis have stolen my child!"

This was a signal for villagers, long trained to repulse such thefts, to rush at us from many sides, and there was fighting. But what stunned me was the arrival of six or eight determined women in chaderies, moving swiftly through the darkness like avenging furies. Their shadowy forms engulfed

Ellen as they tore at her hair, her clothes, her face. One thin figure in a gray chaderi swept in like a ferret and grabbed the child. Seeing that the little girl held a contaminated bracelet, the thin figure tore it from the child's hands and threw it back at Ellen.

"Don't steal our children!" a voice of passion warned. The avengers withdrew, but from the shadows came a gaunt, bearded man rushing belatedly to the brawl and hissing hatred.

"Whores! Whores!" he shouted, maneuvering like a robed ghost in his efforts to spit at Ellen.

Zulfiqar had seen the mullah coming and had deftly swung his horse across the man's trajectory to drive him away. The mullah followed at a distance, screaming impotently; and thus we left the frightened villagers, who remained in excited groups, congratulating each other on having once more thwarted the Kochi kidnapers.

Zulfiqar, concerned over Ellen's welfare, dismounted to assure himself that all was well, and she buried her head in his shoulder, sniffling, "All I wanted to do was give the little girl a bracelet."

"How did it start?" the big Kochi asked indulgently.

"Miller and I were having a peaceful argument . . ."

"About what?"

"I claimed that originally Afghanistan knew the freedom of the caravan, but that willfully the people put themselves in these village prisons under the rule of mullahs."

"You're right about the past."

"Miller claimed that we can never go back to the

caravan. That we will know freedom only when the villages have books and roads and electricity."

"He's right about the future," and before Ellen could protest the decision, he leaped upon his horse to lead our caravan from the niggardly village, but then he galloped back to us and cried, "Some day all of us will live in villages like this. But they will be better villages." And he was gone.

The very next morning I had poetic confirmation that Zulfiqar's vision of the future was more likely than Ellen's, for in the early hours when light was just beginning to break across the peaks of the Koh-i-Baba, we sighted a village where dogs were silent, and we crept upon it unawares and were well inside the confines before we were discovered —great camels lumbering down the main road, peering into windows as the villagers were rising— and at one corner I saw a house lit with candles, and it seemed, there in the shadow of the mountains, like all the warm, homely refuges of the world. It was a small segment of space, walled in against the wandering nomads and the camels. It was one man's home. Not even the soaring freedom of the Kochi tents, pitched beside torrents in the mountain passes, could equal the security of that chance home we saw in the half-darkness of dawn. The village people knew something the nomads would never know, a kind of spiritual freedom, and if they were forced to pay a terrible price for it, perhaps that was their choice.

To my surprise, as I brooded on these matters I looked up to see Zulfiqar, on his brown horse, staring at me and the house, and I think he was remembering our discussion of the morning before, and deciding anew that he and I were right; but a dog began barking, the villagers poured out, and the old antagonism between nomad and villager was resumed.

At first I hadn't realized why the villagers were so apprehensive about locking things up as our caravan approached, but after I had seen flashing Mira at work I understood their antagonism. Whenever we made camp after transiting a village I found that she had acquired some new piece of clothing, or a farm tool, or a kitchen utensil. Ellen once said, "The only thing that child hasn't stolen is a bed. You watch! If somebody leaves a door open some day . . ."

At one camp I caught Mira with a new saw and asked her, "Why do you steal from the villagers?"

"When we march through," she replied, "they look at me with hate and I look right back at them the same way." Then she added, "But do you notice how the men follow me so hungrily with their eyes? They'd like to join the Kochis . . . for one night. I could spit at them!"

Our clan had ten large black tents, but many of the Kochis preferred sleeping on blankets in the open. Zulfiqar, his wife Racha, Ellen and Mira occupied one of the smaller tents, notable because it had an awning held up by two additional poles forming a kind of porch where rugs were thrown and where the camp's social life took place. In the late afternoons, when the animals were at ease, Zulfiqar would sit cross-legged between Racha and Ellen, discussing matters with his people. I often joined them and thus formed the foundation for the friendship which developed between the Kochi leader and me.

He asked me many questions, but I learned more than I taught. The Kochis were Muslims who ignored the tyranny of the mullahs but who held Mecca in as deep regard as any Sunni. As we discussed Islam, with its strong reliance upon nature and a powerful God who motivated all natural things, I better understood how Ellen and Dr. Stiglitz had been able to embrace this religion. One afternoon as we sat under the awning, Ellen said, "I could never explain my apostasy to my parents, and that's the real reason why I can't write to them. You see, I was raised to believe that God personally hovered like an unseen helicopter just above the steeple of the Presbyterian Church on Adams street in Dorset, Pennsylvania"—I had remarked earlier how she loved to reel off that rubric, as if names alone symbolized the focus of her rebellion—"and although He was free to keep a weather eye on the Lutheran church down the street, His real responsibility was our congregation. We were the true religion. All else was delusion. I think that if my parents had only once, while I was growing up, intimated that God might also be personally worried about the Jews, I would still be in Dorset. For that would have made sense."

At the end of this rather protracted speech Zulfiqar asked, "Do all American women talk so much?" I said yes and he shrugged his shoulders the way scar-eyed Maftoon did when he couldn't comprehend the behavior of a camel.

The figure of speech Ellen had used disturbed me. Had she spoken with spurious concern for the

Jews because Stiglitz had warned her that I was one? In English I asked, "Did Stiglitz tell you I was a Jew?"

"You are?" she shouted in real delight. "Zulfiqar! Miller is a Jew!"

The big leader, his bandoleer and rifle beside him on the rug, leaned forward to inspect me. "You Jewish?" I nodded and he burst into laughter.

Ellen said in Pashto, "You should hear what this big fool believes about Jews!"

Again Zulfiqar laughed, attracting other nomads, who gathered to see what was happening. He stood beside me and compared his large Semitic nose to my small Nordic one. "I'm the real Jew!" he shouted, and other Kochis stepped up to compare their faces with mine. A long discussion followed, at the end of which Zulfiqar asked, "Millair, are Jews really as avaricious as we say?"

I thought a moment, smiled at Ellen and replied, "Let me put it this way. Zulfiqar, if you parked your jeep near a bunch of Jews . . . they'd steal the tires while you weren't looking."

It took some moments for the boldness of my reply to sink in, and some of the lesser Kochis caught on before Zulfiqar. They were loath to react until he had set the pattern, but they obviously relished my gall. Then he exploded in rollicking laughter and imitated a steering wheel. "Millair," he laughed, "you scared us when you started for the jeep. We had most of it packed on camels." Then he stopped laughing and looked suspiciously at Ellen. "How did you know about the jeep?"

"In the bazaar at Musa Darul . . . they tried to sell it back to me." My discovery of their duplicity pleased the Kochis, and from that moment Miller the Jew became blood brother to the Aryan nomads.

But to one obligatory aspect of Kochi life I never did become adjusted. As we marched week after week through the treeless valleys a detail of four women worked at the rear of the caravan, moving back and forth across the landscape, and it was their duty to gather the fresh droppings of the camels, the sheep and the donkeys and with their bare hands to mold the manure into briquettes which were carefully hoarded in the panniers carried by the donkeys; for in a land where there were few trees other fuel had to be found, and dried dung was excellent. It burned slowly, like punk, had a pleasing odor which imparted flavor to food cooked over it, and was light in transportation.

The Kochi children delighted in coming upon dried dung which the sharp-eyed women of some former caravan had overlooked, and it was a kind of game for them to see who would spot the next camel dropping. One day Mira and I were following Aunt Becky, who as usual was straying, when the camel dropped a large deposit which the women would probably miss; so I gritted my teeth, turned my nose away, and scooped up the precious stuff, running it to the panniers, where the women tending the caravan cheered. I was blushing when I returned to Mira, who, when she satisfied herself that no one was spying, threw her arms about me and kissed me for the first time. "You're a real Kochi!" she teased, and thereafter when I went to her father's awning-porch it was to see her and not to talk with him; and we took long walks among the deserted hills.

Two days after our first kiss, we were hiking up a narrow valley where flowers were in bloom and I thought: The Kochis know only two seasons, the best of spring and the best of autumn. I looked at Mira and asked, "You never know winter, do you?"

She surprised me by pointing to the mountains overhead and saying, "It's always ready to pounce on us." And there it hung, the snowline of the Koh-i-Baba, an ominous threat which reminded me of our impending arrival at Kabul, when I would have to leave the caravan.

I think Mira must have sensed my sadness, for she kissed me ardently, but the moment was spoiled by the sharp voice of Ellen, who said, "You'd better join the others, Mira."

When the little nomad left the valley, Ellen said with some asperity, "You be careful what you do with that girl. One day in India a camel attacked her and in rage she nearly killed it. She takes nothing lightly, and remember . . . she is the chieftain's daughter." Then she added, "She's also much smarter than most of the girls I knew in college."

"Why don't you teach her to read?"

"You be careful what you teach her," she warned.

It was after this intrusion that I first began to notice that Ellen was also becoming involved in matters which could lead to dangerous conclusions, and that when she warned me about Mira she was perhaps thinking not of me but of herself. For example, on the trail she most often walked with Dr. Stiglitz, ahead of the camels; and under the canopy, when we gathered in the afternoons, she took her seat beside him. One of the reasons why Ellen sought out Stiglitz was that at Bryn Mawr she had studied German and French and could thus converse with him in four different languages, and they maintained long discussions on philosophical matters.

I wondered if Zulfiqar took umbrage at this, for I had read in many books that men of the desert were subject to ungovernable passions where their women were concerned, and certainly in normal Afghan life the chaderi and the high wall topped by broken glass proved that the books were right; and I began to fear that my affection for Mira might get me involved in these nomad rages; but the more I watched Zulfiqar the more confused I became, for he certainly did not act like the vengeful, romanticized sheik of fiction. On the contrary, when Ellen and Stiglitz were hiking together, Zulfiqar often rode by on his brown horse, kicking its ribs expertly, and he would occasionally stop to talk but more often he continued past, according them his professional smile, and I got the clear impression that instead of being jealous of Stiglitz, he was somewhat relieved to have in the caravan a man who had spare time for arguing with his second woman.

With me the problem was somewhat different, for Mira was his daughter. I was sure that once or twice he had seen us kissing, and he must have noticed how we always sat together at the tent or at meals, yet he treated Mira and me much as he did the others: infrequent conversation, inevitable smile.

On the night before we reached Kabul, the Kochis prepared a farewell feast for me. Maftoon impressed some men who formed a noisy orchestra for nomad dancing and songs from many trails in Asia. I tried to keep away from Mira, for leaving her was proving to be extremely difficult, and several times I caught myself staring at Stiglitz and Ellen, thinking: They're the lucky ones. Together all the way to Balkh.

That night as I crept into my sleeping bag I asked Stiglitz, "Have you told Ellen what you told me . . . at the pillar?"

"I've told her I can't leave Afghanistan."

"Have you told her why?"

"Sooner or later everyone knows everything," he replied. "The timetable of discovery is not significant."

"That's not true. When I discovered your history . . . in the caravanserai . . . I might have killed you."

"It would have been of no consequence," he said fatalistically.

"How do you feel about me now . . . as a Jew?" I asked.

He considered this for some minutes, while the camels moved about behind us, and at first I thought he had fallen asleep. Then he replied in evasive fashion, "I've given up my home, my family . . ."

"You called her your filthy wife," I reminded him.

"I was speaking of my children," he corrected. "They were different. I surrendered everything . . . profession, opera, a city I loved . . . so in a

(317)

sense, Herr Miller, I'm a dead man, and dead men have no further responsibility for passing judgments."

I made no comment to this and he continued, "To the Jews I did terrible things. You're a Jew. Believe it or not, Herr Miller, the two facts are completely unrelated. Toward you as a Jew I have no feeling whatsoever. Toward you as a man . . . I'd like to be your friend, Herr Miller."

"Would you stop calling me Herr Miller?" I asked.

"I'm very thoughtless," he said, reaching out from his sleeping bag to grasp my arm. "Please forgive me," he begged, and a cesspool of bitterness began to drain away.

After a long silence he asked, "Do you remember how our discussion at the pillar started? No, I thought not. You were berating me for not having amputated Pritchard's leg at Chahar. I tried to tell you that there are factors in life which go beyond medical comprehension, and I equated Pritchard's determination to die with Sem Levin's determination to live. The point is this, I'm sick with shame and grief over what I did to Sem Levin, because I acted against his will, but I haven't the slightest regret over the case of John Pritchard, because I acted in furtherance of his will. One way or other he had commanded himself to die."

"I'm beginning to see what you're talking about," I admitted.

"With me it's the same way," he added. "I'm dead. If the Russians hang me it's no matter. They're hanging a dead man. But if I'm allowed to live, I have willed myself to be reborn. When you saw me in Kandahar I was a walking corpse, concerned only with my bottle of beer. Now I shall be a human being."

I asked, "Has Ellen accomplished this?"

"Yes," he confessed. "But don't forget, Miller, when you leave us in Kabul you'll be a living man too." He allowed this to sink in, then asked, "Have you ever made love to a woman?"

"Certainly," I lied, counting some frenzied moments in war as qualifiers.

"Well, leaving this nomad girl is going to be a different experience from what you imagine. I am wondering what you will do after Mira vanishes. What will you do, Miller?"

"I'll go back to the embassy," I said brashly. "Pick up where I left off."

"With the smell of camels haunting you? Don't be stupid." He turned over and went to sleep.

From the caravanserai to Kabul had been a distance of some three hundred and fifty miles, which required twenty-five days of marching, but since we occasionally held camp for two or three days at sites with adequate forage, it was not until the middle of May that we came over a pass and saw below us the sprawling capital whose center was filled by the low mountain. I stood with Mira and explained, "My house is over there . . . to the north of that mountain. Tomorrow I'll be sleeping there."

The nomad girl rejected my prediction and took my face in her hands. She kissed me warmly and whispered, "Oh, no, Miller! Tomorrow night you won't be sleeping there."

Few Kochi caravans ever entered Kabul with the

advance excitement caused by ours, and as soon as we pitched our black tents in the traditional nomad area some miles west and south of the British embassy, we were visited by three important emissaries. First Moheb Khan, trim and polished in a new Chevrolet, drove out to investigate my report that Ellen Jaspar was traveling with the Kochis, and he consulted lengthily with Zulfiqar and Ellen while Mira and I lingered outside the tent trying to eavesdrop. I remember her asking me, "Who is this Moheb Khan?" I explained that he was an important official who could do her father much harm if he was made angry and she agreed: "He does look very important."

I avoided seeing Moheb, because I did not want to talk with him at that moment, dressed as I was in Afghan clothes; but after he had gone, a lesser official reported to see Dr. Stiglitz, and they sat in a corner of our tent conversing in German, so I did not understand what they were saying, but the upshot was that Stiglitz was not to be arrested or sent back to Kandahar.

Now came my turn, for Richardson of Intelligence drove out after lunch at the British embassy, lit his pipe with infuriating care, stroked his mustache and said in his deep voice, "Miller, I'm afraid there's hell to pay over that jeep." He watched the effect on me and added, "Going to cost you . . . say . . . six hundred dollars. Miller, they stole everything but the name in front. Nazrullah had to make two trips across that desert."

I threw myself on his mercy: "It was stupid, and I know it. But I did feel that Verbruggen would understand."

"The ambassador is raising hell," Richardson confided, and I could feel the boom being lowered.

"What's the bad word?" I asked.

"Well, you saved your neck by that report from Musa Darul. We notified Washington and at least the senator from Pennsylvania's mollified. But the girl's parents! Why doesn't she write to them?"

"She has written . . . several times. I sat over her while she did the last one. But there's so much to explain she tears the letters up. I've drafted this letter, which we can send them, and this complete report."

"Good, and I don't think you need worry too much about the ambassador. Washington's rather pleased that you rescued Miss Jaspar."

"Rescued her? She's never been happier in her life."

"You mean she's staying with the Kochis?" Richardson gasped.

I thought: If I try to explain everything . . . Zulfiqar, Stiglitz, Islam . . . he'll get all balled up. So I said, "I didn't rescue her. She rescued me."

"Now what the hell do you mean by that?" he asked huffily, drawing on his pipe.

"I'll explain in the office tomorrow."

"Now wait a minute," he protested. Then he changed his mind and asked quietly, "Could we take a walk?"

"Why not? I've just walked three hundred and fifty miles."

"Don't you ride the camels?" he asked, and I looked at him with scorn.

When we were far from the tents he said, "Maybe you won't be in the office tomorrow."

"They sending me home?" I asked with a sort of sick feeling.

"No. Washington's come up with a peculiar idea." He paused to let the drama sink in, then sucked his pipe and studied me. "You ever heard of Qabir?"

"No." Then I reflected. Where had I heard that name? I corrected myself: "I've heard the name but I forget where."

"It's an important meeting place of the nomads," he said. "Somewhere in the Hindu Kush."

"Where?"

"Doesn't show on the map."

"Did you ask the British? They know these areas."

"They know it only as a name," he said. "Qabir. Qabir. Does it mean anything at all to you?"

Then I remembered. "One night the chief was ticking off the route of the caravan. Musa Darul, Balkh. And he said he'd be able to use Dr. Stiglitz at Qabir."

"In what capacity?"

"He didn't say."

Richardson walked away from me and kicked pebbles for some time. Then he asked bluntly, "Miller, could you manage some way to stay with the Kochis till they get to Qabir?"

"Why?"

"It's damned important that our side have someone who's been there. We've no information about it except that every summer the nomads gather there, and we think that Russians, Chinese, Tajiks, Uzbeks . . . the lot . . ."

"Supposing I could get there, what do you want me to do?"

"Just look. Find out who the Russians send and how they get across the Oxus."

"I'd stand out like a sore thumb," I protested.

"That may be an advantage," he said. "Think you can arrange to stay with the caravan?"

"Possibly," I evaded, trying not to show the joy I felt at the reprieve.

"If you could," he said cautiously, "I think we'd forget about the jeep."

I said, "I'm not keen on Qabir. Sounds dull. But I've always wanted to see Balkh. Can I come in to-night for some fresh gear?"

"No. We don't want you around the embassy. Tell me what you need and I'll get it."

"Some money, a few vitamin pills, some nose drops . . . boy, your nose dries out . . . and some note pads."

"Don't take any notes on Qabir," he warned.

"I haven't said I could get there," I cautioned. "If there is such a place."

Late that afternoon, while Mira was scrounging the Kabul bazaars, Richardson returned with my gear and a batch of mail, and in a gesture unprecedented for him shook my hand warmly and said with feeling, "Miller, do you even dimly comprehend the opportunity you have? For seven years we've been trying to get to Qabir. So have the British. For God's sake, keep your eyes open."

"What did the ambassador say?"

"He said, 'Imagine such a job going to such a squirt.'" Richardson left, and I swore to myself: Somehow or other, I'm getting to Qabir.

I sat at the edge of my tent in the twilight and wondered what trick I could use for staying with the Kochis, and as I pondered the problem I realized that I wasn't much interested in Richardson's Russians but I was keenly concerned about continuing with Mira. With no plans at all, I felt: Something's bound to work out.

I turned to my mail. Girls had replied to my letters, but now I couldn't even remember their faces. A letter from my father sounded as if Mr. Jaspar were arguing incomprehensibly with Ellen, and provincial Boston matters which had once been of significance were now tedious. How could a group of Kochi women gathering camel dung seem more important than my aunts in Boston? How could my adventures with a gang of nomads and a mixed-up girl from Pennsylvania preoccupy my thoughts? More particularly, how could I manage to stay with Mira?

My problem was unexpectedly solved by Zulfiqar. Accompanied by Dr. Stiglitz he came to my tent and said half apologetically, "The doctor has official permission to stay with us. He's coming to Qabir."

"Where's that?" I asked, trying to appear nonchalant.

"Where the nomads meet each summer. In the Hindu Kush."

"Hope you have a good trip," I said to Stiglitz. "Sounds a long way off."

"It is," the German agreed. "But what we wanted to discuss with you . . . we need a lot of medicine."

I put on a serious face and said, "I suppose you could buy what you need in the bazaar."

"Yes . . ." Zulfiqar said, "if we had the money."

"This time I have no jeep," I reminded him.

"But the American officer . . . when he came, did he give you any money?"

"Yes," I replied, and waited.

"We were wondering," Stiglitz proposed. "Would you buy us the medicine if . . ."

"If what?" I asked cautiously.

"If we took you to Balkh with us?" Zulfiqar suggested.

I wasted time so that it would look as if I were judging the proposal, then asked suspiciously, "How much money would you need?"

"About two hundred dollars," Zulfiqar replied.

"I have a hundred and fifty," I offered, unable to control my excitement at having tricked him into doing what I wanted.

"Good!" he cried, and four hours later he and Stiglitz returned to camp with a cache of drugs and medical implements that would have done justice to a small pharmacy. They had been blackmarketed from as far away as Paris and Manila, and in the areas where we would be heading they'd be worth a fortune. "You got a lot with my dollars," I observed.

"For what we want to do we'll need a lot," Zulfiqar said briefly. He advised us to get to sleep promptly, for we were off to the high mountains next morning at four.

Stiglitz, tired from the bargaining at the bazaar, followed his advice, but apparently Zulfiqar himself did not, for before I could fall asleep I heard the clatter of horses' hoofs, and since no one was permitted to ride the brown horse but the leader of the clan, it must have been Zulfiqar. There came a scratching at my tent and a boy of eight or nine slipped in to advise me that I was wanted. Throwing a shawl about me, I went out expecting to meet the Kochi but saw instead the stars and a beautiful white horse that Mira was holding for me.

"It isn't right that you should walk, Miller," she said.

"Where'd you get this?" I asked, dumfounded.

"In Kabul," she said softly. "My present to you."

"But, Mira! Where'd you find the money?"

"I was afraid that if you had to walk all the way to Balkh you might leave us," she whispered. "You require a horse, Miller. An important man like you deserves one."

I was about to protest her extravagance when I looked at the right flank of the beast, and there emblazoned deep was the letter W. I was being handed a white horse branded with a memento of the Wharton School in Philadelphia, and when Moheb Khan discovered the theft I could be arrested. I started to upbraid her for having the horse, but I was halted by a powerful doubt as to just how she might have acquired it. I recalled her keen interest in Moheb Khan. Weakly I asked, "How did you know I was staying with the caravan?"

She replied gently, "For days my father and I have been trying to think of some trick that would keep you with us. Last night he told me, 'Go to sleep, Mira. I'll think of something.'"

I thought of my lost hundred and fifty dollars and asked, "You mean that Zulfiqar was trying to get me to stay with the caravan?"

"Yes," she whispered. "How did he manage it?"

"In a very interesting way," I replied.

Slowly, gently she took my hand and told the little boy that it was now time for him to leave us, and she led me and the white horse far from camp to a spot where that afternoon she had cached a blanket and I noticed for the first time that from somewhere—probably the bazaar in Kabul—she had stolen a bottle of perfume, and in a wild embrace we found each other. For each of us, I discovered, it was the introduction to love, under a full moon on the high plateau of Asia; so that when toward four the next morning we headed back toward camp, I had the most persuasive reason in the world for accompanying the Kochis to Balkh.

※

13

For many centuries there had been a circuitous highway leading from Kabul to the historic Vale of Bamian, where Buddhism had flourished centuries before the birth of Muhammad, and gifted travelers from the age of Alexander to the present had described the rugged beauties of this road; but Kochis avoided it, for they knew a caravan route which climbed directly into the Koh-i-Baba, a route so spectacular, passing as it did through gorges and along cliffs, that its grandeur was reserved for those who traveled in the ancient caravan manner. So far as I know, this road has never been described in books, because only Kochis used it, and they did not write.

The mountains were fifteen and sixteen thousand feet high, forbidding bulwarks whose peaks no man had climbed, and wherever we looked they dominated the view; it seemed unlikely that anyone could penetrate them, let alone a caravan of camels. But under Zulfiqar's experienced guidance we headed for one apparently solid wall after another and somehow each barrier provided us with one lucky escape: sometimes a gorge, sometimes a green valley that opened dramatically to the north.

Now the animals grew fat on abundant grass

and on some days even the camels modified their grumbling. I spent hours watching our fat-tailed sheep, those preposterous beasts that looked not like sheep but like small-headed beetles stuck onto very long legs. They derived their name from an enormous tail, perhaps two feet across and shaped like a thick country frying pan covered with wool and rich with accumulated lanolin. The tail bumped up and down when the sheep walked, a grotesque afterpiece that served the same function as a camel's hump: in good times it stored food which in bad times it fed back to the animal. I was told that the lanolin was not solid but could be moved about with the hands; certainly it could be eaten, as we proved in our pilaus, but now that the tails were at their maximum they made the ugly sheep seem like something an ungifted schoolboy had scratched on a tablet, and as I sat watching the huge bustles bounce up and down I used to speculate on how the beasts managed to copulate. To this day I don't know.

Our fat-tails were made to look even more farcical by the fact that we occasionally overtook the caravan of some mountain tribe with a flock of karakul sheep, those superbly built patricians with long necks, expressive faces, deep-set eyes and soft ears. They were the finest animals in Afghanistan and were extremely valuable, since karakul skins were a major item in the nation's trade with the outside world. Whenever one examined the fortunes of men like Shah Khan in Kabul, it was usually found that their wealth derived in some way from karakul. The wool of the older animals was not impressive and had, so far as I know, no particular value, but newborn lambs were covered with the silky, close-matted, curly fur that is treasured in all countries; and to compare these aristocratic sheep with the ungainly fat-tailed clowns of our caravan was all to our disadvantage. I asked Zulfiqar why we had no karakuls and he explained, "I'd like to, but the desert marches would kill them."

Because the mountains of the Koh-i-Baba grew increasingly difficult for the caravan—camels growled at rocky areas—we made shorter journeys than before and were inclined, when we found good pasture, to halt for three or four days. It was in these periods of rest, these peaceful days in the high mountains, that Mira and I had our good times. We would leave my white horse in camp for the children to ride and with a chunk of nan would hike to some higher plateau where we would lie in the cold sun, talk and make love.

To be with Mira was a primitive joy. By now I was able to share her concern with matters of the caravan: "Where should we stop?" "When will the ewes throw their lambs?" "Could you live in a village like the one we saw yesterday?" It was her opinion that six weeks of village life beneath a chaderi would kill her, a judgment that I was prepared to accept.

She was like an elf, old enough to be married but young enough to run after a herd of camels with a stick. She had shown no inclination to accept any of the nomad men as her mate, nor did she think of me as a potential solution. On the fifth day north of Kabul she said, "It would be pleasant if you could ride with us forever, Miller. On the trail you're a strong man."

When I asked her how Kochis organized their marriages she said, "We don't usually consult mullahs. A young man goes to an older man like my father and says, 'I want your daughter Mira. How many sheep do I get if I take her?' Or he may demand some camels. Of course, if they do get married he stays with the clan. That way the animals don't leave. Neither does the daughter."

"Is there a feast?" I asked, still uncertain as to what the ceremony consisted of.

"Drums, flutes, a roasted sheep. The children get colored candies and the bride two new sets of clothing. When I marry I'll get a black skirt."

"Ellen wears a black skirt. Is she married to your father?"

"Oh, no! He didn't give her the black skirt. Racha did, out of kindness, because Ellen's were wearing out."

"Did Racha give her the bracelets, too?" I asked idly as we lay looking at the white clouds seeping over the edge of the Koh-i-Baba as its peaks watched us from the north. Mira explained that Zulfiqar had given Ellen the bracelets, but I did not hear her full reply, for I was thinking: I've been with them eight weeks and not a moment of rain. Not even a cloud. What an amazing world, drifting along like this year after year. Then an irritating thought oppressed me: What's so amazing about it? They probably have the same kind of days in Arizona. But I found consolation in one fact: In Arizona they don't have Mira.

As I ended my soliloquy, she ended her explanation of the bracelets, then asked pertly, "If some-body asks you, 'How did you join the Kochis, Miller?' what will you say?"

"I'll say, 'For the first part of the trip, I had to join because somebody stole my jeep.'"

"Did you know that I helped take off the wheels? When we sold them at Musa Darul I got some of the money."

"For the second part of the trip . . . that's more difficult to explain. Maybe I'll say, 'A beautiful Kochi girl bought me with a white horse.'"

Mira kissed me and ran to a brook to catch a drink of fresh mountain water, bringing me some in her felt cap. "How did you get that horse?" I asked, with a nagging memory of Moheb Khan and the possessive way he had taken the arm of the Swedish girl Ingrid.

"With the money I got from stealing the jeep, I bought the horse. Isn't that fair? Lose a jeep, find a horse?"

My recollection of Moheb Khan reminded me of Nazullrah and I asked, "Did you ever meet Ellen's husband, Nazrullah?"

"I saw him. He has a beard."

"Did your father meet him?"

"Why should he? As my father told you in the caravanserai, we made a three-day camp at Qala Bist . . . because of the desert ahead. At the end of the three days Ellen asked Zulfiqar if she could come with us. Up to then she had never spoken to him, so he had nothing to do with her running away. It was us she loved, the caravan and the camels and the children. It was much later that he allowed her to sleep in his tent."

"Was Racha angry?"

"Why should she be? He allowed her to stay in the tent, too."

"Are Ellen and your father . . ." I didn't know the Kochi words and started again. "Is she his woman?"

"Of course," Mira laughed, using the vulgar Kochi gesture for sexual intercourse. "But not like you and me. Not for great fun under the stars."

"Does she love your father?" I persisted.

"Everybody loves my father," she said simply. "In some clans men try to kill each other. Not in ours. But she doesn't love him the way I love you, Miller." To demonstrate the difference, she grabbed me and we ended up rolling on the ground, then seeking a protected crevice in the rocky walls.

It was tacitly understood that Mira and I would not embarrass Zulfiqar by sleeping together in the camp, since he chose to ignore his daughter's misalliance. We were therefore driven to sleep in the open and it became customary for Mira to make a show of going to bed in Zulfiqar's tent, while I did the same in mine, and then later for her to throw pebbles against the black felt, whereupon I would drag out my sleeping gear and lug it beyond the camels, where we would sleep till just before the break of camp.

Strangely, it was in daylight on the trail that I experienced my deepest sense of love for Mira, and I find it difficult to explain why; but when I was riding the white horse, moving up and down the column like Zulfiqar, I would occasionally overtake Mira when she did not see me, and for some minutes I would watch her, swinging along the road in her loose sandals, her shawl falling across her shoulders and her black pigtails bobbing in the sun, and I would recognize her as the freest human being I would ever know. She envied no one, loved whom she wished, took what she needed, concerned herself only with the immediate problems at hand, and lived on the high plateaus where nature was superb or on the edges of the desert where life was as clearly outlined as man ever sees it. Then she would hear me, and she would look over her shoulder at her man on the horse she had acquired for him, and in her look was both equality and pride, and it was sharing that look which made me feel so much a man. I had survived the war as a courageous boy; on the caravan trails, riding through the Koh-i-Baba on a white horse, I discovered what it was to be a man.

We had been traveling like this for five or six days when I began to detect a marked change in Dr. Stiglitz. The apprehension I had noticed in Kandahar and Musa Darul, when he worried about his tobacco and his beer, had left him, and the strong sense of guilt that had characterized him at the caravenserai was gone. He strode briskly along the trail without turban or karakul, his steel-gray hair close-cropped for sun and wind to play upon. At times he looked even happy, in a studied Germanic manner, and made overtures to extend the mutual respect which had begun to develop on that last night before we reached Kabul.

One day he left his position at the head of the camels and fell back to talk with me. Ignoring

Mira in his German manner, he said, "A man could march on like this forever."

I suggested, "Maybe it's because your health is better . . . the open air."

"I place no great reliance on exercise," he assured me professionally. "In Munich I lived perfectly happily walking a few blocks from my home to my office." He lost himself in contemplation of those good, gone days before the war, then added significantly, "I think what accounts for the difference is the confession I made to you at the caravanserai. To be able to tell those things to a Jew . . ."

"You feel you've purged yourself?" I asked coldly.

"No, Miller! Remember, when we spoke I didn't know you were a Jew. Of what I did I can never purge myself. But I can learn to live with history . . . to accept its full burden. That I'm doing."

"Why was the release deferred until this trip? The evil occurred years ago."

"Ah, so!" he agreed. "But always before I was preoccupied with myself. Could I get out of Germany? Could I enter Persia? Would I be caught and hanged?" He shuddered. "I was pathetic, involved only with myself and my tobacco and my beer."

I asked him what specifically had led him beyond himself, and he said, "Fighting with you in the serai. For years Sem Levin had been a ghost hanging upon my throat. But fighting with you by the pillar made Jews real again . . . quit them from being ghosts. I killed a man . . . a living

(335)

man, but I've paid the penalty. The caravan moves on."

I said bluntly, "I hate to think I enabled you to exorcise your ghosts."

"You did. The caravan moves on. Germany moves on. In a few years America will be begging Germany for friendship. Strange, isn't it?"

"You think this erases the past? A fist fight with a Jew?"

"In a sense, yes. We can bear terror only so long. Then it goes away, either because one fights with a Jew, or because one makes a trip with Kochis, or because the calendar reads 1946 instead of 1943. The pillar remains standing in the serai, with the bodies sealed inside, but in the sunlight the nomads graze their flocks." He looked at me in triumph as he cried to the encroaching mountains, "The terror goes away."

Then, still ignoring Mira, he stopped on the rocky trail and asked, "Miller, as a final act of contrition, may I kiss the hand of Sem Levin?"

I was repelled, but when I saw how much he needed this act of absolution, I had to say, "Yes." As the animals moved past us he knelt on the rocks and kissed my hand. When he rose I clasped his shoulder and said, "What you say is true, Dr. Stiglitz. The terror does go away. I no longer look at you as a depraved animal. You're one of us . . . one of us."

He nodded and walked on to resume his customary place with Maftoon and the camels; but when he was gone, shrewd Mira, to whom he had not once spoken, said in Pashto, "He talks a lot, but his real trouble is . . . he's in love with Ellen. Pretty soon . . ." and she made the Kochi sign for sex.

I asked, "What will happen if they do?"

"You mean?" and she made the sign again.

"Yes."

"Maybe my father kill him," she said without emotion. She told me of the time Maftoon's wife had fallen in love with a bazaar man in the Indian town of Rawalpindi, and Zulfiqar had beaten her savagely, so that she had crawled away from the caravan and gone to hide with the townsman. But Maftoon had followed her and knifed the bazaar man to death. "That's his wife over there," Mira said placidly, and I looked at one of the four women gathering camel dung, a woman somewhat older than Racha, vibrant, laughing, handsome, with a gold medallion piercing the right side of her nose. She suspected that Mira was speaking of her and she came to us in great peasant strides.

"What's that one telling you?" she demanded.

"That Maftoon killed a man . . . for you."

"He did," she laughed. "He broke off this tooth, too," and she showed me the stump. "I'd never have been happy in the city." Then she winked at me and warned, "You go away from Mira, Mira kill you, too."

When she returned to the camel droppings Mira laughed and said "I'm not so foolish. When the time comes, you go. When the time comes, I go."

For two days I studied Stiglitz and Ellen as carefully as possible, and I had to admit that Mira was right. They were in love and Zulfiqar knew it. So far he had kept the German from the tent and of course Ellen was not free to leave her bed at night as Mira did, but I looked for an opportunity to warn her of the danger she was inviting, for in spite of his seeming acquiescence I was convinced that Zulfiqar would kill Stiglitz if honor required.

I had never seen Ellen looking so radiant. We were now in cold country, well above ten thousand feet, with snow only a short distance above us and occasionally in some high pass actually nipping at our ears, and Ellen had acquired a long gray burnoose like those worn by Tajik mountaineers. It was made of raw wool and reached to her ankles; so that even in very cold weather it was comfortable. Into its attached hood Racha had worked gold and silver threads, showing Ellen's lovely blond head to good advantage, and when she rode my white horse, as she sometimes did when I wished to walk with Mira, she created the image of a fair young goddess leading her Aryans to some mountain fortress. I understood why Dr. Stiglitz had fallen in love with her.

Well before dawn on the ninth day out of Kabul I was lugging my sleeping gear back to the camels for loading when I saw that Ellen was standing in the darkness, watching for a chance to talk with me, so I wandered over to her and asked, "You need some help?"

"Not in packing," she replied. "But could we talk?"

I threw my gear to Maftoon and told him, "You can ride the white horse," whereupon Ellen and I started down the trail.

It was a matchless time for the discussion of ideas, since we were about to enter one of the noblest areas of Asia, the great Vale of Bamian. Because we were approaching it in darkness from the west, we would be hiking toward the sunrise, and the silvery cliffs on the north would loom out of the shadowy world just as our bodies and our incorporate thoughts came into being from their own universe of shadow. But it was the vale itself that lured us on: a lush, irrigated valley of historic richness from which Buddhism had spread to China and Japan, a vale crowded with trees and cool brooks and pasture lands. It was lined with poplars like a formal Italian garden, and to come upon it in the darkness, when each step revealed new beauties, when the approach of the still-distant sun brought more and more illumination both to the vale and to the problems we carried to it, was an experience not to be forgotten.

In the darkness Ellen cried, "Miller, I've fallen in love!" and the anguish of her cry, the honest perplexity it echoed, had to be respected.

"Mira told me . . . some time ago."

"We've tried to keep it secret . . . even from ourselves."

"Mira says you could invite great danger," I warned.

"I'm not concerned with danger," she said boldly. "I left Bryn Mawr seeking something like this. I left Qala Bist for the same reason. Now that I've found it . . ."

We hiked in darkness, with now and than a fugitive ray of light streaking across the sky like a scout sent forward by some Mongol army. In the gloom Ellen cried, "Miller! What shall I do?"

The pleading in her voice enlisted my sympathy and I tried to be as helpful as possible. "Let me ask your question another way," I suggested. "What are you already doing . . . hiking along a caravan trail at four-thirty in the morning in Central Asia? Ellen, what are you doing?"

She became defensive and countered, "I might ask you the same question."

"With me it's easy. I was sent here. By the government. To find you."

In the darkness she laughed. "Oh, no! The government didn't send you here. It sent you to Qala Bist, but you came here on your own account." Something of the gentleness that had marked her beginning observations now vanished and she added with some asperity, "You're here because for the first time in your circumscribed little life you're sleeping with a wonderful girl, and I don't blame you a bit. But please don't try to convince Aunt Ellen that the United States government told you, 'Go out and sleep under the stars.'"

"That takes care of me. Now what about you?"

Her gentleness returned, and as new streaks of light appeared in the east she explained, "I was driven here. It wasn't Nazrullah, who was a most considerate husband, and it wasn't Zulfiqar, whom any girl could admire. It had nothing to do with love or men. I suppose I was driven here by what I saw happening in the world . . . I was driven by something I was powerless to fight."

I listened, tried to understand, walked for some time in silence, then said, "Ellen, I've done my damnedest to analyze your behavior, and I've failed. When we were in Kabul I turned in my official report, so this discussion concerns only you and me. Can you please explain in simple words?"

(340)

"I don't think so," she replied thoughtfully. "Either the words I've already used trigger your intellect or they don't. Either you intuitively feel that America is making terrible mistakes, or you don't."

"Well, I don't feel it. America's doing a damned good job."

"I'm talking to an idiot," she groaned in the darkness. "Dear God! I need help so desperately, and You send me an idiot."

"Try it again," I said with resignation. "In the simplest words you can muster."

"I will," she said softly. "Miller, don't you see that we're bound to build bigger bombs and then bigger bombs and finally bombs so big that we can destroy the whole world?"

"What you say could be true, but I take consolation in the fact that America is building those bombs and not somebody else."

"Miller!" she screamed. "Do you think no one else can build them?"

"Of course they can't. Russia? China? They'll never have the technical skill."

"Miller!" she shouted. "Don't be an idiot! We're talking about your soul and mine. Don't you see that . . ."

"Who's been feeding you this line? Stiglitz?"

"Yes, he says . . ."

"Does he also say that he was a Nazi . . . in charge of killing Jews?"

"Yes," she replied softly. "And that's why I must live with him . . . the rest of my life."

I was so infuriated with her garbled nonsense that I raised my hand to slap her, but in the half-light she saw it and drew back. "Talk sense," I growled.

The sun, as if eager to provide an illumination which we could not find for ourselves, crept toward the eastern horizon and sent shafts of light high across the heavens. Ellen, happy that the night was ending, shook the gold and silver cowl from her head and allowed the twilight to play upon her shimmering hair. Looking at me in deep confusion of spirit she said, "I am talking sense. Promise me that no matter what I say in the next few minutes . . . no matter how I outrage your logic, you'll listen and try to understand."

"Out of sheer curiosity, I will."

"Let's say I was a girl growing up in a normal family, in a normal church, with a normal group of friends. Boys liked me, and teachers too. I went to dances, gave parties, did well in college. But one day when I was about fifteen . . . long before the war . . . I saw that everything my family did was irrelevant. We were keeping score . . . I can't call it anything else . . . in a game that simply didn't exist except in our imagination. Did that idea ever occur to you?"

"No."

"I'm sure it didn't," she replied, without rancor. "Well, World War II came and I listened to such nonsense as men rarely display in public. I kept my mouth shut, primarily because Father took it so seriously. He was home safe . . . too old to fight. So he could be pretty heroic. As chairman of the draft board he gave a rousing speech to all the young men he sent away. It would have moved you deeply, Miller. Some of the boys my age told me,

'Your old man makes you want to march right out and do your job . . . and his.' Some of my classmates weren't so dumb."

"Some of my classmates weren't so dumb either," I snapped. "I remember a philosophy major named Krakowitz. He said, 'There's only one thing worse than winning a war. That's losing it.' It was his opinion that when you were fighting Hitler, Mussolini and Tojo it might be true that nobody could win, but it was also true that if you lost, it could be real hell. Krakowitz. He died at Iwo Jima."

"I'm deeply touched," she said, bowing in the morning twilight. "So in college I met this gang of kept professors. What else can you call them? Their moral responsibility was to dissect the world, but they were paid to defend it. I suppose they had a job to do . . . learn, earn; pray, stay; live, give. They had one hell of a system going for them, those professors.

"But there was one who used to drop hints that he knew the world needed dissecting, and he caught on to me very fast. Taught music and wrote to my parents that I was rejecting the world. Boy, was he right! Father bullied him in his best draft-board manner and pointed out that I was doing all right in my 'real' classes. Reminded me of the passage in Plato where citizens looked so long in the mirror they confused image with reality. It never occurred to Father that this befuddled music master was looking at the real world while the others were marking me on attributes that would never matter . . . not even when Gabriel blows his horn."

She paused, leaving me space to confute her if I

wished, but I was so befuddled by her succession of comment—as compared to the ease with which Mira accepted the life of the caravan, and to hell with what was bothering London or Tokyo—that I refrained from entering the argument. I had asked for an explanation, and I was getting it, whether I understood it or not. She continued, "When the worst part of the war arrived, my vision was confirmed. I don't know why I wanted to marry Nazrullah. For one thing, in those days I hadn't discovered that he was exactly like my father. Dear Nazrullah! He'll have paved roads in Afghanistan yet. I suppose I came here because Afghanistan was as far from American values as I could get." She paused, then added a curious comment: "The fact that Nazrullah already had a wife made the decision easier. Do you follow me?"

"I'm lost," I confessed.

"What I mean is, my father described anything out of the ordinary as ridiculous, and I wanted to outrage his whole petty scale of judgment. What was the most ridiculous thing I could do? Run off with an Afghan who had a turban and another wife." She laughed a little, then added, "Do you know what started my disillusionment with Nazrullah? That turban. He wore it in Philadelphia for show. He'd never think of wearing it in Kabul."

"I still don't understand," I replied.

"Lots of young people in America will," she assured me. "They're beginning to reject any society built by men like my father."

"Then God help America," I said bitterly.

"It's the young people like me who will save

America," she responded. "They'll understand what's happening, and they'll change things."

I was pondering this chicanery of mind and thinking: I have to respect the passion of her thought and the sincerity with which she advances it, but I certainly distrust the logic—when the sun burst above the horizon and poured some much-needed light into the Vale of Bamian, illuminating the series of white limestone cliffs that rimmed the northern boundary. They rose high above the vale and were deeply eroded, so that shadows played across them in fascinating variety. The green poplars that grew so plentifully elsewhere stopped at the cliffs, allowing them to stand forth in sharp relief. Then, as the sun grew brighter, Ellen called, "Miller! Look!"

At first I did not see what had startled her, since I was looking for some ordinary thing. Then, looming from a gigantic niche cut in the face of the tallest cliff, appeared a towering statue of a man, many scores of feet high, wonderfully carved from the living rock. It was apparently a religious figure of heroic proportions, but what gave it an eerie quality was the fact that its enormous face had been chopped away: lips and chin remained, big as human beings themselves, but all above was a flat expanse of limestone.

While we stood in awe before the towering statue, the rest of the caravan drew up, permitting Zulfiqar to point with his gun at the faceless figure and announce, laconically, "Buddha."

The caravan moved on to its accustomed tenting space, but Ellen and I remained staring at the hypnotic figure. I asked her to stand for comparison by the mammoth feet while I stood back to calculate how tall the statue was: my rough guesswork yielded about a hundred and fifty feet. Who had carved it here in the heart of a Muslim country? Who had chopped away the benign face?

I was not to find an answer to these questions, but as we studied the gigantic statue I became aware that the cliff beside it was honeycombed with caves, whose windows were literally peppered across the limestone. "What are they?" I asked, and Ellen suggested this might at one time have been a monastery. We looked some more and found an opening which seemed to lead to the caves, and Ellen indicated that she would like to explore them.

We entered a dark shaft that led upward through solid rock and after much climbing and skirting of precipitous ledges came to a small wooden bridge that carried us to the top of Buddha's head. We were now far above the earth and a fall would have been disastrous, but we perched safely on the god's head, surveying the vale that opened out before us. In the distance, in bright sunlight, we could see our tents going up.

From the head we found another passageway leading eastward to an interlocking nest of larger caves, which in the old days must have been lecture halls seating hundreds of monks. We found one especially lovely room whose windows, a hundred feet above the earth, framed a view of the Koh-i-Baba, and it was here that Ellen sat cross-legged on the rocky floor, her burnoose covering her body, as she resumed her argument with me.

"When you see the world for the pathetic thing

it is"—at the moment I was at the window, inspecting one of the most glorious views in Asia—"my mother used to tremble with gratification when we bought a bigger car than the one before or a college missing the whole point of education but congratulating itself on a million-dollar dormitory . . ." She was trapped in a sentence from which there was no escape and laughed nervously. "You decide to turn your back on the whole thing and find some simpler base. I thought Nazrullah was simpler than Dorset. Zulfiqar was simpler than Nazrullah. And now Otto Stiglitz is simpler than all."

"How can you say that? The man's an M.D. from a good university."

"He's simpler because he's a non-man. In Munich he descended into hell. He's carried the memory of it halfway around the world. He's fought free of the world and its burden. He's a non-man . . . the thing from which we begin all over."

"Do you really believe this nonsense?" I pleaded.

"You're the way I used to be, Miller," she said condescendingly. "You honestly think that someone up there is keeping score on your life. If you learn fifteen new birds, you get a merit badge. If you study calculus, you make the junior honor role. If you keep your nose clean in the navy, the old man signs a favorable letter. If you obey the ambassador, he may sign another favorable letter. All these little credits are entered in a big book by what some sportswriter called the Divine Scorekeeper. It's a comforting theory . . . made my father very happy. He built up points and got a bigger car. Because he had the big car he was entitled to a bigger house. He won the house, so he was voted into the country club. And because he was in the country club his daughter was welcomed at Bryn Mawr. See where it leads? If his daughter does well at Bryn Mawr she's entitled to marry Mark Miller, who by the same series of tricks earned the points to enter Yale. Now see what happens? His daughter and Mark Miller have got to start collecting their points, and if they don't, the old folks will be scared stiff.

"No, Miller, you're betting on the wrong game. There's no scorekeeper. Nobody really gave a damn whether or not you kept your nose clean in the navy. And when we reach Balkh and you walk out on Mira, the Divine Scorekeeper ought to kick the living bejeezus out of you and set your score back to zero for having been such a swine. But He won't. Because the Scorekeeper, supposing there is one, will be laughing at what's happened and observing to His cronies, 'That boy Miller's a damned sight better kid than when he joined the caravan.' And at Balkh, when you leave Mira, I too shall leave . . . but I'll go with Otto Stiglitz."

I looked at the old lecture hall in which we sat; from here wisdom had been poured to the ends of the nations, as they then existed, and I felt morally certain that every lesson propounded in this classroom, this curious cell in the beehive of the monastery where men spent years surrounded by rock, out of touch with the earth until their passions were burned away and their vision clarified—almost every lesson had refuted what Ellen was saying. The wisdom of the world, whether Buddhist, Muslim, Christian or Jewish, insisted that there were desirable ends, that society was worth preserving no matter how badly scarred at a given moment in time, and that there was a Divine Score-keeper, man himself perhaps, who did judge some deeds as better than others. To the ancient lessons which came to us from this lecture hall in the cliffs of Bamian I was committed, and if Ellen Jaspar was not, the more pity I felt for her.

"Have you slept with Stiglitz?" I asked bluntly.

"No, but I shall when he asks me."

"I suppose you know that Mira's afraid Zulfiqar might kill Stiglitz . . . or you."

"That's of no consequence to either of us."

"It is to me," I countered.

"But you tried to kill Stiglitz yourself."

"I've grown beyond that."

"Miller! That's what I mean. That's the first sensible thing you've said on this trip. Now can you understand me when I say that Stiglitz and I have grown beyond your prejudices? We have, Miller. We are cleansed of this world, and whether Zulfiqar kills us or not is of no significance."

"Might it be of significance to Zulfiqar?" I asked.

Ellen grew grave and said, "That's a difficult question. I had no moral right to intrude on Naz-rullah, but I excused myself by remembering that he had a wife and a daughter."

"He now has a son, too."

"Oh, Karima must be so happy!" she cried spontaneously. "He wanted a son so much. Well, I also admit I had no right to intrude on Zulfiqar, but he can stand it. He has a good family and a caravan which couldn't exist without him. But Otto Stiglitz has nothing . . . hardly even a job. It's through his regeneration and mine that the world has a fighting chance. Frankly, Miller, with men like you and Nazrullah and Zulfiqar the world neither gains nor loses. You're of no moral significance whatever."

I asked, "You know that Stiglitz could be extradited . . . and hanged?"

"Yes. For that very reason he needs me most. But one of the good aspects of living in a non-nation like Afghanistan is that they don't extradite non-men who have already died."

"At Balkh we're only a few miles from Russia. He could be kidnaped."

"Civilized nations don't kidnap," she argued, and I thought it indicative that she rejected civilization when it suited her philosophy to do so, but fled to it for protection of her desires.

"You forget—or did he tell you?—that he kept day-by-day records of his experiments. 'I'm a real scientist,' he boasted, 'I keep records.' The English have those records, you know. He's a prime war criminal."

"You've stated my case for me, Miller. He's already convicted and dead. I've rejected all the lives I've known, so I'm dead too. I can live only at the bottom . . . at the bottom dregs of an insane world. Where hope is being reborn. Does this at last make sense?"

"No," I said.

"It's strange you're so obtuse," she reflected sorrowfully. She rose and went to the far end of the cave, drawing her burnoose about her as if it were an academic robe. "Every honest teacher who stood on this spot lecturing to his students is listening now to what I'm saying. They're applauding. They know that society becomes corrupt and that men must reject it if they are to remain free. They know that life, to replenish itself, must sometimes return to the dregs, to the primitive slime. The men who stood here know that I am right, even if I can't make you listen."

As she left the cave, she waved to the unseen docents who had instructed generations of Buddhist monks in this rock-girt university, those savants who were already dead and buried centuries before America and Dorset, Pennsylvania, were known. "They'll understand," she whispered, and smiling left them.

14

On the second day north of Bamian I had finished
checking the caravan on my white horse and had
ridden off casually to explore a lateral valley, when
I saw two figures climbing over the rocks above
me. I was about to hail them but stopped, for
when I rode closer I saw that they were Ellen Jaspar and Dr. Stiglitz, and I sensed intuitively that
this day they did not wish either companionship or
surveillance. I became sure of this when they
turned a corner which would hide them from the
caravan and ran to each other in hungry embrace.
In a moment the German started undressing Ellen,
and I withdrew unseen.

I would have returned to the caravan, except
that as I rode away a pebble fell from the rocks
and struck me, and then another, and I realized
that someone perched on the high ledges overlook-
ing the lovers was trying to signal me. I reined in
the horse, scanned the rocks above me, and spotted
a figure in red dress and pigtails. It was Mira, who,
having anticipated the intentions of the lovers, had
gone into the valley before them to sequester herself at a vantage point from which she could observe the proceedings.

I waved to her angrily: Get off that ledge! But

she pressed her fingers against her lips, cautioning silence; then, after watching the lovers for some minutes, she raised her hands triumphantly above her head and made the Kochi sign for successful sexual intercourse. And so the four of us remained gripped in the mountains, Ellen and Stiglitz in their long-delayed passion, Mira spying on them from the overhanging ledge, and I watching her gestures from the valley below. It was one of the most erotic moments I had ever known, but it was colored by a sense of tragedy, for I was convinced that if Zulfiqar discovered their passion, Ellen and her German doctor were self-committed to disaster.

After the lovers rejoined the caravan, I signaled Mira to scramble down from her ledge and join me on the white horse. "You mustn't mention this to the others," I warned.

"They know," she laughed, gripping me about the waist as we galloped back to the caravan.

"How could they know unless you tell them?" I demanded.

"Anybody can look at those two and know," she insisted.

And she was right. By noon, when Zulfiqar halted the caravan, it was known throughout the clan that the long-predicted encounter had taken place and we awaited the consequences. Since Zulfiqar was much larger than Dr. Stiglitz and could presumably strangle him if he wished—I thought it incredible that any woman should trade in the great Kochi for the insignificant German—I supposed there would be a savage beating if not a murder, but to my surprise nothing happened. In the succeeding days Ellen became an increasingly beautiful woman, lovelier even than her high-school photographs or my first sight of her in the caravanserai. Her smile grew more warm. Her freedom of movement was enhanced. Even the manner in which she wore her long gray burnoose became more feminine and alluring, but I remember best the way her blue eyes sparkled during the long uphill hikes.

When Zulfiqar failed to react to their affair, the lovers grew more bold. They began sleeping in the doctor's gear under the stars, along the edge of camp, and in the afternoon Stiglitz no longer went to sit with Zulfiqar and Racha beneath the tent awning. The effect of this upon the German was profound and with one exception good. He was no longer so obviously preoccupied with himself, and often when he fumbled with matches while lighting his pipe, he smiled. His nervousness disappeared and he would sometimes lean against the pole in our tent and actually relax.

The only ill effect occurred on the march, for whenever Zulfiqar rode by on his brown horse, Stiglitz tensed himself in case the big Kochi should leap upon him with dagger unsheathed. No amount of inner glow could halt this involuntary reflex, and I thought: They started this mountain-top love affair as non-people indifferent to Zulfiqar, but the deeper they fall in love, the more scared they become.

The march from Bamian to Qabir required eleven days along the most spectacular portion of the caravan route: we were penetrating the heart of the Hindu Kush, and while there were taller mountains in Asia—indeed, the Pamirs, the Karakorams and the Himalayas were all higher—none surpassed these mountains of Afghanistan for their combinations of rocky grandeur and valley charm. Sometimes we would swing around the end of a ridge and see before us ten or fifteen miles of green valley without a single indication that men had ever been there before. At other times the trail would narrow to an ugly defile down which a river tumbled, and the trail would halt abruptly against the face of a cliff, but a rickety bridge built years ago by nomads would carry it across the river and send it onto higher land. It was exciting, fresh, magnificent.

One aspect of the Hindu Kush reminded me of the desert. On the fifth day north of Bamian we rounded a corner on the trail to see before us a valley of some magnitude. At the far end, say four miles away, rose a striking mountain, and I thought: We'll probably camp under that mountain at noon. But when noon came, the near-at hand mountain was a few miles away. On the next day we resumed march and at noon the elusive peak was still a few miles distant. So on the following day we plugged along until the mountain was almost near enough to touch, but when another day arrived, the damned mountain was still ahead of us! It finally took us four full days and fifty miles of marching to reach a spot which at first had looked as if we would overrun it before lunch.

During the days when we were trying to reach the mountain I saw little of Ellen Jaspar, for she and Stiglitz were so preoccupied with their burgeoning affair that I had no wish to intrude, and we spoke only occasionally when we met lugging our sleeping gear to and from the tents. Then on the day we finally reached the mountain, Ellen came to me as we were unpacking and made the comment which first set me wondering about her basic sincerity. She said, half in earnest, half in jest, something which I could have taken as an honest concern in my future but which for some reason, I didn't: "Miller, this caravan is bound to end one day. Don't injure yourself by taking Mira too seriously." This seemed a most inappropriate comment from a girl whose own love affair with Stiglitz was so intemperate that it could incur even murder, and most contradictory to the things she had said about Mira and me during the trip to Bamian. I was about to question her on these incongruities when Mira came to help me, and Ellen moved on.

"I think Ellen likes you," Mira observed casually, but I was so captivated with Mira herself that I forgot her words.

It was no wonder. For each night we slept under the stars in a series of the most spectacular boudoirs two lovers had ever known: the mountains hovered aloft to protect us, the rivers brought us music, the moon was our night lamp, while not far away the sounds of the caravan reassured us. When we finally went to bed beneath the elusive mountain, Mira was especially adorable, a crazy, elfin thing with an unpredictable insight into human affairs, and the majesty of our surroundings and the knowledge that soon we would leave the Hindu Kush and perhaps the loveliest weeks of our lives forced me to consider what might happen to both of us at the end of the caravan trail. I say forced me to consider because a young man who lives with a girl like Mira slips unconsciously, day by day, from first rapture to deepening realization to the gnawing suspicion that she has become an inescapable part of his life, not to be dismissed easily nor forgotten ever, and he does not willingly explore the future. To my surprise, Mira was willing to do so and with frightening accuracy anticipated each problem that disturbed me. The nimble fingers of her thought ransacked my mind to uncover my most sensitive apprehensions.

When I asked what Zulfiqar might do to her when I left: "He can't do anything. Who would inherit his camels?"

When I asked if she would be able to find a husband within the caravan since all the men knew of her love for me: "If I have the camels, I have a husband."

When I asked what might happen if she had a baby: "What happened to those children over there? Some mothers are dead. Some fathers are unknown."

When I asked what she wanted in life: "In winter Jhelum. In summer Hindu Kush. Any better in America?"

And when I asked her if she loved me: "I bought you a white horse, didn't I?" She kissed me and added, "Go to sleep. It is the woman's job to worry about these matters. After all, we have the babies, not you."

But it was when I had asked no question that I sometimes learned most about this delectable young nomad: I was hiking with Mira, having turned the horse over to Maftoon, who galloped up and down the file like a Kazak, when without preparation she observed, "Ellen is the prettiest woman I've ever seen. I would like to look like Ellen. But I would like to be like Racha." When I asked why, she replied, "All the people Racha touches are made stronger. That is not so with Ellen."

I objected and pointed to Dr. Stiglitz, whom Ellen had transformed. At this Mira chuckled: "He was a dying man. Any woman with a good pair of legs could have saved him. I don't count Dr. Stiglitz at all."

"What's going to happen to him . . . when Zulfiqar gets mad, I mean?"

"My father may kill him," she speculated as before. "On the other hand, my father may be grateful that Ellen has been taken off his hands."

"That's an astonishing thing to say," I exploded.

She ignored my question by saying of Racha, "She helps women in childbirth, and handles the camels well, and knows how to care for sick sheep. You know, Miller, Racha is the only one able to argue with my father in the councils, and he trusts her to put the caravan money in the bank at Jhelum." She paused, thinking of her mother, and added, "Racha wears gold in her nose and does not comb her hair, but she is the heart of our caravan, and Zulfiqar would be stupid to trade her for Ellen. He knows that."

"Did he ever love Ellen?" I asked.

Again she evaded my question. "If you stayed with us, Miller," she promised, "I would be like Racha for you." At this point Maftoon rode up on the white horse and asked, "Would the sahib like to have it back?" and Mira snapped, "Yes, you dirty loafer. It's improper for you to ride while he walks." She cupped her hands to make a stirrup for me, and with a quick heft of her tiny body tossed me onto the horse.

As I left Mira, Zulfiqar rode up flashing excitement. "Follow me, Millair!" he cried, and for several miles I trailed him until he reached the crest of the ridge, where he reined in his brown horse to wait for me.

Pointing to an extensive plateau unfolding below us, he said, "That's Qabir."

Richardson had told me that this was a place of much importance, but even so I had not guessed its magnitude. Across the great plain two rivers came from different ranges of the Hindu Kush and met to form a stately Y. As far as I could see, along both the tributaries and the main river, nomads had erected clusters of black tents. Estimating roughly, I judged there were at least four hundred caravans like ours, which at two hundred persons per caravan meant . . .

Startled by my own figures, I asked, "How many people?"

"Who cares?" he asked in boyish excitement. "Sixty thousand? Maybe more."

It was difficult to believe that for more than a thousand years the nomads had been convening in this remote spot on the confluence of rivers and that no national government was yet sure where the meeting place was, nor who attended, nor how the camp was composed. Now that the war was over, airplanes would soon penetrate the secret, but for the time being this was the last outpost of free men.

"Here we go!" Zulfiqar shouted, and he spurred his horse into a gallop that carried him down onto the plateau and among the gathering caravans. I followed as boldly as I dared, but it was some time before I caught up with my Kochi. When I did, I found him hurrying from one caravan to the next, shouting to old friends, reporting on his winter in India and making plans for trading sessions. It was obvious that he was one of the unifying forces of the encampment.

Finally he remembered that I was with him and crying, "Millair! Follow me!" he galloped along the left bank of the nearest tributary until he found an attractive area as yet unoccupied. "We'll camp here," he shouted. "You wait and tell the others." With this he dug his heels into his horse and sped off to new greetings, but he had gone only a short distance when he reared his horse handsomely, spun him around and came dashing back to me: "As soon as they arrive, tell Maftoon to roast four fat sheep." The horse reared again and he was gone.

It would be an hour before the Kochis could reach us, and the waiting became one of the most poignant times of my life, for around me swirled the enigmatic caravans from the heartland of Asia. I saw beside me men and women from tribes I had never known existed, camels that had crossed the Oxus from areas a thousand miles away, children with round red faces, and women wearing fur boots and wonderful tanned smiles derived from months spent in sunlight. In the distance, at some caravan up the river, a man played a flute and it was like an evocation of the Arabian Nights or the music of Borodin that I had heard at the symphony in Boston. As a stranger on a white horse I attracted attention, and some of the nomads even tried to speak to me in strange tongues, but to all I made it clear that this choice spot by the river was reserved for Zulfiqar and I found that people respected his name.

The poignancy grew more intense when I happened to look toward the Hindu Kush and saw the Kochis coming out of the mountains on their way to the camp ground, and for the first time I saw our caravan in its entirety and realized what an impressive aggregation it was: two hundred people, nearly a hundred camels laden with costly goods, several score of donkeys, some goats and more than five hundred choice sheep. This was my caravan, these were my people; and when I remembered the warm family life I had enjoyed in Boston, I felt grateful that I had been allowed to know this larger family.

And then I saw, marching together, dark little Mira in her red skirt and pigtails and shining Ellen, the hood of her burnoose thrown back, so that her beauty flashed in sunlight, and I was unable to move or think or speak. I merely sat on the white horse and looked at these two persons as they came toward me, the nomad whom I loved so much and the strange, fair woman whom I wanted to help and whom I found so difficult to understand, and as I looked at them the thought came from outside me: They are your life, the essence of your caravan.

In a kind of repose—quiet and unfathomed and undisturbed by the men of Asia moving around me

—I watched as the Kochis approached, until three of our men spotted me and shouted, "Here we are!"

"This is the place," I called back, and with a whip of the bridle I sent the white horse speeding toward the caravan, where I leaped to the ground, kissed Mira in front of everyone and whispered, "I was afraid . . ."

"Of what?" she asked quietly.

"That . . . well, that you might not come."

She did not laugh, nor did Ellen, but she plunged her quick hand into my pocket and asked, "Miller, you got any afghanis?"

I came up with a few local coins and when I handed them to her she smiled like a little child, and rounded up all the youngsters of our caravan and led them across the plateau toward the sound of music. I followed my pigtailed Pied Piper until she brought her charges to a traditional spot where some Russian Uzbeks had erected a primitive mer-ry-go-round: a wooden socket had been sunk in the ground and into it was fitted a strong, upright pillar, from whose top branched out ten arms. At the end of each arm hung a free-swinging iron pole, which ended in a rudely carved wooden horse. In half a dozen different languages the Uz-beks shouted, "The wildest rearing horses in the world!"

"Give them all a ride," Mira told the Uzbeks, and our Kochi children were piled on the rough horses, quivering with apprehension and joy. Then two burly Uzbeks, pressing their chests against poles that projected from the pillar, began moving slowly in a tight circle, which made the pillar and

the horses revolve, and everything was so neatly
balanced that soon the Uzbeks had their contrap-
tion spinning smoothly, whereupon they ran faster
and faster until at last they had to spend little
effort, while the squealing children on the horses
spun at great speed, their little bodies almost parallel to earth.

"These horses are the first exciting thing I can
remember," Mira shouted, as children from scores
of different tribes cheered the flying Kochis.
"When I was young, Zulfiqar always gave me a
ride." Her face was radiant, as if she were again
one of the wild and happy children. Then without
warning, she turned and pressed her head against
my shoulder and whispered, "Oh, Miller! I am
again so happy."

It was in this manner—from Mira's spontaneous
turning to me while mothers from many caravans
watched—that the nomads of Qabir discovered that
we were in love, and if there was any one thing
that made my mission at the encampment easier it
was this fact: as a strange American set down on
the high plateau I was bound to be conspicuous
and ineffective; but a young man in love with a
spirited Kochi girl I was so obvious that the nomads felt sorry for me and I was accorded free-
doms that no other stranger would have been permitted.

Then, as the Uzbeks halted their merry-go-round
and Mira recovered her children, I saw that on the
other side of the circle Ellen had gathered a group
of nondescript children whose mothers were not
present with coins, and she brought these round-
faced youngsters to the Uzbeks and there was

some haggling in Pashto. Finally Ellen took off two of her bracelets and gave them to the Uzbek, who tried to bend them in his fingers. He accepted them, and Ellen's children were placed on the horses and again the burly Uzbeks groaned against the poles to get the pillar spinning; and as the children rose higher and higher, speeding through the air, Ellen stood in the afternoon sunlight, biting her knuckles and watching.

At dusk, when the four sheep were well roasted and Ellen had taken her accustomed place to serve the portions, we heard a shout at the edge of our caravan and Zulfiqar appeared, bringing with him some thirty leaders of other caravans plus an orchestra of Tajik musicians, who found a place by the fire and started banging their drums. "Ellen!" Zulfiqar shouted. "Leave the cooking!" And with a sweep of his arm he brought the American girl into the center of the crowd and danced with her vigorously. The visitors watched, then reached out for Kochi women and launched a hilarious celebration. Soon Zulfiqar passed Ellen along to one of the Russians and came to me, out of breath. "Millair," he laughed, "I want you to meet one of the leaders," and he took me through the gyrating dancers to where a tall, heavy, baldheaded man in his late forties stood in fur boots, rough wool jacket and brass-studded belt. His big face was round and clean-shaven, while the slant of his eyes indicated Mongolian ancestry. Grasping him by the shoulder, Zulfiqar said, "This is Shakkur the Kirghiz. He smuggles guns and sells most of the German rifles on the high plateau. He sold me mine."

The big Kirghiz nodded pleasantly, showing

large white teeth with a prominent space in the middle. "You English?" he asked in broken Pashto.

"American," I replied.

He burst into a generous laugh and made a machine gun with his arms. "Ah-ah-ah-ah-ah, Chicago!" he cried. "I see cinema."

I respected the man's vitality, but was irritated by his view of Americans, and on the spur of the moment I dropped so that I was sitting on my ankles, and with my arms folded I did a poor imitation of a Russian dance. "I see cinema too," I laughed.

"No!" he protested boisterously. He shouted at the Tajik musicians and they began a new selections to which he danced a passage of real Kirghiz violence. Here there was no mock clicking of the heels but rather the heavy-booted stamp and whirl of the steppes. Seeing Ellen standing near the roast sheep, he leaped at her, grabbed her by the waist, and swung her into a sweeping, dipping step which made her burnoose swirl over the earth. They were a handsome couple, and although she could not follow the intricate steps, the Kirghiz kept her moving so easily that it looked as if she were indeed dancing with him. The Tajik orchestra brought its music to a climax and the big dancer swept his partner high in the air, turned her about, and put her down gently beside the waiting sheep.

"Time to eat!" he shouted, and Ellen started handing out chunks of mutton to the hungry visitors.

When the feasting ended, Zulfiqar asked Dr. Stiglitz to stand beside him while he announced, "This is a German doctor. He has many medicines." Turning toward one of the tents he shouted, "Maftoon! Bring the box of medicine," and when the impressive collection was displayed Zulfiqar said, "if you have any sick, bring them here tomorrow."

"What charge?" Shakkur the Kirghiz asked.

"No charge," Zulfiqar assured him, and next morning outside our tent a line of men and women, dressed in many different tribal costumes, sought aid. In caring for them Stiglitz was assisted by Ellen, who acted as his nurse, and once while she talked with patients in Pashto the doctor wandered over to me to observe, "You've no idea, Miller, how refreshing it is to treat a woman patient who takes off her clothes and says, 'It hurts here.' Believe me, if I ever get to Kabul the men will turn their wives over to me and leave. No more chaderies in my office."

I had not been at the sick line long when Zulfiqar appeared, leading my white horse. After noticing the patients approvingly, he said, "Come along," and we rode to the other end of the encampment, where he began a systematic visit to all the caravans. At each he did two things; he advised the traders in that caravan how to earn more profit from their goods, and he invited each group to send its sick to his German doctor.

I was impressed with Zulfiqar as he moved among the caravans: a smile, a joke, a reference to me . . . It all made commercial bargaining something more than a mere business occupation. I found that I was in the presence of a real political talent, a man who knew that his simple smile and transparent honesty could win him rewards that another might miss. He was politicking like mad, but I didn't know what for.

Thus I made my way into the yurts of the north, those brown hide-walled circular tents where men with Oriental eyes laughed easily while their buxom wives served yak cheese and roast mutton. Casually I shared hospitality with nomads who had come from all parts of Central Asia and I learned how they made their pilgrimages, what goods they traded, the condition of life in their valleys. I was satisfied that no Russian soldiers accompanied the nomads and probably no political commissars, but of this latter I could not be certain. The great gathering at Qabir seemed to be just that: one of the largest commercial fairs in the world, rivaling Nizhni Novgorod and Leipzig. But there was one thing I was not allowed to learn, perhaps the most important of all, and my defeat on this score was a disappointment. I never did find out where these Russian migrants crossed the Oxus.

Richardson had ordered me not to take notes, but at night I memorized the various tribes and subdivisions I had been with that day. From India came the true Provindahs, the Baluchis, and the stocky men from the kingdoms of Chitral, Dir and Swat.

From southern Afghanistan came the Pashtuns, the Brahuis and the Kochis.

From central Afghanistan came the Durani tribe of the Pashtuns, who now ruled the kingdom, the Ghilzais, who used to rule it, and the curious Kizilbash, a Persian tribe of gifted traders.

From northern Afghanistan came the Tajiks, Uzbeks and Kirghizes, all of whom had related tribes north of the Oxus in Russia, the Karakalpaks, the Nuristanis, who were supposed to be of Greek origin, and the Hazaras, who were the descendants of Genghis Khan's troops.

From western Afghanistan came the Jamshedis, the Firuzkuhis, the Taimuris and the Arabs.

From Persia came the nomads of Meshed and Nishapur, the Sakars, the Salors, and additional tribes of Kizilbash.

From Russia came its segments of the Tajik, Uzbek, Sart and Kirghiz tribes, plus the Kazaks and traders from the old market city of Samarkand.

From remote areas came the nameless tribes of the Pamirs, the Chinese from Kashgar and Yarkand, and the handsome mountaineers of Gilgit and Hunza.

And from everywhere—Persia, Afghanistan, Russia, China—came members of that mysterious and omnipresent group, the Turkomans, a people not clearly defined but brave and canny traders.

When I had spent some time in the tents and yurts of all these tribes, I began to feel a certain smugness that I, of all the foreigners in Afghanistan, should have been the one to penetrate Qabir, but so far I had seen only the externals. On the fifth day Zulfiqar saddled up the horses and said, "Today you will see Qabir," and he led me to the confluence of the rivers where an area had been marked inside of which only men were allowed, and only the leaders of the men. We pulled up before a large Russian-style yurt, whose primitive sides were made of skins and whose spacious interior was decorated with guns, daggers, sabers and three handsome red-and-blue Persian rugs. This was the center from which the encampment was governed.

At the far end a small, low table stood on a white rug brought down from Samarkand, and on this rug, cross-legged, were seated the two sharifs who controlled Qabir. The first was Shakkur, the Kirghiz gunrunner who had danced at our feast, and as he sat in the place of honor he was impressive indeed, a big hulk of man with shining head and penetrating eyes. The humor that had marked him at our feast was gone, for ruling this large encampment was a serious business.

The other sharif was an elderly Hazara, a man whose Mongol ancestry would have placed him beneath contempt in Kabul, but who had built a substantial trade in karakul, so that a fair portion of the skins bartered that year at Qabir would come under his jurisdiction. He wore the tattered clothes of a peasant and often listened to argument with his eyes closed, but he was known as a shrewd trader. "He was sharif when my father first brought me here," Zulfiqar explained, and I asked if I might speak with the old man.

He spoke good Pashto and told me, "You're the first westerner ever to see this yurt." I asked him if Russians from Moscow had attended the camp and he smiled indulgently, saying, "No Communists." Then he added, "This year we have a special event which will make the bazaar exciting for you." I replied that it already was.

Almost every man I met in that yurt was an authentic epic, but my favorite was an old Mongol in his seventies wearing a Gilgit cap. He had come from far beyond the Karakorams with two donkeys and a horse. Of the men who frequented the yurt he wore the filthiest clothes, yet his white beard and toothless mouth were constantly flapping in negotiation. He had been alone on the highest road in the world for eight weeks, starting as soon as snow melted in the high passes, and he carried a considerable quantity of gold, one of the few nomads who did. He told me, "I've been traveling this route sixty-six years. Everyone knows me as the old man with the gold."

"Ever run into any trouble?"

"Never shot a bandit in my life."

Later Zulfiqar told me, "He's telling the truth. All he shot were honest people. For the first forty years on the trail he was a robber in the Karakorams."

Toward the end of the fourth week a Tajik was caught stealing goods from an Uzbek and the culprit was dragged to the big yurt, where the two sharifs were discussing other business. The Tajik had no defense. Witnesses had apprehended him with the goods and he had to confess.

We gathered about the white rug as the two sharifs discussed the matter, and I realized that no nation exercised any sovereignty over this congregation of seventy or eighty thousand people. By consent these two sharifs, one a gunrunner and the other an outcast, enjoyed absolute control. If they now decided to execute the trembling Tajik, they could, but after a short consultation Shakkur the Kirghiz announced the verdict: the right hand to be cut off.

I gasped at the severity of the judgment and impulsively stepped forward. In Pashto I offered to pay the value of the goods stolen, but the old Hazara pointed out that my gesture made no sense. "The goods have already been recovered. What we try to accomplish is not punishment of this poor thief but prevention of further stealing. Carry out the order."

The Tajik began to whimper, but attendants whom I had often seen in the yurt and had taken as mere loungers grabbed the thief and whisked him outside. There was a pitiful scream, after which an Uzbek returned with a red dagger and the man's right hand.

The Hazara sharif, seeing that I was shaken to the point of sickness, took me aside and said, "We must be harsh. I've been sharif here for many years and this is the last cruel judgment I shall make. Don't think unkindly of me."

"Are you retiring?" I asked.

"Tomorrow," he replied with no regrets, "and there are many who think that your friend Zulfiqar should be the next sharif."

Then it became clear! Zulfiqar, having shrewdly guessed the old Hazara's intention to step down, had been conniving for twelve months to be his successor. He had used Ellen, Stiglitz and me exactly as he would have used us had he been bucking for a promotion at the General Motors office in Pontiac, Michigan. In a perverse way I was delighted with my discovery of Zulfiqar's frailty, for it proved that my view of the world was correct and not Ellen Jaspar's. Men everywhere behaved pretty much like her father in Pennsylvania; they had the same banal ambitions, which they expressed in the same banal phrases. But no sooner had I reached this conclusion than a chilling thought possessed me: This isn't Pennsylvania, and there are differences. If Zulfiqar tolerated Ellen's common-law adultery only because he wanted to achieve a goal here in Qabir, what will he do to Ellen and Stiglitz when he's through using them? Then an even more disturbing thought: For that matter, what will he do to me? Because as sharif of the camp he could order anyone destroyed, and who would halt him?

In this gloomy frame of mind I returned to our tents and hurried to see Dr. Stiglitz. "A dreadful thing happened at the yurt," I began, but my news was unnecessary, for in the glow of a lamp Ellen stood holding the right arm of the Tajik thief while Dr. Stiglitz cauterized the wound.

"How did this occur?" Stiglitz asked.

"In this camp two sharifs hold absolute power. Half an hour ago this Tajik was caught stealing; his trial took about four minutes. This is the clean-cut primitive life you wanted, Ellen."

The sight of the bloody stump, plus my news of how the camp was run, became too much for Ellen, and she started to faint, but the Tajik, sensing that she was about to fall, tried instinctively to catch her, and his bloody right arm tore across her burnoose, lacerating the nerve ends so that he screamed with pain. His cries brought Ellen to her senses and she gripped the table. The sight of her ashen face dispelled any sense of triumph I might have had. Afghanistan was much different from Pennsylvania and I wondered how this beautiful woman was going to extricate herself from the complications into which she had so willingly marched.

The next day Zulfiquar shaved with special care and asked me to accompany him to the yurt, where I entered a formal meeting in time to hear the old Hazara karakul merchant announce that he wished to relinquish his duty as sharif. He said, "You must choose a younger man, who can be depended upon to serve you for many years."

I never knew whether Zulfiqar had the meeting rigged or not, but as soon as the old Hazara sat down, a young Kirghiz who had frequented our tent rose and said, "Since one of our sharifs is my clansman Shakkur from north of the Oxus, I think it proper that the new man come from the south." I considered this a rather nice tactic, for the retiring Hazara did not come from the south; as a matter of fact, he came from about as far north in Afghanistan as one could and still remain in the country.

But the trick worked, and an Uzbek who had frequently shared our hospitality asked, "Why should we not select the Kochi, Zulfiqar? He's reliable."

There were no cheers, but there was quiet discussion, and by a process which I did not understand, my caravan leader Zulfiqar was elected sharif of the great encampment. It was a moment of triumph. Those who could speak Pashto told me, "We supported your friend because we were impressed with the way he shared his medical services . . . free." When I left, Zulfiqar was surrounded by the leaders he had been so assiduously wooing in the preceding weeks.

I rode out to camp and broke in upon Stiglitz and Ellen. "Heard the news?" I cried.

"What?" the German asked, as he tended an elderly Uzbek woman.

"Zulfiqar's been elected sharif of the encampment."

"What does it mean?" Ellen asked.

"You saw the Tajik thief . . . no right hand. It means power." She blanched.

It was Stiglitz who first acknowledged the implications of this election. Slowly he pieced together his conclusions: "Zulfiqar's been plotting this for months . . . must have guessed there'd be an election . . . knew he could impress the caravans with me as a doctor . . . Ellen for entertaining . . . Miller for the money. Damn! He used every one of us."

Ellen protested. "You're making it sound too pat."

Stiglitz continued, "So as long as he needed us for the election . . ." He looked at me and I nodded approval of his analysis.

"I'd leave camp," I added. "Right now."

"No!" Ellen cried. "Miller, you must not spread panic. We will not run away. Otto and I believe what I told you in the caves at Bamian. If this is the way it's to end, it's better than anything I ever anticipated."

She kissed Stiglitz and the two lovers renewed their determination to act as planned. I should have been impressed by Ellen's noble sentiment, but I wasn't; for in recent weeks whenever she had made one of her high-sounding speeches I had remembered my conclusion on the road to Bamian: *I have to respect Ellen's sincerity, but not her logic.* Now, for some subtle reason which I could not explain—perhaps because of her casual dismissal of Mira or her willingness to hurt Nazrullah and Zulfiqar—I was beginning to doubt not only her logic but also her sincerity.

In the days that followed, Zulfiqar treated me as a son-in-law. I cannot believe that he knew I had been commissioned by our embassy to spy out Qabir, but he could not have been more helpful had he been my assistant. He said, "In the camp we hear many rumors that this is the last year the Russians will permit their nomads to cross the Oxus, and that was one reason why I wanted the job of sharif. If next year Shakkur the Kirghiz cannot return . . ."

Thus he exposed his final tactic. He suspected that Shakkur might have to relinquish his job as sharif, which would leave him, Zulfiqar, as leading sharif if not the only one. I asked him why the Russians were threatening to close the border and he replied, "When India becomes a free nation, she'll close her borders, too. The day is coming when Kochis will have to stay home."

"What will you do then?" I asked.

"That's why Racha banks our money in Jhelum," he confided. "We're collecting what funds we can and in a few years we'll buy land." He hesitated, then spoke to me as he would have to a son: "I was discussing this with Moheb Khan when we met in Kabul. When the new irrigation dam is built, there will be much new land available at the edge of the desert."

"And you applied for some—to settle down?"

"A winter base," he replied. "We'll go to India no longer. In the spring, of course, we'll bring our goods to Qabir, but only a few of us. The rest will stay home to tend the fields."

"Do the others know?"

"They wouldn't believe it," he laughed, "but Racha and I have about decided. Soon it will happen."

It was a moment when the sweep of time stood exposed, and I thought of the arguments Ellen and I had conducted on this very problem. "Remember the morning when the villagers thought we were kidnapers?" I asked. "Ellen argued that Afghanistan must go back to the caravan and I argued that the caravan must go forward to the village?" I stopped. It was a hollow triumph. "God," I cried, "how exciting it was to march through those dreary villages at your side. Will your village be any better?"

"When you have known freedom," Zulfiqar said, "there's always a chance."

"Why are you stopping now?" I asked.

"Because the old freedom is slipping away from us. They're sending troops to check us at the borders . . . tax collectors. Next they'll inspect our tents. Qabir . . . how many more years will we assemble here?"

I looked at the sprawling tents where I had been so happy and said, "They'll be here when you and I are forgotten."

"No," he corrected. "The black tents are doomed."

"Does Ellen know you think this way?"

"She may have guessed. Perhaps that's why . . ." He didn't finish his sentence. Instead he gave me his professional laugh and said, "People like Ellen always have fixed ideas about how no-mads should live . . . and think. We aren't like that, and I'm sorry if we are disappointing."

"But you worked so hard to become sharif. If the black tents are doomed, why did you do it?"

"The tents will go, but the trade will continue."

"And you want to become a trader? An important man like the old Hazara?"

"In ten years few of the tents we see today will be here. Just a handful of men like me and the Hazara and Shakkur . . . bringing camels and a few servants to load them. We'll trade twice the goods—five times as much. It's clear, Millair, that four-fifths of this camp is unnecessary. The women and children accomplish nothing."

"Do the others agree?"

"All of us in the big yurt . . . especially the Russians." Then he surprised me by using the phrase that Stiglitz had spoken: "The caravans move on. They move to a distant horizon."

The time had now come for disbanding the camp and I discovered that this event was traditionally marked by a game of Afghan polo. Early one morning Zulfiqar sent Maftoon to find me and the cameleer asked, "You like to play polo?"

I said, "Tell Zulfiqar I know nothing about polo," but Mira clapped her hands and cried, "Tell Zulfiqar he'll play." But when I saddled up she checked the lashings and warned, "Better tie everything twice. This game can get rough."

I joined Zulfiqar and we rode to a field east of the confluence, where children waited, chattering with excitement, and the women of the camp, who made a place for Ellen and Mira. The field was crowded with horsemen clustering about the old Hazara, who was trying to establish some rough-and-ready rules. He did not ride his horse well, for under his left arm he held a white goat who struggled to get free, but the old man did succeed in showing us the two goal lines, about two hundred yards apart. Then he cried, "Shakkur, have your men pass out the arm bands," and the big Kirghiz gave the signal.

Shakkur gave me a white arm band and said, "Fight well."

It was to be south-of-the-Oxus versus north-of-the-Oxus, the Shakkur kept on his team the Uzbeks, Tajiks, Kazaks and Kirghizes, while Zulfiqar had riders from Afghanistan, India, China and Persia. There were about forty to a side, but for reasons which became apparent to me later on, no one bothered to insure that we were evenly matched.

Zulfiqar's White team lined up to defend the eastern goal and the Russians opposed us. In the center the old Hazara held aloft the goat by his rear legs while an Uzbek whipped out a knife and cut off the animal's head. With a savage cry the umpire threw the goat's body high in the air and left the field, not to interfere again. Before the goat, spurting blood, could land, a Tajik horseman swept in, caught the animal and raised it over his head in a mad gallop toward our goal line. He had covered only a few yards when he was hit from three sides by our riders, who tackled, grabbed, gouged and beat him. Finally one of our Turkomans leaped almost clear of his horse, grabbed the goat and wrenched it away from the battered Tajik, who was now bleeding from the mouth.

Our Turkoman set off boldly for the Russian goal, but a force of shouting Uzbeks and Kirghizes slammed into him and not only stole the goat but also knocked down his horse, so that he catapulted across the rocky playing field. No one stopped to see if he was hurt, and after a while he recovered his horse and rejoined the game. Meanwhile, one of our Afghans drew even with the Uzbek who had captured the goat and literally threw himself at his opponent, knocking the Russian rider right out of the saddle, but before the goat touched earth, Shakkur the Kirghiz sped in, caught it by one leg and fought his way through the mob to find himself with a clear path to our goal. The polo game was over, for no White rider could possibly catch him.

At this point, the essential feature of Afghan polo was made clear. When the victorious Russian team saw that their captain was about to score they regretted that the game was ending, so one of their own men, a fiery Uzbek set forth in hot pursuit and just as the baldheaded sharif was about to cross our line, this Uzbek teammate came up from behind, gave him a wallop across the back of his neck, grabbed the goat and brought it back into play. Both sides applauded, and the game continued. Thereafter, when any player threatened to score, his own teammates slugged him, gouged him and tried to knock him from his horse. It was always one rider fighting forty of the enemy plus thirty-nine of his friends, and sometimes it was the latter who did the worst damage.

For nearly sixty bruising minutes we played without my distinguishing myself—it seemed that half the other riders were bleeding from the mouth —when I happened to gallop past the children of our caravan and heard them shout, "Get in the game." I saw Ellen, and she looked a bit stunned by the brutality of the sport, but little Mira was furious. "Why did I get you the horse?" she shouted. "Do something!"

So I dashed into the middle of the fracas, where I accomplished nothing until a north-of-the-Oxus Kazak broke loose with what was left of the goat and headed in my general direction. It was apparent that unless I stopped him, the game was over, so I tried to turn him back into the mob, but the Russian decided that he could scare me into yielding ground, so he drove directly at me, and so far as I was concerned his strategy would have worked, for I was willing to withdraw, but Moheb's horse had been trained for just this kind of challenge and, ignoring my reins, leaped ahead seeking contact. We struck the Kazak with stunning force, spun him around and caused him to drop the goat, which to my surprise I caught.

But before I got started for the Russian goal, I caught a glimpse of Shakkur bearing down on me and in order to escape him tried evasive action. He anticipated my move and with his left arm clubbed me across the back so violently that I nearly pitched over my horse's head. In attempting to regain control I exposed the goat, which Shakkur grabbed, literally tearing it from me. He rode off with the body; I was left with one leg.

Dazed from his blow, I started in pursuit, but

the chase was fruitless, for Shakkur had a clear run for the goal, and even though one of his own Kazaks tried to knock him from his horse, the big sharif defended himself by clubbing the Kazak in the face with the bloody goat. Thus ended our game of polo, the sport of gentlemen.

Of the eighty players, more than half had substantial contusions and cuts, and of these, twenty-two were injured seriously enough to require help from Dr. Stiglitz, who set broken bones, pulled broken teeth and applied antiseptic to several square yards of flesh from which the skin had been abraded in sliding falls across the rocky field. This year, however, there had been no deaths.

As we finished treating the last of the cripples and listened to the sounds of festivity in the tents, where the game was being celebrated, I could not resist observing to Ellen, "Sort of like Saturday night after the Yale-Harvard game, isn't it? Or the country club in Dorset after a golf match?"

She had a good answer for this, I'm sure, but she was prevented from giving it by the arrival of the old Hazara, who had come by to congratulate me: "Your play was a credit to Zulfiqar and he should be pleased. A year ago I warned him, 'In 1946 I shall retire. If you act wisely you could be my successor.' Well, everything he's done this year has been correct and your presence and the young lady's"—he smiled at Ellen approvingly—"has helped him very much." He bade me farewell and rode back to the yurt.

When he was gone I saw that Ellen was trembling, partly from outrage, partly from apprehension. "He's been plotting this for a whole year," she muttered, her composure gone. "He's used us most shamefully. I wonder what he'll do now?"

I should have been sympathetic with her, but for some reason I wasn't, and an irreverent thought possessed me, which I ungallantly shared: "Rather neat trick he pulled, picking you up at Qala Bist and keeping you on ice for ten months."

She glared at me, but ignored the joke. "What do you think he'll do'?" she asked nervously.

Toward me, at least, his friendship increased. The day after the polo we rode to see the Russians dismantling the administration yurt and watched as a colorful procession of Uzbek, Tajik and Hunza caravans wound slowly to the east, heading for the crevices of the Hindu Kush. A visible sadness seized the Kochi leader and he turned on his horse to say, "If they do die, these caravans . . ." He paused, then said quietly, "Who could believe Qabir if he had not seen it? Son"—he had never called me this before—"I wanted you to see this plain with four hundred caravans. I saw it when I was a boy . . . no, when I was an infant too young to see anything. This is how men should live."

But each day we became more lonely. The Nuristanis next to us had departed and so had the Tajiks to the west, and a very real sense of doom enveloped our camp. I was constantly expecting retribution to overtake Ellen and Dr. Stiglitz, and I am sure they were too. In fact, I became so jittery that I began spotting where the guns were, and the knives, in case I was myself attacked, for it seemed to me that the brooding figure of Zulfiqar was everywhere.

Finally even Shakkur the Kirghiz departed with

his eighty camels, and our caravan was alone on the high plateau. I overheard little Maftoon complaining to the other cameleers, "If we don't start soon for Balkh, on the return trip the snows will trap us."

"Zulfiqar will tell us when to move," they assured him.

"He's not thinking of the snows," Maftoon lamented.

The next morning I heard a shouting at Zulfiqar's tent and I rushed over to find him standing with dagger in hand, towering over Dr. Stiglitz, who was unarmed and terrified. In his baggy Afghan trousers and dirty turban Stiglitz made a pitiful contrast to the powerful Kochi.

"Give him a dagger," Zulfiqar commanded, and when there was hesitation he shouted at Maftoon, "Give him yours. It killed a man in Rawalpindi."

Fumbling, Maftoon placed his dagger into the trembling hands of the doctor, who knew no more how to use it now than he had that morning in the caravanserai: he held it in both hands, pointed out from his chest.

I fought my way to the front of the circle and shouted, "Zulfiqar! No!"

"You be still!" the huge Kochi roared, and men grabbed my arms.

At the doorway to the tent Racha and some women held Ellen Jaspar, and I looked beseechingly at Mira, who refused to look back at me. Then Ellen screamed and I saw Zulfiqar, with a quick lunge, dive at Stiglitz, who, in a response born of despair, managed to escape the flashing blade but took no steps to attack his adversary.

Zulfiqar whirled expertly and drove at Stiglitz from the opposite direction, but again Ellen screamed and the doctor jumped aside just in time. He was terrified and was obviously about to be killed, except that Ellen, who had convinced him that death was of no consequence, now shouted, "Otto! Protect yourself!" And with this cry the insignificant man wanted to live. He became wary.

What followed occurred with dreadful swiftness, but each motion was etched on my mind. I shall never forget. I thought: I hope Stiglitz wins. I despised him, both for what he had done and for what he represented, but now that he was close to death at the very moment he had found Ellen Jaspar to restore his life, I wanted him to survive. Dear God, I prayed, let the German live.

A roar went up as Zulfiqar made a savage lunge at Stiglitz, who drew himself in so that the Kochi dagger missed, then stabbed at Zulfiqar as the latter flashed by. Stiglitz had drawn blood and the crowd murmured in astonishment.

I never knew whether Zulfiqar realized he was hit or not, but with a roaring leap he struck his opponent with both boots and knocked him to the ground. Like a cat he pounced upon him and wrenched away his dagger. Applying his knees to the doctor's arms, he stared down at the terrified face.

Ellen screamed as Zulfiqar's dagger flashed in the air and I was caught with horror as I watched it speed downward. I heard the crowd sigh. Then I heard voices.

Zulfiqar had driven his dagger into the soft earth, less than an inch from the pudgy doctor's neck. The powerful Kochi left it there as he pushed himself up, loomed over the fallen man and carefully spat in his face.

"Leave the caravan!" he cried in a terrifying voice.

He then stalked to the doorway of his tent and grabbed Ellen away from the women. With a cruel swipe of his hand he knocked her off her feet. Contemptuously he spat in her face and repeated his order: "Leave the caravan!"

Then he stepped across the two stupefied westerners and grabbed me by the throat with his left hand. With his right he gave me a blow that sent me staggering backward in the dust. "Get out!" he roared. "Get out!"

Finally he grabbed little Maftoon and lifted him off the ground. "They're your friends," he shouted scornfully. "Take them to Balkh. Now! Now!"

In a storming rage he tore into his tent and began throwing out all the possessions that Ellen had accumulated. This done, he rushed to my tent, where he did the same with everything belonging to Stiglitz and me. The doctor's bag landed on one corner and popped open, spilling medicine which the silent Kochis began greedily grabbing.

"Put it back!" Zulfiqar shouted. "We want nothing of theirs."

In this manner he continued, with blood reddening his back, until he saw us packed, with white horse saddled, and Maftoon ready with the camel Becky, who carried a tent for us, and a donkey whose panniers contained some food.

"Get out!" he bellowed, and as we crept away down the river trail toward the confluence where he had gained glory in the yurt, I saw him rip off his shirt to inspect his wound. It was not deep and he yelled for Racha to wash it. That was the last I ever saw of Zulfiqar or his wife Racha.

15

We formed a pathetic caravan as we moved out of the Hindu Kush. Stiglitz, shaken by his approach to death, was allowed to ride the white horse, which he did in silence. Ellen was in a state of unbelief: her jaw was sore and her vanity abused. Confusion was increased by the effect of her gray burnoose, which made her look soft and feminine while her words made her harsh and unlovely.

"How dare he strike me?" she asked several times. "And spit at me? He's no better than an ignorant mullah. I should have killed him myself." She was shaken with anger at the memory of her humiliation, and as I studied these bedraggled lovers I was willing to concede that they had converted themselves into non-people, those rejected dregs on which the world rebuilds, and I was sure they felt confirmed in this claim.

Little Maftoon was equally disturbed, because when he got rid of us at Balkh there was no escape: he would have to rejoin the caravan, and it had been his knife that had wounded Zulfiqar, his friendship for me that accounted for his being with us. The scar-eyed cameleer found no pleasure in this caravan, nor did his enemy Aunt Becky, who like all camels protested any trail that descended, since it threw unaccustomed burdens on her awkward front legs. She growled and gurgled so much that pretty soon somebody in the caravan had better undress and let her fight his clothes or there would be serious trouble.

Nor was I exempt from the sense of melancholy which had been closing in on me for days. I had lost Mira, the elfin spirit of the caravan, and I could imagine her trapped in the mountains by her father's hatred of me. In my loneliness I was forced to admit, for the first time, that I loved her without reservation. On the high plateaus she had laughed and teased her way into my heart, and she would remain a part of me as long as I lived. To have lost her without even a farewell was intolerable. But I had also been abused by her father, who during the preceding weeks had been treating me as his predilected son, sharing with me thoughts he would not confide to others. He had gone out of his way to help me with my mission, introducing me to the Kirghiz sharif, and from watching him at work I had grown to admire his cool calculations and mastery of politics; yet our friendship had ended with his knocking me down, cursing me and throwing me out of his camp. Frankly, I couldn't understand what had happened.

In fact, if one considered the entire complement of our cut-rate caravan, the only member not spiritually wounded was the donkey. He plodded along with panniers banging his sides, content to know that if he didn't work for us, on this trail, he would have to work for someone else, on some other trail.

We had proceeded thus for two silent hours when I heard Maftoon cry, "Miller Sahib! Look!"

I turned to see what new misfortune had befallen us, half expecting to find that Aunt Becky had broken a leg, but instead I saw Maftoon pointing back along the trail we had traveled, and there came Mira, in red skirt and pink blouse, running to overtake us.

"Her father will kill her," Maftoon lamented.

She was more than a mile away, a marvelous little hummingbird skipping across the meadowland, and I started running back to meet her. "Take the horse," Stiglitz offered, but I was already on my way.

Out of breath we met on the trail and rushed into a long kiss, which convinced me of how desperately I needed her, how ashamed I had been at being forced to leave the caravan without speaking to her. I think that as we finished our embrace she was weeping, but I do not know, for in these matters she was proud and she buried her face in my shoulder as I lifted her and carried her along the trail.

The others came back to meet us, all except Aunt Becky, who, when she started downhill, turned back for nothing. We looked at her gaunt brown figure plopping across rocks and began to laugh. It was so joyful to be with Mira, and cock-eyed Maftoon, and the lovers and the beat-up old camel.

As I put Mira down, Ellen ran to embrace her as if they were schoolgirl roommates, and the affection between the girls was real, for to Ellen Mira owed her dress, her manner of doing her hair and her few English sentences; and it was obvious that she was pleased to be with the American girl again.

But Maftoon warned in a doom-laden voice, "You should not have done this, Mira. Your father will kill you."

To our astonishment Mira replied, "He told me to come."

"He what?"

"Of course. I told him, 'I'd like to go to Balkh with Miller,' and he said, 'Why not?'"

"You mean that Zulfiqar . . ."

"He's not mad at anybody," Mira assured us, expressing surprise that we should think so.

"He knocked me down," Ellen protested. "He spat at me."

Again Mira embraced her friend. "He had to do that, Ellen. The others were looking, waiting—the whole caravan."

"He almost killed me," Stiglitz added, rubbing his neck.

Mira looked almost condescendingly at the German and asked proudly, "If my father had been truly angry, do you think he would have missed with his dagger? His honor demanded that he do something about you, Doctor. But he wasn't angry. It was only make-believe . . . in front of the others."

I caught Mira by the shoulders and shook her: "Are you telling the truth?"

She laughed at me as she broke free. "Miller! When my father said good-by just now he was chuckling. He told me, 'Tell that damned German he put up a good fight.' And he sent you this, Dr. Stiglitz." From her pink blouse she produced the

Damascus dagger Zulfiqar had used in the duel.
Handing the silver sheath gravely to the German,
she said, "His wedding present to you. My father
said, 'It will remind the wife that her husband was
once willing to fight for her . . . with daggers.'"

Then she took me aside and explained softly,
"When you left, Miller, my father went to our tent
and threw himself on the rugs. Again and again he
said, 'He was like my son. He was my son. Why
did I strike him?' For a while at Qabir I think he
hoped that by some miracle you would stay with
us and help him run the caravan." There was a moment of intense silence, broken by her sharp cry,
"There goes Becky!"

The willful old camel had spotted, off to one side
of the trail, some grass that she fancied and, having eaten it, now continued straight ahead in the
new direction even though it was taking her into
dangerous rocky areas. Nothing would stop her,
dumb beast that she was, for she would continue
plodding ahead until she destroyed herself, unless
some human teased her into returning to the trail.
By those who know them best, camels are considered the stupidest of animals, and Aunt Becky was
out to prove her claim to the title, but she was
forestalled by Mira, who dashed after the lumbering beast, cursing her madly, and we fell to laughing as the determined little nomad pursued the
huge camel, scrambling over rock and shale until
she had maneuvered Aunt Becky back to safety.

This was the tonic our bedraggled group
needed, and without fully appreciating what I was
doing or its consequences I took Ellen by the
hands and teased her in a schoolboy's way. "Ellen

and her men!" I chanted, waving her arms up and down. "She wants to reject the world, so she runs off with Nazrullah, whose only ambition is to build a big dam. So she drops him for wild free Zulfiqar, who wants to settle down beside the dam. Then she chooses Dr. Stiglitz. Look at him up there grinning on that horse. He's planning to build a hospital on Zulfiqar's land beside Nazrullah's dam."

"Ring-around-a-rosy," Ellen cried, joining in the joke. And with a sudden lilt of her body she began dancing me over the trail, her gray burnoose swinging free in haunting beauty. Then I felt the pulsating throb of life in her hands as they gripped mine and realized that this was the first time I had touched Ellen. She was vibrant and her eyes flashed, making her irresistible and quite different from the troubled young college girl we had discussed that wintry day at the American embassy in Kabul. I was caught by an embarrassment which sprang from reasons I did not then fully comprehend, and I let her hands fall, so that the force of her dancing spun her away in lovely gyrations until she collapsed in laughter on a grassy bank.

Dr. Stiglitz leaped from his horse to lift her to her feet, but Mira reached her first and asked with real concern, "Are you hurt, Ellen?"

"I could dance right out of the mountains," she told the little nomad. Then she reached up and kissed Dr. Stiglitz as he helped her back onto the trail.

In this manner we re-formed our little caravan and, with Mira restoring the levity we had lost, began one of the loveliest journeys any of us would ever know. From Qabir to Balkh was only eighty miles, which we should have covered in about five days, but we were in no hurry and our patient progress through the mountains became an extended joy. It had been one thing to carry on a light love affair with a bright-eyed nomad girl, built of hasty meetings in rocky enclaves; it was quite another to live with that girl twenty-four hours a day, helping her prepare pilau, watching her as she loaded the donkey and sharing her life as if we intended never to part. Once she said, "We should find mountains where it never snows and get us a flock of karakuls," and she laughed when Ellen teased, "Can't you imagine Mark Miller herding karakul sheep on Boston Common?" But her easy laughter did not hide the fact that we were falling deeper and deeper in love, so that our final parting was bound to be a matter of anguish.

At the same time I had a chance to observe Ellen and her doctor as they started their new life freed from the presence of Zulfiqar, and as I watched them I had to admit that there was some substance to Ellen's confused thesis about the non-people. She and Stiglitz worried about nothing. For them there was no past, no future, no responsibility. The days came and went, and the two lovers existed. They were non-people who on a high plateau in Afghanistan had found each other after a series of improbable adventures, and the days of their rebirth from nothingness were brilliant to watch.

Yet as soon as I have said this, I must confess that it was also now that I became aware for the first time of a dark presence when they were with us in the tent, an element of strangeness, almost of tangible foreboding. It was Mira who pointed this out to me. For us, love had been a relaxed and easily accepted experience. To be sure, the little nomad girl reveled in an exquisite passion, which she found joy in sharing, and I, although I am no expert in these matters, felt sure at the time that my response was adequate. But on the first night out of Qabir, when the bunks were made and all four of us had gone to bed in the black tent, Mira and I were astonished at the sounds which came from the opposite side of our quarters. It was as if those other lovers feared that nights were numbered and that at Balkh some tragedy would envelop them. Mira whispered, "We better leave the tent for them," but as we crept away I had the curious feeling that this extraordinary performance in the other bed had somehow been directed at me.

Mira and I walked in the gray light of the full moon, passing the nook where Maftoon slept with the animals, while the white horse, that symbol of leadership and manliness that Mira had brought me, grazed on the hillside. In Pashto Mira said, "I am convinced now that my father was relieved when Ellen started sleeping with Dr. Stiglitz."

"That's still an astonishing thing to say."

"I think he'd had enough of lovemaking," she suggested.

"With a girl like Ellen? You must be crazy."

"Do you remember that first morning?" she asked. "At the caravanserai? My father found you fighting and ran out to warn us, 'Hide Ellen. The American is here looking for her.' So we hid her in one of the little rooms. But only a few minutes later he ordered me to bring her before you."

I tried to recall the scene. Zulfiqar had taken our knife and the Kochis had entered, including Mira, whose saucy pigtails I could still see. Yes, Mira was right. Zulfiqar had sent her out specifically to fetch Ellen, and had he not done so, we need never have known that she was with the Kochis. He had intended me to find her.

Mira and I walked for some hours through the great mountains of Afghanistan, then crept quietly back to the tent where Ellen and Stiglitz were asleep, but on the second night the performance in the other bed was repeated and again Mira suggested that we leave, and in this manner my ambivalent feeling toward the other couple developed: in the day they were persons of feeling and judgment with whom I found an increasing sense of identification; but at night they became something strange. One curious facet of this ambivalence concerned Dr. Stiglitz, for I had gradually been forced to concede that he had transformed himself from a Nazi criminal into a man determined to serve humanity. My hatred for what he had done to the Jews in Munich was exorcised; our weeks together, our long discussions, had made him like a brother. I therefore had to conclude that whatever uneasiness I felt about the couple must stem not from Stiglitz but from Ellen.

For example, on the third evening out we pitched our camp in a rocky gorge that would lead us out of the Hindu Kush, and at the end of day Maftoon spread his little prayer rug on the rocks. Estimating where Mecca stood, he knelt to pray, but he had uttered only a few words when Dr. Stiglitz, impressed by the gravity of the mountains at dusk, joined him, and they knelt as the Koran directed, shoulder to shoulder in that brotherhood which Islam fosters and which is unknown to most other religions.

Women were not allowed to pray with men, so well to the rear Mira knelt and after a while Ellen joined her and I was left standing alone within the circle of rocks, wondering how there could be any connection between that spot and Mecca. I respected Islam, but I had never felt either a part of it or capable of ever becoming a part; but at this moment I remembered Nazrullah's question: *If you lived in Afghanistan permanently, wouldn't you pray as a Muslim?* Impulsively I knelt beside Dr. Stiglitz and felt his shoulder touching mine, and for some minutes the five of us prayed and I heard illiterate Maftoon chanting, "God is great. God is great. I am witness that there is no God but the one God, and I am His servant. For God is great. God is great." At that moment of fellowship I could believe that this strange religion, so difficult for a Jew like me to comprehend, had been specially ordained for deserts and high plateaus, and it had been sent by God Himself to make men in these lonely areas act as brothers. At that moment I experienced an intense sensation of Otto Stiglitz as my brother.

"God is great. God is good. We are the servants of God," Maftoon chanted, and it occurred to me: In all the Muslim prayers I have actually heard recited as compared to those one reads in books, I've heard only of God, never of Muhammad. Maftoon, as if he had overheard my thoughts, ended his prayer, "God is great, and I am witness that Muhammad is His Prophet." When we rose I looked back at the girls, and there was dark little Mira in pigtails still kneeling beside blond Ellen, whose burnoose fell about her stately figure like the robes of some saint in prayer, and there was a sense of beauty hovering above the worshipers so harmonious with the setting that for a long time we stayed in the shadow of the mountains saying little.

On the next day we penetrated the last range of hills separating the Hindu Kush from the arid plains leading to Balkh, and as Aunt Becky stumbled out of the mountains and saw flat ground again, she gave a series of joyful gurgles and started loping across the dusty fields, as if here at last was the true Afghanistan.

The heat became considerable, for this was mid-July, and we had to exercise caution in our use of water. We also reverted to the desert practice of traveling at night, but since the moon was nearly full this added to the beauty of our trip. During the day we slept, Stiglitz and Ellen in the tent, Maftoon with the camel, and Mira and I wherever we could find shade.

"I thought Ellen was your dearest friend," I chided Mira as we hiked through the heat looking for a place to sleep.

"She is," the little nomad replied, "but it will be safer if you sleep away from her."

"Why do you say a thing like that?" I demanded.

At first she refused to speak, then added simply, "It was while she was sleeping with my father that I discovered she was in love with Dr. Stiglitz."

"How could anybody know a thing like that?" I

asked with some irritation, for we were finding no shade.

"I told you at the time, didn't I?" she reminded me.

"How did you know?" I snapped.

"I knew, that's all."

Toward midnight of our fourth day on the plains I was riding the white horse at the head of the caravan when I spotted, in the silvery moonlight ahead, an extensive area denuded of trees but marked by solitary mounds on which grass seemed to be growing in scanty spots. In the semidarkness it looked like a burial ground for giants, but when Maftoon overtook me in the moonlight he said, "That is Balkh," and I rode on to inspect the meaningless sweep of empty earth.

So this was Balkh, mother of cities, fair Balkh where Alexander had married Roxane, the learned city at the crossroads of the world, the leading metropolis of Central Asia! As a boy I had been fascinated by this city, ancient and famous even before the days of Darius. All the remembered travelers of Asia had recorded their impressions of this dazzling treasure house: Ibn Batuta, Hsuan Tsang, Genghis, Marco Polo, Tamerlane, Baber. Its history was resplendent. Its memory was obscured. And now even its outlines were destroyed.

Could this be Balkh, this empty field of arid mounds where herd boys tended goats and wandering Kochis came to camp? This expanse of buried rubble with no plaques, no banners, not even a line of brick indicating where the great libraries had once stood . . . could this be the end of the city?

I felt inconsolably lonely, as if I were lost in the paralyzing sweep of history, a shard left by time. I felt like crying out in protest, and when I saw our faltering caravan approaching—one camel, one donkey, for Balkh—I could not find solace even in the thought that Mira would soon be with me.

At Rome the imperial ruins had also depressed me, but only for a moment, because it required no great imagination to believe that something of that grandeur persisted. But in Afghanistan my depression not only affected me; it also permeated the land and the culture and the people. It was difficult to believe that civilization had ever graced this arid waste or that it could return. At miserable Ghazni, at silent Qala Bist, at The City, at faceless Bamian and here at Balkh nothing remained. Were the generations indifferent to history, allowing their finest monuments to disappear while Rome retained hers? Or was it simply that Asia was different, its conquerors so terrible that western man could not visualize their cargoes of horror?

Many times I had crossed the path of Genghis Khan, merely one of the scourges and not necessarily the worst, and each time I had stood where he had erased a population. Perhaps a society cannot absorb such repeated punishments. Perhaps the scourging does something to the minds of men, converting citizens into frightened nomads who feel safe only when carrying their goods with them under their own surveillance. Perhaps it was Genghis Khan who explained why the Kochis and the Kizilbash and the Tajiks remained wanderers with no fixed civilization to sustain them.

Brooding in the moonlight at Balkh, I found increased respect for men like Moheb Khan, Nazrullah, and my preceptor Zulfiqar, who were determined to build a new Afghanistan that would conserve the memories of Ghazni and Balkh yet build upon the newer ideas of Russia and America. Had I been an Afghan, I would have allied myself to these impatient men.

As I reached this conclusion Maftoon brought his little caravan to the ruins, where for the past centuries the Kochis had camped, and while he and Stiglitz unrolled the tent Ellen came to me in the moonlight and said generously, "I'm sorry, Miller, that we quarreled so much on this trip. I've been struggling to find understanding."

"Found any?"

"Some. When it looked as if Otto might die in the duel, I did learn one important fact. That life of itself is good. I found myself praying that he would live."

"It's lucky he did," I replied. "You and he are bound to accomplish some great thing in Afghanistan."

"The non-people don't accomplish," she corrected gently. "They exist, and from them the world takes hope."

"One thing makes me feel better, Ellen. At last I have a glimmer of what you're talking about. But I'm like Nazrullah . . . committed to working for the civilization I'm caught in."

She smiled warmly and grasped my hands, and the effect was as electrifying as before. "How adorable of you, Miller, how predictable! To say a thing like that at Balkh."

"Why Balkh?" I asked.

"Don't you know that at the apex of their history the people here talked just like you? The mullahs proclaimed, 'Allah has this city in His special care. No harm can befall it.' And the generals boasted, 'Our forts are impregnable. No enemy can reach us.' And the bankers were especially reassuring: 'Last year our gross city product rose four percent. We can all afford two slaves in every kitchen.' And here is Balkh. And here is New York."

"Do you honestly believe that the same thing will happen to New York?" I asked, and immediately I was irritated with myself, for I had to recall my own thoughts when traveling down the ruins of The City: *This is Route One between New York and Richmond.*

"I believe that this is the future," Ellen replied. "But you mustn't. Because you're young. You're destined to go back to Boston and work there the way Nazrullah will work in Kandahar. I shall pray for you both, but I will never believe in what you're doing. It's really of no consequence . . . none whatever."

I told her, "I'll try to explain to your parents," and she was on the verge of speaking about them contemptuously when she changed her mind and kissed me, not politely on the cheeks but full on the lips with that abundance of love which had marked her life, and for a moment I comprehended the passion which had carried her so chaotically to Balkh. The impact of her kiss was like the touch of her hand at the dancing: it conveyed the sense of a woman with tremendous vital power and against my better judgment I was driven to wonder: What might have happened had

I met her in the States? In reply I heard the Haverford College boy telling the F.B.I. agent: *I always felt that somebody else might have kept Ellen on the track. But I will admit this. I wasn't the man to do it.*

I was about to break away when, to my surprise, she gripped my shoulders and kissed me again, desperately. "I wish I'd met you in America. After you'd learned what you have in Afghanistan." She brushed the hair from her forehead and looked at the ruins of Balkh. "No, I'd have been horrid for you. These ruins were in my bones." Laughing nervously she added, "Besides, you're so young and hopeful. And I've always been so very old."

As she said this the moonlight played upon her lovely face. Her body swayed backward in the gray blouse that Racha had embroidered, and her bare legs showed beneath the black skirt of the Kochis. Her ankles were caught by thongs from her sandals and she was beyond comparison the most vital and attractive woman I had ever seen. This time it was I who kissed her, and with a violence of consent she pressed her beauty into my arms and against my face and through my being. I was astonished by the overwhelming power of her response and betrayed my fear that the others might see us, but with a practiced eye she calculated that the men would be occupied for some time with the tent while little Mira would remain engaged in unloading the camel.

"They won't miss us," she assured me as she sought a hiding place among the mounds. She found one and beckoned.

"What are you doing?" I asked in astonishment.

She had kicked off her sandals and was untying the cord that held her skirt. "Didn't we just agree that life of itself was good? Let's enjoy it." When I hesitated she argued, "What difference would it make if they did find us?"

The idea stunned me and I remained where I was. "Mira would make the difference," I stammered.

"Don't you want to?" she asked provocatively, as the skirt fell about her ankles.

"You know I do."

"Then come on," and with ravishing grace she stepped from the fallen garment.

I knew that any man who hesitated at such a moment was bound to look pathetic, both to the girl and to himself, and I longed to join those slim, inviting legs. Instead I heard myself making the most improbable reply: "You shouldn't do this to Stiglitz."

With a kind of disgust—whether at me or Stiglitz or Mira I did not know—she recovered her skirt and refastened the cord. "I've done everything for Stiglitz I could," she said. Barefooted she came to me and whispered, "Besides, sooner or later the Russians are bound to get him."

Her callousness seemed as bleak as the desert and now I was glad that I had not followed her deeper into the dunes. "What happened to your idealism about Stiglitz?" I asked. "A few minutes ago you said you had prayed for him to live."

"He lived."

I thought: I'll bet she used the same kind of argument with Stiglitz when she was inviting him to move in on Zulfiqar. *But Otto, Zulfiqar's busy with other things. He won't care.* And she had been right. "Your flowery ideas about the non-people?" I asked. "You give them up? For a couple of days back there you had me convinced."

"Ideas come and go," she replied. Recovering her sandals, she said, "You know very well what we ought to do. Get us a sleeping bag and leave that tent right now."

"With Mira there?"

"I warned you on the trail that you were taking Mira too seriously. Besides, in a couple of days she'll be back with her father."

I drew away, appalled. "At Bamian you made fun of men who play what you called the point game. Right now I appreciate how important that game is. I honestly believe that if I treat Mira decently I get a point in my favor. And whether you like it or not, if you kick Stiglitz around, you lose points."

"With whom?" she asked contemptuously. "The Divine Scorekeeper?"

"No, damn it all. With me." She started to laugh and I got angry. "You reject religion. I don't. Millions of Jews are dead because they took religion seriously. So do I."

"Miller!" she cried, almost loud enough for the others to hear. "You don't take being a Jew seriously, do you?"

"Skip it," I said impatiently, sorry that I had raised the subject. "But the way you reject religion —what were you, Presbyterian?" She laughed and I added, "You know, Ellen, if you took Islam seriously . . ."

"I might be saved?" she asked mockingly.

"It wouldn't take much to save you. The more I hear you bleat about Dorset, Pennsylvania, the more convinced I become that it must be a pretty fair place. You ought to try it some time."

She laughed again and I became embarrassed with my prosaic philosophy and inept performance as a lover. I started back to camp but had moved only a few steps when she overtook me and grasped my arm. Again I could feel the lovely urgency of her body as she made an honest effort to conciliate our quarrel. Without rancor she asked, "Seriously, Miller, doesn't it make you self-conscious? Sentimental speeches like this . . . at Balkh, of all places?"

Her words were forceful and they made me stop. I looked at the undulating graveyard of the great city and saw, in my imagination, the rise and fall of Balkh—Balkh of the Flying Pennants it had been called, as if the city were proud to advertise its accomplishments, temporary though they proved to be—and I sensed some of the meaning behind my mission. I said, "I don't accept your view of Balkh. Cities crumble and civilizations vanish, but people go on. And damn it all, they eat and make love and go to war and die according to certain hopeful rules. I accept those rules."

"The rules?" she asked quietly. "They don't permit you to make love?" She moved close to me and I saw her in the moonlight, as beautiful a girl as I would ever know, more provocative a dozen times than Mira. "The rules won't permit you?" she repeated.

"Not with Mira over there," I fumbled.

"In the morning? Won't you feel like an idiot?"

"How do you suppose I feel now." I grasped her hands and said, "You're marvelously beautiful, Ellen."

She was pleased that I had done this, and returned to her former imaginings. "Why didn't we meet two years ago?" she asked softly. Then, more desperately, she cried, "Miller! Why didn't you come to Bryn Mawr that spring! In your clean white uniform? With your courage and your hopes?" She dropped my hands and asked quietly, "Why weren't you there?"

I left her and dodged among the mounds until I could present myself casually among the others. Improbably, they had not missed us and soon Ellen slipped inconspicuously back into the group she had been prepared to abuse. Once I caught sight of her unpacking the donkey, and as the night wind tugged at her hair she looked as if she had always been a part of these harsh, impersonal steppes.

It was now about three in the morning, and we made a little tea and pilau before going to bed, and as we sat about the fire Ellen said, through either accident or perversity, "Only a few miles up there is Russia."

A visible chill came over Stiglitz, but no one remarked upon his fear, so Ellen added, "Wouldn't you love to see what Samarkand looks like? They say its public square is the most exciting in the world." No one responded to this, so after a while she said languidly, "I think I'll go to bed," and Stiglitz dutifully followed her.

To share the tent with her that night would have been impossible, so I dragged out my sleeping gear and Mira lugged along a pillow, but before we had left the camp Maftoon took me aside and like a conspirator slipped me his dagger: "You must keep this, Miller."

"Why?"

"Because the German . . ."

"What about him?"

"When you and Ellen were in the dunes, he crept over to listen." The little cameleer sucked his teeth, then added, "And remember, he has Zulfiqar's dagger."

I felt dizzy. "Does Mira know?" I asked.

"It was she who asked me to give you my dagger," he explained. "She watched Stiglitz following you." And he was off.

When I rejoined Mira she said nothing, but ran her hands across my clothes till she felt Maftoon's dagger. "It's safer," she said.

There was nothing I could reply, so we looked for a sleeping place and after a while she observed quietly, "You and Ellen are the best friends I have. All I know about being pretty she taught me. She's a wonderful girl . . . like a sister. I told you, Miller, that she was hungry to sleep with you, but you laughed. After I go back with my father, why don't you and Ellen . . ."

I took her brown hands and kissed them. "I'm here because it's you I love," and I told her of the discovery I made while being expelled from the Hindu Kush without her: "You will be part of my life forever."

"Go to sleep," she said. "We have not many more nights."

The sun was well up when scraggly-bearded

Maftoon hurried to where we slept and warned me. "Important government car from Kabul. Man to see you, Miller!"

I assumed this must be Richardson of Intelligence, so I dressed hastily in order that he should not see me with Mira, but when I reached the tent area I found that it was Moheb Khan looking very official in a tan sharkskin suit and silver karakul cap. He was patting his stolen white horse, behind which, to my surprise, I saw Nazrullah, come north to reclaim his lawful wife. Instinctively I felt sorry for him, and because I had not seen him since his forced trip across the Dasht-i-Margo I hurried first to him, embraced him warmly and asked, "How was the desert?"

"As always, hateful."

"We kept our fingers crossed."

Now Moheb Khan interrupted, speaking with severity: "How'd you get my horse?"

I couldn't tell whether he was truly angry or merely joking, so I temporized: "Mira bought him in Kabul."

Moheb brushed dust from his suit and asked, "You certainly knew it was mine. Didn't you guess it was stolen?"

"Was it?" I bluffed.

Moheb was unable to continue the pose and began laughing. "You know how it is. You find a pretty girl. You roll over thinking, 'This is going to be a night of passion.' And you find that your white horse has been stolen."

"Don't punish her."

"Did she steal it for you?"

"Yes."

"Then it's you I curse. For eight weeks you ride and I walk."

I replied, "You know how love is. Roll over again. There's your white horse, well fed and cared for."

Now Mira appeared on one of the mounds lugging our sleeping gear, which told its own story, and when she saw Moheb Khan, from whom she had stolen the horse, she dropped the bedclothes and started running for the tent, but I caught her by the wrist.

"Little thief!" Moheb snarled.

Mira was like me. She didn't know whether Moheb was joking or not, but her irrepressible nature asserted itself—or perhaps she remembered Moheb in some earlier pose—for she broke out laughing and pointed with derision at the handsome Afghan. Making involved gestures, which could only be interpreted as the pantomime of her escape through a bedroom window to steal the white horse, she soon had Moheb laughing with her.

But then Mira saw Nazrullah and recognized him by his beard. "You're Ellen's husband!" she cried in dismay, and the involuntary manner in which she moved protectively before the tent proved that Nazrullah's wife must be inside. Slowly, step by step, Mira retreated, bowed ceremoniously and ducked into the tent.

"Is Ellen there?" the engineer asked me.

"Yes."

He started for the tent but I stopped him. "Is the big Kochi with her?" he asked suspiciously.

And suddenly I realized that whole new cycles

of adventure had engulfed his wife, none of which I fully understood but some of which I was myself involved in. At any rate, I couldn't explain these new developments to Nazrullah, so I stammered, "Look, this is going to be difficult to get into focus. But that big Kochi . . ."

I was spared by the appearance of Ellen and Stiglitz. What kind of hateful truce they had patched up during the night I couldn't guess, but in the morning sunlight Ellen Jaspar was dazzling, and if her husband was still determined to win her back, I could sympathize, for when I saw her in daylight I had to say, against my own conscience: It's you she wants to leave with, you idiot. Move in. Move in fast.

Nazrullah was bewildered by the facts before him and refused to accept their implications. As if nothing had happened, he stepped forward to greet his wife. "I've come to fetch you," he said. "You remember Moheb Khan. Moheb, this is Dr. Otto Stiglitz."

The tall diplomat bowed gracefully and shook hands. "We'll drive you back to Qala Bist," he said to Ellen with a studied air which seemed to say: We're going to give you one chance. Don't mess it up.

"I'm not going," she said firmly, whereupon Moheb Khan shrugged his shoulders and withdrew from the conversation. He had made a conciliatory offer and it had been rejected.

It was Nazrullah who took over. "Please, Ellen. We have the car waiting."

Stiglitz gave the answer: "She's to stay with me. I'm sorry, Nazrullah."

The engineer was determined not to surrender his wife and appealed to Moheb for support, but the diplomat ignored him and asked me, "Is this what happened? Stiglitz?" My nod triggered a dramatic barrage of decisions announced by Moheb.

First he blew a whistle, which was answered by a group of soldiers who had followed him in a truck. "I want that horse taken back to Kabul," he ordered. "This man," he snapped, indicating Stiglitz, "Is to be kept here under arrest. The American woman is not to leave this tent. You, Miller, get in the car. I want to interrogate you at headquarters in Mazar-i-Sharif. Nazrullah, come along." And while the soldiers moved quickly in response to his commands, he led Nazrullah and me to the car.

We sped toward Mazar-i-Sharif, which lay some twenty miles east of Balkh, but as we reached the city our car was impeded by an extensive camel caravan which was setting forth to central Russia, and we had to wait while some eighty lumbering beasts went by, poking their ungainly heads toward our car and grunting at us as they adjusted to the heavy burdens which they were to carry north. The camel drivers, an unusually dirty and unkempt gang, stared at us like their camels and Moheb remarked with some irritation, "Of all the people you meet in our country, ninety-four percent are illiterate. Are we crazy, trying to build a modern state from such rabble?"

I looked at the camel drivers, barely out of the bronze age, and said to the two impatient men beside me, "If I were an Afghan, I'd certainly make the effort."

"I wish we had a million Afghans like you,"

Moheb replied, as the last camel went by, leering at us. And then I saw, riding a sturdy black horse, the master of this nondescript caravan and I understood why his cameleers had looked so filthy. Their owner had wanted them to look that way lest his camels give the impression of carrying some unusual wealth which might attract brigands.

For this was the caravan of Shakkur, the Kirghiz gunrunner from Russia. He had loaded his camels at Mazar-i-Sharif, and was now on his way to cross the Oxus and the great Pamirs and the steppes of Central Asia. Since his was the most dangerous route followed by any of the major caravans attending Qabir—perhaps this was the last time a caravan of such magnitude would make the trip—he sought to avoid attention.

As he rode by I called to him and he remembered me from the encampment. Stopping his horse near our car, he poked his huge bald head our way and, after studying Moheb with suspicion, asked, "Government man?" When I nodded, he said, "So you were a government spy? I warned Zulfiqar."

"No," Moheb laughed. "We've just arrested him."

The big Kirghiz put his left hand over his forehead and cried, "My sympathy to all prisoners," and he spurred his horse so that he might overtake his eighty camels.

At the government offices Moheb ordered tea and biscuits with honey, reminding me of how primitively we had been eating for the past seventeen weeks; but I was dragged back to present problems when he summoned a secretary—a man, of course—and started arranging papers as he asked,

"Now what shall the official report state regarding that horse?"

"Is this for the record?"

"That's why I'm here. The horse and the American woman . . . both stolen."

"Mira told me she bought the horse."

"Where would a Kochi girl get the money?"

"She said she got it from the jeep they stole."

"Jeep?" Moheb repeated.

"Could I strike that from the record?"

"You'd better," Moheb nodded to the secretary.

Nazrullah interrupted. "What did happen to that jeep?"

"Can I speak confidentially?"

"Of course," Moheb agreed, nodding again to the secretary.

"While I stood not twenty feet away, those damned Kochis stole every movable part."

Abruptly Moheb asked, "Who exactly is Mira?"

"Daughter of Zulfiqar," I explained.

"The same Zulfiqar?" he asked, indicating Nazrullah.

"Yes."

"Now as to the new developments regarding Ellen Jaspar."

"It's difficult to explain," I fumbled.

"We have plenty of time," Moheb assured me, pouring some more tea.

"Well, as you know, she ran away from Qala Bist last September. It wasn't love. It wasn't sex. Nazrullah wasn't at fault. Neither was Zulfiqar. When she joined the caravan she didn't even know who Zulfiqar was."

"Is that what you're going to say in your report to the American government?"

"I've already said it."

"Where did she spend the winter?"

"Jhelum."

"All the way to Jhelum? On foot?" Apparently Moheb knew less about some of his country's customs than I did.

"Was she ever in love with the big Kochi?" Nazrullah asked.

"Never."

"Miller," Moheb asked carefully, "if this secretary has to record one simple reason for Ellen's behavior, what shall he write?"

I pondered this question for some minutes, reviewing Ellen Jaspar's motivation as I understood it. It wasn't sex, because her behavior with Nazrullah, Zulfiqar and Stiglitz had an almost sexless quality; she was neither driven by desire nor faithful to anyone who fulfilled it. I wondered if she might be suffering from some kind of schizophrenia, but I could find no evidence that she was; no one was persecuting her; she persecuted herself. At one point I had thought she might be a victim of nostalgia for a past age, but she would have been the same in Renaissance Florence or Victorian England; history was replete with people like her, and although she despised this age, no other would have satisfied her better. It was true that like many sentimentalists she indulged in an infantile primitivism; if bread was baked over camel dung it was automatically better than bread baked in a General Electric range, but many people were afflicted with this heresy and they didn't wind up in a caravan at

Balkh. There remained the possibility that she suffered from pure jaundice of the spirit, a vision which perverted reality and made it unpalatable; but with Ellen this was not the case. She saw reality rather clearly, I thought. It was her reaction to it that was faulty. And then I heard the dry, emotionless voice of Nexler reading from the music professor's report: *I saw her as a girl of good intention who was determined to disaffiliate herself from our society.* This didn't explain why she acted as she did, but it certainly described what her actions were. I looked at Moheb and suggested, "Put it down as rejection."

"Name one man she ever rejected," he demanded.

I preferred to ignore his condemnation and replied, "She rejected the forms and structures of our society . . . yours as well as mine."

"It's about time somebody rejected her," Moheb snapped. "And I'm the man to do it."

"Don't abuse her," Nazrullah pleaded.

"Would you still take her back?" Moheb asked incredulously.

"Yes," Nazrullah replied. "She's my wife."

"He's right," I told Moheb. "You'd both better get used to Ellen Jaspar," I warned. "Because once you let your women out of chaderi, Afghanistan's going to have a lot of girls like her."

Moheb groaned. "Do you believe that?"

"It's inevitable," I assured him. Then to protect Ellen, who in so many ways merited help, I added, "Give her the benefit of one thing, Moheb. She loves your country. In fact, she plans to live here the rest of her life."

"With Stiglitz?"

I started to say yes, but hesitated, and from the way Moheb Khan looked at me I knew he suspected something between Ellen and me. I was another of the men she had not rejected, but Nazrullah, still fighting to get her back, missed the interplay, so I finished my sentence. "Yes, she's staying with Stiglitz."

"Tell me about him," Moheb said.

"She knew him in Kandahar, but I'm sure nothing romantic happened." Then I was forced again to pause, for I saw before me the caravanserai and my first meeting with Ellen Jaspar, and she was sweeping past me on her way to greet Stiglitz. I heard her clear voice crying, *Dr. Stiglitz! Are you all right?* Now what had really happened became clear to me. When she unexpectedly saw Stiglitz against the wall that morning her lips had begun to form a word, which she suppressed instantly. The discarded word was *Otto,* and I could now see it on her lips. Had they known each other that well in Kandahar? Had her blond, Germanic beauty so deeply affected him there at the edge of the desert?

"Something romantic did happen?" Moheb pressed.

"No," I said firmly. "Now about Stiglitz. On our trip north . . ."

"Who suggested that he come north?"

I had not previously considered this matter, but now I tried to reconstruct additional events from that first day with the nomads, and after a long pause I had to say, "I think it was her idea. I think she planned it all . . . that evening."

(416)

"I thought so, too," Moheb replied.

"At any rate, on the trip north they fell in love. At Qabir there was the dagger fight. Stiglitz handled himself capably and even wounded Zulfiqar. After which we were all thrown out."

"Is she determined to live with him?" Nazrullah asked quietly.

"Absolutely," I lied, as Moheb smiled.

"Could I possibly win her back?" Nazrullah pleaded.

"Never," I said with some assurance.

"Suppose we deported Stiglitz?" Moheb suggested.

I thought I was listening to Ellen's insidious suggestion: *Sooner or later the Russians are bound to get him.* I hesitated, and Moheb continued, "When Stiglitz left Kandahar for this . . . this stupid caravan, he broke our law. We've the right to throw him out. Shall we?" The two Afghans leaned forward to catch my reply.

I hesitated. Here, in a strange room in a drowsy provincial capital, my whole mission in Afghanistan was coming to focus. To calm myself I took a drink of tea and thought: These men want me to recommend his deportation. If I really wanted revenge on Stiglitz, I could get it now. The possibilities were gruesomely fascinating, particularly if I recalled the cage full of Jews he had destroyed; but I could feel against my shoulder, as if it were a real force in that room, the pressure of the German's body against mine as we prayed at evening, and I heard myself diverting Moheb with the question, "Does your intelligence report on me cover the fact that I'm a Jew?"

"It does not," Moheb replied, masking any surprise he might have felt.

"I am. That night at the caravanserai, Stiglitz betrayed the horrible things he had done in Munich. More than a thousand Jews sent to death."

"We know," Moheb observed, indicating his papers.

"I tried to kill him. Would have done it, but Zulfiqar arrived with his caravan. I despise Stiglitz. He's a criminal and he ought to hang. But on this trip I've come to know him. He'll serve your country well, Moheb. You just said you needed men like me. He's much stronger than I would ever be. Don't deport him."

"Why not?" Moheb asked cynically. "His going would solve Nazrullah's problem."

"Don't do it!" I warned.

"Why not?" he repeated.

"Because it would be wrong . . . morally wrong."

Nazrullah broke in: "Is there nothing I can do to bring her back?"

"Nothing," I said with great finality. "Even if you were to hang Stiglitz, you'll never get her back."

The force of my words struck the bearded engineer, and to my surprise he dropped into a chair and buried his head in his arms. For some moments his shoulders twitched while we watched in embarrassment. Then Moheb coughed and said, "Dear friend, Miller's right. You've lost her and there's nothing to do about it."

I remember thinking: It's really ridiculous, carrying on like this over a second wife, but then I recalled Ellen as she had been among the ruins, as she was in bed with Stiglitz in the black tent, and I admitted to myself: He's no fool. No wonder he wants to keep her.

Moheb took my arm and said, "Leave him alone," and he led me to another room, where he dismissed the two government clerks and checked doors to be sure no one was listening. When all was secure he moved close and stared into my eyes. "What did you discover at Qabir?" he asked.

"Nothing," I replied with as much simplicity as I could muster.

"Don't lie to me," he snapped. "Don't you suppose I know why you were sent north?"

"I don't know what you're talking about," I bluffed.

"Miller, for heaven's sake! Richardson drove out to the Kochi camp in Kabul and personally handed you orders: Go to Qabir and see what the Russians are up to."

"He did not!"

"Damn it all, we know he did. How else do you suppose he got Shah Khan's permission?"

The reasoning was logical and I was almost ready to come clean when I thought: What if he's bluffing? I replied with some impatience, "If that's what he was supposed to tell me, he certainly forgot. All he did was raise hell about that stolen jeep."

He had been bluffing. "What'd he say about the jeep?" he asked lamely.

"That they were docking my pay six hundred dollars."

Seeking to catch me off guard, Moheb whipped his long forefinger into my face and shouted,

"Miller! You know damned well the American embassy would never let you wander off to Qabir without orders. What were they?"

"Richardson didn't give me orders. I asked to go."

"Why?"

"Because I'd fallen in love with Mira."

"You mean that you told the American ambassador you wanted leave for ten weeks because," and here his voice dripped with contempt, "you'd fallen in love with a little nomad girl?"

"I didn't tell Richardson about her."

"What did you tell him?"

"I reminded him that Washington wanted me to stay on the Ellen Jaspar case until it was settled."

Moheb dropped his truculence and asked casually, "So what did happen at Qabir?"

"Like I said. Zulfiqar damned near killed Stiglitz."

He slammed his fist on the table. "The Russians?"

"I don't anything about the Russians," I protested. Then I changed my voice. "I did discover one thing. That big Kirghiz we just saw was the leading sharif at the camp."

"How does he get into Afghanistan?"

"I wouldn't know about that."

"What the hell do you know about?"

"That the other sharif was this old Hazara who trades in karakul."

"We know about him."

"But this year he retired."

"He did?"

"And to take his place they elected Zulfiqar."

"Indeed?"

"And since Zulfiqar is eager to settle down on some of that new irrigated land near Qala Bist, you might do a good thing for Afghanistan if you settled his clan on five or six thousand acres."

Moheb tried to mask his irritation over the fact that I knew of this confidential matter and asked quietly, "Miller, if we offered Zulfiqar the land, would he take it . . . and stay put?"

"Positively."

"How can you be so sure?"

"We discussed it."

"Why would he confide in a ferangi? On such a matter?"

I wanted to say something that would help Zulfiqar, so I lied, "One day I mentioned that I knew you, and he said, 'Moheb has power of life and death over those lands.' He didn't ask me to intercede, but I know he hoped that I would."

"Well, at least you found out something."

"Then you'll give him the land?"

"We have many applications," he evaded.

"But none like Zulfiqar. He's a man like you and Nazrullah. He needs the land and you need him."

Moheb looked at me with compassion and said, "Why are you Americans so hopelessly stupid? I'll bet there were a dozen Russian agents in that camp, but you saw nothing except a nomad girl."

"I wasn't worrying about Russians," I laughed. He shook his head in amiable disgust and we returned to where Nazrullah was staring at the wall.

"What must I do?" The engineer asked us, no further in his solutions than when we left.

"I know what I must do," Moheb replied briskly.

He summoned the secretary and asked, "Did you check my portfolio to be sure the alternative papers are in order? Good . . . Nazrullah, Miller, come along."

"To do what?" Nazrullah asked.

"To find three white pebbles."

"No!" Nazrullah cried. "I won't."

"Then I will," Moheb replied matter-of-factly. Then he stopped, reflected and said, "There is another way out for you."

"What?" Nazrullah asked eagerly.

"We'll turn your wife over to a bunch of mountain mullahs. A woman taken in adultery." He laughed at his grisly joke, then added gently, "Old friend, take my advice. Find the white pebbles."

As we left the office the secretary stopped us. "Don't forget your call to the English embassy."

"Of course!" Moheb agreed, sending us ahead, and before we left the building we could hear him shouting into the fragile Afghan telephone, "Hello, hello, hello! Is that you, Your Excellency? Here is Moheb Khan. Your Excellency, I want the British government to be alerted . . ." We did not hear the rest.

On our trip back to the barren fields of Balkh, Moheb consoled Nazrullah by reciting verses from the Persian poets, but when the car stopped at our capsule caravan it was Moheb who started hunting for the three white pebbles. When they had satisfied themselves, Nazrullah walked boldly to the black tent and called, "Ellen."

The soldiers brought her forth dressed in black skirt with gray blouse and three gold bracelets on her left wrist. Her tanned face was radiant in the sunlight, her marvelous blond hair framing it in windblown lines. As her legal husband approached, she looked solemnly at him and waited for his question: "Wife, will you come back with me to Qala Bist?"

"No," she replied in an icy voice, whereupon he raised his right hand and threw one of the pebbles to the ground.

"I divorce thee," he announced. Again he looked at her, beseeching her to rejoin him, but again he had to raise his arm and throw a second pebble to the ground.

"I divorce thee," he announced as Ellen listened without emotion. For the third time he pleaded with her, and for the third time she rejected him. Looking at her with eyes that had filled with tears, he hesitated in hopes she might reconsider, but she remained impassive, and he dropped the last pebble.

"I divorce thee," he said in a ghostly whisper. Unable to look further at the beautiful woman he had wooed in a strange land, he turned and walked with dignity to the car.

As he went, I watched Ellen Jaspar, now legally divorced, standing immobile by the tent. A smile of quiet satisfaction marked her lips, for now she was free, and from the right side of her body she lifted her hand ever so slightly so that she could form with her thumb and forefinger a circle, which she flashed at me, signifying: "All's well."

"Bring out Stiglitz," Moheb ordered, and the German was led forth, blinking in the sunlight. He must have guessed that Ellen intended to desert him, for he ignored her and looked only at Moheb.

"Otto Stiglitz," Moheb began, "we've informed the British government that you're being surrendered to them at Peshawar, in India. You're a criminal of war, and we have no place for you in Afghanistan." He blew his whistle and other soldiers appeared. "Take him to Peshawar," he announced, and an officer started clapping handcuffs about the German's wrists.

But this was to be no easy arrest, for Stiglitz broke loose and threw himself at me. "Jew! Jew!" he screamed. "You've done this to me." He scratched at my face until one of the soldiers tore him away.

Then he lunged at Moheb Khan, pleading, "Excellency, don't believe him. He's a filthy Jew and he told you lies. Why did he lie to you? Because he wants the girl himself. Yes! Yes!"

The commotion brought Nazrullah back in time to hear Stiglitz cry, "Yes, Excellency! Last night this Jew took the girl over there. They committed indecencies. And while they were doing it they plotted my death."

He left Moheb and threw himself at Ellen, who drew back in disgust. "This one made love with the Jew behind that mound. And she told him, Hand the German over to the Russians, they'll hang him. Excellency, the Jew has poisoned your mind."

Moheb ordered the soldiers to pinion the doctor's arms, and when this was done he stood before the German and said, "The Jew you condemn has just spent an hour with us, pleading for your life. At your trial, I'm sure he'll testify for you."

Snapping his fingers, Moheb ordered the soldiers to drag the prisoner off, but as he went he tried to grab my arm. "You will tell the judges what I said at the pillar? There are many Jews in Munich alive today because . . . You will testify for me?"

"I will," I said, and he was dragged away. The truck engine sputtered. The wheels spun in the sand, and the soldiers were gone.

"Take the girl to the car," Moheb ordered Maftoon, and the unshaved cameleer led Ellen away. Since I had assumed that I was to remain in Balkh until Zulfiqar arrived, I supposed that this was the last time I would see Ellen Jaspar, and it was with real confusion that I saw her go. Her fair head was provocative as ever, her lithe body beneath the gray blouse and black skirt as exciting, and her long legs ending in the leather sandals were as alluring. The clever rationalizations I had given at the interrogation seemed irrelevant when confronted by the girl herself.

I broke the spell by turning away and going to Mira, but I was unexpectedly halted by Moheb, who grabbed my arm and said, "You, too, Miller. We start for Kabul . . . now."

"I'm not leaving."

"Shah Khan's orders."

"I've got to say good-by," I protested, bringing Mira to my side.

"Say it. In five minutes we go."

"What about my gear?"

"You," he shouted at Maftoon, "pack his stuff. Hers too."

I led Mira away from the tent to one of the mounds of Balkh, from which we could see the foothills of the Hindu Kush, where we had been so happy. "I hoped we'd be here for a week," I began.

"You will look after Ellen," she replied. "She talks strong but she needs help." She was about to speak further when her nomad boisterousness took command and she cried, "Look at that crazy camel."

We left the mound and walked to where Aunt Becky was searching for grass. Her droopy eyes, ungainly feet and preposterous lower jaw kept her a comedian, even at this painful moment, and in gratitude for her having brought us so far I reached out to pat her in farewell, but she was not one to be tricked by sentiment. She interpreted my gesture only as a preamble to being loaded with burdens and withdrew uttering loud protests, and we were left alone.

"Mira, Mira," was all I could say, for in these last precious minutes there was so much we should have said and so little capacity for speech. Our parting had come so suddenly and was accompanied by so much ugliness that any chance for a decent farewell had been destroyed.

"Qabir, Bamian, Musa Darul," she recited. "When we are at those places . . ." She looked at me, deeply ashamed of the tears forming in her eyes. She blinked them away, laughed, and said, "Without you the caravan will be a marching of ghosts. You were very handsome on your white horse."

At the car Moheb was blowing the horn.

Then I remembered the warning which Stiglitz had sounded in the black tent: *Leaving this nomad girl is going to be a different experience from what you imagine.* But to leave her in this manner . . . a part of my conscience, of growing up, was being torn away.

"Inshallah," I mumbled.

"Inshallah," she replied.

Unable to look back, I hurried to the car where Moheb sat at the wheel with Ellen beside him and Nazrullah in the rear. The engineer, ignoring his former wife, sat gazing through field glasses at the foothills of the Hindu Kush.

"It's uncanny," he mused. "How could she have seen such a distance?"

He handed me the glasses and I saw that Mira had left the ruins and was striding purposefully toward the mountains, out of which her father's caravan had appeared, following those ancient trails which soon the nomads would travel no more.

On the drive back to Mazar-i-Sharif no one spoke. Ellen's presence, following the charges against her that Stiglitz had broadcast, was more than we could cope with at the moment. Besides, I was affected by real suspense concerning her future, for I could not guess Moheb's plans, and he drove in imperious silence, his firm jaw locked in self-counsel. I supposed that when we reached Mazar we would deposit her at the government building, but we did not.

To my surprise we drove straight through the city and picked up an ancient road, thousands of years old, leading to the northeast. Along it plodded a camel caravan, insensitive to our intrusion, and as I looked ahead I saw on his black horse Shakkur, the Kirghiz gunrunner.

"Ho, sharif!" Moheb called from the car, and the Russian galloped up and dismounted.

He saw me sitting gloomily in the rear seat and asked seriously, in broken Pashto, "You taking the criminal out to shoot him?"

"No," Moheb laughed. "We have a passenger for your caravan."

Now the big Kirghiz saw Ellen, with whom he had danced that night at Qabir, and intuitively he grasped the situation. "This one?" he asked.

"Yes."

"She have papers?"

"Yes." From his portfolio Moheb took Ellen's green passport and handed it to the sharif. In Arabic, Cyrillic and Roman writing, signed jointly by Shah Khan and the Russian ambassador, it was stated that the bearer had permission to transit Russia on her way home to America. On a special page, for me to see, was the official notice that Ellen Jaspar, having been legally divorced from her Afghan husband, was free to exit the country. Ceremoniously Moheb Khan handed Ellen the precious document and announced, "Madam, you are being kicked out of Afghanistan."

To the Kirghiz he explained these matters, handing him a substantial number of Afghan gold coins. "This will pay her passage to Moscow. We'll cable her parents, and they'll have the rest waiting there."

"Christ Almighty," I exploded, jumping from the car. "You can't do this."

"I'm not doing it," Moheb protested. "She's doing it herself."

"What do you mean?"

"I came to Balkh with two sets of papers for this girl. One would have restored everything as it was.

The other set kicks her out of the country. I gave her the choice. She made it."

"She didn't know what was involved!" I protested, trying to get Ellen to appeal for a second chance.

The tall Afghan turned his back on us and explained to Shakkur, "The poor boy's in love with her."

The big Kirghiz smiled indulgently, then asked with caution, "Does my friend Zulfiqar know of this?"

"He kicked her out of his caravan," Moheb reported. "We're doing the same."

Apparently the young leaders of Afghanistan were not afraid of making difficult decisions, but in the case of Ellen Jaspar their decisions were wrong, so I went to Moheb and warned him in rapid French, "This could cause serious trouble between our governments. How do you know what will happen to this girl?"

At that moment Moheb was helping Ellen from the car and he replied thoughtfully, "This girl? Nothing will ever happen to this girl." And he escorted her graciously to the Kirghiz, to whom he also delivered her pitifully small bundle of clothes.

At this point I had to interrupt. I took Ellen and Shakkur away from the others and asked, "Ellen, do you appreciate what's happening?"

With infuriating equanimity she ignored me and asked the sharif, "Where are we going?"

Pointing northeast he replied, "We cross the Oxus at Rushan, cut through the Pamirs, then Garm, Samarkand, Tashkent." It was a trip I would have given a year to take, and Ellen appreciated this, for when Samarkand was mentioned she smiled at me with deep satisfaction.

"Will we get there safely?" she asked.

"That's my job," the sharif replied, and I reflected: For ten weeks I tried every trick in the book to find out how the Russian nomads cross the Oxus. Now the top man tells me.

I said, "Ellen, I could force the Afghan government . . ."

"I'm not afraid," she answered, and she looked at me as if she were free and I the prisoner.

I summoned the others and announced, "I want everyone to hear that in the name of the United States government I do protest most vigorously this incredible act."

Ellen laughed and replied, "You heard him, gentlemen. If he catches hell, we'll all have to testify for him." She held out her hands, took mine and kissed me. "I do wish we'd met in America," she said.

With this speech she intended to leave, but decency would not permit her to go without acknowledging Nazrullah, so at last she stepped before him and said, "Dear friend, I am most sorry." They looked at each other without moving and I thought again of how, on the desert, he had consulted the stars before assuring me that Ellen was safe once more in Afghanistan. Now he would follow those same stars till he knew that she was safe in America.

Finally she turned away and swung easily into the rhythm of her new caravan, as if she had been traveling with it for many months. I watched as the big Kirghiz galloped back to the head of his camels, spurring them on; for this caravan, excused from the encumbrance of either sheep or families, did not intend to cover a mere fourteen miles a day. It was headed for towering passes that must be cleared before the fall of snow, and for these travelers to Russia there would be no restful halting at noon.

The last camel passed us and we stood alone on the ancient road, watching the caravan as it lost itself in dust. I last saw Ellen Jaspar with her blond hair and black skirt swirling among the camels, marching east toward the greatest of the mountains.

"It's barbaric," I protested weakly, and Nazrullah agreed.

"She would have destroyed you both," Moheb Khan replied.

Note to The Reader

The scene of this novel is the Kingdom of Afghanistan in 1946. Conditions are described as they existed in that year and as truthfully as research and memory will permit.

The reader may be curious about what has been happening in the intervening seventeen years, and a brief note covering recent developments may prove helpful.

Few nations have experienced a more spectacular growth and change during this period than Afghanistan. Kabul has paved streets (Russian money). Kandahar has an airport (American money). The city of Kabul has a fine public bakery (Russian). And many towns have good schools (American).

Foreigners have been visiting the country with ease and frequency. President Eisenhower was there in 1959, and many Russian leaders arrived both before and after that date. The vigorous struggle between America and Russia for Afghanistan's affection, referred to in this novel, goes on unceasingly with ultimate victory uncertain. An overriding fact is this: Russia abuts on the northern border for nearly seven hundred unguarded miles, while the United States is nearly eight thousand miles away. Under these circumstances it is remarkable that our side has done as well as it has.

Our victories have been the result of selfless work by dedicated men and women like John Pritchard, the fictional engineer of Chapters Nine and Ten. Apparently, when our country needs such men, there is an endless supply, but we rarely call upon them or find a worthy place for them when they are called.

The battle between old and new which is a feature of this novel has produced some interesting skirmishes. In 1959 women were allowed, even encouraged, to dispense with the chaderi in public. A few did; many preferred the isolation and protection of the shroud . . . or more likely, their husbands did. Symptomatic of the future, however, was the plebiscite held in neighboring Iran in 1963 on similar matters of civil freedom and relaxation of mullah rule. In Iran, which is about fifty years ahead of Afghanistan in social change, the vote was on the order of 4,000 to 1 in favor of modernism. Young women wearing no chaderi stormed the streets on election day, begging people to go to the polls. Old-fashioned mullahs interpreted the vote as the end of organized religion, which of course it was not.

The bright young men represented in this novel by foreign-trained Moheb Khan and Nazrullah and by locally trained Nur Muhammad have brought their nation improved administration. They have by no means achieved victory, but they have won a position from which victory is possible. Many such young men find themselves inclining toward Russia; others, thank heavens, see promise in continued links with the West.

The patterns of social life depicted in the novel have changed radically in the past seventeen years. Kabul now has a good hotel, newspapers, radio, a public cinema to which westerners can go, stores other than bazaars, and several restaurants. Amenities in the cities like Kandahar and Mazar-i-Sharif are also better, but Ghazni remains pretty much as described.

The public punishments described in the novel are no longer common. Since the reader may wonder, I witnessed the first execution, but not in Ghazni; as for the second, I arrived in Kandahar only a few days after it occurred and was given a series of photographs taken by an enterprising man who told me that he had prevailed upon the father to work from the other side because the sunlight was better. Afghan polo, properly called buzkashi (goat dragging), still flourishes and is both rougher and more fun than I describe.

The great dam on whose preliminaries Nazrullah worked in 1946 is in being—one of the marvels of Asia —and its electricity is eagerly sought. The land opposite Qala Bist which was to have been irrigated was found, alas, to be too full of residual salts to be productive. In a sense, this failure of one aspect of the Helmand Project had unfortunate overtones not dissimilar to those that grew out of the German bridges: Afghans looked at the mighty dam, at the cost, at the partial failure and asked, "Why bother?" The German bridges, when I traveled the road from Kabul to Kandahar, were exactly as described; but the Afghan bridge built by Shah Khan and Nazrullah's father stood on a different road.

As for the Kochis, restrictions have been placed on them at every turn. They cannot enter Russia. Traders from China can no longer penetrate the Pamirs with goods. Pakistan, the western portion of old India, conducts a running fight with Afghanistan over the nationality of Pashtuns and halts many of the nomads at the arbitrary border. The tents are still black; the women are still superb in their freedom; the fat-tailed sheep are still among the most preposterous of animals; and the camels still protest at everything.

The reader may also wish to check my credentials for writing this novel. My first acquaintance with Afghanistan came in 1952, when I was living in the Khyber Pass and had a chance to scout the Afghan border for many miles north and south of that historic area. It was then that I conceived my determination to visit Afghanistan. It was then also that I came to know several Kochi tribes fairly well—Povindahs, we called them, for I did not hear the name Kochi until later— and decided that one day I might try to write about them.

In 1955 I was able to enter Afghanistan itself and made these journeys: First, Khyber Pass to Kabul; second, Kabul to Qala Bist; third, across the Dasht-i-Margo to the Chakhansur, called in this novel The

City, which is perhaps a more appropriate name; fourth, down to Chahar Burjak, one of the worst trips I have ever made; fifth, up to Herat and back down to Girishk; sixth, Kabul to Istalif and the lower Koh-i-Baba; seventh, Kabul to Bamian and on to Balkh; eighth, Kandahar to Spin Baldak and Quetta. And there was a ninth trip, perhaps the most memorable I have ever taken, from Qala Bist along the untraveled left bank of the Helmand River to Rudbar. This took us across the Registan desert in a caravan that camped at night in sand dunes with little water and less food. It was from the experiences on this trip, not referred to in this novel, that I developed my love of desert life.

On one of these trips I was visited by friends of a European woman who sought my help. Some years before she had married an Afghan and had passed into the limbo described in parts of this novel. I asked to see her and was taken to a pathetic hovel where I talked with her for the better part of an hour, but I was unable to help. Later I heard of similar cases and met with people actively concerned in liberating wives of foreign origin. However, in fairness I must add that I also met several European women married to enlightened Afghans, and these wives led normal, happy lives; they wore no chaderi, visited Europe when they wished, and were pleased that they had come to live in Afghanistan. Today, of course, quite a few American girls have been marrying Afghans without encountering difficulties with citizenship or the right to travel.

Qabir is an invented name, but the facts associated with it are not. The massive nomad convocation met at no regular place, and where it did meet bore no proper name, for the land is unbelievably wild, empty and unknown. It was called merely The Abul Camp and was probably larger than I suggest. Also, the subsidiary camps for attendant families seem to have been farther from the trading center than I have indicated. The Abul Camp was for men only. Until 1954 no known outsider had ever visited the camp, so that events depicted in this novel are anachronistic by eight years.

As for a foreign woman's visiting the camp, there is no record of its having happened.

The archaeological sites referred to—Qala Bist, The City, Bamian, Balkh—are faithfully described. Bamian remains one of the compelling sights of Asia. My notes, penciled hurriedly as we approached from the east, tell the story:

> Bamian: at eastern approach the Red City (name Zak?) high on hill and cliffs several hundred feet high. Note little castles guarding trail all the way up. City 4 main levels. It was here Genghis Khan lost his son. Destruction of Bamian followed. Red City on right bank of Bamian River. City at Bamian named Ghulghulah and stood back at present hostel. KOCHI is Farsi word (those who move).

> Cliffs 350 feet high, reddish tan. Probably over 500 cave entrances visible, each leading to 4 or 5 rooms. Some caves 300 feet high, sheer drop. Magnificent corridors. Frescoes. All faces routed out. Located foot of soaring sepia and purple-brown mountains facing Koh-i-Baba.

> From one room in the highest level of caves I counted 61 snow-covered peaks in midsummer, all over 15,000 feet high.

The Caravanserai of the Tongues, its location and its pillar are inventions, but each is true to the spirit of Afghanistan. I camped in many of these deserted caravanserais, great lonely structures scattered over the land, and never failed to be impressed with their mood and their function. It was at one that I met my first Kochis in Afghanistan and jotted down the outline of a novel much different from this one. As for the pillar, I forget where I heard about an event of similar import; possibly it was at Herat, where Genghis Khan is reliably reported to have slain a million people. One contemporary authority wrote that it was a million and a half.

My contacts with Islam have been consistent and varied: Indonesia, Borneo, Malaya, Pakistan, Afghanistan, the Near East, Turkey. I have written favorably of the religion, have known many of its leaders, and hold it in both respect and affection. My experiences, as the reader may guess, place me in opposition to the rural mullahs.

Practically every Afghan word, when transliterated into the Roman alphabet, can be spelled in alternate ways (Kabul, Caboul; Helmand, Helmund) and consistency in orthography seems at this point impossible. The editors of this book and I drew up lists of many variant spellings. We consulted numerous experts, some with rather exalted credentials, and in the end found ourselves repeating the lament of Omar, the poet from nearby Persia:

> Myself when young did eagerly frequent
> > Doctor and Saint, and heard great argument
> > About it and about: but evermore
> Came out by the same door wherein I went.

It will be some years before the Roman spelling of essential Afghan words is standardized. Those which offered the most interesting variants include:

chaderi, choudhry, shaddry, chadhri, charderi
ferangi, farangi, faranji, ferengi, feringhee
Tajik, Tadjik, Tadzhik
Pashtun, Pushtun, Pushtoon, Pakhtoon, Pathan
Kandahar, Qandahar
Koran, Qur'an
Bamian, Bamyan, Bamiyan
Kochi, Kuchi
Pashto, Pushto, Pushtu, Pukhto
Povindah, Powindeh

I must make it clear that our decision to spell a given word in a given way was never taken without extensive study, but I must also confess that the final decision was usually arbitrary and that consistency from one decision to the next did not seem possible in view of the conflicts existing among the experts.

For two usages I am alone responsible. In 1946 in this part of the world Iran was known as Persia, the Amu Darya river as the Oxus. If I were writing about today, I would of course use the contemporary forms.

In recent years whenever I have been asked which of the countries I have seen I would most prefer to visit again, I have invariably said Afghanistan. I remember it as an exciting, violent, provocative place. Almost every American or European who worked there in the old days says the same. It was, in the years I knew it, what Mark Miller says: "One of the world's great cauldrons."